GIANTS
of the ASH

To my late wife, Teresa.

What though the radiance which was once so bright
Be now for ever taken from my sight,
Though nothing can bring back the hour
Of splendour in the grass, of glory in the flower;
We will grieve not, rather find
Strength in what remains behind ...

Wordsworth ("Intimations of Immortality")

GIANTS
of the ASH

Brendan Fullam

WOLFHOUND

First published 1991 by
WOLFHOUND PRESS
68 Mountjoy Square
Dublin 1

British Library Cataloguing in Publication Data
Fullam, Brendan
        Giants of the ash : a century of hurling greats.
        I. Title
        796.35
        ISBN 0 86327 315 7 hardcover
        ISBN 0 86327 323 8 limited edition

The publishers are grateful to hurlers and their families who supplied photographs for this book, and wish to thank sports photographer Jim Connolly in particular. While every effort has been made to trace holders of copyright material, in a few instances we have been unable to contact the relevant persons. We request that they write to the publishers.

Cover and book design: Jan de Fouw
Typesetting and layout: Wolfhound Press
Colour separations: Pentacolour Ltd
Monochrome photographs scanned by Accu-plate, Dublin
Printed in the Republic of Ireland by the Leinster Leader Ltd

Contents

An Iomáint

Ar dhroim an domhain níl radharc is áille
Ná tríocha fear ag bualadh báire,
Ar pháirc mhór ghlas faoi thaitneamh gréine,
Is na gártha molta ag dul chun spéire.

Dhá fhoireann ghroí in aghaidh a chéile,
Gach fear i mbarr a nirt is a réime;
Camáin á luascadh ar fud na páirce,
Is an sliotar ag imeacht ar luas in airde.

An tríocha fear ag rith is ag léimneach,
Buillí á mbualadh le neart is le héifeacht,
Tapúlacht coise is oilteacht láimhe,
Ar dhroim an domhain níl radharc is áille.

Seán Ó Finneadha

PREFACE

When I began this work in 1980 it was in two parts: a large book in which I set aside a page for each hurler, and which contained the player's autograph, a written contribution from each player (varying from one sentence to several paragraphs), a photograph or two, the major honours won, and some sundry detail; and a separate volume in which I set out the contents of our discussions. This book is an amalgam of both.

It spans all the decades of the GAA. Ten of its contributors were born before the turn of the century. The oldest of these, John T. Power of Piltown, was born in 1883, a year before the GAA was founded. He was in his ninety-ninth year when I met him. One of the youngest contributors, Damien Martin of Offaly, was born in 1946 and played in the Centenary All-Ireland in Thurles in 1984. My original list of players exceeded a hundred and increased as each year passed. I had therefore to think in terms of a second volume at a future date to pay tribute to many players of the recent past.

This book is about remembering: remembering the hurlers of the past decades and the great game they played and fostered. It is also about giving something in return: in return for the countless hours of indescribable enjoyment I got in my young days just going to the hurling-field for hours of practice every evening, and in later years for the wonderful entertainment I got at the many great games I attended at venues throughout the country.

In compiling this book I sought out as a general rule only players who had spent a decade or more at top level. I spoke only with players who had retired from inter-county hurling, because one can reflect more effectively from a position of retirement.

This book reflects views, perceptions, memories, nostalgia, sadness, fulfilment, friendships, and humour. Above all it deals with a great game and the men who made it; a game that decade after decade has sent spectators away from Croke Park, Semple Stadium, Nowlan Park and other venues spellbound by the performances of our hurling men. And the men who made it? Well, these are some of them — just a few. They represent their colleagues, contemporaries and opponents — thousands of them who played a game that is truly unique: an 'unpremeditated art'.

Paddy Downey of the *Irish Times* once described the great game thus: 'Hurling at its best is a beautifully balanced blend of silken skills and fierce man-to-man combat, a spectacle of sport that almost beggars description.' And Carbery had this to say: 'Hurling survives and is indestructible because of its stern naked grandeur'.

Go maire an iománaíocht go deo!

Reaching high, Ray Cummins of Cork gains posession in the 1977 All-Ireland Semi-Final, Cork v Galway. (Photo: Jim Connolly)

INTRODUCTIONS

Seán Ó Síocháin

General Secretary and Director-General of the GAA, 1964–79

Tá éagsúlacht na leabhar faoi imeachtaí Chumann Lúthchleas Gael imithe i líonmhaire go mór le blianta beaga anuas, agus cuirfear fáilte ar leith roimh an leabhar seo — an ceann is neamhghnáiche díobh go léir — a thugann le chéile, in aon chomhluadar amháin, príomhchuraidh cáiliúla na hiomána ó aimsir bhunaithe an chumainn. Is ábhar mórtais dom féin é gur iarradh orm réamhrá a scríobh faoin saothar stairiúil seo.

This is an extraordinary book by any standards, in that it records for posterity the hopes and aspirations and personal motivation of the hurling giants from each decade, who have between them elevated Ireland's finest field game to the world's greatest sporting spectacle. Here we are reintroduced in a very intimate way to the men who made the game and who have enriched our memories through having become legends even in their own time.

One can read through and between the lines the high regard that these all-time greats had for their hurling contemporaries; they are worthy representatives of Ireland's greatest sportsmen. It is in the nature of things that many of them are larger than life; and through their leadership qualities and personalities, in addition to their hurling expertise, they highlighted a tradition, a culture and an art that is unique to Ireland. The book embodies in a very special way the extraordinary unifying effect of a game in getting players to think and act with one mind and the effective force of that unity of thought and action on the vast majority of a nation in helping it to overcome personal and political differences.

Déanaim comhghairdeas leis an údar as saothar na mblianta atá curtha le chéile aige sa leabhar seo, a léiríonn meon agus aigne agus tréitheachas sár-iománaithe na tíre, glúin i ndiaidh glúine. Beidh Cumann Lúthchleas Gael agus na glúine atá fós le teacht buíoch dó.

* * *

Paddy Buggy

President of the GAA, 1982–84

Hurling was old when the nations were young. Our ancient and medieval teachers, as well as the greatest of our modern thinkers and writers, proclaim it. Charles Kickham's Matt the Thresher in *Knocknagow* and Canon Sheehan's Terence Casey in *Glenanaar* are but the re-creations of the hurling heroes of Oisín.

The epic of Diarmaid and Gráinne gives clear evidence of the antiquity of hurling, and its esteem in ancient Ireland is greater than that of any game in world literature. Skill with the camán was part of the schools' curriculum; it was a preparation for their manly skills with arms. The young princes carried camáns with bands of gold or silver according to rank.

Hurling is known in the Irish tongue by the beautiful word *iomáin*, meaning the art of driving, hurling, tossing, whirling, pressing or urging forward, which expresses the life urge and spirit of a great national game. Hurling is a moulder of character; and if the skills and style are present, the budding athlete will derive growing pleasure from every game. The clash of the ash, the physical joy of a hurler's heart, of a flying sliotar well hit, the wristwork, the bodily contact of a physical field game — these are just a few of the joys of this great game.

There is an affinity between all hurling folk, and the game creates a special bond of friendship between the keenest of rivals that lasts a lifetime; and the funeral of the well-known hurler is a sad but revealing testimony to the esteem and friendship that prospers from this rivalry on our hurling fields.

The game draws support from all walks of life, and great players and outstanding games are remembered in song and in story. The author, Brendan Fullam of Millbanks, New Ross, is one of hurling's greatest enthusiasts, and he has spent many years travelling the hurling counties, meeting and talking to many of our hurling greats. This book is a series of anecdotes and memories from the lives of these great athletes and their thoughts on the modern game. I recommend it to all hurling enthusiasts, and I hope that it will be cherished by all who read it and that it will become a research manual for those with the hurling faith.

Is binne glór mo chamáin féin
Ná guth na n-éan is ceol na mbard.
'S ní binne fuaim ar bith faoin ngréin
Ná poc ró-thréan ar liathróid ard.

* * *

Kevin Cashman

Hurling correspondent, Sunday Independent

I cannot recall a time when hurling, hurlers and hurleys did not dominate every conversation — or plan to get one across on someone — in our house. Now that I am tied into the often unreal media business, I recall that the myth-making didn't start yesterday, or the day before. For we would spend hours on the way from school, or long after lights out, over inventions or fond wishes about imaginary gaiscí of our heroes. The foundations in reality of the dream factory are laid early.

But that was all in the long-ago of innocence. Since then I have never ceased to marvel at how hurling discovers and reveals the limits of the human spirit; and lifts, and occasionally ennobles, the like of myself who even now on the downward slope of old age would wish to have attained eminence with the camán rather than the ballpoint.

But the memories and the great days of revelry suffice. And one day small Una

O'Connor of Blackrock with a wrecked ankle and a worse shoulder played QUB (Queen's University, Belfast) by herself. And in that performance all the ecstasy and worth of living given to us by Ring and Mackey and the others was captured and immortalised.

Ar aghaidh leis an iomáint!

* * *

Mícheál Ó Muircheartaigh

Sa bhliain 1887 is ea a tosnaíodh ar chomórtaisí Uile-Éireann a imirt ar dtúis. Tiobrad Árann agus Gaillimh a bhí sa chéad cluiche ceannais úd i mBiorra.

Ever since that historic first final, folklore has preserved the names and deeds that the many giants of hurling created. It adds to the stories when somebody like Brendan Fullam goes to the trouble of recording first-hand recollections from seventy-nine of the said giants.

As the years go by, each word will attain a greater significance — agus beidh na glúnta atá fós le teacht buíoch duitse, a Bhreandáin, agus dar ndóigh do fathaigh na h-iomána freisin.

Go gcúitítear do shaothar leat. *28.8.1991*

Stopping the ball — goalkeeper Pat Nolan in action during the 1962 Leinster Final between Wexford and Laois.

A rare hurling photograph, taken at Croke Park on May 14, 1922. The occasion was the All-Ireland senior hurling final of 1920 in which a Faughs-powered Dublin team beat Cork by 4:9 to 4:3. Cork's Jimmy (Major) Kennedy, complete with soft hat, runs onto a loose ball to score one of the two goals he registered in that game. (Photo: The Cashman Collection)

Kevin Armstrong (Antrim), fourth from left, during the Railway Cup Football game, Munster v Ulster in 1943.

Kevin Armstrong (right) exchanging views with star Tipperary forward Jimmy Doyle.

"

I was delighted to have played hurling and football. I got great enjoyment out of the games, and they made my life just wonderful. To meet players and people like yourself makes the GAA the greatest sport in the world.

I have played hurling and football against great men of all the provinces. I look back on those days as the greatest days of my life. But the GAA also needs the back-room men, who form a very important part of the structure of the GAA; also the sports writers, who make the game and the players.

This book is an added dimension to the GAA.

My boyhood heroes were Mick Mackey and Bobby Beggs.

"

Born 1922

You don't find Antrim figuring in the list of major hurling honours; and yet the county has a long hurling tradition. The game has flourished for decades in the Glens of Antrim and elsewhere throughout the county.

Over the years the men of Antrim suffered from lack of serious competition. A time there was when Antrim automatically entered the semi-final stages of the hurling championship but usually fell easy prey to the champions of Munster and Leinster. But defeat never daunted them, and they kept playing and promoting the game they loved. No wonder then that a great sense of pride stirred in the Glens in 1983 when Loughgeil Shamrocks won the All-Ireland senior hurling club title by defeating St Rynagh's of Offaly after a replay at Casement Park.

Many fine individual exponents of the hurling art came out of Antrim, but none more famous than that great dual player Kevin Armstrong. You will not meet a greater enthusiast or warmer personality.

While I was primarily interested in Kevin the hurler, it was of course impossible to ignore Kevin the footballer. His football career spanned the years 1937 to 1957. He played several times for Ulster and enjoyed Railway Cup success. He stood out in a great Antrim football team that won Ulster senior honours in 1946 and repeated the success in 1951. In 1946 they failed by only three points to Kerry in the All-Ireland football semi-final in a game where Kerry used the professional foul to full advantage and brought about the downfall of what many will tell you was a superior and indeed outstanding Antrim fifteen.

Kevin recalled three special memories

from his football days:

— the triumph in Ulster in 1946 that ended thirty-three years of waiting;

— his selection on the Ulster Railway Cup football team in 1942, when he played with the élite of Ulster that included great names like Jim McCullough of Armagh, Vincent Duffy of Monaghan, John Joe O'Reilly of Cavan, Alf Murray of Armagh, and Big Tom O'Reilly of Cavan; Ulster won the competition and took the trophy to the northern province for the first time;

— being captain of the Ulster football team in 1947; again they won the trophy, and Kevin had the honour of being the first man ever to take the cup across the border. The great sense of achievement felt in Antrim is reflected in the action of Séamus McFerron in re-presenting the Railway Cup to Kevin in the Ulster Hall in Belfast.

But let's now turn to Kevin the hurler, whose prowess with the camán enabled him to win a place at left-half-forward on the Centenary team of players who never won an All-Ireland medal. Chosen with him in that forward line were Josie Gallagher (Galway), Martin Quigley (Wexford), Jimmy Smyth (Clare), Christy O'Brien (Laois), and Mick Bermingham (Dublin).

Kevin belonged to the O'Connell club in Belfast. It was founded in 1916, and those closely associated with its foundation were John Harvey, Liam Harvey, John Harte, and John Gaynor. At the first meeting someone asked, 'What will we call the club?' And the reply came, 'What will we call it? We'll call it after that man up there on the wall: Daniel O'Connell, the Liberator.' And so it was agreed and the club was named O'Connells. As Kevin finished the story about the foundation he reflected sadly that the club had ceased to exist that year.

Throughout the decades Kevin recalls that tremendous work was put into fostering the game of hurling. It began with the foundation of the Antrim County Board in 1901. Laurence O'Neill was chairman; Bulmer Hobson from Holywood, an ardent Gaelic League man, was secretary; George Martin, a Belfast solicitor, was treasurer,

and he later became president of the Ulster Council. Very soon Antrim became the top Ulster county, winning hurling and football titles yearly. They were kingpins in hurling: no side could compete with them in the province.

Kevin chuckled as he told me that he had won more Ulster senior hurling titles than Christy Ring had won Munster titles. But in Ulster it was easier. Oppositon came only from Down and Donegal, and neither county provided a real threat to Antrim's supremacy.

In recent years it has become the practice to take under-age players down to Cork during the summer and involve them in local competition. They have also had the benefit of tuition under the guiding hand of Justin McCarthy, former Cork star. Justin has been very impressed by the Antrim boys, who were able to hold their own with their Cork counterparts, and Kevin hopes that as time passes Antrim will benefit from this experience. He feels that participation in the Leinster championship would greatly improve Antrim hurling and give them the kind of top-class competition that is vital for success.

Without a doubt Antrim's most successful decade in hurling was the forties. The junior championship was suspended because of the war, and this left Antrim out in the cold. However, the Central Council agreed to allow Antrim take part in the senior championship. In 1943 they played Galway in Corrigan Park, Belfast, in the quarter-final. Few expected the result that emerged — Antrim 7:0, Galway 6:2. It was a Noel Campbell goal from a sideline puck in the closing minutes that snatched victory from Galway. Another Antrim man who played a leading role that day was Danny McAllister, who scored four goals.

So, Antrim moved on to the All-Ireland semi-final against Kilkenny. The game was played at Corrigan Park. It was an August Sunday, and Kilkenny were favourites. But the hurling world was in for a shock. Antrim hurled extremely well. Midfield was controlled by Jackie Bateson and Noel Campbell; the defence was solid, and the attack combined well. It all added up to another great Antrim victory, and they were on their way to Croke Park to the final against Cork.

Unfortunately, the fairytale did not continue. Kevin is convinced that Antrim were better than the final score of 5:16 to 0:4 would suggest. Men who had played a great game in Corrigan Park against Galway and Kilkenny appeared to freeze in Croke Park. The occasion was too much. And of course Cork, in Kevin's opinion, were 'a super side — maybe the best ever to leave the Leeside'.

But it wasn't all gloom, because from that defeat sprang the origin of the present Casement Stadium. Kevin told me that Corrigan Park was purchased in 1927 for £1,600. It had an uneven surface of heights and hollows, and was partly blamed for the heavy defeat at the hands of Cork. It was resolved that Corrigan Park should get a surface like a billiard table that would improve Antrim hurling. That led to the setting up of a committee to raise funds, and eventually ground was bought at Andersonstown and the building of Casement Park began. When it was opened, on 1 June 1953 by Cardinal d'Alton, it was free of debt, having cost £101,000 — a truly remarkable figure to have raised in those times.

Over the years Antrim gave many great men to the GAA, including two presidents, Séamus McFerron and Paddy McNamee. But the one that Kevin feels should have a monument erected to his memory is F. D. McKerrigher. The man was dedication personified. In the troubled times he left his home near Corrigan Park and travelled by bicycle to Dublin to attend the convention. He returned to Belfast, dodging Black-and-Tan forces on the way, and brought news and details of the Dublin convention to his colleagues in Antrim. Kevin often tells this story of dedication and commitment, and Cavan officials have often remarked to him, 'We still have no-one to beat your man on the bike'.

Kevin was a regular choice on the Antrim and Ulster senior hurling teams. He was part of history on 20 February 1944 when Ulster took part for the first time in the Railway Cup competition but went under heavily to Munster in Croke Park with a score 9:3 to 3:1.

A year later more history was made. Ulster shocked Leinster in Belfast by beating them in the first round of the Railway Cup by 3:1 to 2:3. The final showdown was at Croke Park on St Patrick's Day against Munster, who won well on the score 6:8 to 2:0. But it was no disgrace. Munster were star-laden: Jim Ware and Andy Fleming of Waterford, P. J. Quane of Clare, Tommy Purcell of Tipperary, Willie Murphy, Paddy O'Donovan, Jim Young, Con Cottrell, Christy Ring and Johnny Quirke of Cork, and Peter Cregan, Jackie Power, Paddy McCarthy, Dick Stokes and Mick Mackey of Limerick.

Kevin at centre-forward for Ulster was opposed by Jackie Power. He felt honoured to have played in such company in 1945, and he was still good enough to play on an Antrim team almost twenty years later, having played his first game with them in 1940.

The team he would have liked to have captained is a mixture of friendships, opponents, and childhood heroes. It is as follows:

Ollie Walsh *(Kilkenny)*

| Con Murphy *(Cork)* | Nick O'Donnell *(Wexford)* | John Doyle *(Tipperary)* |
| Willie John Daly *(Cork)* | Paddy Clohessy *(Limerick)* | John Keane (Waterford) |

Jack Lynch *(Cork)*   Jackie Power *(Limerick)*

| Christy Ring *(Cork)* | Mick Mackey *(Limerick)* | Kevin Armstrong *(Antrim)* |
| Jimmy Doyle *(Tipperary)* | Nicky Rackard *(Wexford)* | Eddie Keher *(Kilkenny)* |

Born 1935

John Barron places great emphasis on sportsmanship and clean play. He was very glad to see the 'third man tackle' abolished, and believes this will contribute greatly to the development of the game. He also welcomes the rules that have been designed to protect players being 'pulled on'. He does, however, add that if a back or forward puts up his hand to grab a ball and gets his hand hit because his opponent pulls first time on the ball, then the opponent should not be penalised. To penalise in such cases discourages first-timing the ball and overhead play.

He likes to recall a story of true sportsmanship. It happened in the 1958 All-Ireland semi-final between Tipperary and Kilkenny. Jimmy Doyle was in sparkling form and scored something like eight points off no less a defender than Paddy Buggy. After the game someone said to Paddy, 'What happened you — why didn't you hit him?' Paddy's reply was, 'Why should I? He didn't hit me'.

John was glad to see the ban go. He considers that it was retained for far too long and that it led to unnecessary dissension within the GAA and within counties. He also feels that some counties adopted a tougher vigilance policy than others. John was a victim of the ban. He was suspended for six months at the age of sixteen, and recalls that Seumas Power, his fellow-countyman, also incurred suspension under the ban.

He welcomes the development of social contact among players and officials, and feels that this was an aspect of GAA life that was neglected for too long. He remembers a gold watch tournament final at Bruff in 1959 when Waterford played Limerick.

66

I consider myself very fortunate to have played hurling when the game was especially strong in Waterford; to have had as my team-mates Seumas Power, Phil Grimes, Mick Flannelly, Austin Flynn, Tom Cunningham, Tom Cheasty.

My greatest disappointment was losing the 1957 All-Ireland final. This was dimmed somewhat, however, by our victory in 1959.

The players I remember with great affection are Jimmy Brohan, Liam Moloney, Nicky Rackard, Jimmy Doyle, Denis Heaslip, and Paddy Barry. 99

After the game both teams were entertained to a fine meal, but when the meal was over they all dispersed. There was no real intermingling. The late Mick Mackey was at the meal, and John regrets that he did not go over to Mick, whom he greatly admired, and have a chat with him.

John always had a special admiration for Tommy Doyle, and he regarded Jimmy Doyle as one of the great artists of the game. One of the nicest fellows he ever played on was Liam Moloney of Limerick. 'Any time I played on him he got several goals off me,' said John.

His greatest hurling memory is the 1959 All-Ireland win over Kilkenny following a replay. In the second game John and his opponent, Dick Carroll, were sent off in the second half 'for very little'. John vividly remembers Seumas Power's great equalising goal in the dying seconds of the first game, and reminded me that from the puck-out Seumas gathered the ball at midfield and was barely wide with a great effort for a point. The puck-out brought the final whistle.

A close second comes his first Munster medal in the 1957 victory over Cork; and his greatest regret is the manner in which Waterford let the 1957 All-Ireland title slip from their grasp against Kilkenny, who were to become their bogey team.

Following the recent death of Mick Mackey we saw the publication of many photographs, including the now famous one of Mackey and Ring on the occasion of the Tipperary v. Cork Munster championship match at Limerick in 1957. John has the story surrounding that photograph first hand from the late Dick Dalton — 'a great GAA man and a great De La Salle Club man' — who was umpire that day.

Mick Mackey was the goal-flag umpire at the city end. Dick Dalton was the other umpire at that end. Cork were defending the city goal. It was the first half. In came a high lobbing ball to the square. Tipperary forwards came thundering in too. Ball and forwards reached Cashman, the Cork goalkeeper, simultaneously.

Now Cashman had the ball in his hand, and the next thing was he was in the back of the net and Mackey was waving the green flag for a Tipperary goal, satisfied that the ball was over the line. Meanwhile Dalton had his hand up for a seventy. Tipperary fans were cheering wildly with joy, and those behind the Cork goal were screaming at Dalton to take down his hand. Then the referee was running in, and Ring was also making his way up from the other side of the field.

What Mackey hadn't noticed was that as Cashman was being bundled into the net he palmed the ball across the goal to Dick Dalton's side (some say he threw the ball) and over the line for a seventy.

By now Ring was in the goal area and the crowd were still roaring. Mackey had gone into the net and come out with Cashman's hurley — the goal-flag seemed inadequate. The referee was talking to Dalton. 'What happened?' 'It went over for a seventy,' said Dalton. 'For God's sake keep your hand up or we'll all get killed,' said the ref. The seventy was awarded.

In the second half Ring had to retire with an injured wrist. He came round by the city goal. As he passed Mackey the exchange took place. 'You never lost it,' said Ring. 'And neither did you,' said Mackey. Then the camera clicked and a famous moment was recorded.

Talking of Ring brought another memory to John's mind. It was in the late fifties. John and fellow-countymen Phil Grimes,

John's ideal team from the men of his era reads as follows:

Ollie Walsh *(Kilkenny)*

John Doyle *(Tipperary)*   Austin Flynn *(Waterford)*   Bobbie Rackard *(Wexford)*

Jim English *(Wexford)*   Pat Stakelum *(Tipperary)*   Jimmy Finn *(Tipperary)*

Sean Clohessy *(Kilkenny)*   Seumas Power *(Waterford)*

Frankie Walsh *(Waterford)*   Christy Ring *(Cork)*   Jimmy Doyle *(Tipperary)*

Phil Grimes *(Waterford)*   John Barron *(Waterford)*   Eddie Keher *(Kilkenny)*

Seumas Power and Frankie Walsh travelled westwards to play Galway in the first round of the Railway Cup. It was a cold Saturday in February. It was also Lent, and in those days that meant no meat at the evening meal. But John and his colleagues were cold and famished, and they ordered steaks and chips. They were enjoying the meal when Ring arrived with Corkmen Paddy Barry, Jimmy Brohan, and Mick Cashman. The waitress came out and Ring personally placed the order for everybody: 'Boiled eggs' — and eggs it was. Barry, Brohan and Cashman had to settle for the taste of eggs and the smell of steak.

In 1964, at the age of twenty-nine, John got a severe attack of pneumonia that laid him low for several weeks. At the time it badly affected his energy, and he never made it back to county level. Hurling lost one of its great gentlemen and sportsmen.

Paddy Buggy (in striped jersey, underneath the telephone pole, left background). Action near the Kilkenny goal in the 1953 All-Ireland Semi-Final, Galway v Kilkenny.

Born: 1929

My first visit to Paddy took place in 1981, when we chatted in general about the game of hurling, which he played at top level for twelve years between 1949 and 1960. A National League title eluded him, but he won all the other major honours the game had to offer in those years.

Paddy is a great advocate of good sportsmanship and discipline. He believes that much could be done to enhance and encourage these qualities. He believes too that a spirit of innovation and experiment — an opening of minds; a widening of horizons — could bring new dimensions to the organisation.

Paddy had the honour of being president of the GAA from 1982 to 1984 — an honour that was further enhanced by the term of his presidency coinciding with the Centenary celebrations of 1984, when a great organisation looked back with pride on the achievements and progress of a hundred years.

In our meetings I sensed the great depth of feelings both of loyalty and dedication that he had for the game of hurling and the Gaelic Athletic Association. I therefore approached him again before publication of this book to write an introduction that would encompass the traditions and folklore associated with this ancient game. This he has done in a unique and splendid fashion.

66

I regret that such skills as the drop puck, ground pucking and the overhead striking of the sliotar are gradually fading from the game of hurling, and I consider that scores should not be allowed unless struck with the hurley.

My greatest game was a National League game, Kilkenny v. Cork, when I played on Christy Ring; and a couple of other games which stand out in my memory are the 1959 All-Ireland v. Waterford — the drawn game; the county final Slieverue v. Tullaroan, when my club, Slieverue, won its only senior hurling title; and the Railway Cup game Leinster v. Munster when Leinster defeated Munster for their first Railway Cup title in thirteen years.

Among the players I admired were Christy Ring, Bobbie Rackard, Vin Baston, Jimmy Langton, Ollie Walsh, Jimmy Doyle, and Tim Flood. 99

Born: 1895

Feargus de Búrca
(Frank Burke)

"

As a Kildare man I felt honoured to have played for Dublin in 1917 against a great Tipperary team and to have won my first All-Ireland medal.

Some of the greats I played against were Johnny Leahy, Stephen Hackett, whose brother by the way was playing that day for Dublin.

We had an under-strength team against Wexford in 1918 and paid the penalty. One of the famous men that played for Dublin that day was Harry Boland.

"

I visited Frank Burke at his home in Rathfarnham, Dublin, on the evening of the 1981 All-Ireland senior hurling final between Offaly and Galway. I was sorry to learn that Frank, who was eighty-six years of age, had had a serious operation earlier in the year and was still recovering.

Before I met him, Frank's daughters had told me that during his illness he lost inter-est in everything except hurling and football. These were the great loves of his life. They took root in childhood. His college days began in Knockbeg in Carlow. Frank arrived complete with hurley. He was taken aside and told 'We play cricket here'. It was a bit of a setback. Hurling opportunities were rare. Frank stayed for one year.

He had watched the match live on television in the afternoon and would watch it again on "Sportscene" that night — truly a measure of his great enthusiasm for hurling. He would live every moment of it and burn considerable energy in the process.

Frank came to Dublin in his young days from Co. Kildare, and played football and hurling with Collegians — a club that is now defunct. Those were the days when Ireland was gaining its independence. Frank was a great admirer of Pádraig Pearse; displayed in his living-room was a photograph of the patriot. He spent Easter week with the 1916 leader in the GPO. He was there, believing in a cause — "in bloody protest for a glorious thing". Frank was destined to follow in this patriot's footsteps and to teach in Scoil Éanna.

He was most friendly and genial, and obviously enjoyed recalling hurling memories. My immediate feeling was that I was talking to one of the grand old men of hurling. Uppermost in his mind was a point scored by Eugene Coughlan for Cork from a kneeling position in the second game of the 1931 All-Ireland final against Kilkenny.

He felt that in general there was too much lifting of the ball nowadays, and not enough first-timing it on the ground and in the air. He was devoted to hurling and football all his life, and he had a very special love for our native language too.

The horrors of Bloody Sunday were vivid in his memory. No wonder: he was playing that day for Dublin at Croke Park in the football game against Tipperary.

Frank was a candidate for the position of general secretary of the GAA in 1929. He was defeated, however, by one vote by the late Pádraig Ó Caoimh.

His first inter-county hurling game was with Dublin in the 1917 final. It heralded the beginning of a golden era in Dublin hurling that was to last for a decade. Before the final he was naturally apprehensive, as Dublin were up against the previous year's champions, Tipperary, who had a great reputation and were again captained by the renowned Johnny Leahy. In the 1916 final Tipperary were represented by a Boherlahan selection, and had beaten a famed Tullaroan selection from Kilkenny by 5:4 to 3:2. But 1917 was to be Dublin's year, on the score 5:4 to 4:2, and Frank Burke collected his first All-Ireland senior hurling medal. The Hackett brothers played on opposite sides that day: Martin with his adopted Dublin, and Stephen with his native Tipperary. Frank recalled the brilliant display of Brendan Considine in the 1917 final and the great goal he scored very early on in the game. That goal followed from a pass by Frank Burke that was doubled on first time by Brendan. Brendan Considine came on as a sub almost immediately after throw-in, because a Dublin player went down injured and had to retire. It seems that Brendan's omission from the first fifteen was because of training sessions missed.

I asked Frank how he felt about Offaly's win over Galway. Like all of us he hated to think of either team losing but felt that Offaly's win would be a great boost for the game in the midlands and would almost certainly encourage the spread of hurling.

Frank then returned to the 1917 team and reminded me that there was not one Dublin-born player on the selection. Munster supplied twelve players, from Limerick, Tipperary, Cork and Clare. The three Leinster men were Tommy Moore from Kilkenny, Joe Phelan from Laois, and Frank himself from Kildare.

Frank was a dual player. After winning hurling titles in 1917 and 1920 he went on to collect three successive All-Ireland titles with his adopted Dublin, in 1921, 1922, and 1923. He has the unique honour of being the only player ever to have won more than one All-Ireland medal in both hurling and football.

Michael Collins (with hurley) and Harry Boland at Croke Park.

Born: 1939

The county players I admired most in my time were Liam Devaney, Donnie Nealon and Babs Keating of Tipperary. Ray Cummins of Cork was a great forward to get possession.

99

"

Hurling is a game that I have got great enjoyment from and at the same time has been very good to me. Like every youngster I had an ambition to win a medal at the game. After what seemed ages I achieved my goal at sixteen years of age when I won a Leinster Colleges junior medal with St Kieran's.

After making the breakthrough I was lucky enough to win an All-Ireland Colleges medal. On making the Kilkenny senior panel I had one great wish: to win an All-Ireland medal with Kilkenny.

The win over Waterford in 1963 was my greatest thrill, but the sweetest win for me was the 1967 victory over Tipperary. The reasons for this were:

— Tipperary were the best team in my era;
— Kilkenny were waiting so long for this victory;
— my next-door neighbour, the late Bill Kenny, had played on the 1922 Kilkenny team.

My greatest regret in hurling was not winning a senior championship medal with Lisdowney.

D rama attended the early moments of my meeting with Ted Carroll at his home in Kilkenny. We were just settling down to a pleasant chat when a large window-pane was badly shattered. When the initial shock passed, the message dawned. Ted's son, who had been playing in the back garden, had hit the wrong target with the sliotar.

Ted hurried out and, it seemed, with drastic action in mind. However, by the time he reached the back garden his mind had travelled back to his own youth, and similar misdeeds were recalled. I don't think that even a yellow card was shown.

Ted still enjoys hurling with his club, Lisdowney. He would relish a county title win with his native parish, but tradition is not on his side in having this expectation realised. He cherishes his Leinster Junior Colleges medal and All-Ireland Senior Colleges medal, won in 1957 with that great nursery of Kilkenny hurling, St Kieran's College.

A first All-Ireland medal is always special, and so it was with Ted in 1963 when Kilkenny defeated a fine Waterford team in a high-scoring game.

Probably his most satisfying hour in the black-and-amber jersey was in the All-Ireland final of 1967, when Tipperary were conquered. It broke a long tradition of defeat going back over forty years. Ted was proud to have been part of a Kilkenny team that broke the Tipperary spell.

The third All-Ireland medal came in 1969 when he had one of his finest hours and Cork were defeated on the score 2:15 to 2:9. Additional honours came his way in 1969, when he was selected as Texaco Hurler of the Year.

In all, Ted took part in five All-Ireland finals. The odd-year ones were won: 1963, 1967, 1969. The even-year ones were lost: 1964 and 1966. In 1964 they met an all-conquering Tipp fifteen and had to be content with second-best. In 1966 they entered the final with the tag of favourites, but an unfancied Cork team playing first-time, no-nonsense hurling surprised Kilkenny on the score 3:9 to 1:10.

Ted had only one Railway Cup success. It came in 1965, a year when Leinster and All-Ireland honours deserted Kilkenny. He manned the centre-back position, and flanking him on the right was fellow-countyman and supreme stylist Séamus Cleere. On the left wing was the uncompromising Offaly man Paddy Molloy. It was a fine half-back trio, each with a very different style.

Ted will always be associated with two defensive positions: centre-back and right full-back. He filled both with distinction for county and province.

This was the Kilkenny team with which Ted won his first All-Ireland medal in 1963:

	Ollie Walsh	
Phil Larkin	J. Whelan	M. Treacy
Séamus Cleere	Ted Carroll	Mick Coogan
Paddy Moran	Seán Clohessy	
Denis Heaslip	Johnny McGovern	Eddie Keher
Tommy Walsh	Billy Dwyer	Tommy Maher

Born: 1929

Martin Codd.

front of me no matter how far I moved out the field.

If I were asked who the best player was I would have to say Ring, but on his day Bobbie Rackard had something that no other player I ever saw had. I can't find a word to describe what I mean, but it was a combination of skill, courage, sportsmanship, and gentlemanliness.

"

"

The highlights of my hurling career would be, first, the 1956 All-Ireland final against Cork before a crowd of near 100,000 people; my second great memory would be of when we played Cork in the Polo Grounds in New York in 1957. Both these games gave me everything most players only dream of. To have been part of a team that brought excitement and joy to the people of Wexford is something that still gives me great satisfaction.

The saddest and most heartbreaking memory would be the premature death of Nicky Rackard and the sadness and tragedy that came into his life when he had given so much joy to others.

The two best players I played on would both be centre-half-backs. Pat Stakelum of Tipp always gave me a lot of trouble under the falling ball because like myself he could hit directly above his head, but he was very strong and could hold his ground against one. The other man who gave me a lot of trouble was Martin Óg Morrissey of Waterford, who always seemed to be in

Wexford first called Martin Codd to the purple-and-gold jersey of senior hurling for the league campaign in November 1949. He was selected for the last time when he was recalled in 1965 to man the full-forward berth with a view to adding punch to the attack: 'Wexford were looking for a full-forward'. In between those years there was a glorious era in Wexford hurling.

Martin didn't command a permanent place on the county team, but he hovered on the brink all the time. He was on and off the selection for a number of reasons.

In the fifties Wexford produced three fine midfielders in Séamus Hearne, Ned Wheeler, and Jim Morrissey — 'a man who did a lot for Wexford hurling.' They were automatic choices. Martin was perceived by the selectors as a midfielder, and a midfielder only. This kept him from holding a permanent place. No real effort was made to slot him into the attack, where his weight and height might well have troubled many a defender. Injuries too were a problem with Martin, and these kept him sidelined for long periods.

Every player brings some aspects of his character and personality to bear on his style of performance on the field. Where Martin was concerned he tended to lack aggression. In a Railway Cup game against Ulster in 1951 he 'eased off in sympathy' after Leinster had gone six or eight goals up. The next thing was he was replaced. 'The Wexford selectors would have understood me, but the Leinster selectors didn't. Anyway, in similar circumstances I would do the same again. I found it very hard to display aggression — to develop aggression. I preferred to play on a "sore" player rather than a quiet one: that could get me going.'

And yet in the League final against Galway in 1951 reaction replaced gentleness. It was the time when forwards and midfielders all lined up at midfield for the throw-in. Martin was third or fourth from the front. Referee Con Murphy of Cork threw in the ball, and immediately Martin's counterpart lashed across his ankles — no ball in sight. Reaction was swift as Martin up-ended the Galway man with a fist to the jaw (Martin has a very big fist). 'It was the only time in my career that my name was taken'.

Four games in particular stand out in his mind. Pride of place goes to the 1956 All-Ireland final against Cork. 'You see, nobody accepted we were great after beating Galway in the 1955 All-Ireland. I was a stopgap centre-forward in 1956.' I suggested to Martin that it was a master stroke to have played him there. 'Yes, it was — it worked. I had already been tried in a Walsh Cup game against Kilkenny. Padge Kehoe or Tim Flood could have been in the centre, but they were more effective on the wings. I never played in a game like it before or after. The crowd was so big; they kept roaring the whole time; you got a feeling of being hemmed in; you wouldn't hear an opponent coming.'

In preparation for that game Martin didn't read any newspaper previews. He didn't train after the Friday week before the game. Nick Rackard said to him, 'Do it whatever way you want to'.

He would regard the 1956 team as the best Wexford team he played on. He would see it as superior to the 1954 side, mainly because they had been together longer, were more experienced, and had gained in confidence. After the 1956 win over Cork, Wexford's confidence reached a new level. Martin too got a new-found confidence. He was never afterwards 'badly played out of a game, and rarely finished without scoring'.

The second game he talked about took place at the Polo Grounds, New York, in 1957. Again Cork were the opponents. As Martin stood to attention for the Irish and US anthems he felt a double sense of pride. 'You see, my mother was American'.

In the parade before the game Jim Barry, the Cork trainer, had marched between the two captains, chest out. He wore a red jersey. *Jim Barry* was written across the front; *Cork* was written across the back.

Victory went to Wexford. Martin was delighted. To have defeated Cork on two prestigious occasions — the All-Ireland of 1956 and at the Polo Grounds in 1957 — elevated Wexfordmen to new levels. 'I never saw Ring and Barry so crestfallen,' said Martin, 'and the Cork supporters from New York were equally disappointed. Ring never wanted to lose, no matter how unimportant the game, so you can imagine how upset he was to have lost in front of the exiles. I particularly remember that day the way Bobbie Rackard contained Ring. The field had no corner flags then, because the shape was oval. Any time Ring got possession out near the flags Bobbie used to stalk and shadow and dispossess him.' In the League final against Tipperary in 1956 and in the All-Ireland final against Cork in 1956, and again against Cork in the Polo Grounds, Martin feels that Wexford were well-nigh unbeatable. 'When the pressure came on we were able to withstand it, hold our composure, and lift our game.'

The best game of hurling he ever played in was the League final of 1958 against Limerick. 'It had everything. It was incredibly fast and open. I was at corner-forward on Dermot Kelly. In the closing stages, when Limerick were pressing fiercely, I came out to make a third midfielder in an attempt to take the pressure off our backs. Limerick should probably have won. Indeed they would have only that Billy Rackard and Nick O'Donnell in the last line of defence did things that no-one in their right senses would do.' The fourth game he talked about was the 1951 National League final against Galway. 'We lost that one. I generally have no recollections of games I lost, whether playing with Wexford or' Rathnure. But I remember that 1951 game. We were very keyed up beforehand. It was our first taste of the big time. A trip to America was at stake. We were still green. The winning days still lay ahead of us.' Hurling has always meant a great deal to Martin. 'I couldn't live without it.' He spent about four months working in England in the early part of 1950. When he heard that Wexford had beaten the Leinster champions, Laois, in the championship he declared to himself, 'I'll be home for the Leinster final.' And he was — and played in his favourite position, centrefield, against Kilkenny.

From his young days Martin was always closely associated with Rathnure minor teams and 'got a lot of enjoyment from it'. He trained two very fine Wexford minor teams in 1980 and 1981. The 1981 side 'was very unlucky to lose to Kilkenny in the Leinster final,' following which Kilkenny went on to beat Galway by two points in the final.

Nowadays Martin trains the Wexford county camogie team and watches his daughter and niece carry on a proud tradition.

The best hurling combination Martin ever saw in action was the Bennettsbridge team of the fifties. 'They had the best understanding and were the most organised fifteen I ever saw play.' He also had a special admiration for the Tipperary team of the early fifties. 'I liked the traditional style of hurling they served up. I was always impressed by Tommy Doyle. I liked his first-time style and his good ground hurling.'

The two opponents he admired most were Pat Stakelum of Tipperary and Martin Óg Morrissey of Waterford.

Martin had other talents too. He was a competent musician and a good singer. When he was in England in 1950 he was offered £10 to sing three nights a week, and even though it was nearly twice what he was earning on the building, he laughed off the offer and didn't take it up. Around 1965 Martin was part of a group that played in fleánna ceoil. He then formed a band with some Cork musicians under the title 'The Herdsmen'. 'I made no money at it,' said Martin, 'and after a couple of years I returned to farming.'

After Martin had picked out the following team from the men of his era that he would like to have captained, he added, 'I picked these men on the basis that they would be at their best on the day,' and of his right-half-back, Séamus Cleere, he said, 'He was poetry in motion.'

Ollie Walsh *(Kilkenny)*

Bobbie Rackard *(Wexford)*   Nick O'Donnell *(Wexford)*   Jimmy Brohan *(Cork)*
Séamus Cleere *(Kilkenny)*   Pat Stakelum *(Tipperary)*   Denis Coughlan *(Cork)*
Martin Codd *(Wexford)*   "Chunky" O'Brien *(Kilkenny)*
Christy Ring *(Cork)*   Liam Devaney *(Tipperary)* Jimmy Kennedy *(Tipperary)*
Eddie Keher *(Kilkenny)*   Nicky Rackard *(Wexford)*   Tim Flood *(Wexford)*

Born: 1903

Patrick Collins

Paddy Collins is a quiet and retiring man who has made a great contribution to hurling both as a player and an administrator. He arrived on the county senior scene in 1929, and so as a player is associated with the great Cork era of 1926–31. His club, Glen Rovers, has been central to his way of life since his youth.

When you ask Paddy about his greatest hurling memories he does not hesitate to name the 1931 All-Ireland campaign and the 1934 county championship. In 1934 Glen Rovers and Paddy Collins won county senior honours for the first time. From then on the club was to grow in fame and fortune and become one of the outstanding clubs in the country.

The campaign of 1931 is clearly etched in his mind. He described it as 'a long, testing championship that made great demands on stamina and endurance. It took us seven games to get custody of the McCarthy Cup, and none of the games was easy,' he said.

The first game was against Clare, and won on the score 3:4 to 1:6. In the next round Tipperary provided the opposition, and were beaten 3:5 to 2:3.

Then came the Munster final against Waterford. It was a draw the first day; and a controversial draw it was from a Waterford point of view. It was in the eighth minute of 'lost' time that Jim Hurley scored the equalising point for Cork, following which the final whistle was blown. The replay saw Cork through on the score 5:4 to 1:2.

The All-Ireland final made history. It took three games to decide the issue. The score was 1:6 each in the first game, and

"

I have special memories of the three games against Kilkenny in the 1931 All-Ireland final. I played on Dan Dunne in all three games. It was the hardest All-Ireland I played in. We had beaten Waterford in a replayed match in Clonmel.

I enjoyed playing the game, especially in the local club competitions.

These are the men I admired a lot: Christy Ring, Martin Kennedy, Phil Cahill, Phil Purcell, Mick Mackey, Jack Lynch, Mick King, John Joe Doyle, John Keane, Christy Moylan, Paddy Phelan, Jim O'Regan, and Timmy Ryan.

"

2:5 each in the second game. Seven scores to each team in both games show how close and tight the exchanges were. Paddy was part of history when Cork triumphed 5:8 to 3:4 in the third game.

No more major honours were to come Paddy's way. He continued to hurl until 1938 and had departed the county scene when Cork entered another great and record-breaking era in 1939. But Paddy the selector and club man remained on in the administration field, and his contribution is aptly and beautifully described by Jim Young in his article on "Fox" Collins in *The Spirit of the Glen*.

'Since 1919 to the present day Fox has been player, Administrator, Selector and inspiration to every generation of Glen men. His record both for the Club and County puts him among the immortals but he has been more than that to all of us. Whether mending hurleys after a hard day's work, training with his team or choosing the men for the coming match, he exhibited a kindness, loyalty and integrity that inspired all those around him. His was the stuff of heroes, the skilful, courageous, strong defender. He never bowed the knee in defeat, he never gloated in glory. He accepted the up and downs of Club life with equanimity. His versatility was shown when he designed the medals for the 1941 and 1942 Cork county championships. He was always there just like he is today. No match is unimportant, no distance too great. When Glen men ask "Who was at the match" the answer invariably is "Well, Fox of course and — ". He has seen the Club through the lean years, he has been part of the success. He has seen many staunch comrades go to the "happy hurling grounds" and he has seen the old order changing. The swinging lefthander with the red hair is as vibrant today as when he wore the Glen and Cork colours. His love of hurling is as great as of yore. Just to have him around gives a sense of purpose to the Club and a faith to guide it in the years ahead.'

John Connolly, Galway, in action. (Photo: Jim Connolly)

Born: 1948

"

I was born in Leitir Móir, Connemara, and when we moved to Ballybrit, beside the world-famous Galway Racecourse, at the age of five years, hurling became as much part of my life as sleeping or eating.

Although my father had never seen a game of hurling played before then, his interest in it had a great effect on me. I remember him carrying me on the crossbar of his bike the five miles to Pearse Stadium in Salthill to see the Galway team play. The look of admiration and expression on his face as he pointed out to me the Galway stars of the day made a huge impression on me as a young lad.

Our great club, Castlegar, had at that time their playing-pitch at the front field of the racecourse, which was directly across the road from our house. Evening after evening I would spend my time pucking the ball around as they trained, running after it for them when it went over the bar or went wide, listening to them talk as they togged out or togged in, and all the time talking hurling.

That was the foundation of our hurling,

and as my six younger brothers — Pádraic, Michael, Joe, Jerry, Tom, and Murth — started to grow up it was many a great tussle and row we had as we played a game called five goals in . Later, as we all hurled for our club, which was known by everybody as Cashel , the greatest day of my sporting life was the day the seven of us won seven All-Ireland medals when we won the All-Ireland club final, beating the great Antrim team Ballycastle in the final.

It was also a tradition of ours, even after us getting married with our own homes, we would all meet in our old home place the morning of a match, known to everybody in Galway as Mamó's, which was an old name for Grandmother's. We would chat about the game, and without realising it we built up a kind of spirit that stood for us on the field. Then as we left Mamó's she would always shake the bottle of holy water on us, saying, 'Mind yourselves and don't be fighting, and don't come back here if ye lose.' Of course we had many a fight, and we lost plenty of times, but we were always welcomed home.

Of course the other great day in our lives was Galway winning the All-Ireland in 1980. You must remember that we were beaten so often for so long by so little to realise what it meant to Galway. On that great Galway team Michael, Joe and myself played, while Pádraic was a sub. Joe played a real captain's part, and crowned it all with a famous speech 'as Gaeilge' afterwards.

Hurling then has been a great part of my life and our family's, and although Nuala, my wife, spent many an evening and Sunday on her own with the kids, she also loved the involvement. It's now starting all over again with our sons, Shane and Cathal.

Apart from hurling I also played football with a city team called St Michael's and played with Galway minors and under-21s, and in 1968 with a lot of the stars of the great three-in-a-row senior football team. When I was seventeen a local boxing club was started by that great boxing man "Chick" Gillen. I joined with a few of the lads, and went on to win the Connacht junior light-welterweight championship that year. However, I soon came down to earth when a fellow called Mike Berry beat the hell out of me in a local tournament.

Anyway, I thank God for the ability to play hurling at top level. That game has helped me to be a better person in many ways; helped me to accept disappointment on and off the field and bounce back. It has given me the opportunity to make and meet friends from all around the country that I'll have until the day I die.

" "

John Connolly had no personal hurling heroes in his youth, but he was always wonderstruck by the way his father, who was normally a calm man, became elated and excited as he watched Joe Salmon and Paddy Egan and other Galway stars perform; and he would utter aloud their names to his young son John. The performance of the hurling heroes appeared to mean so much to his father that when John began his county hurling he always hoped that he too would bring joy and entertainment into the lives of many of the spectators.

His first senior match was in the championship in 1967 against Clare (Galway played in Munster from 1959 to 1968), and, like many a Galway hurler over the decades, he was to learn all about the frustrations of narrow defeats. Those frustrations peaked after the defeat by Kilkenny in the 1979 All-Ireland final. In John's opinion it was one of the weakest Kilkenny teams ever to win an All-Ireland. Galway failed to convert opportunities; conceded unnecessary scores; and failed to capitalise on

our strengths and take a grip on the game. On the way home his wife turned to him and said, Ye'll never win an All-Ireland now. John was well aware that there was a belief in Galway that a curse hung over the hurlers. But I always laughed at the idea. However, on the way home, after what my wife had said, I began to think that maybe there was some substance in it.

The Pope came to Ireland in 1979 and was given a magnificent reception. '1980 was a good year on the hurling-field. We beat Limerick in the All-Ireland final and had whatever luck was going that day — the first win since 1923, when Limerick were also beaten. We won the Railway Cup. My club won the All-Ireland club championship, and I was honoured with the Texaco Hurler of the Year award. Maybe the Pope had lifted the curse.'

Well, if he did it was only a temporary measure — a form of partial indulgence — because John 'will never understand how Galway lost to Offaly in the 1981 final,' and he thinks about the goal he scored in the first half — 'and the umpire waved the green flag but the referee disallowed it.' The sound of the final whistle heralded a feeling of despondency that represented a nadir in John's hurling life.

But there were high moments too, and one memory that will never fade was the occasion of the All-Ireland club semi-final in 1980 against the Cork champions, Blackrock. Athenry pitch was thronged. 'Parish rivalry was cast aside and every Galway man became a Castlegar man that day. I never remember scores, but I'll never forget that score, 2:9 to 0:9, and we beat a Blackrock team that had nine county players, including Frank Cummins of Kilkenny.'

As he looks back now his biggest regret is the depth of remorse and upset he used to feel after losing a match. 'I would go back over every movement and every missed stroke and all the opportunities and analyse the might-have-beens. If I could start all over again I would promise and undertake to myself as a top priority to set out to enjoy every match.'

He singles out three hurlers as exceptional — Frank Cummins of Kilkenny, Ray Cummins of Cork, and Mick Roche of Tipperary — and he wonders 'if we will ever again see a forward unit like what Kilkenny had in the mid-seventies: Crotty, Delaney, Fitzpatrick, Brennan, Purcell, and Keher.'

Brendan Considine (p.32) on the right, while on the run, with his brother Tull behind, and a professor of St Flannan's College, Ennis.

66

Now that the years have passed I look back as a young fellow on the preparations that counties undertook to win a Munster and All-Ireland championship. Clare gave more attention to this procedure than many other counties. We in Clare were amongst the most enthusiastic in this regard. Kerry were the tops; they trained conscientiously. Clare were the second.

For the 1914 All-Ireland and provincial matches and during the lead-up we spent almost six weeks — Lehinch, Quin, Lisdoonvarna, and Kilkee — in training.

Our supporters are the best in Ireland, and due to their generosity and enthusiasm we reached a higher level of fitness than our opposing rivals. Overall it is sad to recall that despite this generous support our county has not reached the top level of distinction to which at least our supporters were entitled.

99

Born: 1897

As well as being a great exponent of hurling, Brendan Considine also played football and rugby with distinction. He did some boxing too, but of all games hurling was his favourite.

He was one of seven brothers who, listed alphabetically, were as follows: Brendan, Dermot, Joseph, Pat, Sylvie, Tull, and Willie — better known as "Dodger" . All distinguished themselves on the sporting field. In 1914 Willie and Brendan won Munster and All-Ireland honours with Clare. Tull wore the county jersey when Clare won their second Munster title in 1932.

Brendan was a young man when Ireland was gaining its independence, and in common with many hurlers and footballers of those days he took part in the national movement. At one time he spent forty-two days on hunger-strike. He also spent some time on the run. To take the heat off him his employers, the Munster and Leinster Bank, transferred him out of Dublin.

The photograph in this book is a historic one. It was taken during a visit to his native Clare while he was on the run. At the back of the photograph is his brother Tull, and to Brendan's left is a professor from St Flannan's College, Ennis.

Prominently displayed in his sitting-room was the 1916 Proclamation, and also a photograph of Dev and himself that was autographed by Dev.

All through his life he felt a tremendous pride in our culture, heritage, history, and language.

Brendan's job in the bank took him around the country, and in his time he played hurling with Clare, Cork, Waterford and Dublin. He played against "Tyler"

Seeking possession. Cork's Crowley and Fenton
with Delaney of Offaly in mid-air.

The GAA stadium at Croke Park, Dublin on All-Ireland Final day.

The Cork team enter the pitch at Croke Park for the 1990 All-Ireland Final.

John Commins, Galway. 1990 All-Ireland semi-final.

OPPOSITE:
John Fenton, Cork. 1986 All-Ireland final, Cork
versus Galway.

Denis Walsh, Cork and Nicky English, Tipperary in the Munster Hurling final, 1990.

OPPOSITE: Team talk — the Kilkenny Camogie team. Page 40 TOP: Seán Kearns of Dublin during the Dublin/Waterford clash in 1990. Page 40 BOTTOM: P.J. Cuddy (Laois) in the Laois/Westmeath game, 1986.

Jimmy Barry Murphy, Cork 1984.

Mackey and remembered him as being very strong — a fine forceful hurler — with a black curly head of hair. He played with Cork in their Munster final victory over Limerick in 1920. He told me that Limerick objected on the grounds that he was illegal. Happily, however, good sense prevailed and the objection was withdrawn.

As he browsed through the names in this book he came across that of John T. Power of Piltown. He remembered him well, and recalled that he had the reputation of being a great goalkeeper. Turning to more modern times he recalled the great natural hurling ability of Des Foley and particularly his displays in his college days.

Brendan told me he always felt a great feeling of loyalty towards his native Clare. He spoke of the county's wonderful supporters, and regretted, as indeed all hurling lovers do, that Clare's great contribution to hurling down the years had not been reflected in titles won. His dearest wish would be for Clare to win its second hurling title and to see the McCarthy Cup cross the Shannon.

The Clare team with whom he won his first All-Ireland Senior Hurling medal was as follows: Ambrose Power, Jackie Power, M. Flanagan, E. Grady, Tom McGrath, Pa "Fowler" McInerney, J. Shalloo, Willie Considine, Brendan Considine, Martin Moloney, Robert Doherty, J. Fox, J. Clancy, J. Guerin, J. Spellisey.

'They were a fine body of men. Most of them were six foot or over. Many of the team were highly skilled in the art of doubling on the flying ball. The captain of the team was Amby Power and, at six foot four, he was the team's giant.

'The Dodger — that was my brother Willie — played a wonderful game in the final. He had strength and courage above the ordinary.

'Martin Moloney, who was better known as "Handsome", was a beautiful player and a lovely striker of the ball.

'Tom McGrath from O'Callaghan's Mills was a fine full-forward. He had great drive and speed.

'Bob Doherty from Newmarket-on-Fergus always played with determination and distinction, and he later hurled with Dublin.'

Brendan told me that the Clare forward line of that era was known as 'the forwards machine'.

He recalls that the 1914 victory was an occasion of great rejoicing. Clare had a good win over Limerick, and they defeated Cork by a point in the Munster final. The All-Ireland final against Laois was a fine contest, but the margin of victory, at 5:1 to 1:0, was more than Clare had expected. They were, however, very well prepared and trained throughout the whole campaign under the watchful eye of Jim O'Hehir, for whom all the players had a deep respect.

When it was all over, Brendan, who was still a student, returned to St Flannan's College, Ennis, and to celebrate the occasion there was a special day's leave for all.

In a career that lasted until 1930 his only other All-Ireland success was with Dublin in 1917.

...ory Meagher (left) and Eudi Coughlan shake hands prior to the start of the first of the 1931 games between Cork and Kilkenny at Croke Park. Behind Eudi stand Jim Hurley, Willie Clancy, "Balty" Aherne and "Hawker" Grady. *Opposite:* Eudi Coughlan wearing a skullcap, which each member of the team was presented with after the 1931 victory. He captained the side.

Born: 1900

receiving the cup for Blackrock Club in winning the county championship.

" "

"

It was my ambition as a boy to become a Blackrock hurler, and it happened when Carrigtohill beat them in the 1918 championship. The club was reorganised, and 1919 saw a new team — about eight of us were put on the team — and we never looked back up to 1931, winning seven county championships, four All-Irelands, five Munster Championships, two national leagues for Cork (Blackrock selection).

Cork took the selection from my club in 1932, so that finished my time for Cork. I never put on a red jersey for them again.

The Cork team from 1926 to 1931 was among the greatest ever. It was one of Cork's great eras, if not the greatest. The game was very fast then; if a player did not get rid of the ball he was tackled by a man, and the ball was pulled on without ceremony. By comparison the game now is like tennis, as players have to handle the ball before they can strike it.

While winning the 1931 All-Ireland after two replays was a very special memory, I got as much if not more pleasure in

I t was Johnny Quirke who arranged my meeting with Eugene Coughlan at his home in Blackrock, Co. Cork. When Johnny explained the purpose of my visit, Eugene said to him, 'Who would want to be bothered with old fellows like us now?'

The truth of course is that the name Coughlan, and in particular Eugene Coughlan, will always be recalled and remembered in hurling circles. It was men like Eugene — known to hurling fans as Eudi — that made and fostered the game of hurling. They were heroes in their playing days, and after their retirement legend grew around them.

I was glad therefore to meet and talk to this great hurler of the twenties. His many cups, trophies and medals were displayed in the living-room. Some medals he had given away, but he 'gave up that practice'. His wife told me that he used to say, 'I earned those medals the hard way; I sweated hard to win them; I'll give no more of them away.'

Eudi was captain in 1931. The final of that year was to go down in GAA history as a historic occasion. It was the first time that it took three games to decide the final issue. Each occasion was filled with drama; but in the end the glory rested with Cork. Victory gave them their eleventh title and put them joint leaders in the honours list with neighbours Tipperary.

As well as his All-Ireland medal, Eudi took with him as part of the spoils of victory the three sliotars that were used in each of

those epic games. They are on display in his living-room, with the score from each game neatly recorded on the relevant slio-tar: 1:6 to 1:6, 2:5 to 2:5, 5:8 to 3:4. Cold statistics, behind which lie the heat of battle.

To commemorate the uniqueness of the occasion and the famous victory, each member of the team was presented with a miniature gold hurley. Eudi took his from its place of display among his trophies and proudly showed it to me.

The famous 1931 team was as follows: Eugene Couglan (captain), J. Coughlan, E. O'Connell, J. Hurley, P. O'Grady, M. Aherne, P. Aherne, P. Delea, M. O'Con-nell, M. Madden, Paddy Collins, D. B. Murphy, Jim O'Regan, W. Clancy, T. Barry, G. Garrett (sub in replays).

He also showed me a plaque presented to him in 1961 by Gael-Linn and on which was written the following inscription:
Rogha iománaí na hÉireann, Eugene Coughlan, a roghnaíodh mar an leath-tho-sach ab fhearr riamh.

This great half-forward felt that players nowadays are allowed too much scope by the rules to play around with the ball. 'In my day,' said Eudi, 'if you didn't get rid of the ball quickly you got a flake of a man and the ball was flaked away from you. If you put your hand up for the ball, it was strictly at your own risk.' He strongly dis-agrees with some interpretations whereby players who have their hand hit when they put it up for a ball are awarded a free.

He told me that life in his day was simple, and all his spare time was devoted to hurling. He told me how hard he worked in his young days, when he was employed by Ford in Cork. Later he was to get a job with the Harbour Board.

Club hurling was very competitive in his young days, and Eudi expressed the view that it was as hard, if not harder, to win a Cork county medal as it was to win an All-Ireland title.

Hurling was very much in Eudi's blood. His father, Patrick — known as 'Parson' — and his Uncles Dan, Denis, Ger and Tom all hurled and won All-Irelands with Cork. His brother John also wore the Cork jersey and won All-Ireland honours. His mother's family also had a strong hurling tradition.

From his early youth it was his ambition to become a Blackrock hurler. He achieved this and won major honours with Black-rock and Cork. He was furious when Cork took the selection of the county team away from his club in 1932. He packed up county hurling in protest, and said to me, 'So that finished my time for Cork: I never put on a red jersey for them again.'

Tall and spare, amiable and affable, Eudi's views and convictions were laced with steel and determination as he recalled events from the past and voiced his opi-nions on many issues.

With Eugene, parish loyalty and club honour came first. His association with the Blackrock club goes back over eight de-cades, and even today he is still part of the club, guiding and helping and counselling. It seemed to me that his loyalty, dedication, commitment and lifelong contribution to the Blackrock club was at all times, in the immortal words of Charles J. Kickham, 'for the honour of the little village'.

Born: 1919

1955, I thought they were the grandest people I ever met. We had our good times — laughs, fun — and disappointments. We still meet on and off and still have a laugh or two. As regards other inter-county players outside of Cork, it was always a pleasure to meet or play against them.

And I don't mind telling you we were no angels on the field.

Looking back to my playing days brings to mind happy memories and friendships. I had my ups and downs, but I was a patient man, and it brought its rewards in the end.

"

"

I remember 1954 in particular at Croke Park. When coming on the field before the game and looking around, it seemed that all the spectators were on the field. I thought all the stands would collapse, there was such a large crowd. I was to hear that the entrance gates were broken down by people trying to get in. There must have been over ninety thousand people at the game. In my opinion it was one of the memorable finals. We were lucky to win.

They say it's better to be born lucky than to be born rich. During my inter-county days I met some of the nicest people that one could wish to meet. From my early days, 1938, to my last year with Cork,

Not all stories of fairytale dimensions belong to the long-ago. Dave Creedon's hurling career is a good example.

He loved all games — hurling, football, soccer, rugby — and in his young days played them all whenever he got the opportunity. But those were the days when the GAA banned "foreign games". Under that heading came soccer, rugby, hockey, and cricket. GAA players caught playing or attending such games were suspended. Suspicion, not to mention proof, made you a bad risk, and you could be dropped from the panel. Such was Dave's fate.

'I was dropped from the minor panel in 1937 because of suspicions about my eligibility. I saw Cork go on to win the All-Ireland minor title in Killarney that year. It was a lost opportunity — and a disappointment. A narrow sense of nationalism pervaded large segments of the GAA at that time. But I suppose it reflected the mood of the nation in those days. I was a sub on the senior team beaten by Waterford in Dungarvan in 1938. Later that year I was suspended for playing a "foreign game". I served my suspension then, but I was caught again in the early forties and served another term.

'Between 1940 and 1954 I won nine county senior hurling titles with Glen Rovers.' It is surely a little ironic then that in 1952, when Dave finally made the Cork team permanently, he got there because of a chain of circumstances that involved a chosen goalkeeper being dropped for allegedly playing soccer!

For the first-round match against Limerick, Jim Cotter of St Finbar's was Cork's goalkeeper. He fell ill. Mick Cashman of Blackrock was then called upon and subsequently had to cry off because of injury. Cork's next choice was Seánie Carroll of Sarsfields. He was delighted to be chosen. Then came disappointment. His soccer escapades reached the ears of the powers that be. Seánie was sitting on the bridge in Riverstown with some pals when a car arrived out from the city. He was quizzed and had to admit playing a soccer match the previous November. Exit Seánie.

Now for Cork's fourth choice of goalkeeper (all coincidentally beginning with the letter C) enter Dave Creedon, his *persona non grata* days now behind him. 'I was visited by Fox Collins at my place of work in Beamish and Crawford's and asked if I would play against Limerick. I said I would help out. I got on OK in that game, and coming off the field I said to the selectors, "I'll play the next time if you pick me, but don't make me a sub".'

Why object to being a sub? 'Well, all along my career I had played the role of sub, except for occasions when I played in League games or challenge games, and often I stood in the depths of mud in the pouring rain. I began off by being sub goalie in the senior team in 1938. After that I was sub goalie to Jim Buttimer and Tom Mulcahy. That's where I was for the finals of '46 and '47 — won and lost respectively. I loved being on the panel and assembling for training sessions and meeting colleagues. I enjoyed the banter and the crack. When we stayed in hotels we used carry on like children — knotting sheets and tossing each other out of the bed — but it was all harmless.

Coming off the pitch after the victory over Limerick I decided it was now going to be a case of first choice or not at all. When I got married the previous year — 1951 — I decided to retire from hurling. Maybe I might play a few games with the club; anyway, I was then in my thirty-third year — about time to be thinking of calling it a day.

'I remember listening in to the Tipperary-Wexford final of 1951 — I was on holidays in Salthill. Little did I think that I would be playing in Croke Park twelve months later.'

How did he find championship hurling? 'Those games against Limerick and Tipperary brought home to me the difference between club hurling and inter-county championship stuff. The hectic man-to-man combat; the speed; the intensity; the tension, and of course the atmosphere, all lifted the game onto a much different plane.

'I let in two goals in the Munster final against Tipperary that I should have stopped. They were both struck from about forty yards out. Apart from that I was pleased with my performance, but I was learning that championship hurling demanded total concentration for the full hour.'

Was there any one occasion that stood out above all others? 'Winning the All-Ireland final in 1952 against Dublin was a moment apart. I'll always remember coming off the field after the final whistle. Supporters had put me up on their shoulders; a delighted girl handed me a pear — I don't know who she was, but 'twas the sweetest thing I ever tasted: you know the way you can get dry with the excitement of a game.

' 'Twas John Lyon's first medal too. And there we were like two children hugging and embracing each other. But then I always was and still am a terrible sentimentalist. I realised that day too the difference between being part of a winning team on the field of play and being a sub. The sense of elation is completely different: you have to be part of the action to really taste the sweetness of victory.'

Three games of hurling stand out in Dave's memory. He played in two of those. The 1952 Munster final against Tipperary, when they halted Tipperary in their bid for four in a row in Munster and in All-Irelands, was very special. Dave collected his first Munster medal as a playing member. He was in his thirty-third year.

The second game was the 1954 All-Ireland final against Wexford. 'Croke Park was packed like sardines. Wexford should have won — they should have won well: they got countless chances — but they failed to convert them. For us it was a memorable win against the run of play. It was historic too. It completed three in a row for me and for Cork.'

The third game was the 1971 Munster final at Killarney between Limerick and Tipperary. Dave regards it as one of the truly great games in the history of hurling: 'the day Babs Keating will always remember, and fortune favoured Tipperary'.

Dave holds a unique record. In three successive All-Ireland finals he was beaten only once. Wexford slipped one past him in 1954. Dublin and Galway drew blanks in 1952 and 1953, respectively. An action photograph from the 1952 final shows Dave diving full length across the goal to bring off a breathtaking save while Tony Herbert of Dublin is seen leaping into the air, believing that the ball must surely have entered the net. 'I used my hands a lot. I had big hands — I was a cooper by trade. Sometimes there are invisible holes in the hurley.

'You could never be sure how things would work out in goal. I remember playing in the Cork county final in 1940 against Sarsfields. I was terrible: I think I let in seven goals. But the other fellow was worse: he let in more — ten, I think. And the following Sunday we played again in a

'suit lengths' tournament, and the two of us were the best players on the pitch.'

Interestingly, he would not regard the 1952–54 teams of which he was a member as being on par with the 1946–47 teams on which he was a sub. 'The '46 team was very talented. It was also very skilful. It was full of hurling ability and had many very good individuals. As a unit it was very effective — definitely ahead of the '52–54 team'.

Had he any particular hurling philosophy, and any particular view of the present-day game? 'I was one of those people that wanted to win every match. It didn't matter whether it was challenge, league, tournament, or championship — I always had a determination to win. I never gave up hope until the final whistle blew.

'I was never a believer in lifting the ball if you hit it first time on the ground — it makes such a difference to a game. I hate to see players lifting the ball unnecessarily.

'I saw hurling in the thirties, forties, and fifties. Standards were very high. The standard is gone down now. A lot of what I see now is cat: too much poking; too much lifting — why can't they get rid of it first time on the ground? Anyway, there is far too much protection for the man in possession. Those who frame the rules must never have played the game.

'You can't touch a goalkeeper now. I enjoyed full-blooded hurling: dust flying in the square. I never minded forwards coming in; it all added to the excitement.'

Speaking as a goalkeeper about goalkeepers, Dave has no doubt at all about who were the kingpins. 'Paddy Scanlon was the greatest I saw. I would put Tony Reddin second.'

Down in Cork, when they chose the Cork Centenary team in 1984 their choice of goalkeeper was Dave Creedon: sub in 1938 in the early spring of his career; hero in the All-Ireland campaigns of 1952, '53, and '54; memorable performances in the late autumn of the career of a most dedicated hurler.

Born: 1917

of Cork; Jim Mullane of Clare, Josie Gallagher of Galway, Johnny Ryan and Mutt Ryan of Tipperary.

I also had four brothers who played with Limerick: Tom, Joe, Maurice, and Willie. Tom won a minor All-Ireland in 1940 and a National League in 1947 and a Railway Cup in 1948.

I myself won four Railway Cup medals with Munster, and I played six times for Munster.

"

I played my first match with Limerick in 1937. We won the National League in 1938: we beat Tipperary in the final in Thurles. I played in the first Oireachtas final; we beat Kilkenny in 1939. 1940 was Limerick's year. We drew with Waterford in Killarney; we beat them in Clonmel in the replay. I marked the great Willie Barron.

We met Cork in Thurles and drew the first day, and we beat them in the replay. I was marking the great Christy Ring both days — fair but hard. We went on to beat Galway in the semi-final, and we met Kilkenny in the final and beat them. I was marking the wily Langton that day. Jim was a great hurler.

I played centre-back for Croom. We won seven West Limerick medals and we won two county championships — we beat Ahane in 1940 and '41. I was marking the great Mick Mackey.

I also played minor centre-back for Limerick in 1935 and 1936. I played on great players like Dr Jim Young, Johnny Quirke, Paddy Healy and Mossie Riordan

Peter Cregan was engrossed in a GAA article when I called at his home. He retired from inter-county hurling early in 1947 at the relatively young age of 28.

I asked him to explain what seemed to me to have been a premature retirement. He told me of the sacrifices he had to make when training for the county team. He remembered on many occasions paying a woman two shillings — a princely enough sum in those days — to milk the cows while he went to train with his fellow-players. His farm management work also involved ploughing and harrowing the fields with a team of horses. 'I couldn't afford to suffer injury,' said Peter. So it was mainly his way of life that forced him into early retirement.

Though small in stature, Peter was very strongly built. He used to pull tug-o'-war, and as part of his training for this sport he would throw a rope across the limb of a tree, attach a weight to it, and then hoist the weight. He was capable of lifting three stone more than his own weight.

Looking back on early memories, he recalled being a spectator at the Munster final in Cork in 1937 when he experienced the disappointment and agony of defeat as he saw his heroes and red-hot favourites, Limerick, go under to a gallant Tipperary fifteen. He made a special mention of the outstanding display of Jimmy Cooney for Tipperary at midfield that day and the terrier-like performance of Tommy Treacy at centre-forward.

Pressed to recall a particularly satisfying hour from his own career, his mind went back to an autumn Sunday in 1941 when his native Croom played Ahane in the Limerick senior hurling final. Earlier that year the 1940 final had been played and Croom beat Ahane. However, because of a family bereavement John and Mick Mackey did not play for Ahane, so Croom folk felt that they had to beat Ahane in the 1941 final before they could really relish the 1940 victory.

The task on hand was daunting. Ahane had nine of the county team in their ranks. In a tense, fiercely fought contest Croom emerged as winners for the second year in a row. On that day in the 1941 final Peter played at centre-back for Croom, and at different times during the course of the hour found himself opposed by John Mackey, Mick Mackey, and Jackie Power. One of those three would be enough in any game, but that day Peter was equal to the occasion and had one of his finest and most memorable hours.

Victory was all the sweeter because it was by the narrowest of margins, 4:2 to 4:1 (in the 1940 final the score was 4:2 to 3:1). So Ahane at the height of their glory had been beaten in 1940 and 1941 by Croom, and but for these defeats would have won sixteen successive Limerick hurling titles.

Fresh in his mind too were the two Munster final games with Cork in 1940. He described the exchanges as fierce and the atmosphere as electric. Both were gruelling games, with Limerick emerging winners in the replay. It was a cherished victory, because in the 1939 final a last-minute goal had given Cork a two-point victory in what was an equally pulsating and epic final.

Peter played on Christy Ring in 1940 and many times afterwards, and he always regarded him as a very determined but fair opponent. In the 1940 All-Ireland final Limerick met Kilkenny, who were reigning champions, having beaten Cork in the 'thunder and lightning' final of 1939 by a point scored by Jimmy Kelly in the dying seconds.

Peter recalls a sports page headline posing the question 'Who will hold the wily Langton?' The task fell to Peter, and he was as pleased with his performance on Jimmy Langton that day as he was when he had the task of marking him in the 1939 Oireachtas final, which Limerick won.

He described the 1940 campaign as a very tough one. The first-round match with Waterford was a draw. The replay was won by two points, with the winning goal coming in the closing stages.

The Munster final against Cork ended in a draw. The replay was as gruelling as the drawn game, with Limerick emerging with two points to spare at the end. There followed a hard game with Galway, and then the final against Kilkenny. 'It took six of the hardest games I ever played,' said Peter, 'to win the 1940 championship, and in the process we had to beat both of the previous years' finalists.'

He regretted that the efforts of subsequent years failed to bring him another All-Ireland medal.

The Limerick team on which Peter figured in 1940 lined out as follows:

Paddy Scanlon

| Jim McCarthy | Mick Hickey | Mick Kennedy |
| Tommy Cooke | Paddy Clohessy | Peter Cregan |

Timmy Ryan   Jim Roche

| John Mackey | Mick Mackey | Dick Stokes |
| Ned Chawke | Paddy McMahon | Jackie Power |

Born: 1925

associated with this book, and all good wishes to it.

99

“

Happy memories of the great game of hurling — playing against some wonderful players from Tipperary, Limerick, Kilkenny, Wexford, Waterford, Clare and Galway.

In my opinion the greatest men that played the game were Jamesy Kelliher, Dungourney, Mick Mackey of Limerick, and Christy Ring of Cork.

I am disappointed at the standard of the game at this time. The entertainment value is gone from the hurling with the new rules that apply: first-time hurling and the fair shoulder are now forbidden. Hurling and football are team games, and co-operation is necessary when possible. Overhead hurling is gone. We have too much stopping the ball and picking off the ground instead of first-time hurling.

At the moment there is too much hand-passing. Therefore, we have no long deliveries from the half-back line as in the great games of the forties and fifties.

Hurling has been wonderful to me — meeting and making friends throughout the country. I am delighted and honoured to be

Willie John's earliest GAA memories go back to 1931, when he was only six years old, to the second replay between Cork and Kilkenny in the All-Ireland final. Lory Meagher, then a household name and a hero of Willie John's even at that tender age, would not be playing for Kilkenny. He had rib injuries from the first replay.

There were only three radios in Carrigtohill in 1931, and Willie John had gathered with the others at O'Briens' house to listen to the broadcast. Coming up to half-time, local hero Tom Barry had the ball in his hand when the radio went dead. There was a stampede as everyone headed for one of the two remaining radios.

Cork won the day, and Willie John was happy. He now had county and All-Ireland ambitions, and got a red geansaí. From then on hurling became a way of life with Willie John. He had other interests too, particularly hunting, snaring rabbits, and seeking birds' nests. He loved nature. He never knew the meaning of the word boredom.

He loved listening to the grown-ups of his youth talking about the hurlers of the past, and one man in particular stood out. He was Jim Kelliher of Dungourney; and from what Willie John heard of him he had no hesitation in bracketing Jim Kelliher with Mick Mackey and Christy Ring. Here is some of what Willie John used to hear said.

'Kelliher was great. He was something

out of the ordinary. He was a great horse-man too. He was very fit from the hurling, and when training his horses he would, after jumping a ditch, dismount from the horse and run across the field beside the horse so as to spare the horse. He brought the same level of thoughtfulness to the game of hurling. He used to take some close-in frees off the ground, and was capable of scoring goals from the ground shot. He was a man of great intelligence.

Willie John's big moment came on the Monday before the 1947 All-Ireland final, when he was picked among the subs, and thereafter for a decade he was a regular with Cork.

He recalls that in his early training sessions with the senior squad he felt like a plough-horse among racehorses. The ball was flying by him, passing him up and down. 'They were so accomplished — Lynch, Ring, Lotty, Kelly, and company — all adept; all masters.' But Willie John learnt quickly. By 1956 he was a seasoned veteran.

Cork faced the reigning Munster champions, Limerick, in the final at Thurles. Willie John was at centre-back. 'We knew Limerick would be flying. We saw what they did against Clare in 1955. We were concerned about their speed. They were a fine team,' he said.

'My instruction to my wing men that day was to hold our line and not be caught out of position. I knew I would match any opponent in a twenty-yard dash, but after that I felt I'd be caught. They were very fast — after all, Prendergast was sprint champion.'

Willie John admits to having one of his greatest hours in the red jersey in that 1956 game against Limerick. Time and time again he repulsed and broke up the Limerick onslaught. Yet despite his brilliance it began to look mid way through the second half that Limerick would triumph as they went two goals up. And but for Willie John they would have been further ahead. It was then that lightning struck three times.

According to Willie John, Dónal Broderick, the Limerick corner-back, who for fifty minutes had totally contained Ring, momentarily lost concentration. The consequences were shattering, as Ring proceeded to raise three green flags. It was one of Ring's great moments of magic. Before the goal-scoring spree Willie John recalls that Ring ran out to the sideline to Jim Barry and changed his hurley for an old one.

Despite Ring's contribution they will still tell you in Limerick that it was Willie John who beat Limerick in 1956, and he was reminded of it in Mick Hickey's pub in Castleconnell on the occasion of Mick Mackey's funeral, when they talked into the early hours of the morning and 'the hospitality was incredible'.

One of his most satisfying games was the Munster final of 1952 against Tipperary. A great Tipp team were heading for four in a row in Munster and All-Ireland titles. It was important in Cork that Tipp should be halted.

The game was entering its closing stages, and the suspense was great. The score read Cork 1:11, Tipperary 2:6. Willie John was at centre-back. Tipperary won a sideline cut. 'Is there much time left?' said Willie John to the referee. 'Clear this one and it's all over,' came the reply.

Pat Stakelum took the sideline cut for Tipp. 'It hopped lovely. I dived for it and completely missed it; my heart sunk, but Gerald Murphy, Lord rest him, caught it and cleared it upfield, and the final whistle sounded,' said Willie John.

In that moment of victory his mind went back to 1949, to the same venue, to the first-round replay between Cork and Tipp. 'With two minutes to go Cork were three points ahead and were awarded a free about twenty-one yards out. Jack Lynch stood over the ball. Ring said to him, "Put it over the bar." "Don't worry," said Jack. The ball went wide. I heard Pat Stakelum shout, "Come on, lads, we have 'em!"

'From the puck-out the ball came up the field. Sonny Maher was at full-forward for Tipp. Jim Young was corner-back for Cork. Would you believe it, Jim Young and myself went for the same ball with Sonny Maher. I went to take Sonny, feeling that Jim Young would clear it. But didn't Sonny scoop the ball over to the unmarked Jimmy Kennedy; his hand was shaking; he gathered; struck — goal. Extra time, and we lost.'

Willie John had tremendous admiration for Christy Ring. He believes that Christy came into his own in 1946, and he considers the Cork team of 1946 to be probably the best all-round team to represent Cork. 'It had ability all the way from Tom Mulcahy in goal to Joe Kelly at corner-forward,' he said.

According to Willie John, Ring used to say, 'I'd never disallow a goal — it's too hard to get one.' He used also say, 'We should do away with the full-back and full-forward — what are they at but pulling and dragging one another?' That was of course before the third-man tackle rule altered the role of full-backs and full-forwards.

Commenting further on Ring, he said, 'Christy had perfect control of his hurley: it was an extension of him. He always used a heavy hurley with a wide pole. He had strength, speed, guts, courage, determination, dedication, and supreme confidence in his own hurling ability.'

Willie John had observed the duel between Ring and Doyle in the first drawn game of 1949. Doyle was under pressure, for Tipperary had set him the specific task of containing Ring. He was under no illusions. Any faltering on his part and Tipp would be out of the championship.

Ring was fully aware of the strategy. He too knew what was at stake. The hurling world would be watching the outcome of every tussle. Whatever the ebb and flow of battle, judgement would be reserved until after the contest was decided. All kinds of honour and pride and glory were at stake.

In the first game Ring got one point. All the time it was hip to hip and shoulder to shoulder. In the second game Willie John knew that a different strategy was called for. It was playing right into Doyle's hands for Ring to be standing shoulder to shoulder with him. A number of times Willie John said to Ring, 'Keep away from him, keep away from him.' The intention was to put pressure on Doyle by making him follow a roving Ring and possibly create a gap in the Tipperary defence. But Ring refused to respond: his reply was, 'The crowd, what about the crowd, what will the crowd think?' That's how it was in those days. That's how great the pressure was.

Willie John loved and revelled in the old style of hurling: hip to hip, shoulder to shoulder, the third-man tackle, ground hurling, first-time hurling, overhead striking.

He thinks you can have too much coaching. 'When the ball is thrown in, you're on your own and it's then you have to fall back on your own resources. That's when you must have confidence in yourself and concentrate on every ball.' He abhors the stupid foul, and says that we see a couple in every game and that quite often they cost a team the game.

Even though he played his best games at centre-back, his favourite position was left-half-forward; and while he met many opponents in his time he had no hesitation in naming Mickey Byrne of Tipperary as 'the hardest man' he ever met.

On Tuesday 30 June 1981, under the title 'This is Your Life', a presentation was made to Willie John in the parish hall at Carrigtohill. Here is an extract from the book.

A great man who was in the truest sense a sportsman who carried through his life the sense of chivalry and fair play that marked his conduct on the field.

A man of unfailing good humour. His pleasant disposition and colourful personality made him a popular colleague not only in sport but also in other areas of his life.

It is certain that in paying this tribute and in recording the details of his exciting career, many happy memories will be evoked, by both his contemporaries and his present day admirers alike. Memories of successes achieved for Carrigtohill and further afield, for his dedication to his native parish, as a leader, as a sportsman, as a family man, as a great historian in his own right. Willie John Daly, This is Your Life.

One of Willie John's constant companions during his childhood was a donkey called Baram, and anywhere that Willie John was seen, so was the donkey. He used to spend all his sixpences on oats to feed Baram. Whether or not he overfed him, one day Baram unexpectedly dropped dead while passing Barryscourt Castle. Willie John was of course broken-hearted at this sudden loss of a close companion. Nevertheless, he claims that to this day there was never a funeral as big as Baram's seen in Carrigtohill.

Willie John's hurling career ended with the Cork team in 1958, along with his fellow-players Tony O'Shaughnessy, Matt Fuohy, Gerald Murphy, and Josie Hartnett. The five players had formed the veritable backbone of the 1952–54 sides.

Willie John was then invited to train the Cork team, and it was under his guidance that the senior hurlers won the 1973 Oireachtas competition for the first time since its inauguration in 1939, when they defeated Kilkenny by 1:8 to 1:6. He continued to train the team for a further three years.

There were two Carrigtohill men who played a major part in building up Willie John's career from an early age: Tom Barry, a three-time All-Ireland medallist himself and now a great admirer of his, and Denis Conroy, who in Willie John's own words influenced him the most.

When I asked Willie John to pick a team that he himself would like to have captained, he chose the following:

Paddy Scanlon *(Limerick)*

Brian Murphy *(Cork)*   Seán Óg Murphy *(Cork)*   Jackie Power *(Limerick)*

Seán Herbert *(Limerick)*   Pat Stakelum *(Tipperary)*   Paddy Phelan *(Kilkenny)*

Jim Kelliher *(Cork)*   Lory Meagher *(Kilkenny)*

Eudi Coughlan *(Cork)*   Mick Mackey *(Limerick)*   Jimmy Langton *(Kilkenny)*

Willie John Daly *(Cork)*   Ray Cummins *(Cork)*   Christy Ring *(Cork)*

Born: 1905

Michael Daniels

could, I would give you the five stone and it would do both of us good.'

I played on Mackey in an army final and the pulling was also tough. The ref thought it was time to talk to me, and Mackey thought he was going to put me off and he ran over and abused him, saying we were only playing fair. It shows the sportsmanship of the man.

99

"

My first love was hurling. I played senior with Dublin, 1930, and a hard task was given to me to mark Tommy Leahy of Tipperary. We were beaten by Tipp that day. I played against Limerick in 1934 and the first match was a draw. The replay was a good game — Limerick won.

I have great memories of all the great lads of Limerick: Mick Mackey and John Mackey; Timmy Ryan (who was marking me) — a great hurler.

My greatest thrill was 1938, when we beat Waterford in the final. It was a pleasure to play against such a great team: John Keane, Willie Barron, Jack Feeney. Our team had some great stars that day: Tom Teehan, Jim Byrne, Harry Gray, and Christy Forde.

I had some great laughs in some of our games. One day in Cork in the National League final against Cork I was playing on Jim Hurley and the pulling was tough, and Jim said to me, 'If you play the game with me I'll play the game with you.' So I said to him, 'So well you could, and you five stone heavier than me.' And Jim said, 'If I

W hen Dublin faced Waterford in the All-Ireland Final of 1938 a unique piece of history was created. Mick Daniels was captain of the Dublin team. Mick Hickey skippered Waterford. Both hailed from the same locality — born within shouting distance of each other: Mick Hickey in Carrickbeg in the county of Waterford, Mick Daniels in Carrickmore across the River Suir in Co. Tipperary.

Victory went to Dublin, and Mick Daniels collected his only All-Ireland medal. It ranks as his most cherished hour.

His greatest disappointment was in 1934, when Limerick defeated Dublin in a replay after two wonderful games. Mick feels that Dublin had taken a grip on the replay and were pressuring Limerick, when the Dublin mentors introduced an unfit Charlie McMahon to the team. Mick has always felt that this was a blunder. Charlie had an injured hand. His prowess as a defender would place him among the great corner-backs of the game; but Mick is adamant that an All-Ireland final is no place for anyone who is not one hundred per cent fit in every respect.

When Mick first lined out with his adopted Dublin in 1930 he was joining a county that had established a proud hurling tradition. They had won All-Ireland titles in 1917, 1920, 1924, and 1927. The 1927 team was a superb combination. It beat one of Cork's greatest teams in that year's final.

It speaks volumes therefore for the 1938 Dublin team when Mick describes it as being as good as any team that Dublin ever fielded. This is high praise indeed, especially when one takes into account the brilliance of the 1927 team and the outstanding achievement of the 1934 team, which halted Kilkenny at the height of what many consider their greatest era by defeating them 3:5 to 2:2 in the Leinster final.

But with names like Harry Gray, Christy Forde, Tom Teehan, Mick Butler, Charlie McMahon, and Mick Gill, they had to be great in 1938. He remembers the thirties as a great decade for hurling, with Limerick and Kilkenny really outstanding, and fine teams too emerging from Tipperary, Waterford, Cork, Clare, Galway and Dublin.

As he looks back now he would have found it hard to believe in 1938 that forty-four years would pass and that Dublin would still be without further senior hurling successes at All-Ireland level. He feels that a hurling revival in Dublin backed by an All-Ireland victory would be a great boost for the game.

As he talked about some of the great players he encountered he singled out two in particular: Pa "Fowler" McInerney of Clare and Dublin, whom he described as one of the quietest players ever to play the game; and Mick Mackey, with whom he had many encounters and relished every one of them. Of Mick he said, 'He gave and took hard knocks in the same sporting spirit.'

One of his proudest moments was in 1936 when he won his only Railway Cup medal with a Leinster team that lined out with such greats as Paddy Larkin, Peter Blanchfield, Tommy Leahy, Paddy Phelan, Mattie Power, Tom Teehan, Charlie McMahon, and the Byrnes. They triumphed over a powerful Munster team by just one point, 2:8 to 3:4.

Those were the days when to play for your province was a wonderful honour. It made you the envy of your colleagues. 'To win a Railway Cup medal was a proud achievement,' said Mick.

Our meeting being on the eve of the 1982 hurling final, it was inevitable that we would exchange some views on the prospects of Cork and Kilkenny. While the consensus was that there would be a narrow win by Cork, Mick said that Kilkenny had the ability to outfox opponents and on occasions beat better teams than themselves. He was hinting at a Kilkenny victory, and as I write the final is over. Kilkenny are celebrating. But it was not a case of outfoxing a better team. They outmanoeuvred and outflanked the hot favourites to win a famous victory.

A selection from around Mick's era that he would like to have captained:

Tommy Daly
(Clare)

John Joe Doyle	Pa "Fowler" McInerney	Bobbie Rackard
(Clare)	*(Clare & Dublin)*	*(Wexford)*
Mick Daniels	John Keane	Paddy Phelan
(Dublin)	*(Waterford)*	*(Kilkenny)*

Lory Meaher
(Kilkenny)

Mick Gill
(Galway)

Tommy Treacy	Mick Mackey	Mick Darcy
(Tipperary)	*(Limerick)*	*(Tipperary)*
Jackie Power	Martin Kennedy	Mattie Power
(Limerick)	*(Tipperary)*	*(Kilkenny)*

Born: 1935

mensely, and made many friends. I always looked on hurling as a game to be enjoyed. The vast bulk of opponents want to play the ball. I never looked for trouble down the years; I have always maintained that anyone who looks for trouble will get trouble.'

Liam was a man of many positions. Versatility was his hallmark. In his years on the Tipperary team he played in fourteen positions; the only place he never manned was the full-back berth.

He took part in eight All-Ireland finals, and it is interesting to recall the positions he played in: 1958 full-forward, 1960 centre-forward, 1961 left-half-forward, 1962 centrefield, 1964 sub in the second half (to replace Larry Kiely in the forwards), 1965 and 1967 left-half-forward, 1968 left-full-forward.

He reflected on some of those All-Ireland games. He would rate the 1958 team as a moderate one. But it brought him his first All-Ireland medal, and that made the occasion extra special, even though the final itself was not a memorable one.

In 1960 Tipperary were supremely confident. 'We hit the field first and we were red-hot favourites,' he recalled. 'Then Wexford came out, and Theo English and myself observed their two midfielders: Jim Morrissey and Ned Wheeler. Both were big men and looking very fit, but that didn't dent our confidence. I was playing on Billy Rackard. I never really liked playing on him. I could never really manage him,' Liam admitted. The result was a humiliation for Tipp. Liam learnt that day that there are no certainties in sport. Of Wexford he said, 'They were a fine team and a fine bunch of men.'

He agrees that Dublin should have won

"

To win is great and a proud moment. So my great joy was to win a county final with my club, Borrisoleigh, at nineteen years of age — the year 1953. I won a lot of games and lost a lot of games, but hurling to me was a joy to play — and the friends I made on and off the field.

My second joy was to play for Munster with Christy Ring, Jimmy Doyle, and all the stars. As I look back and recall fond memories of past games, I realise that the memories become more important as I get older. I always believe in good sportsmanship on and off the field, and in my hurling days it was always my wish to aim at high standards and a spirit of give and take.

My greatest rivals were Johnny McGovern, Billy Rackard, Tom Neville, Larry Guinan, and Paddy Philpot.

"

Over a long career Liam Devaney 'got a lot out of the game, enjoyed it imthe 1961 final. In many respects that was Liam's final. He was switched to centre-back, and I can well recall his display. He steadied a Tipperary defence that was under great pressure. He dealt with everything that came his way with confidence and authority. His normal style had a panache about it, but in the final of 1961, as he stood supreme at centre-back, there was an added exuberance to his performance that made him stand apart. It was his day.

He won the Caltex Award of 1961, and he was also the journalists' choice as Hurler of the Year. Strange as it may seem, Liam does not regard the All-Ireland final of 1961 as his best day. His choice goes to the game against Clare in the Munster semi-final at Limerick in 1955. A very promising Clare fifteen had beaten Cork in the first round. They continued on their victory trail by beating Tipperary 1:6 to 0:8, but of that Tipperary total, Liam contributed either six or seven points. Though vanquished, he still cherishes his display on that day.

He regards the 1964–65 Tipperary combination as an excellent one. It was the best Tipperary team he played on. They made a clean sweep of titles in those two years, winning Munster, All-Ireland, National League and Oireachtas honours. There was strength in their subs, a sure measure of a good team.

He remembers training in Thurles for the 1964 All-Ireland final. At the last training session Paddy Leahy called Liam and Larry Kiely to the back of the stand. 'We're going down now to pick the team,' said Paddy. 'The two of ye are hurling terrible well,' he added. 'But we can't play the two of ye — ye will get a half an hour apiece.' And so it was. Larry Kiely played the first half, and Liam took the field early in the second half. It was a reflection of the talent of a great team.

As Liam took the field, the crowd responded with a rousing cheer. He had that kind of effect on the supporters: he always created an expectancy. Tipperary fans had not long to wait.

He gathered and controlled a ball on the wing; timed and measured his pass to Dónie Nealon; it was quickly dispatched to the net.

Liam had great praise for Paddy Leahy, 'who could motivate players in training, lift their spirits from the sideline, and inspire them to great deeds in the dressing-room at half time.' In his own county there was none he admired more than Paddy Kenny, and if Liam was picking a team Paddy would be a must for the corner-forward position. Tipperary had many great goalkeepers whom Liam admired, but he reserved special words of praise for John O'Donoghue. Of the 1964–65 forward line-up he had this to say. 'I look upon Jimmy Doyle as a hurling genius and comparable to Ring in many respects. McKenna and McLoughlin brought those around them into the game, and didn't always get the recognition they deserved. Keating and Kiely fitted into the Tipperary forward line like a glove.' It all added up to a forward combination that fired on all cylinders, moved with a deadly precision, and devastated many an opposition.

It was Liam's first-hand experience of this kind of teamwork that causes him to oppose such things as 'Man of the Match', 'Hurler of the Year', and 'Highest Scorer of the Championship'. He believes that such awards can offend many players and can turn some individuals from being team-centred to being self-centred and selfish.

He feels he was fortunate that his hurling career coincided with a great Tipperary era and that he was lucky to have got his place at a time when so many hurlers in Tipperary of above-average ability were challenging for a place on the county team.

His admiration of hurling artists is such that he would have settled for fewer honours to see players like Kevin Armstrong of Antrim, Jobber McGrath of Westmeath, Joe Salmon of Galway and Jimmy Murray and Christy O'Brien of Laois win some major national title.

Liam feels that players' sense of pride has diminished somewhat in recent years. In his day there was a great feeling of pride when you donned the club jersey. To be handed a county jersey was a really great honour, and under no circumstances would you miss an opportunity to play for your county. But to be selected for Munster and take your place beside Ring and his likes was an honour to be cherished for a lifetime.

I asked Liam if he could account for the descent of Tipperary hurling into the "black hole" since 1973. He feels that in general club hurling is not as good as it used to be, and that you must have very good clubs if you are to have a good county team. It is also his opinion that Tipperary have changed their style of play, moving away from the first-time stuff to something more akin to a soccer-style approach. As well as that, Tipperary seem to be unable to find three or four players around whom they could build a good unit. Unlike bygone days, the flow of talent no longer produces the two or three players annually that are the bloodstream of any successful team.

Then of course there is the matter of Lady Luck. Tipperary attempted on a few occasions to emerge from the "black hole". They nearly did it in style in the Munster final of the centenary year of 1984. They were hurling like warriors inspired and ready to be decorated, when suddenly everything went wrong and there was no time left to put it right.

Liam, however, is hopeful that success is not too far away. Given the breaks it could be a real possibility. Many would say it is a "must".

For there is no doubting that Munster and hurling need a vibrant and successful Tipperary — champions again in 1991!

Born: 1922

of far better men that put a lot more into the game and have but memories to show.

"

"
The game of hurling is a noble art of the best field game, but I am sorry to say it has lost some of its basic skills, such as ground hurling, the drop puck, and the clash of the ash as the centrefields fought in the air for possession.

I made many lifelong friends with the men I had the honour to play with and against, and many is the enjoyable hour I spent chatting about the match we could have won, but never the one we should have lost!

Some of the most frightening moments of hurling years was marking Dick Stokes in the Munster final, 1945, and Jackie Mulcahy in the final — both class hurlers with two very different styles.

To name the great men of hurling during my short time would take too long, but some come to mind: Mick Mackey, Bill O'Donnell, Jackie Mulcahy, Jimmy Langton, Johnny Ryan, Dick Stokes, Jackie Power, John Keane, Andy Fleming, Willie John Daly, and Jim Young.

Thank God and my fellow-hurlers for all I got from the game; but there are hundreds

Jim Devitt's inter-county career was a relatively short one — cut short in the end by health considerations. It was a pity. Jim was a sterling defender in the true Tipperary mould, all nine stone eight of him, and would have been a candidate for the Tipperary defence in any era.

In his short innings, however, he won All-Ireland, National League, Munster and Railway Cup honours. And much more lay around the corner at the time of his untimely retirement.

That was in 1949, and a wonderful year it turned out to be in many ways for Tipperary and its hurlers. They had three representatives on the successful Munster Railway Cup team on St Patrick's Day. Jim Devitt and Tommy Purcell were the wing-backs; Willie Carroll was corner-forward.

Very few would have thought then that within six months Tipperary would be All-Ireland champions. No-one, however, could have foreseen that none of Tipp's Railway Cup men would take the field in the All-Ireland final. Tommy Purcell played his last hurling game on St Patrick's Day. He fell ill, and departed this life the following September. Willie Carroll faded from the hurling scene after playing in the opening matches of the championship. Jim Devitt, too, took part in the opening games of the Munster championship and was left with memories that could never be forgotten. I refer of course to those drawn games against Cork at Limerick, and the extra time that saw Tipp win through.

'Was it Tipp's youth?' I asked Jim. 'No,' he replied. 'It was Lady Luck: there was only a hop of a ball between us.'

Jim is a Fine Gael supporter, and from time to time he meets people whom he regards as fanatical Fianna Fáil supporters. So to rise them he tells them this story from the game against Cork in 1949. 'Jack Lynch was in possession and got a dart of a hip from Tony Brennan. Jack lost his hurley, but continued with the ball at his feet. More tussling saw the ball rise into the air about a foot from Jack's head. I tipped it one side and let fly. If I thought then that Lynch was going to be Taoiseach for Fianna Fáil I'd have taken his head clean from the shoulders and finished him off.

'I get a great kick from rising the Fianna Fáil fellows with that story,' said Jim.

Jim belonged to an era of tough man-to-man combat, when exchanges could be fierce and no quarter asked or given. It was an era too when you didn't dally with the ball. It was a foolish man who would put his hand or foot in the pathway of the sliotar.

The following story from Jim illustrates how things could be. Tipp were playing Kilkenny in a League game in 1947. Jim was marking the late Jack Mulcahy, who had an iron reputation. At the end of the game, which saw some furious exchanges between the two, each of them had a split lip, and their bloodstained jerseys made matters appear considerably worse than they really were.

They were advised to get medical aid for their wounds, and headed off together to the local hospital. Jim entered the surgery first, and on seeing him the young doctor on duty said, 'Good gracious, what beast did that to you?' whereupon Jim just pointed his thumb backwards towards Jack Mulcahy, who was following close behind. On learning that each was responsible for the condition of the other, she could not believe that they could both arrive together in such friendly fashion for medical treatment. It was so like the story of Ferdia and

Cú Chulainn from Irish mythology. But as Jim said to me, 'when the game was over we shook hands and were the best of friends.'

The incident, however, had a sequel. Years later, by which time Jack had died, Jim was in Kilkenny playing cards, and in the company was Mrs Mulcahy. They were introduced to each other, and on hearing his name Mrs Mulcahy said to Jim, 'So you're the man that split my man's lip. Do you know that I didn't get a kiss for six weeks because of you!'

He regretted that he never had the honour of winning a county senior hurling title. Not that the opportunity did not present itself: he could have thrown in his lot with Ahane of Limerick in the early forties, but he declined the offer. He was in the army in Limerick at that time, and won an All-Ireland army medal on a team captained by Mick Mackey in 1943. He could have joined fellow-countryman Paddy O'Shea from Kilfeakle in the Ahane colours, but opted instead to remain with his native Cashel. As things turned out, Paddy O'-Shea played wing-back with Limerick against his native Tipperary in 1945, and also won five Limerick senior hurling titles with Ahane.

Among the players he admired were Micky Byrne of Tipperary; and if a team of practical jokers was being selected, Micky would be first on the list. Tim Flood of Wexford he regarded as a brainy hurler and a great artist of forward play. Martin Kennedy of Tipp and Paddy McMahon of Limerick he would rank among the great full-forwards of the game.

His greatest wish would be to have shared in the glories of Tipp's successes from 1949 onwards, and especially the three-in-a-row All-Ireland victories between 1949 and 1951. If he had been there he might well have been in the wing-forward position, because Paddy Leahy had plans for him there and had tested him in the League campaign against Laois and Dublin in 1948.

But it was not to be, for fate ordained otherwise.

Born: 1922

Shem Downey

S hem received word in 1946 to go into training for the championship. 'I thought it was the greatest thing that ever happened to me,' he said. He remembers cycling to the training session the first evening, and would have walked if necessary, so great was his enthusiasm to make the Kilkenny team.

It is somewhat rare to find a Kilkenny man who preferred football to hurling. Yet such a man is Shem Downey of Ballyragget. Although he played football with Kilkenny, it is of course as a hurler that he is better remembered.

He got his baptism of fire in his first senior All-Ireland final. The selectors placed him at centre-back and he had the task of marking Christy Ring. Shem recalls that for twenty-nine minutes he held him, and then Ring broke away, gathered the ball well outfield, and headed for goal, with Shem in pursuit. The backs fell away and opened out as each defender covered his man. This made even more room for Ring. Shem intended hooking him, but with a short swing Ring batted the ball, which, according to Shem, went in off Jim Donegan's shoulder into the Kilkenny goal.

At half time Kilkenny switched Dan Kennedy to centre-back, and Shem went to midfield. Ring's contribution to the second half was devastating. 'He was capable', said Shem, 'of doing it on any man, but if he had done it on me I would be gone for good, as I was making my debut. In a free-scoring game Cork won decisively, 7:5 to 3:8.'

Both teams were back in Croke Park the following year. This time Shem was corner-forward and marking the veteran

"

I remember the following in particular: In the 1947 League against Limerick I sent a ball from ten yards, which Collopy saved, and it bounced back away out the field. It was a crucial save.

In the 1953 semi-final I got the ball from the throw-in. I turned and struck and the ball sailed over the bar. But we lost.

In the 1951 Railway Cup against Munster I was corner-forward on Dan McInerney. 'Stay outside that line,' said Dan to me. When the next ball came in I pulled on the drop and goaled. 'Did you score that?' said Dan to me. 'I did,' I said. 'Then you will score no more.' I repeated it again five minutes later.

I enjoyed all my hurling days, and love to see my twin daughters, Angela and Ann, enjoying camogie so much.

Some of the men I admired included Christy Ring, Bill Walsh, Jimmy Kelly, and Dan Kennedy. From childhood I admired Paddy Phelan, Lory Meagher, and Mattie Power.   **"**

Shem Downey with his twin daughters, Angela, left, and
Anne, both leading camogie players.

and teak-tough defender Din Joe Buckley.
In a classic match Kilkenny triumphed 0:14
to 2:7, and Shem contributed two points of
that total.

The year 1950 was one of disappointments. In the All-Ireland final Tipperary
won by 1:9 to 1:8. Kilkenny had enough of
close-in frees to have won the game, including a dying-moments 21-yards free
that would have given them a draw, but the
stylish and usually reliable Jimmy Langton
had an off day, and Tipp collected their
second title in a row.

Earlier that year the same teams met in
the League final. The prize: a trip to
America. Here is how Shem remembers a
game that they lost 3:8 to 1:10.

'I was a sick man for that match. I didn't
want to go out that day. Talk about being
in form! I took punch on Saturday going to
bed. I went to Mass on Sunday, and was
beside a fellow called Roundy Lawlor, who
won an All-Ireland with Kilkenny in 1932
— he used to make hurling balls. "Go
home," said he, "and go to bed; you're not
fit to play."

'I went home and took more punch. I
might as well be drinking water. Anyway,
I went to Dublin and stripped off, and I
went to Paddy Phelan and said, "I'm bet;
I'm gone from the two knees down. I can't
play." "Oh, my God," said he, "and Langton off. You'll have to play. You'll forget
it when you go out on the field."

'Well, I never hurled such a game in all
my life. The strange thing was that for a
fortnight before I never caught a hurley in
my hand. I just did a bit of a run and got
massaged. There is no use in talking about
being in form. If I put out my tongue the
same day, the ball would come to me.'

Reporting on the match the following
day one sports writer wrote: 'If ever a
player deserved a trip to America, Downey
did.' It was suggested in some quarters that
Shem should travel and referee the match,
but Shem wasn't prepared to do this, as he
felt he didn't know enough about refereeing.

But 1950 did have the compensation of

a Leinster title. It was achieved over Wexford at Nowlan Park. This is how Shem recalls it.

'Wexford were only coming at the time. I was playing at midfield. My instructions were to stop Bobbie Rackard if he came up the field on a solo run. He did; I went to meet him and struck him in the chest with my two knees and knocked him down. Sure if it was now I'd be sent to the line. Anyway, he didn't come any more.

'I was playing on Jim Morrissey — a big man. The ball came down between the two of us and I jumped for it. Morrissey didn't jump at all but caught it over my head and side-stepped me and sent it over the bar from eighty yards. The next one came; he did the same thing. Begod I was a small man.

'They changed me at half time and brought me centre-forward on Bobbie Rackard. The ball was coming in low, and I scored a goal and three points against Bobbie.

'We won the game, but Wexford could have won it. They had served notice. They were on the march. With time running out, Wexford got a 21-yards free. They were one goal down. Nicky Rackard had a go at one of his specials. It was blocked. The game was over.'

According to Shem, there are no easy games. He remembers the intensity with which the semi-finals of 1947 and 1953 were contested against Galway, and in one of those games a colleague, feeling the white heat of the exchanges, turned to Shem and asked, 'Is it worth it?' From what he has heard, read and remembers he considers the 1935 Kilkenny team as the best ever to leave the county. And then he names them: Lory Meagher, Tommy Leahy, Jimmy O'Connell, Johnny Dunne, Padge Byrne, Paddy Phelan ... Other Kilkenny men he admired were Jimmy Heffernan, Jimmy Walsh, and Jimmy Kelly. He considers Willie Walsh one of the best he ever played against. Outside of Kilkenny he mentioned Willie Murphy, Christy Ring and the O'Riordan brothers of Cork; Pat Stakelum, Jimmy Finn, Jimmy Kennedy, Tommy Doyle and Tommy Purcell of Tipperary, and John Mackey and Jackie Power of Limerick.

Nowadays Shem's sense of satisfaction from the game of hurling is renewed as he watches his twin daughters — Ann in defence and Angela in attack — give dazzling displays of craft, skill and expertise as they proudly wear the black-and-amber for the Kilkenny county camogie team.

1967 All-Ireland, Tipperary and Kilkenny. Left to right: Mick Brennan (K); John Doyle (T), see p.64; Claus Dunne (K); Len Gaynor (T) and Kieran Carey (T).

Born: 1930

John had won enough honours when they spiked his bid for a record-breaking ninth All-Ireland medal and instead restored Kilkenny's pride by granting them their first major win over the premier county since 1922.

John is honours-laden, with All-Irelands, National Leagues, Railway Cups, Oireachtas titles, and county titles. He genuinely and sportingly spares a thought for the countless wonderful hurlers who won very little in the way of medals and in some cases no major trophies at all.

He arrived on the hurling scene in 1949 and just seemed to drift on and on from year to year with Tipperary teams that were at times great but never less than formidable. He seriously considered retiring in 1957. Being an only son and occupied in the running of a large farm was extremely demanding and very time-consuming. He weighed things up carefully and discussed matters with hurling colleagues and mentors. It was the late Paddy Leahy, a shrewd judge of a hurler's worth to a team, who prevailed on John to reconsider and keep himself available to Tipperary.

John's presence in the Tipperary defence contributed significantly to many a subsequent Tipperary victory. He could lift and inspire a team. His hurling was at all times fearless and full-blooded. He portrayed a "Matt the Thresher" image.

Three memories in particular stand out for John in a career that was highly eventful. Winning his first All-Ireland medal has always remained special. It was won rather easily at the expense of Laois in 1949, on the score 3:11 to 0:3. In fairness to Laois, they did not strike true form on All-Ireland day, and were a much better team than the

"

From an early age my big ambition was to be on the Tipperary team, and nothing was going to stop me. I must say I was fortunate enough to get on a great Tipp team at the start of my career.

I would say the fact that I was lucky enough to win eight All-Irelands and eleven National Leagues is not that which has meant most to me; it was the sheer enjoyment I got out of playing the game over two decades. I must say I was very lucky when I think of all the great players who never won any major competitions.

Hurling is one of the greatest field games in the world, and I hope it will continue so.

"

Fate was kind to John Doyle when, at the tender age of nineteen, he was guided by it to an All-Ireland senior victory with his native Tipperary in 1949. Eighteen years later, in 1967, the gods decided that

The 1950 Tipperary team — one of the great teams. *Back row, left to right:* Phil Purcell, Paddy Leahy, Jack Ryan, Dinny Ryan, Philly Kenny, Seamus Bannon, John Doyle, Pat Stakelum, Tony Brennan, Sonny Maher, Phil Shanahan, Jimmy Kennedy, Paddy Kenny, Fr John Ryan.
Second row: Gerry Doyle, Ned Ryan, Tommy Doyle, Mick Ryan, Micky Byrne, Jimmy Finn, Tony Reddin, Jim Devanney.
Front: Tommy Ryan, Sean Kenny, John Everard. *Mascot:* John Purcell

score might suggest.

Next comes the trip to America in 1950 to play the League final against New York. The Tipperary party flew out from Shannon about mid-September and arrived back by ship in Cóbh almost a month later. For John it was the experience of a lifetime. They returned as League champions, but only after an extremely hard-fought encounter. New York had in their line-out such accomplished players as Terry Leahy of Kilkenny, Phil Grimes of Waterford, and Steve Gallagher of Galway, and were cheered on by a crowd of about thirty thousand. Thirdly, there was the Munster final clash with Cork in 1960. As far as John is concerned it was a game that had absolutely everything, and was the greatest game they ever played. He described it as a titanic struggle. It reminded old-timers of the Cork-Limerick clashes of the late thirties and early forties. So energy-sapping was it that some have held that it contributed to Tipperary's poor performance against Wexford in the final of that year.

Like all hurlers, John had his childhood heroes. Mick Mackey came first. Then there was Christy Ring, who John was destined to play with and against in later years. Within his own county he had special admiration for John Maher, Johnny Ryan, and Tommy Doyle.

Paddy Leahy was a major influence on John in his youth, and he attributes much of his success to him. He considers Jimmy Smyth of Clare, Paddy Barry and Christy Ring of Cork, Eddie Keher of Kilkenny and Tim Flood of Wexford to be among the best he played on, and he regards his team-mate Jimmy Doyle as one of the most outstanding forwards the game has known.

At county level he was never particularly concerned about who he might have to mark. 'But at club level it could be different. An opponent who would never even make the county team might want to make his name and might attempt to frustrate you or spoil you or harass you, with a view to throwing you off your game. But this was something you had to live and cope with.'

He feels that some of the manliness has gone from the game, and laments the outlawing of the old-fashioned shoulder and the body check. He feels it has become too much a game of getting possession, running with the ball, and sometimes playing for a free, and that all this has taken from the game as a spectacle. He doesn't like the way players can go on solo runs nowadays and get an almost free passage, compared with bygone days; he feels it is insulting to opponents the way players on solo runs are allowed such latitude. In the past the style of tackling and body checking forced the player to release the ball, and he feels that that's the way it should be.

John readily admits that one of his greatest disappointments was the defeat of his native Tipperary in the Munster final by Cork in the Centenary championship of 1984. 'We haven't recovered from it yet,' he said, 'and right now the outlook is not good.' As he watched that game with six minutes to go, Tipperary were leading by four points. They looked like increasing their lead. He had expectations of celebrations and a great revival.

Cork were on the rack. Tipp were hurling superbly. Another sweeping attack was launched on the Cork goal; it threatened to seal Cork's fate. Then a Tipperary pass was intercepted. Suddenly and unexpectedly from the very depths of their defence Cork counter-attacked. Twice the Tipperary fortress fell. A dream had become a nightmare.

John still wonders how Cork got through for two goals and finished four points ahead at the final whistle. He didn't say it, but I'm sure he has often reflected that many a Tipp rearguard of yesteryear would in similar circumstances have taken no prisoners and conceded no goals.

Born: 1906

“

I started my inter-county senior hurling career in the 1926/27 National League, and I got a baptism of fire in my first two games: first it was Mattie Power, who was playing then with Dublin, and the second was Mick King of Galway. Apparently I didn't do too badly, for I was kept on the Clare team up to 1938.

One memory which stands out was our remarkable win over Galway in the All-Ireland semi-final of 1932. With twenty-five minutes to go, Galway were leading by sixteen points when Tull Considine started on a scoring rampage, which will hardly ever be surpassed so close to an All-Ireland final. He scored six goals and a point that day, which was mainly responsible for Clare winning by five points. However, Kilkenny beat us in the final by just one goal, 3:3 to 2:3. Sad to say, Clare hasn't won a Munster final since then, even though they contested the final many times. We are always living in hope.

Some people think the hurlers of today aren't a patch on the hurlers of thirty, forty or fifty years ago. Personally, I think that there are excellent hurlers today, as good if not better than those of the past; but the rules have changed the game a good deal. I think there is too much lifting and running with the ball. No hurler, no matter how fast, will travel as fast as the ball when well struck. Some think the game now is a lot faster; I don't agree. I accept that there is a lot more running, but the ball will travel faster when well struck. Besides, the non-stop for injuries gives the impression that the game is faster.

Nowadays it is hard to know who charges who when a defender attempts to stop a forward on a solo run. A player can be whistled for a foul if he pulls on an overhead ball and while doing so unintentionally strikes an opponent who prefers to put up his hand where his hurley should be. I agree with the rules which nowadays protect the goalie. I think that all scores should be made with the hurley instead of the hand ball.

Hurling is a great game — probably the greatest of all field games; and I hope it will last while grass grows and water runs in our dear old land.

*And when the Great Recorder marks your score against your name,
'Twill matter not who won or lost, but how you played the game.*

”

Hurling still plays a large role in the life of John Joe Doyle, who places great importance on clean play and good sportsmanship. He is still active with Tulla GAA Club and is involved with the Dr Tommy

Daly Park committee.

He would love to have seen Clare hurlers take an All-Ireland crown in the seventies. Clare's consistency in that decade brought them League victories over Kilkenny in 1977 and 1978. Those were the years when it seemed as if an All-Ireland triumph would have come Clare's way, but fate was most unkind. In the 1977 Munster final against Cork their full-back, Jim Power, was sent to the line in the first half, and Clare lost by five points. The following year, when Cork had a slender lead at half time after playing with the wind, it seemed that a Clare win was on the cards, but they failed to take scoring chances and appeared at times to be rooted to the ground. Their defeat, on the score 0:13 to 0:11, was all the more galling when one considers that John Horgan, the Cork corner-back, got the major portion of the Cork scores.

Hurling followers will know John Joe better as "Goggles" Doyle, a name he acquired because he used to wear goggles, specially designed and made by himself, over his glasses as a form of protection. The goggles worked extremely well for him, but there would be occasions during a game when they would get fogged up and John Joe would have to await a break in the play (in those days the non-stop play rule did not apply), when he would hurriedly wipe them clear.

Naturally, one of his great regrets is his failure to win an All-Ireland medal. He came closest to this in the 1932 final against Kilkenny. Clare came up against a Kilkenny team that was powered and back-boned by most of the seasoned warriors of the gruelling 1931 final against Cork, which took three games to decide the issue.

Clare came very close. At the end it was 3:3 to 2:3 in Kilkenny's favour. There were moments Clare would recall with regret, in particular two beautifully taken sideline cuts by Lory Meagher that floated into the square and were finished to the net by Martin White. In the case of one of those goals it was felt that Martin was in on the goalkeeper before the ball arrived. Years later, John Joe was to remind Martin of that goal, and sportingly he did not deny that it was of a doubtful nature.

John Joe recalls that towards the end of the game Tull Considine was going through for what seemed a certain goal. Some maintained he was fouled and got no free, but John Joe, who was at the other end of the field, did not have a clear view of the incident and could not say what really happened. Tull, he says, was a wonderful and great-hearted player; a stylist who also had the ability to mix it.

He recalled how much he used to enjoy the Thomond Feis tournament games each spring in Limerick, in which Cork, Limerick, Tipperary and Clare used to participate. He spoke too of the fine teams Waterford used to produce, and recalled some great displays by Charlie Ware, the Waterford full-back — 'a man of small stature but a very fine full-back'.

Then 1930 was another year when Clare might have won an All-Ireland title. In their great game against Tipperary in the Munster final they matched them throughout the field, but Tommy O'Meara in the Tipp goal had the game of his life. Said John Joe: 'He would have stopped the whole of Co. Clare that day.' Clare folk watched with envy and regret as Tipperary proceeded to defeat Galway and then go on to capture the All-Ireland crown at the expense of Dublin.

So, with great names like Tull Considine, John Joe Doyle, Dr Tommy Daly, "Fowler" McInerney, and Larry Blake, Clare failed to win an All-Ireland crown. 'I feel we were worth at least one title between 1928 and 1932,' said John Joe, and no hurling lover will disagree with that.

Born: 1918

of the reigning Munster and All-Ireland champions.

Limerick were heading for five-in-a-row Munster titles, and also for five successive All-Ireland appearances. After the victory over Limerick, Tommy was carried shoulder high through the streets of Thurles. 'It was an overwhelming experience for a chap of nineteen. It was a memory that can never fade; it was a dream debut — it doesn't often happen that way.'

And then he told me of another memory. It happened in 1949 when he was mature in years and a veteran hurler. He had decided to retire from hurling, but a chance meeting with John Joe Callanan, one of the selection committee, altered that decision, and what followed is the stuff that dreams and fairytales are made of.

Tipperary met Cork in the first round of the Munster championship of 1949, and to Tommy Doyle fell the unenviable task of marking Christy Ring. If he could contain Ring, Tipp's prospects would be enhanced; if not ... When the final whistle blew, the teams were level, and Christy Ring on the scoreboard had a personal contribution of only one point. Came the replay and the final whistle. Once again it was a draw, and incredibly Ring was on this occasion scoreless. Doyle was carving a name for himself among the hurling immortals.

The game went into extra time: two periods of fifteen minutes each. When the marathon ended Tipperary were in front and Ring had but one point to his credit. So, after 150 minutes of play Tommy Doyle's name had entered history for his magnificence in containing the Cork maestro and, apart from one point, rendering him ineffective where scores were concerned.

"

One of my greatest memories was beating one of the greatest hurling teams of all times: the Mick Mackey team of 1936 in 1937. I can recall that day getting away from Mickey Cross, racing away from Paddy Clohessy and racing in to Paddy Scanlon, scoring two great goals.

Men of my time that I admired were John Joe Doyle, Christy Ring, Mick Mackey, Jack Lynch, Larry Blake, Paddy Phelan, Seán Herbert, Jackie Power, and Johnny Quirke.

"

When I asked Tommy Doyle to record a great memory, he decided without hesitation to opt for the first major game of his hurling career: the Munster final against Limerick in 1937 at the Cork Athletic Grounds. His youth, speed and enthusiasm, coupled with the scores he got that day from the left-half-forward position, were major factors in Tipperary's surprise defeat

After he had recounted the event Tommy fell silent for a little while. He was in a pensive mood as he reflected on the encounter. It was as if he was reminding himself that it did really happen and that it wasn't a dream. Surfacing from his thoughts he said, 'I'm not sure if it could be done again.'

It was a rare achievement, but Doyle had the temperament to do it. Tactically his approach was right, and he achieved his success by his commitment and dedication to the task on hand, an indomitable spirit, and total concentration allied to first-time hurling.

The fairytale did not end there. Tommy went on to win three more Munster and All-Ireland titles, as well as two League victories.

He recalled for me the lean years between 1937 and 1949, particularly those that might have borne fruit. Tipperary looked like a very good bet to retain their All-Ireland title in 1938, but then came the famous "Cooney Case" (see p.155); and when Clare's objection was upheld Tipp were out of the championship. An outbreak of foot and mouth disease kept Tipperary out of the championship in 1941; however, in a delayed Munster final played in the autumn of 1941 Tipp faced Cork, who by then had won the All-Ireland title. Tipperary won convincingly on the score 5:4 to 2:5. 'I have little doubt but we had the ability to capture the All-Ireland crown in both 1938 and 1941.'

The lean spell was temporarily interrupted in 1945 after Tipp had surprised Cork in the Munster semi-final and went on to take the All-Ireland crown. However, it was back to the desert again in 1946, 1947, and 1948, when Tipperary experienced heartbreaking first-round defeats at the hands of Limerick and John Mackey; for Mackey in those years was still a power and used to cause havoc in the Tipp defence.

However, the arrival of 1949 heralded an era of glory for Tipperary and immortality for Tommy Doyle.

On the wall of his living-room hung a portrait of himself. It was presented to him by Cork admirers, and bore the inscription, "Tipperary's Greatest Hurler".

Mick Hickey leaving the pitch at Croke Park after Waterford's 1948 triumph. (See pp.99–100 below.)

Born: 1922

"

While I have many happy memories of my hurling days and Gaelic football days, the one I like best to tell is about the day we played a county match in the Loughrea Hurling Club grounds. It was during the Emergency. Petrol was restricted, and transport was not readily available. How were our club officers to get the team to Loughrea, twenty miles away?

After several meetings a friend of one of the hurlers had a turf lorry, which was engaged, and with great secrecy we all met there from the city centre at appointed place, known to the racing world: the famous Ballybrit Racecourse. Time: 11 o'clock a.m.

After several detours, trying to avoid all the official checkpoints, we arrived two miles from Loughrea town — this was to be the pick-up point after the match; walked to the field; played our game and won; had some refreshments — money was scarce: sweets, biscuits, and red lemonade.

On making our way back to the appointed place, word came that our transport was spotted, and, to use an expression from the past, our turf lorry was 'on the run'. So we started to walk back to Galway, getting to Craughwell village tired and hungry. Anyone that knows the area is aware of an orchard beside the road; enough said. Again we got word our lorry was the Galway side of Craughwell, up a side road. All aboard, and home sweet home. Five miles from Galway city our turf lorry broke down — time, 2.30 a.m. Two of the hurlers, Tommy Hughes and Charlie Hughes, had a friend in the area, Carnmore Cross; knocked up Roddy Grealish and saddled the pony and trap. Some of us got in and made for home. I got out of the trap at the crossroads — now a roundabout — and walked to my home at College Road; walked in — no lock on the front door — had a cup of tea.

That's just one of my many happy memories of my days on the hurling-field. I met so many nice friends — that is what it is all about. Much would be missing from our way of life without the hurlers and Gaelic footballers.

These are the hurlers I have played against who gave so much enjoyment to us all and asked for nothing in return: Kevin Armstrong, Seán Clohessy, Jackie Power, Pat Stakelum, John Mackey, Christy Ring, Dan Heffernan, Mick Mackey, Dick Stokes, Kevin Matthews, Vin Baston, Jimmy Langton, Jimmy Kennedy, Frank Cummins (Dublin), Jack Lynch, Paddy Rustchitzko, Tim Flood, Harry Gray, Nick Rackard, Tom Ryan, Padge Keogh, W. J. Daly, Paddy Scanlon, Jimmy Smyth, Matt Nugent. **"**

Seánie Duggan wonders how much more enriched the GAA would be today were it not for the War of Independence, the Civil War, and emigration. Each of these phenomena in our history left its own particular legacy.

'Much of our activities were too politically based: our thinking and aims became blurred; we tended to be very inward-looking. The Civil War left us with a loss of unity of thought, purpose, and objectives; all three events drained us of our young manhood, and we suffered the great loss of the energies and idealism of our youth.'

When he compares today with yesterday he sees the concept of "the good old days" as containing a great deal of myth. An uncle of his who spent fifty years in America remembers the past in Ireland as "the bad old days" when he calls to mind vivid pictures of hunger, deprivation, ill health, and unemployment. 'And yet these conditions that impelled people to emigrate indirectly caused the establishment of our games in foreign lands.'

As far as Seánie is concerned, the most important thing in the GAA is the club, and he emphasised this many times during our chat. Next in importance would come our youth, and in this regard he is very pleased with the good work being done by Féile na nGael.

He is a keen student of history and believes we can learn much from it. On the question of the future of the GAA and its games, Seánie draws a parallel with the famous revolutionary march of Mao Tse-Tung and says, 'It will succeed and progress as long as it has the support of the people; the club is the cell of growth and renewal.'

When he was a youngster in Galway he used to stand behind the goal and retrieve the ball for Paddy Scanlon, the famed Limerick net-minder. 'He did leave in a few,' he smiled as he recalled the legendary Paddy, who played club hurling for a time with Liam Mellows.

Seánie played minor for Galway at sixteen and spent two seasons in those ranks. He recalls his minor days with special affection, and saw them as the springboard to his senior career. He remembers in particular a minor semi-final against Kilkenny when Galway lost by about nine goals. After the game he overheard a supporter express the hope that he had 'seen the last of that fellow in goal.' Fortunately his wish was not fulfilled.

Seánie moved to senior ranks and established himself as one of the great goalkeepers of hurling history. He played in an era when goalkeepers had to cope with the inrushing forwards as well as the sliotar; and when I asked him what he thought of the task of the goalkeepers of the present day and the protection they were now afforded, he simply said, 'Good luck to them'.

Greatness is generally measured by performance and comparison. Seánie scores highly under both headings. He played many superb games. His understudy in Galway was Tony Reddin, and when Tony moved to Tipperary and was honoured by the county selectors his genius and brilliance between the posts gave him a permanent place among the ranks of the great hurling goalkeepers. But in Galway Tony had to play second fiddle, so one need search no further for proof of the calibre of Seánie.

His superb qualities were recognised and rewarded in 1984 when he was chosen on the Centenary team of hurlers who never won an All-Ireland medal. Also on that team was "Jobber" McGrath of Westmeath, a player greatly admired by Seánie, and he made special mention too of Des Dillon of Clare.

His choice of childhood hero goes to Mícheál O'Hehir — 'the man who brought hurling games in vivid form to the people of rural Ireland at a time when television was unknown and transistors unheard of.'

The games he enjoyed most were the Oireachtas finals of 1950 and 1952 against Wexford — both won by Galway (2:9 to 2:6 and 3:7 to 1:10). He remembers the games for the sheer splendour of the hurling, and he probably had his finest hours.

He would like to see Galway participate in either Leinster or Munster. 'Down the decades when Galway had some great men and very fine teams, games were lost through lack of competition. That vital edge was missing in close finishes — it cost us several games and possibly titles over the years.'

For Seánie there is one memory that will never fade: the 1951 National League final against New York at the Polo Grounds. With time ticking away and Galway one point up, New York were awarded a 21-yards free. 'Up stepped Terry Leahy — great hurler, master scorer. My mind was very uneasy: would it be defeat all over again? Leahy bent, lifted, and struck, but his shot was saved and cleared.' Seánie recalls that before the final whistle Josie Gallagher had two further points, to give Galway a three-point win. The final score was Galway 2:11, New York 2:8. (In the home final: Galway 6:7, Wexford 3:4.)

'To have won at home against an up-and-coming Wexford team and to win a major national trophy before thirty thousand exiles at the Polo Grounds is still clear and vivid and pleasing; and of course a trip to New York in 1951 — when many people never went outside their own county — was the treat of a lifetime.'

Seánie retired somewhat prematurely after receiving an accidental eye injury in 1953, but in any event 'the fences were getting wider; the agility of youth was fading.' Now at sixty-five years of age as he reflected on the hurling evenings and Sundays of his younger years — 'on a game that is an art apart, its extent and depth perhaps not fully realised, rather merely accepted' — the fact that he didn't win an All-Ireland medal seemed less a loss than it did twenty-five years ago or earlier; he thought mainly of 'the friends and the friendships, for that is really what it is all about.'

Dan Dunne (signature)

living: Dan Dunne, Martin White, and Jack Duggan.

Dan has a record of having won seven gold medals in one year — a record that is unlikely ever to be equalled. The victories in 1932 were:

Dublin senior hurling title with Young Ireland;

Dublin senior League title with Young Ireland;

All-Ireland championship;

National League 1932/33;

Railway Cup;

Leinster title;

Tailteann Games.

"

We lost our chance in 1931 in the drawn game.

"

B efore my visit to Dan at his home in Rathgar, Dublin, he had suffered a number of illnesses. I was glad therefore to find him in good spirits and recovering well.

He told me that he was regarded as the best schoolboy hurler in Kilkenny in his young days. At the age of fifteen he left school and went to Drogheda to serve his time in the grocery business. There was no hurling in Co. Louth, so during his seven years there opportunities of making the Kilkenny team were lost. In 1931 he returned to Kilkenny, and after twelve months he went to Dublin and joined the Young Ireland Club. He made an immediate impact, and was selected for the great Kilkenny team of 1931. At the time of writing only three members of that team are

After 1933 he played no more; this is the great regret of his career. 'I had to quit the game when I was only a boy,' he said. When he was in Drogheda he injured his knee roller-skating. It gave him considerable trouble on the hurling-field, and towards the end of 1933 he had to retire. He felt that but for the knee injury he would have played on into the forties and shared in many more Kilkenny successes.

So his career turned out to be a very short one. Yet it had many moments and victories to be cherished.

There was the success-laden year of 1932 already referred to. And there was of course 1931, when Kilkenny failed at the last hurdle but only after three gruellers with Cork. That was the only time the hurling final ended in two draws and had to go to a third game. Dan is very proud to have been part of that very special piece of hurling history.

He feels Kilkenny lost their chance of taking the title in the first game. After ten minutes of the second half Kilkenny trailed by 1:5 to 0:2. They staged a great recovery, and a game that might have been won ended on level terms, at 1:6 each.

He recalls that in the replay Kilkenny started well and went into an early five-point lead. After that it became a game of changing fortunes, but at the end of the hour it was level pegging again, this time 2:5 all. Dan felt it was a fair result.

But fate was to take a hand in the third game before it even started. Lory Meagher broke three ribs in the second game and was now sidelined. Missing too was defender Paddy Larkin, and Bill Dalton. Now with their forces depleted, and particularly with the genius of Lory not available, Kilkenny fell to superior Cork forces on the final score of Cork 5:8, Kilkenny 3:4. Dan recalled with a special sense of achievement that he was the only player to have found the net in all three games.

He felt there had been too many changes in the rules of the game, and preferred it as it was in his day. He did agree, however, with the rule that abolished "charging" the goalkeeper, but felt that when he is in possession of the ball it should be permissible to tackle him, even in the small parallelogram. 'It's too easy to get frees nowadays,' he said.

Dan went on to recall that there was an abundance of great hurlers in the thirties. 'They grew on trees' was how he put it. Men he particularly admired were Garrett Howard, Mick Gill, Tommy Treacy — 'he never drew back, was full of life, would tackle a steamroller' — Tommy Daly, Larry Blake, Tull Considine, and Jackie Power — 'one of the greatest of them all'.

He regarded Kilkenny and Limerick as the outstanding teams of the thirties. He felt Clare were most unfortunate not to have won a couple of titles between 1927 and 1932, and he took the view that Cork could never be underestimated.

He remembered Dublin club hurling as being of a very high standard and very competitive. There were some great teams, including Garda and Army Metro. He made special mention of a Tipperary man, Tom Teahan, who played centre-back for Army Metro and whom he rated highly.

As our discussion drew to a close I asked Dan if he would like to name the team he would like to captain from all the players he had seen. He opted mainly for a Kilkenny selection, supported by a few guest outsiders.

John T. Power *(Kilkenny)*

Dan Kennedy *(Kilkenny)*   Jack Rochford *(Kilkenny)*   Garrett Howard *(Limerick)*

J. Lennon *(Kilkenny)*   Tommy Moore *(Kilkenny & Dublin)*P. Phelan *(Kilkenny)*

Eddie Byrne *(Kilkenny)*   Lory Meagher *(Kilkenny)*

Christy Ring *(Cork)*   Sim Walton *(Kilkenny)*   Jackie Power *(Limerick)*

Dan Dunne *(Kilkenny)*   Martin Kennedy *(Tipperary)*   Mattie Power *(Kilkenny)*

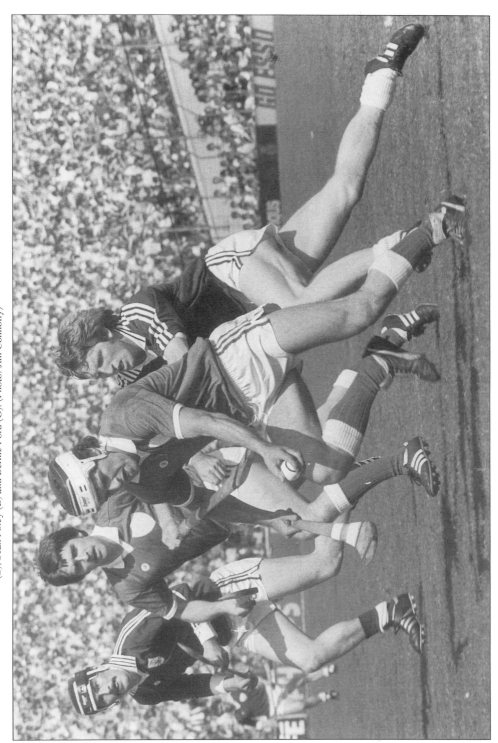

1981 All-Ireland Semi-Final between Galway and Limerick. (Left to right) Joe Connolly (G), Leonard Enright (L), Sean Foley (L) and Bernie Ford (G). (Photo: Jim Connolly)

Born: 1916

Andrew Fleming

" Some of the greats of my time that I played against were Christy Ring, Mick Mackey, Jack Lynch, Dr Jim Young, Dr Dick Stokes, and Josie Gallagher.

"

"

I would like to mention several great players I played on during my career on the playing-field. One was the great Christy Ring. I recall playing on him in Dungarvan in the National League. On the same day the game was not going so well for him, but near the end he gave me three stitches in the head, and while looking at me on the ground he said, 'I should have done it an hour ago.' That was the spirit on the field; but we were always the best of friends after the matches.

One of the greatest moments of my life was when the final whistle was sounded in Thurles when we beat Cork in the Munster final in 1948 by one point, after Christy Ring (RIP) had missed the last chance of equalising.

When Andy Fleming left school in 1935 he abandoned hurling and spent the next three years playing football with Stradbally. In 1938 he played two junior hurling games with Kilmacthomas — having been persuaded by the Kilmacthomas selectors to line out. Some of the Waterford selectors saw him in action and were impressed. Andy joined the county panel in 1938, and remained there until his retirement in 1951.

His approach to the game was marked by a deep dedication. He trained regularly the whole year round, and told me that he played with total commitment in all matches. He never believed in giving up or throwing in the towel, no matter how much his team might be losing.

There were many occasions in the thirties and forties when Waterford had All-Ireland winning combinations, but fortune never seemed to favour them, and they lost matches that they might have won.

Andy recalled two particularly frustrating games. One was the 1940 first-round Munster championship match against Limerick in Killarney, which ended in a draw — Limerick 4:2, Waterford 3:5. (Limerick won the replay 3:5 to 3:3 with a goal in the closing stages.) The second was the 1943 Munster final against Cork. Waterford were matching Cork in all positions, and with about ten minutes to go, a high ball came in that was going wide. Backs and forwards stretched for it, and the ball deflected off a hurley and into the net. It was the losing of the game, as the final whistle left Cork leading by two points — 2:13 to 3:8. Their disappointment was even deeper when they heard that Antrim had beaten Kilkenny in the other semi-final.

In both these cases Limerick and Cork went on to record All-Ireland wins.

The most memorable county final was against Tallow. John Keane was at centre-back and opposed by a six-foot-plus garda from Galway. Things were not going well for John, but when he was forced to leave the field with a severe head injury early in the first half it looked very bleak indeed for Mount Sion, as Tallow appeared to have a firm grip on the game. It was then that Andy was moved from right-full-back to centre-back, and the entire trend of the game changed. In the second half a very high ball came lobbing down between himself and the garda. Both pulled and finished up with split heads, but it was Andy who connected and cleared. As they lay on the ground the ball returned, and Andy recalls getting up and sending it over for a point. Words were exchanged between himself and his opposite number, who shortly afterwards was moved to full-forward. Mount Sion by now were in the ascendency and finished comfortable winners.

He recalled an incident from a great Railway Cup final against Leinster in 1943. It was a closely fought encounter right from the throw-in, and Andy remembers that there was never more than one point between them. Entering the closing stages of the game he gathered a ball in the half-back line. Glancing down the field he saw Christy Ring sprint along the wing waving, and shouting, 'Andrew, Andrew — '

Andy dispatched a ball of low trajectory that fell ahead of Christy, who gathered, soloed to the twenty-one and sent the ball crashing in to the net. Munster won 4:3 to 3:5. Whenever Christy and Andy met, Christy used to love to recall that movement. He would say, 'You could never again repeat that shot — it was so perfect.'

It was the beginning of a long friendship.

Andy also recalled for me a game between Cork and Waterford in 1944. It was the Brother Ignatius Rice Tournament final. He was playing right-half-back, and after ten minutes went down with a head injury, but was bandaged heavily and played on. Indeed the selectors wouldn't hear of him going off. It was important to beat Cork. In the second half Jack Lynch was switched to mark him, but this was Andy's day, and he continued to dominate. The bandages were changed when necessary. With ten minutes to go and the game as good as won it was suggested to Andy that he could now come off, but having gone so long he had no intention of giving up at that stage when all was over and won. He cycled to the hospital and had seven stitches inserted in the head wound, and then went home and went to work the following day.

An encounter with Mick Mackey in a Limerick v. Waterford game is worth recording. Mick was being marked by John Keane, and as they awaited an incoming ball Andy came in from the wing and caught Mick with an unexpected shoulder that rattled him. About twelve minutes later Andy put his hand up for a ball, only to find hand and ball getting the contents of Mick's hurley, with Mick adding, 'Tit for tat, Andrew,' and off he went smiling.

Andy has two cherished mementoes in his house. The first is a citation from the Mount Sion Club on the occasion of his wedding in 1946. The second is an address from Mount Sion Club after the 1948 All-Ireland victory:

In token of our appreciation of your sterling work and gallant service to Club & County, we the members of Mount Sion Club felicitate and congratulate you on this auspicious occasion of our County's Senior All Ireland hurling victory in which you played so active and so memorable a part.

Andy told me of an interesting episode in relation to the Railway Cup final that took place in 1945. There was considerable criticism of the hurling team chosen by the Munster selectors. They accepted a challenge from a second Munster fifteen, and the selectors added, 'We never presumed to be infallible.'

The game was played at UCC grounds on 25 February, the proceeds to go to the Augustinian church building fund. The prize for the winners was a valuable set of gold medals. Andy recalled that it was a fine game of hurling, with the original selection winning and vindicating the judgement of the selectors.

The late P.D. Mehigan ("Carbery") in a preview of the game in *Gaelic News* wrote:

Munster's Railway Cup fifteen, dealt with elsewhere, make familiar names in every hurling household. They will leave nothing to chance on February 25th, for their future places may be in the balance. This is a game to set hurling pulses beating high, every man of the thirty a star hurler, battling in a noble Christian cause. The turnstiles up the picturesque Dyke will click merrily:

'Oh for the clash of the Ash so sweet,
The flying ball and the hurlers fleet.'

Satisfied with progress? Paddy Grace (see pp.88-89 below), second from left, in the Kilkenny dug-out.

Born: 1927

Jim Flood,

ways thought that in my time Wexford hurling was very clean and sporting, and I believe it's because of this that the county team established the reputation it had for sportsmanship.

Among the players I admired were Christy Ring, Mick Mackey, Pat Stakelum, John Doyle, Johnny McGovern, Jimmy Duggan, Des Ferguson, Billy Rackard, Nick O'Donnell, and Johnny O'Connor.

99

"

I remember the 1962 final as the best we played in and one that I wish we had won. I was in the autumn of my career, and indeed most of the other players were also. It would have been great to have finished on a winning note, but in a finely balanced contest the scales tipped in favour of a great Tipperary team.

I remember the 1954 final for the chances I missed, and the outstanding display of Bobbie Rackard: fifteen minutes of the greatest display I ever saw in a hurling-field.

To have played inter-county hurling was a great honour. For me, however, I got even more enjoyment from club hurling. I al-

Tim Flood played his first game for Wexford in a League match against Dublin in 1947, 'but I was taken off shortly after half time' — "bíonn gach tosú lag". He played his last game for his native county against Waterford in the League campaign of 1962–63. In between those years he shared in all the glories of a great Wexford era. All-Ireland honours, however, were slow in coming. A series of setbacks, including All-Ireland defeats in 1951 and 1954 at the hands of Tipperary and Cork, respectively, were beginning to lead to some self-doubt and frustration.

But victory came at last in 1955. 'If we hadn't won that one we might never have won at all.' I suggested to Tim that Clare might have been a different proposition if their paths had crossed in 1955. 'Yes, Clare would have been harder than Limerick in the semi-final of 1955. They were convincing in their wins over Cork and Tipperary, but fell in controversial circumstances to Limerick in the Munster final on a sweltering hot July day. Clare had beaten us in the Oireachtas final — we were a bit unlucky,

I thought. They were a strong and quite talented team, but I think we would have beaten them, though it would not have been an easy passage.'

Why didn't Wexford win more in those golden years? 'I suppose we were unlucky in 1954 and 1962 — it was a puck of the ball on both occasions. I had the winning of it in 1954 — I was awful disappointed. There are always a few teams as good as you, so it is hard to come out on top all the time.'

Had he a childhood hero? 'Ah, yes: Mick Mackey. I was very young, but I saw him play and I used to listen to the matches on the radio. My mother was from Limerick, so we used to follow them. Mick was so good that every time you went out playing hurling you assumed his name — you became Mick Mackey. He changed hurling, and of course invented the solo run. I was always taken by his strength and ball control. I have no doubt but Mackey and Ring were on a plane apart.'

I asked him to reflect on the fifties and the memories uppermost in his mind. 'I suppose over the decade the rise of Wexford helped to change hurling a little bit. There were many great players I had admiration for: Tony Wall and Pat Stakelum of Tipp, and of course Jimmy Doyle. I played against the Cork backs — the cleanest backs I ever played against: Jimmy Brohan, John Lyons, Matt Fouhy, and Tony Shaughnessy. I played on Vin Twomey. You could hurl on him for a lifetime and you wouldn'ι get hit.

'I felt Waterford were the best team in Munster at that time. They should have won more. They played a most attractive brand of fast, spirited hurling and had several outstanding individuals — among them Seumas Power, Philly Grimes, John Barron, Tom Cheasty, Johnny Kiely, and Austin Flynn.

'I think the two best games of my career were against Clare in the Oireachtas of 1954 and against Laois in the first round of the championship in 1953. If I could start all over again I would put a lot more thought into the game. It was only after I finished that I began to think how a team

should play. As a half-forward I would concentrate on getting the ball in quickly to the full-forward line — full-forwards should be good tacklers. I would play more fast ground hurling and mix the game more. Billy Rackard perfected the "catch and strike" style for which Wexford were renowned, but I think Wexford played too much of this. The full-forwards could on occasions profitably play the ball out to the half line.'

His favourite position was left-half-forward or centre-forward, where he played for his club. If he had to pick two contemporaries to play on the wings in the half-forward line with him they would be Christy Ring and Padge Kehoe — 'a very brainy player'.

On trends at the present time Tim had this to say: 'The game is surviving very well. I don't agree with all the emphasis on fitness. Players are under too much pressure all the time now. They are even under pressure at training. I think this causes the skills to suffer. Billy Rackard wasn't too far wrong recently when he said that no-one plays for pleasure any more. A tendency to play a lot of passes has crept into the game, and I don't think that is really on. I feel that the very talented Galway teams of the eighties have tended to overdo the pass — and to their disadvantage on many occasions.

'I would like to see the youth playing the game for the enjoyment of it. A lot of money is going into the game now in a whole variety of ways. It's getting a bit professional. Somehow I don't like that.'

The name Tim Flood is synonymous with hurling, but it has also found honour in the world of music and dogs. He began learning the banjo at thirty. There was no musical heritage in his family. Learning it didn't come easy to him, but he persevered and was good enough to take part in competitions and fleánna between 1960 and 1967, when he was accompanied by his brother-in-law Gerry Forde, who was an accomplished fiddler.

He has been very successful with dogs. 'I suppose it might seem a terrible thing to say but the dogs gave me the greatest enjoyment of all. I was always interested in dogs. In the early days it was greyhounds, but towards the end of the fifties I got a border collie.' Thus began a team relationship between man and dog that brought Tim great enjoyment. His many successes include victories in Ireland and Britain.

Hurling glory and the sound of music are now things of the past, but Tim and his dogs continue on their way, still going strong and looking forward to the future and to more successes.

Josie Gallagher, Galway, with his daughter Ann. See pp.86-87 below.

Born: 1940

As I talked with this great Gaelic sportsman at his home in Kinsealy in north Co. Dublin, there was no doubting the great regret of his sporting career. It was the losing of the 1961 All-Ireland hurling title to Tipperary on the score 0:16 to 1:12. Although Tipperary had injury troubles they had a powerful team that included such greats as Kieran Carey, John Doyle, Michael Maher, Tony Wall, Jimmy Doyle, Liam Devaney, and Dónie Nealon. Twenty years later he didn't hide the sense of deep disappointment he felt when the final whistle blew on that sunny first Sunday in September 1961.

Des recalled that Dublin had many chances that day, and victory might well have meant a hurling revival in the capital. Unfortunately, opportunities went a-begging. With ten minutes to go Dublin had gone two points ahead, but Tipperary pegged them back, and Jimmy Doyle pointed to give Tipperary the lead. In the dying moments Dublin got a free some distance out on the Hogan Stand side, but the effort went wide.

Des was in no doubt that this was a good Dublin team. They had beaten the All-Ireland champions, Wexford, in the Leinster final by 7:5 to 4:8. They were well served in goal by Jimmy Gray; the full-back line was strong and solid, manned by Des Ferguson, Noel Drumgoole, and Lar Foley. Fran Whelan and Des formed a good midfield partnership.

The Dublin forwards, who moved the ball well on the ground, had fine strikers in W. Jackson and the Boothman brothers, Achill and Ben. In the Railway Cup final of 1962 Leinster selectors fielded eight of the Dublin team, including the entire full-

"

I regret not having won an All-Ireland hurling medal. I loved the game and all the friends I made from it. Special memories would be the 1961 All-Ireland and all the Dublin championships, hurling and football, with my club, St Vincent's, who came first for me, and the comradeship while playing the game for Dublin, which lasted into later life.

Having failed to win the '61 All-Ireland there was compensation by winning the two Railway Cups in 1962, where it was a joy to be associated with the greats of Dublin, Wexford (for whom I had a great grá), and Kilkenny.

More time should be spent on the basic skills of hurling, which I feel are vital to the game. Among the greats of my day were Christy Ring, Jimmy Doyle, Joe Salmon, Ned Wheeler, Billy Rackard, and Norman Allen.

"

back line. They defeated Munster by 1:11 to 1:9, and it is interesting to recall the Munster full-forward line: Jimmy Smyth; Christy Ring; Seumas Power. Des points to all this as evidence of the quality of the Dublin team of 1961.

He went on to talk about what it took to win an All-Ireland title, whether in hurling or football: courage, dedication, determination, commitment; a great deal of sacrifice; and above all, especially at that level, the breaks — or what many call luck.

He talked about all the things that can happen on a particular day. An entire team can hit an off day. A key player vital to a team's morale can play below par. Early scores given away, especially goals, can be demoralising, as indeed can scores to an opposing team against the run of play. 'There are so many things — so much that can go wrong,' he said.

Turning to personalities, Des talked in glowing terms of Jimmy Doyle of Tipperary — his immense hurling skills and his great sportsmanship.

With the name Doyle fresh in his mind, he recalled an encounter he had with John Doyle of Tipperary in a Railway Cup game against Munster. Des got possession around midfield and made his way past several opponents. He was moving at great speed as he neared the 21-yard line, at which time he saw John Doyle take off from the full-back line to tackle him. He sent a pass to Eddie Keher, who was lying loose; but when all this was happening,

John Doyle kept coming, and Des finished up flattened on the ground from a Doyle shoulder long after (or so it seemed to Des) he had passed the ball to Eddie Keher. 'What did you do that for?' asked Des, and John's reply was something like, 'What else could I do? I had to keep coming, I couldn't stop.'

Des talked about the superb artistry and hurling skills of Eddie Keher, which were clearly evident even in his college days, when he played against him in the Leinster schools championship.

He has a very special admiration for the Wexford hurling teams of the fifties and early sixties, and felt that they were unfortunate not to have won a few more All-Ireland titles. Ned Wheeler's sportsmanship and hurling style made a particular impression on Des.

He recalled too the great hurling prowess of Billy Rackard. He had clear memories of the Leinster final in 1961, when he played on Billy for most of the game. Throughout it was a battle to determine who would catch the ball as it came down from the sky, since both of them favoured this style of play.

Des was also an outstanding footballer and won an All-Ireland title with his native Dublin, but he preferred hurling, and I couldn't help feeling as we talked that an All-Ireland medal would in many ways have meant more to him than his football triumph.

The Dublin team of 1961 that failed to Tipperary by the narrowest of margins on the score 0:16 to 1:12 lined out as follows:

		Jimmy Gray		
Des Ferguson		Noel Drumgoole		Lar Foley
W. Ferguson		C. Hayes		S. Lynch
	Des Foley		Fran Whelan	
Achill Boothman		M. Bohan		L. Shannon
Ben Boothman		P. Croke		W. Jackson

Born: 1922

66

I enjoyed every moment of my hurling life. I made many friends. I often regret I never won an All-Ireland medal — so many times so near.

I hope the game will never die.

I recall some of the great men: Christy Ring — an artist — Pat Stakelum, Bobbie Rackard — wonderful hurlers. The greatest man I ever saw was Jackie Power.

I won a Fitzgibbon hurling medal with UCG. They were allowed three outsiders: Seán Duggan, Vin Baston, and myself.

99

Over a period of thirteen years in inter-county hurling Josie Gallagher hasn't got many great moments to relish. Heartbreaking defeats have left their imprint.

He remembers four All-Ireland semi-finals in particular. In 1944 against Cork at Ennis they lost by one point, 1:10 to 3:3. It was a powerful Cork combination heading for four in a row, and they were battle-

hardened after two epic encounters with Limerick in the Munster final. Scores were level in the last minute when, if Josie remembers rightly, Seán Condon got the winning point for Cork. The defeat became even more depressing after Cork beat Dublin 2:13 to 1:2 in the All-Ireland final.

In 1945 at Birr it was Kilkenny 5:3, Galway 2:11 — another one-point defeat. Josie recalls that Galway were two goals up after two minutes. They led by seven or eight points at half time. Nearing the end of the game Kilkenny had whittled down their lead. Then Langton equalised with a point from play for Kilkenny, and added the winning point from a free.

In 1947 Birr again proved to be Galway's graveyard, and again the margin of defeat was one point, the score Kilkenny 2:9, Galway 1:11. It was a great and exciting game of hurling. Galway seemed destined for victory. With two points up and lost time being played, the crowd thought the referee had blown the full-time whistle and rushed onto the pitch to cheer off their Galway heroes. But no; it seems a whistle had been blown by someone in the crowd. In the lost time that remained Kilkenny had points from Jimmy Langton and Terry Leahy, and dead on the final whistle Langton got Kilkenny's winning point. A photograph of the Galway team published after the game carried the caption, "So near and yet so far". Defeat brought bitter disappointment to a Galway team that had many outstanding hurlers, including Seánie Duggan, John Killeen, Paddy Gantley, and Willie Fahy; and yet Josie looks back on that 1947 semi-final at Birr as the most memorable game he played in.

Five years later, 1952 saw the string of

defeats continue when Galway lost to Cork at Limerick by 1:5 to 0:6. By now Josie was convinced that good Galway teams had the odds stacked against them in All-Ireland semi-finals when they met teams from Munster and Leinster who had put tough provincial campaigns behind them.

Josie considers the 1947 Galway team to be the best he played on. We have seen how they failed to Kilkenny by one point at Birr; but earlier that year they gave evidence of their class when they defeated a Munster team in the Railway Cup final that included John Keane, Willie Murphy, Christy Ring, Jackie Power, Tommy Doyle, and Alan Lotty.

1957/58 League final between Wexford and Limerick — a game that ranks with the great games in the history of the GAA.

On changes in the rules, he was very glad to see the third-man tackle go. Obstruction, he feels, didn't help the game of hurling. He is not too happy, however, about the scope now given to a goalkeeper. While he would be opposed to charging and dangerous play, he feels a fair shoulder charge should be allowed.

Talking about goalkeepers, he reminded me that Tony Reddin was a Galway man and that he once played at full-forward for Galway on Tony Brennan in a Monaghan Cup game against Tipperary in London.

The Connacht team — all from Galway — was:		
	Seán Duggan	
D. Flynn	P. Forde	Willie Fahy
M. J. Flaherty	Jim Brophy	B. Power
John Killeen		Paddy Gantley
Josie Gallagher	H. Gordon	P. Jordan
M. Nestor	Tadhg Kelly	Steve Gallagher

Josie was playing senior club hurling at fifteen. His boyhood heroes were Lory Meagher, Mick Mackey, and Paddy Phelan.

A game that gave him great personal enjoyment was an Oireachtas semi-final against Limerick in the mid-forties when he scored four points from sideline cuts at different angles from each side of the field. Indeed, those who saw Josie play will remember that he rarely lifted close-in frees; he preferred to cut them over the bar.

He felt privileged to have refereed the

When Tony Reddin joined Tipp, Tony Brennan was his full-back.

As we talked about Galway's great and historic All-Ireland win over Limerick in 1980 Josie pondered for a while and then said, 'Better Galway teams failed to win an All-Ireland' — surely a measure of the calibre of the Galway teams of the '42 to '54 era.

He summed up his sporting attitude to the game when he said, 'If you can't meet a man afterwards and shake his hand, then there is little point in playing the game.'

See also photo p.83 above.

Josie's ideal team, drawn mainly from the men of his era, reads as follows:		
	Seán Duggan *(Galway)*	
Bobbie Rackard *(Wexford)*	Nick O'Donnell *(Wexford)*	Jim Treacy *(Kilkenny)*
Jimmy Finn *(Tipperary)*	Pat Stakelum *(Tipperary)*	Jim Young *(Cork)*
Paddy Gantley *(Galway)*		Mick Ryan *(Tipperary)*
Christy Ring *(Cork)*	Mick Mackey *(Limerick)*	Jackie Power *(Limerick)*
Jimmy Doyle *(Tipperary)*	Nicky Rackard *(Wexford)*	Matt Nugent *(Clare)*

Born: 1917

"

When we beat Tipperary in the minor final of 1935, after many defeats at the hands of Tipp, it was a great breakthrough. It was also a surprise win, which made it all the more special for me.

I greatly remember the good years as well as the bad years, but I enjoyed them all equally well.

These are some of the men I admired: Paddy Phelan, Mick Mackey, Jack Lynch, Nick Rackard, Bobbie Rackard, Jim Langton.

"

GAA affairs have always been central to Paddy's life. That is very evident to anyone who visits the Grace household.

As the sun was setting on his county hurling career, Paddy found himself in the position of newly elected county board secretary in 1948. He has remained in the position ever since, and looks like staying there until the Lord calls him.

Paddy Grace and Kilkenny hurling are synonymous, and in many respects Paddy has become an institution in himself. Nowlan Park is special to him. He is particularly proud of the contribution he has made towards making it the fine stadium it is today.

His interest in GAA affairs, and the game of hurling in particular, is boundless. One of his special concerns is the spread and preservation of the game, especially among the youth. Strangely enough, or so it seemed to me, his senior playing days don't now evoke any great depth of enthusiasm in him. The task on hand now as county secretary has become an all-absorbing one, and he seems to concentrate solely on this.

When we did discuss his playing days it was very obvious that the minor triumph over Tipperary in 1935 meant a great deal to him. His interception and clearance that led to Terry Leahy scoring the winning point in 1947 had taken a back seat.

Secondary too was the great win of 1939. That final was played in a Hitchcock-like setting. Thunder roared and lightning flashed, and rain came down in torrents. Kilkenny stole the day from Cork when Jimmy Kelly from Carrickshock produced that magic touch that brought a point and the winner in the dying moments. It ranks as one of the memorable finals.

So now let us return to those days that have remained so special: Paddy's minor days of 1935. In a way it is easy to understand why the minor victory in the '35 All-Ireland against Tipperary has remained so special and vivid.

The competition began in 1928. It was

every young hurler's dream to win a minor All-Ireland; it would be a gateway to senior ranks.

Kilkenny were beaten by Tipperary in the 1930 final. They won their first minor title in 1931 with a victory over Galway. In 1932 they fell victims again to Tipperary. But Paddy had not yet arrived.

By 1935 Tipp were appearing in their fourth-in-a-row final and seeking a four-in-a-row win. Paddy was the Kilkenny captain. What an honour it would be to halt Tipp!

Paddy and his under-age colleagues had but one objective: the Tipperary victory march had to be stopped and the minor crown and glory brought to the Noreside. The objective was achieved. It was very close — six scores each at the final-whistle — but Kilkenny were superior on goals, at 4:2 to 3:3.

That success of Paddy's early youth still lingers on, a memory that time cannot dim, indelibly imprinted on his mind — a triumph that has for Paddy remained "forever amber."

This was the victorious Kilkenny panel, many of them later to become household names: Paddy Boyle, B. Brannigan, Tom Butler, J. Cahill, Tom Delaney, P. Giles, Paddy Grace, W. Henebry, B. Hinks, B. Holohan, Terry Leahy, Jim Langton, P. Long, M. McEvoy, Jack Mulcahy, S. O'-Brien, T. Prendergast, E. Tallent, T. Teehan, P. Walsh.

Paddy Grace, a familiar figure at Croke park.

Born: 1929

Ring, Tony Wall, John Keane, Jim Langton, Bill Rackard, Tom McGarry, John Kiely, Joe Salmon, Austin Flynn, and Paddy Barry.

99

"

· My greatest memory of course was winning the 1959 All-Ireland. My saddest moment was of course the 1957 All-Ireland, in which I had the honour of being captain of the Waterford team. I consider myself lucky to have played with Water-·ford in their greatest years, from 1947 to 1965 — the years that they contested their All-Irelands of 1948, 1957, 1959, 1963, and of course the one and only National League of 1962/63.

When I arrived in New York the first thing that struck me most was the standard of play in both hurling and football, which was so high. The dedication of the players and officials was great. They would have to travel long distances to get in one hour's practice — maybe one or two hours by train. Some of the prominent players that played in New York were Terry Leahy and Steve Kelly of Kilkenny, Joe Looney of Cork, Des Dooley and Seán Craven of Offaly, and of course the Galvin brothers of Waterford. In my years in New York I played with Tipperary.

Opponents I admired were Christy

Phil Grimes had three childhood heroes: Christy Moylan, Mick Hickey, and John Keane. He had a closer association with John Keane, because they came from the same district and belonged to the same club — Mount Sion. Indeed, in many ways John was a father figure.

In his young days, when he had no jersey, Phil recalls receiving from John Keane a present of one of his Railway Cup jerseys and feeling ten feet tall when he wore it. Another kindly act that Phil recalled about John went back to 1945, when the minor championships were revived. Phil was picked to play with Waterford; but two weeks before the match he broke his collarbone. On the day of the match he was standing at the Tower Clock, feeling very dejected as he watched his colleagues take off for the game. John Keane saw him, opened the door of his car, put Phil sitting on his knee and took him to the match.

Phil told me that John was a great all-round athlete, and likes to recall that people remember that John in his young days used to go part of the way to school walking on his hands. In later years when travelling to matches with the Waterford players they would stop to stretch their legs, and John would travel fifty yards down the road walking on his hands. Those recollections typify the man that was John Keane:

kindly, simple, devoted to youth and the game of hurling.

Phil played with Waterford in the first round of the Munster championship against Clare in 1948. After that he emigrated to America, where he played with the Tipperary team. 'We had some great games against Kilkenny,' he said.

In his first game with Tipperary against Kilkenny he was opposed by the great Terry Leahy. He played with New York in the 1949/50 National League final against Tipperary in New York. Terry Leahy had a great game that day on Pat Stakelum, but it wasn't sufficient to carry the day for New York, who went down on the score Tipperary 1:12 to New York 3:4.

Gaelic Park was the Mecca of all Gaels each Sunday. A field day was held for a different county weekly, and that county association would receive a percentage of the gate. Crowds of up to six thousand would gather for the Sunday game, and many would assemble in John Kerry O'Donnell's bar in Gaelic Park after the game. Phil was surprised at the standard of hurling in New York. It was very competitive. But once the game was over and you walked outside Gaelic Park no-one discussed the game with you: you realised you were 'in far foreign fields'.

Back in Ireland within two years, Phil resumed his hurling in Waterford. The 1961 and 1962 county finals against Erin's Own stand out in his memory. Both went to replays, and the honours were shared.

Phil welcomed the rise of Erin's Own. Up to then Mount Sion were more or less accepted as annual favourites, and when they were beaten it was as often as not due to complacency. But opposition that challenged Mount Sion supremacy was welcomed by Phil, because it tended to lift the standard of hurling, and this of course was good for Waterford.

He then went on to recall the dedication that he and his early contemporaries had to the game. As dusk would be falling, Jack Ryan, the caretaker, would want to lock up and he would shout at Phil and the other players, 'Why don't you bring up your beds altogether?' But as time passed by, Phil saw the changes that were coming. The young players would want to leave training sessions early; there were growing counter-attractions; even what the trainer might say could be challenged.

As we talked we wondered if the GAA authorities were too slow to recognise the changing climate. Should film libraries of hurling games have been set up? Should we have had museums? Should we be changing some more of our rules now that the modern game is evolving — for instance, ought the palm goal be disallowed; ought the kicked goal be disallowed; should it be permissible, within the rules, to shoulder a goalkeeper inside the small parallelogram?

He then turned his thoughts to their golden era, 1956–63, which saw Waterford win League, Oireachtas, Munster and All-Ireland titles. But one All-Ireland, 1959, does scant justice to the quality of Waterford's performances during those years. It's hard to know why more All-Irelands were not won; 'perhaps at times there was a tail on the team; perhaps the depth of talent wasn't sufficient,' said Phil. This is hardly the full answer, because Waterford lost games on the scoreboard that they had dominated and dictated outfield.

Waterford showed themselves capable of matching great Tipperary teams during their golden era; but against Kilkenny they tended in some way to change their style of play and pay the penalty.

It was inevitable that the name Christy Ring should come up, for they were contemporaries. 'Ring', he said, 'was perfectly balanced, and this factor contributed to his greatness. On the field he would chat you up with a view to distracting you or putting you off guard.' Phil remembered being a spectator at a Cork-Tipperary Munster final in Limerick in the early fifties. An incident he related demonstrated that Ring revelled in the unorthodox. The ball was thrown in — Ring was wing-forward on Connie Keane. Before Ring had got into his position Cork had got a 21-yards free. Ring took it and goaled. As he moved outfield towards his position Connie Keane, meeting him for the first time in the game, shook hands with him, but Ring kept going up-

Phil Grimes with friend and county team-mate, Seumas Power.

field and was back in defence when Tipperary were awarded a 21-yards free and he was on hand to clear it after it was taken. So before the game had even warmed up Ring had scored a twenty-one, saved a twenty-one, and had yet to clash with his immediate opponent.

Knowing that Phil had played in most positions, I asked him if he had a favourite one. Without hesitation he said left-full-forward. He loved the position. When playing there he always got the feeling of total confidence. It didn't matter to him who he was marking. He felt supreme.

If Phil could go back in time he would want to play all over again the 1962 Oireachtas final and the 1963 League final against Tipp. But pride of choice would go to the Munster final against Cork in 1959. He lined out at centre field. From early on it was obvious that Martin Óg Morrissey was having considerable difficulty in containing Paddy Barry — 'a great forward'.

Phil was switched to centre-back, a position he often wanted to play in, and he proceeded to dominate the scene and give a supreme display. His presence sealed the road to goal.

Ring moved out from corner-forward in a switch with Barry, alternating this tactic from time to time, but without success. This was Phil Grimes' day. When the referee blew full time, Grimes collapsed exhausted. Ring came over and picked him up. 'Go the whole way now,' said Ring, and they did.

This is Phil Grimes' ideal team from the men of his era:

Ollie Walsh *(Kilkenny)*

John Doyle *(Tipperary)* Nick O'Donnell *(Wexford)* Andy Fleming *(Waterford)*

Billy Rackard *(Wexford)* Pat Stakelum *(Tipperary)* Phil Grimes *(Waterford)*

Seumas Power *(Waterford)* Vin Baston *(Waterford)*

Jimmy Doyle *(Tipperary)* John Keane *(Waterford)* Frankie Walsh *(Waterford)*

Christy Ring *(Cork)* Nicky Rackard *(Wexford)* Paddy Barry *(Cork)*

Born: 1925

Jimmy Heffernan

"

I was born in Glenmore, a rural parish on the Kilkenny-Wexford border. I made my first visit to Croke Park in 1936 to see the famous Kilkenny v. Limerick All-Ireland. Kilkenny had great players in Lory Meagher, Paddy Phelan, and Paddy Larkin. Limerick had the famous Mick and John Mackey. I remember sitting on the sideline. It was a day to remember, even in defeat.

I also remember the old tram cars, which were very much part of old Dublin. Although I was from Kilkenny I won my first minor hurling championship in Wexford in 1941, with a team from New Ross called O'Hanrahans. In 1942 I was picked on the Kilkenny minor hurling team. The Leinster final was not played until 1943 — as a curtain-raiser to the Cork-Antrim senior All-Ireland final. We won the Leinster title at the expense of Dublin.

In 1944 I came onto the Kilkenny senior team, and we played Wexford in New Ross — a game which Wexford won. We had disappointing All-Ireland defeats in 1945 and '46, but we won against Cork in a great 1947 final.

My brother Mick was a very good hurler; he played minor and junior for Kilkenny and played senior in 1943. In 1944 he played on the Wexford senior hurling team that beat his native Kilkenny. A few years later he played senior hurling for Waterford and Mount Sion.

I played my senior club hurling with Mullinavat in the forties. I remember playing the 1943 county final against Carrickshock — the club that I later won a county title with in 1951.

What I remember most about the 1943 final was a wild swing I made that connected with Jimmy Walsh's leg. He had won All-Ireland medals with Kilkenny in 1932 as captain, 1933, 1935, and 1939 again as captain. He was a veteran. I was a chap of eighteen. The stroke was more careless than deliberate. Jimmy called me back as I was going away. He placed his hand on my shoulder and said quietly and firmly, 'There are lots of things I would let a chap do to me on the hurling-field, but I wouldn't allow him to do that.' For discipline and humiliation the lesson was worse than if he had hit me. I never forgot it. It was his approach that made the lasting impression on me. Ever after that I had great respect for him.

"

Jimmy Heffernan was eleven years old in 1936 when he sat on the sideline in Croke Park on All-Ireland final day and watched in awe as Mick Mackey led his all-conquering Limerick team in the pre-match parade. Before the team came onto the field a spectator beside Jimmy asked, 'Did you ever see Mick Mackey, son?' 'No,' replied Jimmy. 'Well, you'll see him today, and you'll never forget him.'

Ten years later he played on opposite sides to Mackey in a Railway Cup match. Father Time had taken his toll, 'but to have played on the same pitch with him was an honour to be remembered.'

Jimmy arrived on the senior scene at the early age of nineteen, and played his first championship match against Wexford in New Ross in 1944. In donning the black-and-amber jersey he was acutely conscious of the standards he had to live up to. Right through the thirties his native Kilkenny had witnessed a golden era in hurling. This was reflected in performances, victories, and hurling men whose deeds and skills would be talked about around the firesides for as long as hurling lived.

In that decade Kilkenny produced household names in almost every position. Honours came aplenty. Between 1931 and 1940, inclusive, they appeared in eight All-Ireland finals — missing out only in 1934 and 1938 — and were victorious on four occasions. And there were lots of names to inspire the youth: Lory Meagher, Paddy Larkin, Johnny Dunne, Paddy Phelan, Peter Blanchfield, Jimmy Walsh, and Mattie Power, to mention but a few. Yet, strangely enough, Jimmy's heroes were not the seniors but the minors of 1936. 'I saw them win the All-Ireland; I wanted to follow in their footsteps. My ambitions and dreams identified with them rather than the seniors.'

Jimmy was a versatile performer. 'I could hurl almost anywhere. I played in all the half-back positions. I preferred midfield best — you had room and freedom there. I also played in the half-forwards and corner-forward.'

His hurling career coincided with part of the war years and the postwar days of rationing, scarcity, and frugal living. Hurling was part of everyday life, and a very serious part of it. 'If you played a bad game or felt you lost a game for your club or county, you felt bad about it and felt somewhat in disgrace. You cycled to the club matches and togged out by the side of the ditch. Clothes were rolled up in a bundle and left on top of a stone or under a sheltering bush. Only the major venues had dressing-rooms, and most of them were very basic.'

He feels the elimination of the third-man tackle has helped the game evolve. 'In my day you stuck to your position and held off your opponent whenever necessary. As a defender one of your jobs was to ensure that the forwards did not get in on the goalkeeper. Nowadays there is more carrying of the ball and tactical play, but I think some skills have declined, like ground hurling and overhead striking. The ball is better now: it's rainproof. In my time it got soggy and heavy in the rain. It's a neater ball now; the leather at the stitching doesn't protrude as much.'

Jimmy's first All-Ireland final was in 1945. 'Jimmy Maher, the Tipperary goalie, beat us that day. Mícheál O'Hehir came into the dressing-room before the game and spoke to me; he always did that with new players so as to get to know them. He asked me where I went to school; I said Mount Sion, and he probably announced that on the radio.

'We were back again in '46, but Cork beat us. We got the blend and tactics right in 1947 and defeated Cork in a thrilling finish: no goals but enough of points to do the job — 0:14 to 2:7.'

The team he would like to captain reads as follows:

Ollie Walsh *(Kilkenny)*

| "Fan" Larkin *(Kilkenny)* | Nick O'Donnell *(Wexford)* | Bobbie Rackard *(Wexford)* |

| Jimmy Heffernan *(Kilkenny)* | John Keane *(Waterford)* | Martin Coogan *(Kilkenny)* |

Lory Meagher *(Kilkenny)*   Timmy Ryan *(Limerick)*

| Christy Ring *(Cork)* | Mick Mackey *(Limerick)* | Jimmy Langton *(Kilkenny)* |

| Eddie Keher *(Kilkenny)* | Nicky Rackard *(Wexford)* | Jimmy Doyle *(Tipperary)* |

He retired from hurling at the relatively young age of twenty-eight, having played at club, county and provincial level. 'They approached me three times to make a comeback, but I declined.' His last inter-county game was against Galway in the 1953 semi-final. 'We lost a big lead that day and finished up losing by a point.' After that farming took first place in his daily life, 'although hardly a Sunday passed that I wouldn't be at some match'.

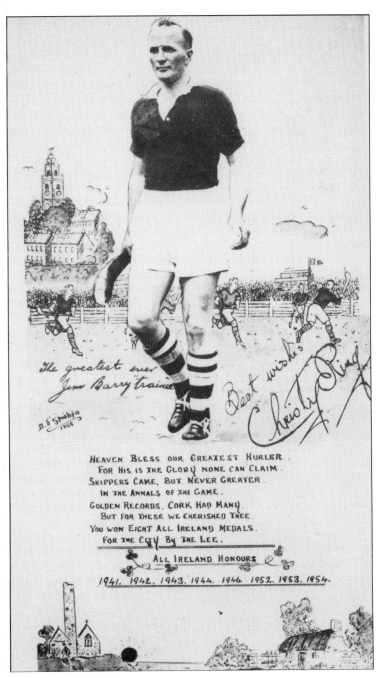

"The greatest ever" Jim Barry trainer

D.S Snooby 1965

Best wishes Christy Ring

HEAVEN BLESS OUR GREATEST HURLER.
FOR HIS IS THE GLORY NONE CAN CLAIM.
SKIPPERS CAME, BUT NEVER GREATER.
IN THE ANNALS OF THE GAME.
GOLDEN RECORDS, CORK HAD MANY,
BUT FOR THESE WE CHERISHED THEE.
YOU WON EIGHT ALL IRELAND MEDALS.
FOR THE CITY BY THE LEE,

ALL IRELAND HONOURS
1941. 1942. 1943. 1944. 1946. 1952. 1953. 1954.

See below pages 208-09.

Seán HERBERT 1942–1953 Limerick and Ahane

Born: 1923

Seán Herbert. Taken after the National League victory over Kilkenny in 1947.

"

In the thirties, when I was growing up in the parish of Ahane, hurling was the chief topic. This was the Mackey era, known after as the golden era of Limerick hurling. The Thomond Feis tournament held in Limerick every year between Cork, Limerick, Tipperary and Clare was a pointer to the championship. I saw some great games and some great players — George Garrett, "Fox" Collins, Eugene Coughlan, Jim Hurley, Jim O'Regan (Cork), Phil Purcell, Phil Cahill, John Maher, Tommy Doyle, Tommy Treacy (Tipperary), "Fowler" McInerney, Larry Blake and John Joe Doyle (Clare), and of course our own Mackeys, Timmy Ryan, Paddy Scanlon, Paddy Clohessy, Garrett Howard, Jackie Power, and Paddy McMahon.

I remember my father taking me to the Munster final in 1937 against Tipperary. The whole world caved in on me that day as my heroes were beaten. That day my favourite player was Tommy Doyle — he had everything a hurler needed. Little did I think that day that I would play with him on Munster teams, and against him with Limerick. We became great friends over the years.

Jackie Power was my hero in my young days. I grew up with him, and he was a great character. Jackie was also a very good athlete. The greatest moment of my life was when I was notified that I was picked to play against Cork in the League, 1942. I had been a minor in 1941 — rule 27 knocked me out of a minor All-Ireland in 1940. My opponent that day was Jim

96

Young, one of the best half-backs ever to come out of Cork.

The greatest backs I played on were Jim Young, Tommy Doyle, Tommy Purcell, Bobbie Rackard, Jack Quaid, Andy Fleming, and John Keane. The best forwards I played against were Josie Gallagher, Jack Mulcahy, Jimmy Smyth, Mick Ryan, Hauley Daly, Willie John Daly, and Tommy Doyle.

The one regret I have is that I did not win a Munster or All-Ireland medal after playing for twelve years. I played in five Munster finals without success. Nevertheless, it was great to have played with and against all those fine players. It would be wonderful to meet all those lads together and go down hurling's memory lane. I would love to get their views on coaching and the state of present-day hurling, especially Jim Young.

99

S eán Herbert will tell you that when he was growing up two topics dominated the Herbert household. These were politics and hurling. Seán's father's house was burned by the Tans during the struggle for independence, and the memory didn't die easily. The independence movement found very strong support in Seán's native district of Castleconnell. He mentioned in particular Seán Carroll, a local fisherman and Irish-speaker who was to become OC of the East Limerick Flying Column.

So much local involvement led to the disbanding of the Castleconnell club around the year 1918. Between then and 1927/28 hurlers in the locality played with

a variety of different clubs. Then a new club was formed, under the name Ahane. It was destined to make its mark on the hurling world.

It is hard to believe that in twelve years in inter-county hurling, Seán failed to win either a Munster or an All-Ireland medal, despite playing in five Munster finals. Admittedly there were several near misses, and Seán recounted some of them.

He remembers as a spectator at the 1939 Munster final marvelling at the skill of Johnny Quirke, a most versatile hurler, as he doubled on an overhead ball that Paddy Scanlon in the Limerick goal never saw as it flashed to the net. But his admiration turned to heartache in 1944 when, as a member of the Limerick team, he saw Johnny send in a low ground ball from around midfield that travelled all the way to the Limerick net. An epic game that might have been won was drawn.

The replay was even more heart-breaking. Again fortunes ebbed and flowed. With fifteen minutes remaining and Limerick five points clear, Mick Mackey had the ball in the Cork net only to have it disallowed for a free on him as he went through (advantage rule?); the free was missed. With the final seconds approaching, Limerick were now level, but then Christy Ring found the net, and prompted one sports editor to head the report, "Ring's wonder goal keeps title in Cork."

The following year, 1945, Limerick suffered defeat at the hands of Tipperary in a game in which Limerick dominated and had 70 per cent of the play; but the Tipperary defence, and in particular little Jimmy Maher in goal, were superb. In those days your championship form determined whether or not you made the provincial

His ideal team from the men of his time is:

	Paddy Scanlon *(Limerick)*	
Bobbie Rackard *(Wexford)*	Nick O'Donnell *(Wexford)*	Alan Lotty *(Cork)*
Seán Herbert *(Limerick)*	John Keane *(Waterford)*	Jim Young *(Cork)*
	Timmy Ryan *(Limerick)*	Harry Gray *(Laois)*
Christy Ring *(Cork)*	Mick Mackey *(Limerick)*	Tommy Doyle *(Tipperary)*
Johnny Quirke *(Cork)*	Nicky Rackard *(Wexford)*	Jackie Power *(Limerick)*

team. As Seán walked disconsolately from the field Johnny Ryan of Tipperary came over to him and told him he would be on the Munster team. At the time, however, it was poor consolation.

Then there was 1949 — again against Tipp — when Jackie Power had the ball in the net after a great solo run only to be whistled back by the referee, Con Murphy of Cork, for allegedly carrying the ball too far. The losing margin was one goal. Seán was captain that day, and as such regards the 1949 Munster final defeat as his greatest disappointment.

Despite these and other near misses, Seán relished all his hurling days, and was rewarded with League, Railway Cup and county honours. The 1947 National League victory over Kilkenny stands out as his most memorable occasion. It was his first time playing in Croke Park. The fact that Kilkenny were All-Ireland champions and had defeated Cork in a classic added further lustre to the Limerick win. According to Seán it was a Limerick team of very considerable potential with a very tight defence.

The first game ended in a thrilling draw — Limerick 4:5, Kilkenny 2:11. In the replay Seán formed part of a powerful Limerick half-back line, all from Ahane. It read: Seán Herbert, Jackie Power, Thomas O'Brien. Seán's brother Mick was at fullback. Limerick triumphed by 3:8 to 1:7.

A feature of the replay was the outstanding display of the Limerick goalkeeper, Paddy Collopy. Twice he saved point-blank shots from the Kilkenny men from a range of 10 or 12 yards. The game and exchanges were far closer than the score suggests. A Monday sports page carried the headline, "Goalkeeper Collopy's wonderful saves."

There were other memories too. All through the forties, when Limerick met Cork, Limerick players never looked upon Christy Ring with particular fear. They tended to worry more about players like Johnny Quirke, Joe Kelly, and Seán Condon. Seán recalled the first-round championship game against Cork in Limerick in

1942 — a game that Jim Young described as the greatest game he ever played in. In Seán's opinion Jackie Power played the greatest game of his career that day on Christy Ring. He was high in his praise for Harry Gray of Laois, equally adept left or right, and second only to Timmy Ryan in overhead play.

We then talked about the various types of attire worn by players in bygone days. Barefoot players were not uncommon in the early part of the century. Peaked caps were quite common; as well as keeping the sun out of the eyes they also protected the head. Some players who hadn't hurling boots used to play in their everyday shoes or boots. It was not unusual to see a team (at club level of course) with one or two players playing in long trousers tucked inside their socks. Funds were scarce in those days, and togs were not always available for all members of the team.

Seán witnessed something on the field that I had never seen. When very young he travelled on the bar of a bicycle to a match at Marketsfield in Limerick and there saw one of the players displaying his hurling skills while wearing a hard hat.

Seán has studied all aspects of the game and loves to talk about tactics. If he had power, there is one change he would like to make. He feels that it is extremely difficult for a defender to cope with an incoming forward as the rules stand, and would like to see the frontal shoulder block allowed. (Bobbie Rackard was in full agreement with this when I talked to him.) In advocating this change, it is interesting to note that Seán does not speak as a defender only. It must be remembered that he won Railway Cup honours as a half-back, midfielder, and half-forward.

Seán's inter-county career ended rather abruptly. In the 1953 Munster championship Limerick were trounced by Clare. Seán was disconsolate, and decided to quit the county scene, despite the pleadings of Jackie O'Connell. It was a pity. In the years that followed Limerick could have done with his experience.

Mick Hickey, proudly displaying the hurley used by his father in the 1888 "invasion" of the United States by the Irish athletes.

Born: 1911

and others that I admired were Christy Ring, Mick Mackey, and Vin Baston.

"

As I look back I can recall the many near misses the Waterford team had against teams like Cork, Tipperary, and Limerick: Cork in 1943, and in 1937 in particular against Limerick at Clonmel.

It was great to have played at a time when hurling was at its best, in the thirties and forties.

I regret one game in particular: the final in 1938. On that day I allowed Bill Lough-nane score a goal that won the game for Dublin.

The best man I ever played with or against was Christy Moylan of Dungarvan;

Dusk was falling when I arrived at Mick Hickey's home near Portlaw, Co. Waterford. Both Mick and his wife looked with interest through the book, and recalled qualities and feats of those who had already contributed.

Mick is a fund of history, lore, and stories, and soon we were travelling back through the decades, and penetrating deep into the early years of the last century. On the wall hung a framed photocopy of a description of the lands in his locality around 1565. Reference is made to a "ploughland", a term used in those days to signify several hundred acres of land. The term "musket shot" was also used to denote a measure of land.

Close by hung a photograph of Mick's father, a man of fine athletic physique and standing six foot four, who had accompanied the Irish athletes in the US "Invasion" of 1888. No championships were played in Ireland that year. Mick showed me a photograph of the team of athletes that travelled on the *Wisconsin*. He was able to identify Maurice Davin and Pat Davin of Tipperary, Hunt of Dublin, Carthy of Tipperary, and of course his father.

The Irishmen of those days were men of considerable athletic prowess, and were more than a match for the competition they faced in America. They also played several exhibition games.

Mick gave me a photograph of himself

in which he is holding the hurley his father used in the American tour. It is interesting to compare it with today's hurley: the model of 1888 was shorter and more like a hockey stick.

According to Mick, his father was the first man to take a hurley into his native Carrick-on-Suir. He walked from Carrick to Mooncoin to get a pattern and, having returned, set about making a hurley.

Now Mick is reciting a poem he remembers reading in an article by "Carbery":

'Twas coming from the fair of Ross
I spied that bend of growing ash
And swore I'd cut that makin's true
Before the night was done.
Though tyrants held the woodland then,
Close guarded by Black Thady Nash,
I shouldered home that supple tree
Before the morning sun.

Yes, those were the days of landlord rule, and Mick's father often recalled that in his young days if you were caught taking an ash tree from the landlord's estate you could finish up in Van Diemen's Land. He remembers too being told about the last man who was hanged from the shaft of a cart in Carrick-on-Suir about 1820, and left there for three days. The offence: stealing apples.

We then talked about Mick's own playing days, and I reminded him of an article I came across in a scrapbook Andy Fleming game me to look through. It seems that Mick always trained with dedication. Waterford played Cork — who had won the 1944 All-Ireland championship — in the final of the Ignatius Rice tournament in Waterford, and confounded the critics by recording a resounding eight-point victory. "Taobhlíne" in his "Gaelic Notes" recorded that Mick did a spot of road running in preparation for the match. When passing his own house his mother saw him. 'Is that Mickey?' she enquired from a neighbour. The reply was in the affirmative. 'I declare,' replied the good woman. 'Will he ever grow up!'

Mick regards Christy Moylan as the finest exponent of the game he ever played on. He considers the Kilkenny teams of the 1967–75 era as ranking with the great hurling teams of GAA history.

Three generations of Hickeys have held close links with the GAA: Mick, whose county hurling career stretched from 1936 to 1948; his father, who travelled with the athletes to the United States in 1888; and his son Martin, who played for Waterford until recently for a period of over a decade. So three generations of the family have spanned almost a century of GAA activity, a fact that Mick is justifiably proud of.

History repeated itself in the recent past when Martin captained the Portlaw senior hurling team that won the county title, an honour that fell to Mick in 1937.

Mick recalled the 1938 final against Dublin. It followed Waterford's first provincial success in Munster after several near misses and years of dedicated endeavour. It was a close, hard-fought game that Dublin won on the score 2:5 to 1:6. Croke Park inexperience probably cost Waterford the title that day, but Mick himself felt particular tinges of regret after the game as he reflected on a goal scored by Bill Loughnane that he still believes he might have cut off.

In 1948 Dublin again provided the opposition. To strengthen the defence, Waterford recalled Mick Hickey from retirement to man the wing-back position in the final. Earlier in the year they had recalled Christy Moylan to the team; so it was a team of seasoned campaigners that took the field against Dublin. John Keane, Christy Moylan and Mick Hickey had been there in 1938 and they were now supported by such veterans as Jim Ware, Andy Fleming, Vin Baston, and Mick Hayes. The blend was good. Waterford triumphed on the score 6:7 to 4:2 and recorded a historic first.

Mick himself was not pleased with his form in the final. He was as fast and as fit as ever, he said, but his timing and sharpness were not what they used to be. Be that as it may, the acquisition of an All-Ireland medal brought a fairytale ending to Mick's hurling career.

See also photo p.70.

Garrett HOWARD
1921–1936
Limerick and Croom, Dublin and Garda, Tipperary and Toomyvara

Born: 1899

> Over the years I have always admired Mick Mackey, Paddy Clohessy, Éamon Cregan, Pat Hartigan, Moss Carroll, Paddy Phelan, Phil Cahill, Dinny Barry Murphy, Jim O'Regan, John Doyle, and John Keane. **"**

Garrett was completely engrossed in the action of the Ireland v. Romania rugby match on television when I arrived at his house in Newtown. When the match was over we got down to talking about hurling.

Mick Mackey had said to me that Garrett was a "mine of information." How right he was! He also reminded me that Garrett was the only Limerickman to win five All-Ireland senior hurling medals — three with Limerick and two with Dublin.

Garrett talks about the game with the same enthusiasm that he played it with. Here was a man who had a wide-ranging hurling career, winning major honours with two provinces, two counties, and three clubs. I put to him a series of questions designed to evoke a cross-section of his greatest memories. What was his most memorable inter-county game? 'From many memorable games I finally select the All-Ireland final of 1927, Dublin v. Cork. The Garda club formed the backbone of the Dublin team — a team that didn't include any native of Dublin. Cork were All-Ireland champions, and favourites to retain the title. They included in their ranks Jim Hurley, Jim O'Regan, Dinny Barry Murphy, Eudi Coughlan and the Aherne

"

I regret that the Limerick team of the thirties didn't win at least three more All-Irelands, which they could and should have won. I look particularly at the years 1933 and '35, and also 1937. Other victories might have been between 1939 and '44.

My most memorable recollection is winning my first All-Ireland with Limerick in 1921 — played in 1923. In my estimation the team of this era would rank with most of the great teams of any period.

Hurling is still a game of all the skills, and in my estimation has no equal as a field game.

brothers, and Seán Og Murphy.

'Dublin led right through; every man, from the great Tommy Daly to left-corner-forward, the wily Mattie Power, struck form. Cork never got going in their usual style as Dublin went on to win comfortably.

'I was proud to be part of this team, a team which also included Mick Gill, Pat "Fowler" McInerney, and Martin Hayes. This victory gave me great satisfaction, as I rated the Cork team 1926–31 one of the best ever.

What was his most memorable club game? 'I choose the Tipperary county final of 1930, between Toomyvara and Boherlahan. At the time I was stationed in Toomyvara, where they lived and breathed hurling. Wedger Meagher's greyhounds were a household name. It was up to us to maintain a proud tradition. Boherlahan, powered by the Leahys, Captain Johnny, Paddy and Tommy, Ned Wade, Paddy Dwyer, were synonymous with hurling.

'The game was played in Thurles — a tough, uncompromising match, which ended in a draw. Before the replay Toomyvara trained as never before — even coming in for sessions during the early afternoon.

'The replay drew a huge crowd to the show grounds in Nenagh. Toomyvara settled down quickly, and after twenty minutes went ahead, a lead they never relinquished. Jack Gleeson and Jack Gilmartin held sway at midfield. "Swimmer" O'Brien played a tremendous game at right-wing-back. Martin Kennedy, the great full-forward, led the attack. Every man played his part: Stephen Hackett, Tom Gleeson, the O'Mearas and Kelly brothers, Tom Burns, and Jack Kennedy.

'This victory meant something special to Toomyvara. It was great to be part of it. The following year it was repeated in a game which featured two of the greatest goals I ever saw — scored by Martin Kennedy.'

What was his most memorable inter-provincial game? 'Definitely the inaugural Railway Cup game in 1927, when I lined out for Leinster against Munster. Both teams were star-studded. The midfield duet — Lory Meagher and Mick Gill, against Tull Considine and Jim Hurley — was worth travelling to see. Phil Cahill, Eudi Coughlan, Martin Kennedy, Ga Aherne were terrific forwards opposing Leinster backs. Mattie Power, Ned Fahy, Din O'Neill and myself faced Seán Óg Murphy, Dinny Barry Murphy, Jim O'Regan, and "Marie" O'Connell.

'The game was a thriller right through, great hurling and very sporting. Leinster won by two points. It was considered by many to be one of the best games ever in the Railway Cup series.'

Could he recall some of the events of the 1935 final? 'The 1935 All-Ireland final, Limerick v. Kilkenny, was the most frustrating game I ever played in. The conditions were atrocious: torrential rain fell during the entire game. It was difficult to hold the hurley; good hurling was out of the question.

'At half time Kilkenny led by a point,

I asked him to select his ideal team — including himself — from all the players he had known. Was this a hard one? 'Yes, I agree, this is a hard one. Why? For the simple reason that there are so many great players to choose from for each position. I could select at least a dozen teams, any one of which I would be happy to be included in. However, as the onus is on me —'

Tommy Daly *(Clare)*

Bobbie Rackard *(Wexford)*   Seán Óg Murphy *(Cork)*   John Doyle *(Tipperary)*

John Keane *(Waterford)*   Jim O'Regan *(Cork)*   Garrett Howard *(Limerick)*

Timmy Ryan *(Limerick)*   Jim Hurley *(Cork)*

Phil Cahill *(Tipperary)*   Mick Mackey *(Limerick)*   Mick King *(Galway)*

Christy Ring *(Cork)*   Martin Kennedy *(Tipperary)*   Mattie Power *(Kilkenny)* as far as I can recall. Efforts were made to call off the game, but not everyone agreed. The second half saw Kilkenny forge ahead, but Limerick came back with a goal and a point, leaving Kilkenny one point ahead. In the dying seconds Limerick were awarded a 21-yards free. Mick Mackey stepped up to take it. All we needed was a draw. However, fortune was against Limerick; the ball failed to rise and was cleared by Kilkenny.

'No doubt Kilkenny were a very good side. However, Limerick reversed the result in no uncertain manner in the 1936 final.'

Could he recall the hurling heroes of his boyhood and anything special he remembered about them? 'In my native Croom I learnt my hurling from the local heroes, the Mangan family: Ger, Mick, Pat, Jim, and Tom. They had a great influence on me and taught me all the skills. I cannot leave out their sister Ellie, who was as good as any of the men. With my brothers Martin and Willie I spent many hours with the Mangans and other neighbours — Hogans, Roches, and Bennetts — playing hurling.

'Others whom I admired and from whom I learnt a lot were Mick Feely, Jack Shea, Mick Mullane, Egan Clancy, Stephen Gleeson, Paddy Flaherty. I was influenced also by John Tyler Mackey, Martin Hayes, Tom Hayes, Ned Treacy. Outside of Limerick the men I heard most about were Tom Semple, Hugh Shelly, Paddy Brolan, and Jimmy Murphy, the Demon from Horse and Jockey, Jack Radford, Simon Walton, and the wee Doyles from Mooncoin, James J. Kelliher, and Connie Sheehan.

With muscles brown, although you are growing old and frail, it is seldom you let Cork go down.'

Our chat was wide-ranging, covering many counties, decades, and players. He always looked upon Timmy Ryan as the supreme midfielder. There was a great horse on the go around that time called Golden Miller that won several major honours and was full of energy. Timmy had tremendous stamina: he would keep going for ever and cover acres of ground. He used to remind Garrett of Golden Miller, so Garrett used to call Timmy "the Horse."

He recalled a blistering championship game between Limerick and Cork in 1935. Limerick lost Paddy Clohessy after ten minutes, when he was put off. The exchanges were uncompromising. Mick Ryan at midfield for Limerick pulled on a ball as Cork player Kelly stumbled headlong in front of the hurley and got hit on the head. He fell and was out cold. Mick turned to Garrett and said, 'Do you think he's dead?' The players knelt in prayer and were joined by the crowd as Kelly was stretchered off the field. Happily he recovered and was back in action the following year.

Garrett strolled as far as the car with me, and enquired how Mick Mackey was, and then, grasping my arm, said to me, 'You know, in many ways John was as good.' As I prepared to go it seemed as if all the years had rolled back as he said with a laugh, 'I was only an altar boy when I played my first senior game with Croom.'

Born: 1916

Hurling, to the hurling man, is very much the story, and perhaps the legend, of larger-than-life figures, from Cú Chulainn to Lory Meagher, Mick Mackey and Christy Ring and to our own giant of the hurling scene in Decies, John Keane of Mount Sion.

John Keane sprang from a family steeped in Gaelic tradition, and from his earliest days he manifested a lively interest in our native games. Reared in a strong Gaelic neighbourhood and schooled in that cradle of Waterford hurling, Mount Sion, John took to the games like a duck to water. A fine, strapping youngster, daring and fearless, his potential as a hurler was quickly realised by the Brothers in Barrack Street, and Keane's feet were firmly set on the road to hurling fame and stardom.

In 1934 the young minor played more than one man's part in bringing All-Ireland junior honours to Waterford, and in that jubilee year of the association he was one of a grand Mount Sion team

that won the county junior championship and ushered in a new name and a new era in county senior hurling. John Keane, yet a minor, had made his mark, and for almost twenty years to come his was to be the outstanding name in Waterford's Gaelic story.

1935 witnessed his advent to the County Senior fifteen as a corner back. The following year saw the further development of the young star, and then, in 1937, we saw the full blossoming of a great centre half back, whose skill and daring and incomparable sportsmanship were to fire the blood and grip the imagination not only of Waterford but of all Ireland. Few who saw Waterford's battle with unconquerable Limerick in 1937 will ever forget John Keane's inspired display on the greatest ever forward, Mick Mackey of Ahane.

The barely twenty-year-old Waterford man took the honours in one of the best man-to-man tussles I have ever seen on a hurling field. That day John Keane and Mick Mackey became firm friends and the hurling maestro from Limerick is one of our hero's greatest admirers. That, I think, is indicative of the character of John Keane. He was a great player, who played the game with verve and fire but always in truly Gaelic spirit.

His Railway Cup record equals that of the legendary Martin Kennedy of Tipperary and the irrepressible Mick Mackey of Limerick.

He was the idol of hurling fans everywhere and one of the greatest drawing cards in Munster hurling.

The McCarthy Cup: All-Ireland trophy.

Cork supporters celebrate their team's homecoming in 1990.

Seán Silke of Galway during the 1984 match against Waterford.

Mark Corrigan shoots for Offaly, against Laois opponents.

Eamonn Cregan of Limerick in action in the 1981 Munster Hurling Final.

Concentration from Noel Skehan, Kilkenny.

Iggy Clarke, Galway, 1984.

Joe McKenna and Matt Rea of Limerick in the 1984 National Hurling League final against Wexford.

John Callinan of Clare.

Ray Cummins of Cork in 1985.

Eugene Coughlan of Offaly, 1985.

Ger Henderson of Kilkenny meets Galway opponent B. Lynsky.

TOP: Tony Doran of Wexford in the battle against Kilkenny.
BOTTOM: Tipperary's Kennedy and Cleary, and Cork's Fitzgibbon in the 1990 Munster Hurling Final.

The Munster team of 1943 with John Keane (back row, top left). It contained some of the greatest exponents of the game that hurling has known: (back row, left to right) John Keane (Waterford), Dick Stokes (Limerick), Batt Thornhill (Cork), Willie O'Donnell (Tipperary), Jack Lynch (Cork), Andy Fleming (Waterford), Mick Mackey (Limerick), Willie Murphy (Cork), Jim Barry, Trainer; (front row, left to right) Johnny Quirke (Cork), Jim Young (Cork), Tommy Doyle (Tipperary), Christy Ring (Cork), Jackie Power (Limerick), Peter Cregan (Limerick), Jimmy Maher (Tipperary).

Cork 1943
Back row, left to right: Johnny Quirke, Jim Young, Tom Mulcahy, Con Murphy, Jack Lynch, Alan Lotty, Ted O'Sullivan. *Middle row, left to right:* Din Joe Buckley, Batt Thornhill, Sean Condon, Mick Kennefick, Mick A. Brennan, Christy Ring, Jim Barry (trainer). *Front row, left to right:* Con Cottrell, Willie Murphy.

He never spared himself. He turned out in match after match, county and inter-county, championship, challenge and tournament, winter and summer, never counting the personal cost where the honour of his Club or his County was concerned.

Still the coveted All-Ireland medal evaded him. For years the Waterford defence had defied the might of Munster, but a lack of decisiveness in attack could not command the victory a sterling defence deserved. The advent of John Keane to the forty yards made all the difference. He brought a new type of play to the attack and turned his great experience as a defender to good account in outwitting the best backs in Clare, Cork, Galway and finally Dublin in the great victorious All Ireland of 1948.

Looking back briefly in one final glance at the saga of one man's herculean efforts for the cause of Gaeldom, memories come crowding in. The writer recalls 1937 at Clonmel. The strapping figure in blue and white thwarting the great Mick Mackey; the blonde, curly head bobbing as Keane threw back attack after attack in one of the really great games of the Munster championship.

Then came the greatest display of courage and determination and perhaps his greatest personal triumph — his epic display at Dungarvan in 1943 against Tipperary, when with a badly injured ankle he stood at centreback and almost alone broke the back of every Tipperary attack. Well I do remember cutting the boot from his swollen leg at the end of that excruciating hour. And I recall, too, the old wizened man of Tipperary who pushed his way through the crowd to where John lay, to shake, as he said 'the hand of John Keane, the greatest man in Ireland.'

(Condensed from an article in *An Déiseach*, 1974, with the kind permission of the author, Pat Fanning, GAA president 1970–73.)

There are occasions in life when certain strange forces converge and combine to urge people onwards to special missions. Such was the case with John Keane. He was unwell. He journeyed to Kilkenny; back to his native Waterford; onward to Cork; thence to Tralee to his former Limerick rival and Munster colleague; then onward to Limerick; and more than likely he had planned to come back through Tipperary to Waterford. Pat Fanning told me the rest of the story when I visited him in 1990.

'John Keane died in November 1975, and to the day of his death on a lonely road between Tralee and Limerick he loved and breathed the spirit of hurling and remained the happiest of men in the company of hurling men. John knew he was ill, and one suspected that he knew he was not long for this world. But the courage that, allied to a great natural skill, had made him one of the hurling giants, sustained him in that last illness, an illness with pain that might have withered a lesser man. The story of his last few days deserves telling, if only to illustrate his love of hurling and of the hurling rivals whose friendship he treasured.

'He was ill, and he travelled to Kilkenny, where he spent a night with Jim Langton, recalling past encounters. Back to Waterford, a fitful night's rest, and off to Kinsale in Co. Cork, there to rake up old memories with great-hearted Jack Barrett. Then on to Tralee, where he met and talked with a man he admired greatly, Jackie Power of Limerick. The following morning he took off for Limerick, anxious to meet old enemies and great friends like Mick Mackey and Paddy Clohessy and Timmy Ryan and the rest of them. He had a particular grá for the Limerick men of that era. He never reached Limerick: he died by the wayside, his journey incomplete. They took him to Limerick, where all Munster honoured him before he was taken home to his beloved Waterford and Mount Sion.

'I choose to regard John's last journey as the pilgrimage of a man who knew his days were numbered and who wished to meet again some of the men with whom he had given so much of himself on the fields of Ireland. John Keane couldn't have had, nor would he have wished for, a more fitting end.'

114

Eddie Keher with John T. Power of Piltown,
Kilkenny's star of an earlier generation.

❝

It is impossible to describe in words the enjoyment I have got and still get from the game of hurling. Looking through the famous names in this book it seems only yesterday that I started collecting the photographs of these great players and pasting them carefully into a book which I used read out loud twenty times a day. The great Waterford team of 1948 is my longest memory, though I never saw them playing. I remember my mother bringing me over to shake the hand of Jim Ware in Tramore one day and boasting about it for years afterwards. I never thought I would have the honour of sharing a book with these great men as I am doing now.

I enjoy everything about the game: watching, playing, training, practising. Whereas All-Irelands are the glamorous occasions, some of my greatest memories are from club championship or tournament games. I suppose "firsts" are inclined to be the memories, and my first school county

Born: 1941

medal in 1952 (under-14) is high on the list. My first appearance with Kilkenny in 1959; my first win, 1963; captain of a winning team in 1959; my first and only county championship with Rower, Inistioge, in 1968 — all have their own significance. 1972 against Cork was probably the best eighty minutes of hurling I have had the pleasure of playing in.

But as I said, there were many more aspects of my involvement in the game that I love: talking to people who have an obvious appreciation of hurling; friends I have made; trips to the USA and other countries — all have their own particular place. I loved being a part of such a great Kilkenny era of the sixties and early seventies. Every player on each team played his own part, and so many games would not have been won but for the "do or die" effort of each man. Some of the famous Kilkenny men I admired belonged to an era when as many titles didn't flow Kilkenny's way, but nonetheless inspired us to try to emulate them. I suppose if it were possible to turn the clock back a few years just for one hour I would love to get one more chance of playing with the Delaney-Purcell-Crotty-Brennan-O'Brien combination of forwards which I enjoyed so much.

❞

*A*ll these trifles lead to perfection, and perfection is no trifle. Eddie Keher is honours-laden. The list includes National Leagues, Railway Cups, All-Irelands, Leinster titles, All-Star awards, Oireachtas titles, a county title, and Hurler of the Year in 1972.

I wondered if such a range of achievements could have left him with any regrets or unfulfilled ambitions. 'I played in four minor championships, lost one semi-final to Galway, lost two All-Ireland finals to Tipperary, and only tasted victory once. In those early years I would have cherished more success.

'At county level I won one county title with my club, the Rower, Inistioge. There were a number of near misses and disappointments. We were capable of winning more, but we played in an era when there were some very good teams around: the Fenians, James Stephens, and towards the end of our day the Shamrocks arrived as a force. In a different era we would have won more.'

Eddie was one of the great forwards in the history of the game. Throughout his career he was a prolific scorer. In the 1963 All-Ireland final Kilkenny scored 4:17 against Waterford's 6:8. Eddie scored fourteen of the Kilkenny points — ten from frees.

It wasn't by accident he pointed frees from all angles with incredible consistency. He practised the art regularly. He strove for perfection. His mastery of this facet of the game won many a match for Kilkenny. Every skill, every stroke, every detail was studied and practised diligently. If he failed with a free he would make arrangements the following week to go out with a colleague, critically examine his technique, and practise frees from the angle from which he had failed. It all added up to a hurling master who was fortunate to have played with a great county during a golden era. The presence of so many excellent hurlers around him enabled him to demonstrate his range of talents to the fullest and win wide acclaim.

Eddie would like to see more players go out to practise in addition to the organised training sessions, and set about eliminating their deficiencies and shortcomings. Examples cited by Eddie included a bad left hand, the sideline cut, the bat-down, doubling on the ball in the air and on the ground and pulling against the coming ball in the air and on the ground. 'It is this kind of practice with a few friends that builds confidence and lifts a player to a higher level.'

He sees a more uniform interpretation of the rules as a most desirable priority.

Eddie likes to be involved with teams, but he found the job of manager desperately demanding where time was concerned and therefore found it somewhat unrewarding. He feels there is far too much focusing on the managers nowadays. He doesn't like it. 'Players start to depend too much on them. I can never understand when I see a player looking to the sideline for guidance and directions when taking a free. He should know instinctively what to do.'

It is difficult for him to find a common yardstick against which to measure the standards of various decades. 'Pitches are better than ever; there are more of them; more are playing the game. The game has changed, though basically not drastically. We have witnessed great minor and under-21 games; we have seen some great championship and League games. Somehow we tend to measure the health of hurling by the quality of the All-Ireland final or the Munster final or the Leinster final. This can lead to a wrong conclusion. Also there can be a tendency in some quarters to say the game is in decline or the standard has dropped if Tipperary, Cork or Kilkenny aren't on top. There is no evidence to support such a view.'

His management policy would be to define the tactics and strategies in broad outline, produce a general pattern, and encourage the players to use flair and initiative within that framework. 'I would like to see a little more flair on the part of players and teams.'

Where did the hurling brilliance come from? Not particularly from his antecedents. His mother was a Co. Kilkenny woman, but no strong evidence of hurling existed on her side. His father hailed from Co. Roscommon. He played football with Garda teams; also played football with Kilkenny — together with Kieran Purcell's father — decades ago when apparently standards in Kilkenny were considerably higher than they are today. His uncle on his father's side went to live in Mayo and hurled there.

Still, there is nothing in any of that to suggest that great hurling was in the genes. So that brings us back to his college, St Kieran's; his county, Kilkenny; the example of so many outstanding county men; and probably most likely and important of all, his own extraordinary levels of fitness, commitment, dedication, diligence, and remarkable attention to detail.

Eddie Keher steps up to take a penalty in the 1975 All-Ireland final against Galway. *Left to right:* Seán O'Connor (referee), Seán Silke of Galway, Eddie Keher (Kilkenny) and Kieran Purcell of Kilkenny.

Eddie Keher, Kilkenny captain, holds aloft the McCarthy Cup on winning the 1969 All-Ireland Final. On the right is Seamus Ryan, President of the GAA. (Photo: Jim Connolly)

Born: 1925

Rackard, Pat Stakelum, Nicky Rackard, Joe Salmon, Tim Flood, and Seán Clohessy.

"

And tho'
We are not now that strength which in old days
Moved earth and heaven; that which we are, we are;
One equal temper of heroic hearts,
Made weak by time and fate, but strong in will
To strive, to seek, to find, and not to yield.

"

I suppose any player of Gaelic games has in his heart at some time longed to be a member of an All-Ireland winning side. I was naturally delighted to be one of the Wexford team who brought the All-Ireland title back to Wexford after so many years, and of course it fulfilled my youthful aspiration.

However, I think I got nearly as much satisfaction at club level, and I can honestly say I really enjoyed every game I played. I always wanted to win, but once the game was over and if defeated I looked forward just as eagerly to the next game, be it club or county.

To have played with Nick Rackard, Nick O'Donnell etc. was as great as it was to have played against such as Jimmy Finn, Jim Langton, Christy Ring, and a host of other stars during that period. To have made so many friends throughout the years was an extra bonus that brings back happy memories.

Some of the greats I played against were Christy Ring, Harry Gray, Jim Langton, Nick O'Donnell, Jimmy Finn, Bobbie

A ptly indeed do these words from Tennyson's "Ulysses" describe the Wexford of 1962. They had tasted glory and scaled great heights in the fifties. In major competitions they had defeated all the leading hurling counties: Cork, Tipperary, Limerick, Clare, Galway, and Kilkenny. But they had known disappointment too.

They confounded the critics in 1960 by comprehensively defeating Tipperary in the All-Ireland final. Could they repeat the win in 1962? The bulk of the 1960 team was still there, and five of the team had been there on the first Sunday of September 1951 when Wexford lined out against Tipperary to contest their first final since 1918. Would time begin to take its toll?

Padge admits that with ten minutes to go he began to feel the stamina going. He was now thirty-seven years of age. Others too were feeling the hectic pace — "made weak by time". At the final whistle, the score

Padge Kehoe about to strike, with Kilkenny's Tom Walsh on left. (Photo: Jim Connolly)

was Tipperary 3:10, Wexford 2:11, in a really great final. It was a game Wexford might well have won but, though still "strong in will", they were not now "that strength which in old days moved earth and heaven." It was Wexford's swan song, and a glorious one at that.

Padge's first visit to Croke Park was in 1931. He was only six years of age, and his father took him to see Cork and Kilkenny in action. The game itself is a mere blur in his memory, but the names of all the Cork players of that great 1931 team have remained firmly imprinted on his mind.

His father, Pádraig, was a great influence on him. Padge describes him as a poet, a dreamer, a patriot, and a Gael. He wrote many articles in the *Enniscorthy Echo* under the pseudonym "Hy Kinsellagh," and he represented Wexford in Dáil Éireann.

Padge quoted his favourite verse from one of his father's poems:

But give me that river cleaving
From Bunclody to the sea,
Through the heart of rebel Wexford;
Enniscorthy town for me.

He wrote a play too, *When Wexford Rose.* It dealt with the Rising of '98 and was performed in the Abbey in the 1916–22 period. He was always deeply involved in GAA affairs and was a selector in the 1914–18 years when Wexford had a golden era in football.

When Padge was young his father used to take him out into the field and spend time throwing the ball to him, and it was in this manner that Padge learned his early skills of hurling. He remembers his father talking about the great Wexford hurlers of the early part of the century, and in particular about the prowess of Paddy Mackey, Seán Kennedy, and Mike Cummins, who were on the victorious 1910 Wexford hurling team.

From his youth Padge remembers the Kilkenny trio of Lory Meagher, Paddy Phelan, and Peter Blanchfield — 'lovely clean hurlers who always played the ball.' He had tremendous admiration for Jimmy Langton, a delightful ball-player.

We then talked at length about the rise of Wexford as a hurling power. Some results around the mid-forties began to suggest that Wexford were in the ascendant. Padge gives much of the credit to Nicky Rackard for Wexford's rise to fame. According to him, Mick Mackey had been Nicky Rackard's idol. He loved his dashing and his daring and the strength of his charge as he headed for goal. He drew inspiration from Mick, modelled himself on him, and tried to emulate his style and tactics.

Another important factor in the rise of Wexford was the good sporting relationship that existed between Rathnure and St Aidan's. This spirit of comradeship manifested itself at county level.

In 1948 there was a growing feeling among Wexford hurlers that the day of the breakthrough was not too far distant. At Bellefield, Enniscorthy, Wexford failed by two points to Dublin. The defeat was even more disappointing when it was learnt that Laois had beaten Kilkenny. Psychologically Wexford felt they could handle Laois, but in those days the Kilkenny hurdle had a "Beecher's Brook" dimension attached to it.

In 1950 in the Leinster final Wexford were desperately unlucky to fail to Kilkenny by 3:11 to 2:11. They deserved at least a draw, and there was strong evidence

His ideal team from the men of his time would be:

Ollie Walsh *(Kilkenny)*

Bobbie Rackard *(Wexford)*   Nick O'Donnell *(Wexford)*   John Barron *(Waterford)*
Jimmy Finn *(Tipperary)*   Pat Stakelum *(Tipperary)*   Willie Walsh *(Kilkenny)*
Harry Gray *(Laois)*   Jim Morrissey *(Wexford)*
Seán Clohessy *(Kilkenny)*   Mick Ryan *(Tipperary)*   Jimmy Langton *(Kilkenny)*
Paddy Kenny *(Tipperary)*   Nicky Rackard *(Wexford)*   Christy Ring *(Cork)*

Padge Kehoe going into action after the throw-in in the All-Ireland Final of 1954 against Cork.

of the potential that lay in this team. Padge recalls that "Wilkie" Thorpe had a fine game that day for Wexford. He had the ideal temperament for the big occasion. Indeed, the bigger the occasion the better he liked it.

Padge was captain in 1954, and he doesn't hide the disappointment he felt about the defeat at the hands of Cork, and very much against the run of play too. But the forwards failed to capitalise, and paid the penalty. Before the '54 final Jimmy Langton expressed the view that if Nicky Rackard stayed in on the edge of the square on John Lyons, Wexford would win. It was probably a sense of frustration at wasted chances that brought Nicky foraging out-field, but the farther he went from goal, the less the sense of pressure this Cork defence felt. Padge would have wished to have a second chance in 1954. 'We could never

miss so much again.'

Padge would love to be hurling now. He feels there is greater scope now that the third-man tackle is gone. He considers that the goalkeeper is over-protected. We have gone from one extreme to the other, he says. He would like to see a revival of the overhead hurling skills, and would favour the abolition of hand-passed and kicked goals.

He had special words of praise for Pat Stakelum, 'a great centre-back equally adept in the air and on the ground.' He talked about the amount of 'hurling the ball' that Nick O'Donnell did at a time when many full-backs played the role of "stopper."

Padge commented on Nick's droll sense of humour. After Nicky Rackard had scored something like 7:6 against Antrim in the 1954 All-Ireland semi-final, Nick O'Donnell muttered after the game, 'He might have kept a few of those for the game against Cork!' In 1960 in the opening stages of the game against Tipperary Jimmy Doyle slipped John Nolan and ran headlong into a full-blooded shoulder from Nicko. It rattled Jimmy. Nicko turned to John Nolan and said, 'You should be able to manage him now, John.'

Hurling was a way of life with Padge. His father enkindled a love of the game that still remains. He loved playing for his province and county. He enjoyed even more playing for his club. He holds a unique record with his now disbanded club, St Aidan's. During its lifetime he had the honour of being on all the teams that won county titles at all levels in hurling.

Like many hurlers at all levels, Padge found immense satisfaction in spending hours in the local pitch 'just pucking about.'

Born: 1899

"

My first Munster match was against Seán Óg Murphy — the best full-back that played the game. It was in Cork we played. I scored four goals.

Hurlers I have always had a special admiration for: Seán Óg of Cork, Mick Mackey and Garrett Howard of Limerick, Mick King of Galway, John Maher and Liam Devaney of Tipperary.

"

Martin was relaxing in his chair when I called to him at his home a few miles from Nenagh. Wherever hurling is talked about and full-forwards discussed, the name Martin Kennedy crops up, for it is synonymous with full-forward play at its best. In his day he was unrivalled, and when Tipperary toured America in 1931 Martin made history with his goal-scoring feats.

Together we looked at the autographs; and the names of many of Martin's contem-

poraries evoked for him memories and thrills of bygone days. Of Seán Óg Murphy of Cork full-back fame he spoke with deep admiration. There were many great clashes between them as the tide of battle ebbed and flowed. Fortune changed from game to game, with Seán Óg supreme one day and Martin getting telling and decisive scores on the next occasion.

As we spoke of Tipperary's decline in the hurling world, something that afflicts all counties at some stage, Martin expressed the hope that Tipperary would soon make a comeback — a hope that has since been realised.

I asked him if there were any prospective hurlers in the household, and I was told that his grandson, aged eleven, was keen and enthusiastic.

As Martin wrote in the book, I turned to his daughter-in-law and asked, 'Is the story about the feathers true?' Whereupon Martin paused briefly, looked at me quizzically but never uttered a word, all the time smiling, and then went on to write again; but his daughter-in-law confirmed that the story has substance. The story goes that Martin in his hurling days used to take two feathers with him and place one in the ground at each side of the outer extremities of the parallelogram. Thus did Martin initiate his own radar system for sending sliotars goalwards.

He then took me to the sitting-room, where he showed me his collection of medals and trophies. The centrepiece was a fine silver cup presented to the Tipperary team when they toured America. Inscribed on the cup were the names of the touring team.

The Railway Cup competition was inaugurated in 1927, and Martin Kennedy must surely hold some kind of record in this series. From its inception until his retirement in 1935 he was a regular choice each year on the Munster team. From his nine successive appearances in the finals, he collected six medals.

In those days players took an intense pride in being selected for their province, and competition for places was incredibly keen. It speaks volumes for Martin's hurling prowess that at the end of his days he was still, in 1935, able to command his place on the Munster team. Indeed, in that year he was Tipp's only representative.

He will tell you that in nine years of Railway Cup appearances he played with and against some of the greatest exponents of hurling the game has known, while spectators were treated to some wonderful games. But from a great career of many memories Martin has never forgotten his first encounter with Seán Óg in the Munster championship in Cork in 1922.

Seán Óg's reputation as a formidable and uncompromising full-back was well established. Martin, an unknown, had yet to arrive. But arrive he did with a bang in that encounter against Cork in 1922. He netted four goals. The hurling world sat up; it heralded the arrival of a full-forward who would grow in stature and become a master of the art of full-forward play. Martin was most modest about his prowess and hurling feats, but he didn't hide the fact that the memory of that debut performance remains very special and undimmed.

For one of his moments of regret Martin went back to the 1922 All-Ireland final against Kilkenny. Tipperary seemed to have victory sewn up, but a very late flurry by Kilkenny brought a succession of scores that left Tipperary dumbfounded and trailing by 4:2 to 2:6 when the final whistle sounded. However, 1925 brought compensation when victory over Galway gave Martin his first All-Ireland medal.

He still cherishes the memory of that day, so let us recall the line-out, which was as follows:

Johnny Leahy (captain), A. O'Donnell, M. Mockler, M. Darcy, J. J. Hayes, Martin Kennedy, S. Hackett, J. Power, P. Leahy, P. Cahill, T. Duffy, J. Darcy, W. Ryan, P. Power, P. O'Dwyer.

Born: 1919

"

Kilkenny versus Tipp, 1945 — Jimmy Maher, the Tipperary goalie, was in fine form. He was the difference between the two teams. I thought we had the best of the game out the field, but when the final whistle sounded, the score is what counted, and best of luck to Tipp.

Some of the stars of my time were John Keane, Mick Mackey, Paddy Phelan, Jack Mulcahy, Jimmy Walsh, John Maher, Nicky Rackard, Christy Ring, and Vin Baston.

"

Winning your first All-Ireland has to be special, Jim told me, and it is extra-special when you are only twenty years of age, as Jim was on that first Sunday in September 1939 when Kilkenny pipped Cork by one point. The attendance matched the date, at just over 39,000. But the conditions were atrocious. Thunder and lightning and torrential rain were the order of

the day. The referee's togs and jersey were all one colour as the dye ran freely from the saturated jersey. In the circumstances the game, according to Jim, was a marvellous one.

He reminded me that in those days the forwards and midfielders lined up for the throw-in. There were too many involved, and not infrequently players got a bad belt in the opening seconds. He likes the change that leaves the throw-in between the four midfielders.

But more about the 1939 final and how Jimmy remembers it. 'Five of the 1935 team were still there — Jimmy O'Connell, Paddy Larkin, Paddy Phelan, Jimmy Walsh, and Peter Blanchfield — and into this team had been blended many of the minors of a very good 1935 side. Kilkenny got off to a great start with two early goals, and led by that margin at half time.

'Cork steadied in the second half, and with a couple of minutes to go Willie Campbell goaled for Cork to bring them level. It began to look like a draw, and considering the appalling conditions under which the game had been played, probably all thirty players would have settled for a second meeting.

'But it wasn't to be. On the stroke of time Jimmy Kelly collected a weak clearance after a Paddy Phelan seventy had fallen short, and sent it over the bar for a winner.'

Jimmy feels he played his best game in Birr in 1947, against Galway in the All-Ireland semi-final. 'Galway thought they had it. They were very unlucky: they had a great team, from Seánie Duggan in goal right out the field to corner-forward.'

One game he would like to have had a

second shot at was the 1945 All-Ireland final against Tipperary. He is loud in his praise of Jimmy Maher, who was outstanding in goal for Tipperary in that final.

Jimmy remembers cycling to Cork in the forties for a championship game between Limerick and Tipperary, and vivid in his mind is the sight of John Mackey at full-forward for Limerick going in on top of Jimmy Maher in the Tipperary goal and belting the crossbar with the hurley in an attempt to unnerve the Tipperary custodian.

He has always felt that the 1935 Kilkenny team was the best to leave the county. In the final of that year Lory Meagher reached great heights as he captained his men to a famous victory over a star-studded Limerick team on the score 2:5 to 2:4. On a day when rain fell relentlessly to produce a sodden pitch, Lory's words to his men were, 'Keep the ball on the ground. Hit it first time. Keep it on the move.'

In recent times, however, Jimmy is beginning to feel that the teams of 1972–75 and 1982–83 would match the best. He considers that Pat Henderson has done a wonderful job on the present team and that Ollie Walsh and Noel Skehan have made major contributions through their superb goalkeeping to the Kilkenny victories over the past twenty years.

As Jimmy looks back on his own hurling days he says that he enjoyed them all. He enjoyed the moment of victory, but he found reward in the lean years too. The weeks leading up to an All-Ireland final were great: the lads coming to the field to train; the crowd gathering to watch; the excitement of the build-up; the glamour of the occasion. Yes, win or lose, he found it all enjoyable.

Both of his All-Irelands were won by a single point. Both were won on the call of time. He knows how close it was. He knows he might have won none. And it is because of this that he sympathises with all those hurlers down the years who have made hurling the great game it is but who never had the honour of winning an AllIreland medal.

He is generous in his praise of other counties and the men who represented them. There have been great men too, he says, at club level who for a variety of reasons were unable to gain recognition on county teams. What a kind thought from a man of Jimmy's stature! He was delighted to see Offaly rewarded in 1981. He feels Galway were worth three in a row; 'We robbed them of one,' he said as he referred to 1979.

By and large he considers that hurling is as good as ever. 'It hasn't changed all that much. The abolition of the third-man tackle does give the forward more scope; the "advantage rule" isn't allowed as much as it might be.' Nowadays he rarely misses a game, and looks forward to a match every Sunday.

Terry Leahy (See p. 126)

Born: 1918

"

My memory goes back to the great All-Irelands in 1931: the two drawn games — I used to watch the great Jim Regan, Eugene Coughlan, Lory Meagher, Eddie Doyle, and Paddy Phelan. I was only thirteen years old, and I was watching every movement of the great ones. I learnt a lot of hurling from those great heroes.

I used to copy Lory's great drop puck, which was a great asset to me for years after. I remember a great drop puck I scored in the 1939 final off the great John Quirke — which we won by a last-minute point.

Then on to the '47 final, when our policy was to go for points, because we knew the great backs of Cork — Alan Lotty, Paddy Donovan, Willie Murphy, Dr Jim Young, Con Murphy, and the great goalie Tom Mulcahy — were like the Rock of Cashel. There was terrible temptation to go for goals when Cork were leading by two points. But we didn't fall into the trap. Tom Walton was fouled, and I was elected to take the all-important free.

Mícheál O'Hehir of course was broadcasting, and he said 'the old pro Terry Leahy is going to take it and I wouldn't be in his boots for all the tea in China. But he bends, looks, and strikes, and you know by the roar of the crowd where the ball has gone.' The Cork goalie pucks out the ball; goes up to Paddy Grace; hits a long ball down to the Cork square, and Jim Langton hits it in to the Cork goalie. He stopped it, and I knew he would clear it to Hill 16. I ran before Alan Lotty; I gathered it and sent it straight between the posts for the winning point. The game was proclaimed a classic, and although it was a victory for Kilkenny it was a triumph for hurling.

Two years later I left for America and set about organising the Kilkenny team in New York. Success came our way, and we trained very hard and won the 1950 and 1957 championship. Hurling was a great link with the homeland. It helped me to settle down quickly in America. I made many, many friends there from every county and brought a lot of enjoyment to Irish exiles.

"

In the late 1940s Terry Leahy emigrated to New York. Employment was difficult to find in Ireland, and Terry was glad to make a new life for himself in New York, where he found a secure job with a transport company. He took with him his hurley and his hurling skills. These were to be his link with the homeland. They would open doors for him in his adopted country; they made him feel less an exile. Whenever possible, he would make a trip home for the All-Ireland hurling final, and August 1981 was one of those occasions.

It was Eddie Keher who arranged my meeting with Terry one Sunday evening in Kilkenny. It was a pleasure to meet and chat with this enthusiastic Kilkennyman.

He recalled his boyhood heroes, the wonderful Kilkenny hurlers of the early thirties, and added, 'Hurling is as fast now as it was in my playing days, but what I do miss is the lack of overhead striking as it was in the thirties and forties. One great rule that is in force now is the protection for the goalie. Remember, in my time a high ball coming in to the goal-mouth, the poor goalie had no protection except from the full-back and he was driven — ball, hurley, and all — to the back of the net.'

Terry would pause occasionally to glance at the autographs of the players I had visited. Every so often he would say, 'He was a good one.' He delighted in reading the names aloud; it conjured up the past, it personalised the memories. He was reliving it all: green flags, cheering supporters, white flags, memorable points, the timely shoulder, the opportunity lost, the fury of the clash, the friendly handshake, the drop puck, the classic score.

Yes, the drop puck. This was a skill Terry enjoyed talking about, because he often used it. He remembered in particular two successful drop puck attempts that soared over the bar. One was against Cork in the 1939 final, from the Hill 16 side of Croke Park. The other one happened in the Polo Grounds in the fifties against Tipperary. The New York goalie pucked out the ball and Terry doubled on it on the drop and sent it over for a point and up into the stand.

Terry's two All-Ireland successes came at the beginning and end of his hurling career in Ireland — in 1939 and 1947. Both finals were cliff-hangers and rank among the great games of hurling. Both saw Kilkenny snatch victory from Cork by the narrowest of margins in the dying seconds.

In 1939 it was Jimmy Kelly of Carrickshock who scored the winning point in what was to become known as the "thunder and lightning" final. In 1947, in beautiful weather, it was Terry Leahy who stole the limelight in a hurling classic. With time running out he scored the equaliser, and in lost time he sent over the winner.

In New York he continued to give dazzling displays, and hurled up to 1957. At the time of his arrival in New York, Tipperary were the dominant hurling power. Gradually, under Terry's leadership and inspiration, Kilkenny (New York) were moulded into an enthusiastic combination and became a force in the New York hurling world. To the followers, Terry was a hero. With all the skills that are part of Kilkenny hurling he did things with the ball that were never before seen in New York, and for the spectators it was sheer magic to watch. In America he was "Mr Hurling."

Before we parted, he told a hurling tale. Paddy and Mike were great hurling fans. Mike was dying, so Paddy went to see him. 'Mike,' said Paddy, 'when you go up above get back to me somehow, long distance.' 'Okay,' said Mike. 'Let me know is there hurling up above.' He was dead about two weeks when the phone rang at midnight. 'Hey, Paddy, this is Mike from Up Above.'

'Oh, great,' says Paddy. 'Is there hurling up there?' 'Well,' says Mike, 'I've good news and bad news.' 'Give me the good news first.'

'There's hurling up here — never saw anything like it on earth.' 'Great,' said Paddy. 'Give me the bad news now.'

'You're playing in goal next Sunday.'

Of all the games throughout his career with Kilkenny, Dublin, Faughs, and New York, pride of place in Terry's memory goes to the 1947 All-Ireland final. That team read:

Jim Donegan

Paddy Grace		Paddy Hayden	Mark Marnell
Jimmy Kelly		Peter Prendergast	Jack Mulcahy
	D. Kennedy	Jimmy Heffernan	
T. Walton		Terry Leahy	Jimmy Langton
Shem Downey		Willie Cahill	Liam Reidy
Sub: E. Kavanagh.			

Born: 1917

which grows so abundantly in our land. Can anything be more racy of the soil — the game itself, the camán, the men who play it?

99

66

I have always unashamedly claimed that hurling is the best field game in the world. I won't deny that this is a subjective assertion. I have not seen all field games in reality, but I have seen most of them in reality and the rest on television. My opinion still holds.

I think that hurling typifies the Irish character and tradition more than anything else, with the exception of our language. It has a combination of skill, courage, speed of thought and action, and calls for a spirit of give and take more than most games.

Its main implement is a stick skilfully hewn and fashioned from the ash tree,

I met Jack Lynch by appointment at his office in Dáil Éireann. As he glanced through the book I was compiling, it seemed as if something jogged his memory, and he said to me, 'What date is it?' 'The eighteenth of February,' I replied. It turned out to be a historic day: 'This is the thirty-third anniversary of my entry to the Dáil.' I offered my congratulations.

I recounted for him my earliest recollections of Gaelic games and of his participation in them. It was the 1945 senior football final between Cork and Cavan — a day when Jack was to carve for himself a special place in GAA history by adding a football medal to his successive hurling victories of 1941 to '44. It was to be followed in 1946 by a further hurling success: six All-Ireland medals in a row.

In 1947 he was on the losing side in the hurling final against Kilkenny: seven All-

---

Jack's ideal team, which was not chosen specifically for me and therefore does not include himself as captain, is as follows:

Paddy Scanlon *(Limerick)*

Fan Larkin *(Kilkenny)*   Nick O'Donnell *(Wexford)*   Willie Murphy *(Cork)*

Tommy Doyle *(Tipperary)*   John Keane *(Waterford)*   Billy Rackard *(Wexford)*

Eudi Coughlan *(Cork)*   Timmy Ryan *(Limerick)*

Christy Ring *(Cork)*   Mick Mackey *(Limerick)*   Jimmy Langton *(Kilkenny)*

Eddie Keher *(Kilkenny)*   Nicky Rackard *(Wexford)*   Josie Gallagher *(Galway)*

Ireland finals in a row.

I told him I had a bet of sixpence (old pence!) with my father on Cork against Cavan in 1945. I didn't give my father any choice of team: being a Longford man from very close to the Cavan border, his allegiance and support, I presumed, would lie with Cavan. Anyway, even at that young age I had a feeling Cork were going to win. 'That was a lot of money in those days!' said Jack. How very true! 'Your judgement was sound — did you collect?' Yes, I got paid.

As we talked about the way the game of hurling had evolved and developed over the years, Jack made particular reference to the amount of handling of the ball that goes on nowadays, and wondered if the game would benefit from perhaps a little less handling. He expressed the view that it was very difficult, if not impossible, to compare men of different eras.

We talked for a while about his "firsts," which are interesting to record. His first visit to Croke Park was in 1931, when he was a spectator at the first drawn game between Cork and Kilkenny. He played his first senior hurling club game with Glen Rovers in the semi-final against Shandon in 1934. 'It wasn't a very successful debut, and I failed to find a place on the first fifteen that played in the final.' His first senior county game was against Limerick in the League in 1935, when he was opposed by John Mackey. He made his senior championship debut against Clare in 1936.

Thurles was his favourite hurling ground. 'There isn't a hurling pitch in the country to equal it. It's the full size, has a great sod, and of course it has a unique atmosphere.' I recalled what Garrett Howard once said of Thurles pitch: 'If a man can't hurl in Thurles, he can't hurl.'

While the forties were particularly rewarding to Jack and his native Co. Cork, 'there were many occasions in the thirties when I thought I would never win an All-Ireland medal.'

Somehow 1939 has a special nostalgia for Jack. 'It was the year we broke through in Munster after being out of it since 1931. We met a great Limerick team in the Munster final. They were still a mighty force in hurling, and included Mick and John Mackey, Paddy Scanlon — who was the best goalkeeper I have seen — Jackie Power, Paddy McMahon, and Timmy Ryan. Having beaten them by two points in an absolute thriller — actually we only clinched it with a goal in the final moments, and indeed nearly lost it a few seconds later — we were very confident of beating Kilkenny in the All-Ireland final.'

Cork lost that game by one point, and yet strangely enough Jack sees it as one of the most memorable he played in. It was of course his first All-Ireland final. 'I remember more facets of that game than any other I played' — but then I suppose if you play in thunder and lightning and torrential rain, it is hard to forget. It was a game that might have been won. But Cork, who hadn't come out of Munster since 1931, were raw to the big time. 'It took a little longer before the breakthrough came, and when it did come we just kept on winning — and made up for all the disappointments of the thirties.'

The records show Jack Lynch as having won three Railway Cup medals, but quite a few more were won on the substitute bench. 'In those days competition for places on the provincial team was incredibly keen. Players felt highly honoured to be chosen. The Railway Cup was a prestige competition, and the medals were greatly treasured.'

Our chat had gone on for quite some time. Jack wrote his contribution; and as he recorded some of the hurlers he admired — Christy Ring, Mick Mackey, Timmy Ryan, Christy Moylan, Paddy Phelan, Harry Gray, Paddy "Fox" Collins, and Jim Young — he remarked, 'I'll be in trouble over this.'

During what had been a most pleasant meeting I could sense those qualities that had prompted Liam Cosgrave to say of him, after he had stepped down as leader of Fianna Fáil, that he had been 'the most popular Irish leader since Parnell.'

Mr Jack Lynch, Taoiseach (Prime Minister) from 1966–73 and 1977–79.

Some statistics on the featured players

	Born	County	Club	Era	All-Star Awards (1971–)	All Ireland Medals	National Hurling League Medals (1926–)	Railway Cup Medals (1927–)	County Titles	Provincial Titles	Oireachtas Titles (1939–)	Visited
Kevin Armstrong	1922	Antrim	O'Connell's (Belfast)	1940-61					5	21		1985
John Barron	1935	Waterford	De La Salle	1954-64			1	4		3	1	1983
Paddy Buggy	1929	Kilkenny	Slieverue	1949-60		1		1	1	5	2	1981
Frank Burke	1895	Dublin	Collegians	1917-23		2			4	4		1981
Ted Carroll	1939	Kilkenny	Lisdowney	1961-71		3	1	1	1	5	3	1982
Martin Codd	1929	Wexford	Rathnure	1949-65		1	1		3	1	2	1987
Paddy "Fox" Collins	1903	Cork	Glen Rovers	1928-38	Sp	2	1	1	7	2		1981
John Connolly	1948	Galway	Castlegar	1967-81	2	1	1		6	1	1	1991
Brendan Considine	1897	Clare (Dublin)		1914-30		2				4		1981
Eugene Coughlan	1900	Cork	Blackrock	1919-31	Sp	4	2	3	7	5		1981
Dave Creedon	1919	Cork	Glen Rovers	1952-55		3	1		9	3		1988
Peter Cregan	1918	Limerick	Croom	1937-47		1	1	4	2	1	1	1981
Willie John Daly	1925	Cork	Carrigtohill	1947-57		3	2	2	4	2	1	1984
Mick Daniels	1905	Dublin	Army Metro	1930-39		1	1	1	3	2		1982
Liam Devaney	1935	Tipperary	Borrisoleigh	1955-68		5	8	3	1	8	6	1986
Jim Devitt	1922	Tipperary	Cashel	1944-49		1	1	3	1	2		1981
Shem Downey	1922	Kilkenny	Tullaroan	1946-54		1			1	3	1	1983

Name	Born	County	Club	Career								Year
John Doyle	1930	Tipperary	Holycross	1949-67		8	11	5	3	10	6	1986
John Joe Doyle	1906	Clare	Newmarket	1926-38	Sp			3	6	1		1981
Tommy Doyle	1918	Tipperary	Thurles Sarsfields	1937-53	Sp	5	3	3	7	6		1981
Seán Duggan	1922	Galway	Liam Mellows	1943-53		5	1	1	5		2	1987
Dan Dunne	1908	Kilkenny	Young Ireland (Dublin)	1931-33		1	1	2	1	2		1982
Andy Fleming	1916	Waterford	Mount Sion	1938-51		1		7	6	1		1981
Tim Flood	1927	Wexford	Cloughbaun	1949-61		3	2	2	2	5	4	1982
Des Foley	1940	Dublin	St Vincent's	1958-69				3	4	1		1981
Josie Gallagher	1923	Galway	Gort	1942-54			1	1			2	1983
Paddy Grace	1917	Kilkenny	Carrickshock & Dicksboro	1939-50		2		1	5	6		1982
Phil Grimes	1929	Waterford	Mount Sion	1947-65		1	1	2	13	3	1	1981
Jimmy Heffernan	1925	Kilkenny	Mullinavat & Carrickshock	1944-53		1	1		1	5	1	1990
Seán Herbert	1923	Limerick	Ahane	1942-53			1	5	8			1981
Mick Hickey	1911	Waterford	Portlaw	1936-48		1			1	1		1983
Garrett Howard	1899	Limerick	Croom; Garda (D); Toomyvara	1921-36	Sp	5	5	2	8	8		1980
John Keane	1916	Waterford	Mount Sion	1935-51		1	3	7	8	2		
Eddie Keher	1941	Kilkenny	The Rower (Inistioge)	1959-77	5	6	3	9	1	10	3	1982
Padge Kehoe	1925	Wexford	St Aidan's	1946-62		3	2	6	3	6	4	1983
Martin Kennedy	1899	Tipperary	Toomyvara	1922-35		2	1	2	4	3		1981
Jimmy Langton	1919	Kilkenny	Éire Óg	1938-53	Sp	2			7	8	1	1984
Terry Leahy	1918	Kilkenny	Young Ireland & Faughs	1938-49		2			7	5	1	1981
Jack Lynch	1917	Cork	Glen Rovers	1935-51	Sp	5	3	3	11	6		1981

Name	Year	County	Club	Period								
Johnny McGovern	1932	Kilkenny	Bennettsbridge	1952-62	2		1	1	11	5	2	1982
Pa "Fowler" McInerney	1893	Clare (Dublin)	O'Callaghan's Mills & Garda	1913-33	2	Sp	1	1	7	5		1981
Paddy McInerney	1895	Limerick	Young Ireland	1918-25	2			2	2	3		1981 W/t
John Mackey	1914	Limerick	Ahane	1933-48	3		6	7	15	5	1	1980
Mick Mackey	1912	Limerick	Ahane	1932-46	3	Sp	5	8	15	5	1	1980
Paddy McMahon	1911	Limerick	Kildimo & Ahane	1935-40	2		4	2	2	3	1	1980
John Maher	1908	Tipperary	Thurles Sarsfields	1929-45	3			1	9	4	1	1983
Michael Maher	1930	Tipperary	Holycross	1956-66	5		6	3	3	6	5	1986
Damien Martin	1946	Offaly	St Rynagh's	1964-86	1	1		1	12	4	5	1991
Lory Meagher	1899	Kilkenny	Tullaroan	1926-36	3		1	2	5	6		
Christy Moylan	1916	Waterford	Dungarvan	1935-49	1	Sp		5	1	2		1983
Con Murphy	1922	Cork	Valley Rovers	1941-51	4			2		5		1991
Mick Neville	1887	Wexford	Castlebridge	1904-18	1			1	1	2		1981
Matt Nugent	1921	Clare	St Joseph's (Ennis)	1945-58			1	3	2		1	1983
Nick O'Donnell	1925	Wexford	St Aidan's	1947-62	3		2	1	7	6	4	1981
Jim O'Regan	1901	Cork	Garda (Dublin) & Kinsale	1926-36	4		2	2	1	5		1981
Jackie Power	1916	Limerick	Ahane	1935-49	2		5	7	15	2	1	1981
Jim Power	1894	Galway	Tynagh	1918-28	1			6	6	1		1982
John T. Power	1883	Kilkenny	Piltown & Mooncoin	1907-25	4			2	2	6		1981
Seumas Power	1929	Waterford	Mount Sion	1948-64	1		1	5	12	3		1983
Dan Quigley	1944	Wexford	Rathnure	1964-72	1		1	3	8	3		1990

Name	Year	County	Club	Career								Award
Johnny Quirke	1911	Cork	Blackrock	1932-46		4	2	7	3	4	1	1981
Billy Rackard	1931	Wexford	Rathnure	1949-64		3	2	4	3	6	4	1981
Bobbie Rackard	1927	Wexford	Rathnure	1947-57		2	1	1	4	4	4	1988
Tony Reddin	1919	Tipperary	Mullagh & Lorrha	1943-56		3	5	5		3		1988
Christy Ring	1920	Cork	Glen Rovers	1940-62		8	4	18	12	9		1982
John Roberts	1895	Kilkenny	Dicksboro	1918-28		1		1	2	2		1982
Johnny Ryan	1914	Tipperary	Moycarkey-Borris	1936-48		1		1	3	3		1984
Timmy Ryan	1910	Limerick	Ahane	1930-45		3	5	5	15	5	1	1980
Joe Salmon	1931	Galway	Liam Mellows & Glen Rovers	1949-64			1		5		3	1986
Jimmy Smyth	1931	Clare	Ruan	1948-67				6	5		1	1981
Pat Stakelum	1927	Tipperary	Holycross	1949-59		3	6	5	3	3	1	1986
Dick Stokes	1920	Limerick	UCD	1940-53		1	1	5	1	1		1980
Jim Treacy	1943	Kilkenny	Bennettsbridge	1963-75	2	4	1	3	6	7	3	1982
Tommy Treacy	1904	Tipperary (Dublin)	Young Ireland	1926-42		2	1	3	4	4		1981
Ollie Walsh	1937	Kilkenny	Thomastown	1956-71		4	2	4		9	5	1990
Charlie Ware	1903	Waterford	Erin's Own	1923-38				3	10	1		1981
Jim Ware	1908	Waterford	Erin's Own	1926-49		1		3	11	1		1983
Ned Wheeler	1932	Wexford	Faythe Harriers	1949-65		3	2	3	3	7	4	1981
Jim Young	1915	Cork	Glen Rovers	1935-49		5	3	4	8	6		1981

* Sp = Special Award

Statistics On All-Ireland Finals, 1887-1990

County of Referee	No. of counties to supply ref (cum)	Referee	No. of times All-Ireland ref (cum)	No. of times County supplied ref (cum)	Score	No. of times Runners-up (cum)	Runners-up	Year[3]	Championship Appearances by this Team	Championships won by this Team (cum)	Winners[2]	Score[1]	Captain	No. of times Winning Captain (cum)	Attendance
Offaly	1	P. White	1	1	0:0	1	Galway	1887	1	1	Tipperary	1:1	J. Stapleton		
Dublin	2	P. Tobin	1	1	1:6	1	Clare	1889	1	1	Dublin	5:1	E. O'Shea		
Limerick	3	J. Sheehy	1	1	2:2	1	Wexford	1890[4]	1	1	Cork	1:6	D. Lane		
Dublin		P. Tobin	2	2	1:5	2	Wexford	1891	1	1	Kerry	2:3	J. Mahony		
Waterford	4	D. Fraher	1	1	1:1	1	Dublin	1892	2	2	Cork	2:4	W. O'Callaghan		
Dublin		J.J. Kenny	1	3	0:2	1	Kilkenny	1893	3	3	Cork	6:8	J. Murphy		
Dublin		J.J. Kenny	2	4	2:0	2	Dublin	1894	4	4	Cork	5:20	S. Hayes		
Dublin		J.J. Kenny	3	5	1:10	2	Kilkenny	1895	2	2	Tipperary	6:8	M. Maher	1	6,000
Dublin		D. Wood	1	6	0:4	3	Dublin	1896	3	3	Tipperary	8:14	M. Maher	2	
Dublin		J.J. McCabe	1	7	2:4	3	Kilkenny	1897	1	1	Limerick	3:4	D. Grimes		
Dublin		J.J. McCabe	2	8	3:10	4	Kilkenny	1898	4	4	Tipperary	7:13	M. Maher	3	
Dublin		A. McKeogh	1	9	1:4	3	Wexford	1899	5	5	Tipperary	3:12	J. Condon		
Kilkenny	5	J. McCarthy	1	1	0:6	1	London	1900	6	6	Tipperary	2:5	E. Hayes		
Kilkenny		J. McCarthy	2	2	0:4	1	Cork	1901	2	1	London	1:5	J. Coughlan		10,000
Dublin		L.J. O'Toole	1	10	0:0	2	London	1902	6	5	Cork	3:13	J. Kelliher		
Kilkenny		J. McCarthy	3	3	1:1	3	London	1903	7	6	Cork	3:16	S. O'Riordan		
Limerick		M.F. Crowe	1	2	1:8	2	Cork	1904	5	1	Kilkenny	1:9	G. Doheny		
Limerick		M.F. Crowe	2	3	2:9	3	Cork	1905r	6	2	Kilkenny	7:7	D. Stapleton		
Cork	6	T. Irwin	1	1	3:8	4	Dublin	1906	7	7	Tipperary	3:16	T. Semple	1	
Limerick		M.F. Crowe	3	4	4:8	4	Cork	1907	7	3	Kilkenny	3:12	D. Drug Walsh		
Cork		J. McCarthy	4	2	1:5	5	Dublin	1908r	8	8	Tipperary	3:15	T. Semple	2	
Limerick		M.F. Crowe	4	5	0:12	1	Tipperary	1909	8	4	Kilkenny	4:6	R. Drug Walsh		
Limerick		M.F. Crowe	5	6	6:2	1	Limerick	1910	4	1	Wexford	7:0	R. Doyle		

Att.	Captain	Winners	Score	(a)	Runners-up	(b)	Score	Year	(c)	Referee	Referee County
18,000		Kilkenny	W/O	5	Limerick	2		1911	9	M.F. Crowe	Limerick
25,000	S. Walton	Kilkenny	2:1	6	Cork	5	1:3	1912	10	M.F. Crowe	Limerick
13,500	R. Walsh	Kilkenny	2:4	7	Tipperary	2	1:2	1913	11	J. Lalor	Kilkenny
15,000	A. Power	Clare	5:1	1	Laois	1	1:0	1914	2	W. Walsh	Waterford
	J. Finlay	Laois	6:2	1	Cork	6	4:1	1915	2	W. Walsh	Waterford
12,000	J. Leahy	Tipperary	5:4	9	Kilkenny	5	3:2	1916	11	W. Walsh	Waterford
10,000	J. Ryan	Dublin	5:4	2	Tipperary	3	4:2	1917	7	W. Walsh	Waterford
	W. Hough	Limerick	9:5	2	Wexford	4	1:3	1918	4	W. Walsh	Waterford
	J. Kennedy	Cork	6:4	7	Dublin	6	2:4	1919	13	W. Walsh	Waterford
	R. Mockler	Dublin	4:9	3	Cork	7	4:3	1920	9	T. McGrath	Clare [7]
18,000	R. McConkey	Limerick	8:5	3	Dublin	7	3:2	1921	5	W. Walsh	Waterford
26,119	W. Dunphy	Kilkenny	4:2	8	Tipperary	4	2:6	1922	13	P. Dunphy	Laois [8]
	M. Kenny	Galway	7:3	1	Limerick	3	4:5	1923	2	P. Kennefick	Dublin
	B. Aylward	Dublin	5:3	4	Galway	2	2:6	1924	11	P. Ó Caoimh	Cork
26,000	J. Leahy	Tipperary	5:6	10	Galway	3	1:5	1925	14	P. McCullagh	Wexford [9]
	S. Óg Murphy	Cork	4:6	8	Kilkenny	6	2:0	1926	15	P. McCullagh	Wexford
	M. Gill	Dublin	4:8	5	Cork	8	1:3	1927	12	D. Lanigan	Limerick
	S. Óg Murphy	Cork	6:12	9	Galway	4	1:0	1928	17	J. Roberts	Kilkenny
	D.B. Murphy	Cork	4:9	10	Galway	5	1:3	1929	18	S. Robbins	Offaly
	J.J. Callanan	Tipperary	2:7	11	Dublin	8	1:3	1930	15	S. Jordan	Galway [10]
31,935	E. Coughlan	Cork	5:8	11	Kilkenny	7	3:4	1931r	19	S. Robbins (2); W. Walsh	Offaly; Waterford
34,372	J. Walsh	Kilkenny	3:3	9	Clare	2	2:3	1932	16	S. Robbins	Offaly
45,176	E. Doyle	Kilkenny	1:7	10	Limerick	4	0:6	1933	17	S. Jordan	Galway
30,250	T. Ryan	Limerick	5:2	4	Dublin	9	2:6	1934r	8	S. Jordan	Galway
46,591	L. Meagher	Kilkenny	2:5	11	Limerick	5	2:4	1935	18	T. Daly	Clare
51,235 [1]	M. Mackey	Limerick	5:6	5	Kilkenny	8	1:5	1936	10	J. Regan	Cork
43,638	J. Lanigan	Tipperary	3:11	12	Kilkenny	9	0:3	1937	16	J. Flaherty	Offaly
37,129	M. Daniels	Dublin	2:5	6	Waterford	1	1:6	1938	15	I. Harney	Galway
39,302	J. Walsh	Kilkenny	2:7	12	Cork	9	3:3	1939	21	I. Flaherty	Offaly
49,260 [2]	M. Mackey	Limerick	3:7	6	Kilkenny	10	1:7	1940	11	J.J. Callanan	Tipperary [11]

Attendance		Winning captain	Score	Winners			Year	Losers		Score			Referee	County
26,150		C. Buckley	5:11	Cork	12	21	1941	Dublin	10	0:6		2	W. O'Donnell	Tipperary
27,313		J. Lynch	2:14	Cork	13	22	1942	Dublin	11	3:4		3	M. Hennessy	Clare
48,843		M. Kennefick	5:16	Cork	14	23	1943	Antrim	1	0:4	1	12	J.J. Stuart	Dublin
26,896		S. Condon	2:13	Cork	15	24	1944	Dublin	12	1:2	2	4	M. Hennessy	Clare
69,459		J. Maher	5:6	Tipperary	13	17	1945	Kilkenny	11	3:6		9	V. Baston	Waterford
64,415	1	C. Ring	7:5	Cork	16	25	1946	Kilkenny	12	3:8	3	7	J. Flaherty	Offaly
61,510		D. Kennedy	0:14	Kilkenny	13	25	1947	Cork	10	2:7		3	P. Purcell	Tipperary
61,742		J. Ware	6:7	Waterford	1	2	1948	Dublin	13	4:2	1	5	C. Murphy	Cork
67,168		P. Stakelum	3:11	Tipperary	14	18	1949	Laois	2	0:3		5	M.J. Flaherty	Galway
67,629		S. Kenny	1:9	Tipperary	15	19	1950	Kilkenny	13	1:8	2	6	C. Murphy	Cork
64,322		J. Finn	7:7	Tipperary	16	20	1951	Wexford	5	3:9	1	10	W. O'Donoghue	Limerick
71,195		P. Barry	2:14	Cork	17	27	1952	Dublin	14	0:7	2	11	W. O'Donoghue	Limerick
71,195	2	C. Ring	3:3	Cork	18	28	1953	Galway	6	0:8		8	P. Connell	Offaly
84,856	3	C. Ring	1:9	Cork	19	29	1954	Wexford	6	1:6		6	J. Mulcahy	Kilkenny
77,854	1	N. O'Donnell	3:13	Wexford	2	8	1955	Galway	7	2:8	1	4	B. Stakelum	Tipperary
83,096		J. English	2:14	Wexford	3	9	1956	Cork	11	2:8		12	T. O'Sullivan	Limerick
70,594		M. Kelly	4:10	Kilkenny	14	27	1957	Waterford	2	3:12		13	S. Gleeson	Limerick
47,276		T. Wall	4:9	Tipperary	17	21	1958	Galway	8	2:5	1	9	M. Spain	Offaly
77,285		F. Walsh	3:12	Waterford	2	4	1959r	Kilkenny	14	1:10	1	14	G. Fitzgerald	Limerick
77,154	2	N. O'Donnell	2:15	Wexford	4	10	1960	Tipperary	5	0:11	1	10	J. Dowling	Offaly
67,866		M. Hassett	0:16	Tipperary	18	23	1961	Dublin	15	1:12	2	15	G. Fitzgerald	Limerick
75,039	1	J. Doyle	3:10	Tipperary	19	24	1962	Wexford	7	2:11	2	11	J. Dowling	Offaly
73,123		S. Cleere	4:17	Kilkenny	15	29	1963	Waterford	3	6:8	1	1	J. Hatton 12	Wicklow
71,282		M. Murphy	5:13	Tipperary	20	25	1964	Kilkenny	15	2:8		6	A. Higgins	Galway
67,498	2	J. Doyle	2:16	Tipperary	21	26	1965	Wexford	8	0:10	1	5	M. Hayes	Clare
68,249		G. McCarthy	3:9	Cork	20	31	1966	Kilkenny	16	1:10	2	2	J. Hatton	Wicklow
64,241		J. Treacy	3:8	Kilkenny	16	32	1967	Tipperary	6	2:7	2	6	M. Hayes	Clare
63,461		D. Quigley	5:8	Wexford	5	13	1968	Tipperary	7	3:12	3	12	J. Dowling	Offaly
66,844		E. Keher	2:15	Kilkenny	17	33	1969	Cork	12	2:9	1	16	S. O'Connor	Limerick
65,062		P. Barry	6:21	Cork	21	33	1970	Wexford	9	5:10	3	3	J. Hatton	Wicklow

61,393	T. O'Connor	5:17	Tipperary	22	29	1971	Kilkenny	17	5:14	1	7	F. Murphy	Cork
66,135	N. Skehan	3:24	Kilkenny	18	35	1972	Cork	13	5:11	2	13	M. Spain	Offaly
58,009	E. Grimes	1:21	Limerick	7	12	1973	Kilkenny	18	1:14		7	M. Slattery	Clare
62,071	N. Orr	3:19	Kilkenny	19	37	1974	Limerick	6	1:13		5	J. Moloney	Tipperary
63,711	W. Fitzpatrick	2:22	Kilkenny	20	38	1975	Galway	9	2:10	2	17	S. O'Connor	Limerick
62,684	R. Cummins	2:21	Cork	22	35	1976	Wexford	10	4:11		7	P. Johnson	Kilkenny
63,168	M. O'Doherty	1:17	Cork	23	36	1977	Wexford	11	3:8		18	S. O'Grady	Limerick
64,155	C. McCarthy	1:15	Cork	24	37	1978	Kilkenny	19	2:8		2	J. Rankin	Laois
53,535	G. Fennelly	2:12	Kilkenny	21	40	1979	Galway	10	1:8	1	6	G. Ryan	Tipperary
64,895	J. Connolly	2:15	Galway	2	12	1980	Limerick	7	3:9	1	13	N. O'Donoghue	Dublin
71,384	P. Horan	2:12	Offaly	1	1	1981	Galway	11	0:15	2	8	F. Murphy	Cork
59,550	B. Cody	3:18	Kilkenny	22	41	1982	Cork	14	1:13	2	14	N. O'Donoghue	Dublin
58,381	L. Fennelly	2:14	Kilkenny	23	42	1983	Cork	15	2:12		19	N. Duggan	Limerick
59,168	J. Fenton	3:16	Cork	25	40	1984	Offaly	1	1:12		8	P. Long	Kilkenny
61,814	P. Fleury	2:11	Offaly	2	3	1985	Galway	12	1:12	2	7	G. Ryan	Tipperary
63,451	T. Cashman	4:13	Cork	26	41	1986	Galway	13	2:15		15	J. Bailey	Dublin
59,550 [1]	C. Hayes	1:12	Galway	3	16	1987	Kilkenny	20	0:9		20	T. Murray	Limerick
63,545 [2]	C. Hayes	1:15	Galway	4	17	1988	Tipperary	8	0:14		14	G. Kirwan	Offaly
65,496	B. Ryan	4:29	Tipperary	23	31	1989	Antrim	2	3:9		3	P. Delaney	Laois
63,954	T. Mulcahy	5:15	Cork	27	42	1990	Galway	14	2:21		10	J. Moore	Waterford
64,500	D. Carr	1:16	Tipperary	24	32	1991	Kilkenny	21	0:15		9	W. Horgan	Cork

Notes

cum. = cumulative

1. r = replay.
2. 1887–91 teams had 21 players.
   1892–1912 teams had 17 players.
   1913– teams had 15 players.
3. 1887–91 No relationship between goals and points.
   1892–95 1 goal = 5 points.
   1896– 1 goal = 3 points.
4. 1890 game was abandoned, and awarded to Cork.

Born: 1932

"

The game I remember most is the All-Ireland final of 1957, when Kilkenny beat Waterford by one point. It was a game that could have gone either way, as Waterford were a wonderful team, having some outstanding hurlers like Phil Grimes, Seumas Power, and Mick Flannery.

Other hurlers I rated highly were Christy Ring, Tim Flood, Pat Stakelum, Jimmy Finn, Jimmy Smyth, and Harry Gray.

"

Johnny McGovern's twelve years in inter-county hurling were rewarded with only two All-Ireland medals. It could have been more, and it might have been none.

Johnny belonged to an era that was dominated by Cork, Wexford, Waterford, Kilkenny, and Tipperary. Galway too produced formidable combinations.

Winning an All-Ireland medal was difficult. A great Wexford team adorned

that era. Johnny expressed deep admiration for them and their contribution to hurling.

He remembers as a youth of nineteen being at the Munster final of 1951, when Christy Ring had a magnificent game for Cork but even with his brilliance couldn't halt Tipp's march for three in a row. After the game he recalls being gathered in a group as fans and admirers discussed the game with Ring. Later he remembers being among Tipperary supporters where Pat Stakelum and other heroes were being feted. Secretly he hoped he would play against both counties in an All-Ireland some day and clash with these Munster hurling heroes he admired so much. But it wasn't to be.

Fate sometimes plays strange tricks. In the period in question Kilkenny were to contest all their All-Ireland battles with Waterford. They met in the finals of 1957, 1959, and 1963. All four games were memorable; 1959 went to a replay. Maybe this is one reason why Johnny is so generous in his praise of the Waterford team of the late fifties and early sixties — an era when they played a brand of delightfully attractive hurling that was a mixture of Munster and Kilkenny styles at their best.

Kilkenny won in 1957 and 1963, and only a last-minute goal in the drawn game of 1959 by Seumas Power denied Kilkenny victory. But Johnny readily admits that all three finals might just as easily have gone to Waterford. In 1957 he recalls that with about twelve minutes or so remaining, Waterford led by two goals and looked as if they would win by even more. For this was a game they were dominating.

I watched that game from under the

Cusack Stand near the canal goal end. I remember clearly the superb display of Ollie Walsh in the Kilkenny goal. Three times in the space of seconds in the first half he saved point-blank raspers from Waterford forwards — miracle saves; he kept Kilkenny in the game. Six goals and eight points would have won most titles since 1887, but in 1963 it was not enough for luckless Waterford when Kilkenny scored 4:17.

In 1963 Waterford could be termed unlucky. But in 1957 it seemed to supporters and neutrals that the fury and vengeance of the gods had turned on them. By full time in that game Kilkenny had edged a point in front. Was it Kilkenny magic — point magic? Well, it wasn't the first time they had pulled off the one-point victory trick. They did it in 1935 and 1939 and 1947, and at other times too. But on that September Sunday afternoon in 1957, as the final whistle blew and the score stood at Kilkenny 4:10, Waterford 3:12, Waterford fans sat numbed and shattered.

Johnny then talked about the great Kilkenny teams of the thirties that were full of household names and now form part of Kilkenny hurling folklore. Turning to more modern times, and to defenders in particular, Johnny had a very high regard for the half-back hurling qualities of fellow-countyman Martin Coogan, and Tipperary's Jimmy Finn.

If he struck lean years with his county he certainly struck gold with his club, Bennettsbridge. Between 1952 and 1971 they were the dominant club in Kilkenny, and Johnny won thirteen county titles with them.

He cherishes each of those county successes and is proud to have been part of a club that meant as much to Kilkenny hurling during those years as Mooncoin and Tullaroan did in earlier decades.

Johnny McGovern with his son.

Born: 1893

I had often heard and read about the hurling qualities of Pa "Fowler" McInerney, who hurled with distinction in the jerseys of O'Callaghan's Mills and his native Clare, Garda and his adopted Dublin, and the provinces of Munster and Leinster. I looked forward therefore to meeting him, and set about finding him in Rathfarnham, Dublin, where he lived with his daughter.

As he browsed with interest through the autographs, memories, moments, games and tussles came flooding into his mind — a very clear and alert mind.

As a youth he recalled meeting one day Dr Fogarty, Bishop of Killaloe. The good clergyman enquired from Fowler how he had spent Sunday. 'Hurling, my lord,' came the reply. 'What any healthy boy should be doing,' said Dr Fogarty.

Fowler told me he was the third-oldest living man with an All-Ireland senior hurling medal. The oldest was of course John T. Power of Piltown, then in his ninety-ninth year, followed by Mick Neville of Castlebridge, in his ninety-fifth year. I learnt from Fowler's daughter that her father, despite being eighty-eight years old, used to spend quite a lot of time each day working in the garden. He still looked a strong man, and when I visited Johnny Quirke of Cork, he told me that Fowler was one of the biggest and strongest men he ever played against.

When Fowler came to the autograph of Mick Mackey he recalled that he played not only against Mick but also against his father, Tyler. As he came across some Kilkenny names he remembered that sideline cut Lory Meagher took in the 1932 All-Ireland final — a beautifully taken and

"

I played the game with hurlers of the best that the game has produced, and enjoyed every hour of it.

Some of the men I played against were Anthony Kelly (Galway), Jack Roberts (Kilkenny), Martin Kennedy of Tipperary, "Major" Kennedy (Cork), and Ned McEvoy of Laois.

"

well-directed shot that reached the Clare goal-mouth and finished up in the back of the Clare net. Fate was unkind to Clare that day, for it was a game they might well have won. Indeed, as Fowler recalled, it was won and lost in a six-minute spell early in the second half, when Kilkenny got through for three goals.

He then recalled a game against Cork when Mick Leahy, the Cork forward, ran in under Fowler's hurley and got his eyebrow cut off. He was replaced by Dr Kearney, who put his hand up for the first ball that came his way and scored a point. Fowler had refrained form pulling on that ball when the hand went up, and he suggested to Kearney that he shouldn't put his hand up again. He did, however, whereupon Fowler pulled, and Kearney had to go off with a broken bone in his hand. Years later Fowler met Dr Kearney on his way into Croke Park and they both recalled the incident as they reminisced and recalled the past.

In the same game Mick Leahy came back onto the Cork team after receiving attention, and sportingly admitted to Fowler that he had 'walked into the hurley'.

Noticing Jack Lynch's name, he said he had always made the game of hurling look simple, 'liked the open spaces, and always seemed to be in the right place'.

While there was less handling of the ball in his day, he felt that at county level, hurling was as good as ever, but that there was less hurling at club level now than in his day.

He regretted that Clare couldn't make the breakthrough. He thought they might have done so in the 1970s, when they won two League titles and gave many displays that suggested they had what it took to take an All-Ireland crown. He felt it could have been done in 1932. He saw it as a chance lost, without in any way detracting from the Kilkenny victory.

As I left this fine character I felt that he had enjoyed the memories, and it seemed to me that what he recorded in the book summed up his feelings about the great game of hurling: 'I played the game with hurlers of the best that the game has produced, and enjoyed every hour of it.'

Born: 1895

great spirit to win, which we did. Our next great win was against Dublin, 1921 — a super team of hurlers, but our boys won easily. 1923 arrived v. Galway, which unfortunately was lost — being without our star goalkeeper, Mick Murphy (RIP).

I'm glad to say the grand old game made many great friendships with the great players of each county, which lasted down the years. During those years I will mention some of the greats I most admired: number 1, Tom McGrath (later Colonel McGrath); Paddy Scanlon, Jack Keane, Willie Hough, Dinny Lanigan, Willie Gleeson, Seán Óg Murphy, Paddy Leahy, Bob Mockler, Tommy Moore, John Power, Mick Gill — all gone to their eternal reward, less John Power, who is still hale and hearty at ninety-eight years; many more which I don't name.

Not having the chance to see the game now I must refrain from offering my opinion as regards the quality of the players of those days and the present.

" "

"

As the saying goes, I was born with a hurley in my hand. Hurling holds a great love in my heart. Every moment I could spare I devoted it to the grand old game, and it was a great pleasure to me to take my place on the GAA fields with my fellow-players and opponents. I always believed in ground hurling and tried to get to the ball first and let it go — no picking — before the opponent had a chance to arrive.

I hold special memories of my first All-Ireland victory with Limerick v. Wexford in 1918, which we won by a big score. The county board decided to send the team to Foynes under a great trainer, Jim Dalton (RIP). We arrived at Croke Park with a

Paddy is one of the few surviving hurling veterans of the pre-1920 era. It was Séamus Ó Ceallaigh, the Limerick GAA historian, who is a columnist in the *Limerick Leader* under the pen-name "Camán", who put me in touch with Paddy at his home in New Mexico. They still communicate, and Séamus told me that Paddy regularly inquires about his former club, Young Ireland, and regrets that its fortunes have declined.

Paddy was born in Co. Clare in 1895,

and won hurling fame in the Limerick and Young Ireland jerseys. He had the honour of captaining Limerick in the 1923 championship, when they were victorious in Munster, but failed to Galway in the All-Ireland final.

Paddy sent me some written memories for my book after I had communicated with him in August 1981. Deep nostalgia runs through his sentences as he recounts how much the great game of hurling meant to the Ireland of his youth and the men who played the game.

He sent me a photograph taken in June 1981, about two months before I wrote to him. He had the hurley in his hand; no doubt where Paddy was concerned it was a link not only with the past and with hurling but also with his homeland. He is now the only surviving member of the great Limerick team of the 1918–23 era, which in Garrett Howard's opinion should have won a lot more. It had a great half-back line, with Dinny Lanigan and Jack Keane on the wings and Willie Hough in the centre. So effective were this trio that they became known as the "Hindenburg Line," and have been reckoned by many to rank with the greatest half-back lines the game has known.

Paddy had tremendous regard for Willie Hough. On hearing of his death he wrote to Séamus Ó Ceallaigh. Here is an extract from Paddy's letter:

Willie was a prince of princes in GAA ranks, likewise in social life, beloved not only by the Gaels of Limerick but of all Ireland, because his name was a household word throughout the land as being one of the best centre-backs the game ever produced. When his time came to hang up the camán that he loved, he had the honour to be elected as Treasurer of the Munster Council, a post he held for twenty six years without a contest by any Gael of the Munster province, and could have held it to the end if he hadn't pleaded with the delegates to allow him to resign as he felt the post should pass to another worthy Gael.

The Council was sorry to see him go as he had done such a magnificent job in his post, and to show their appreciation they gave him a gift in the form of a trip to the USA.

In subsequent correspondence Paddy wrote: 'As regards thinking I might pay a visit to Ireland I'd love to see those green fields of Éire once more. However, I'm afraid I can't look forward to a visit. It would mean from here ten thousand miles round trip — too much for an old veteran, and away from family.'

The 1923 team Paddy captained was:

Paddy McInerney, J. Hanley, Dave Murnane, Willie Hough, Dinny Lanigan, Willie Gleeson, Jimmy Humphries, Mick Neville, John Joe Kinnane, Jack Keane, Tom McGrath, Mickey Cross, Bob McConkey, J. O'Grady, Mickey Fitzgibbon.

Born: 1914

cannot dim. He sums it up like this. 'Limerick came out of Munster in 1933 but lost the final to Kilkenny. We were gaining in experience all the time, and the highlight of my career came in 1934 when we won the All-Ireland — the first All-Ireland medal I won. For me that Munster championship in 1933 and the All-Ireland in 1934 surpass everything else I achieved.'

John played minor with Limerick from 1929 to 1931. Here is how he remembers those early days. 'On the fourth of August 1929 I lined out for Limerick at Dungarvan against Waterford in the opening round of the Munster minor hurling championship. It was my first time playing for Limerick in any grade. The Waterford lads won, and went on to take the All-Ireland title. Three of the Limerick minor team, Mick Hickey, myself, and my brother Mick, afterwards won senior All-Ireland hurling honours with Limerick. Waterford had Jackie and Declan Goode and D. Wyse — great men all. In 1932 I was sent in as a sub at left-half-forward against Cork at Thurles in the Munster senior championship. Our hour had not yet arrived this was Cork's day.'

John made many appearances in the Munster jersey, but his most memorable Railway Cup game was the 1935 final. Munster won by 3:4 to 3:0 over a star-studded Leinster team drawn from Dublin and Kilkenny.

On the club scene he felt few matches could surpass the clash between Ahane and Thurles Sarsfields at Newport in May 1947 in a tournament final. The bulk of the thirty players had county experience, and he recalled some of the names on the Thurles Sarsfields side: John Maher, John Lanigan, Tommy Doyle, Gerry Doyle, Dan Mackey,

"

1934, winning my first All-Ireland, is my most cherished memory.

Some of the men I played against and admired a lot were George Garrett, Paddy Phelan, Larry Blake, Philly Purcell, Paddy Clohessy, Mickey Cross, Garrett Howard, and Timmy Ryan.

"

For John Mackey the success of the early days of his hurling career carry a special lustre as well as memories that time

T. Mason, "Bunny" Murphy; in the Ahane line-out: the Mackeys, the Herberts, Timmy Ryan, Dan Givens, Jackie Power, Mick Hickey, Paddy Kelly, Tom Conway.

Ahane were slight favourites, but everyone knew there would be little in it at the finish. It was hip-to-hip stuff. There was no compromise; there was no drawing back; there was no mercy. It was like that for the entire hour. At half time Ahane led by four points. At full time Thurles Sarsfields were two points to the good. But it could have gone either way; it was that kind of game. 'It was a great game,' said John.

He then recalled some of the opponents he met in his time: Paddy Phelan (Kilkenny), Jim Young (Cork), Jack Barrett (Cork), Larry Blake (Clare), Tommy Doyle (Tipperary), John Keane (Waterford), Charles McMahon (Dublin), John Joe Doyle (Clare), Phil Purcell (Tipperary), Christy Forde (Dublin), Tom Teahan (Dublin) — all these were great hurlers, he said.

The defeat at the hands of Kilkenny in the 1933 All-Ireland final was John's greatest disappointment. Here is how he recalls it. 'Limerick came out of Munster in 1933 — it was my first Munster medal. It was also my first time in an All-Ireland final. Kilkenny had a great set of backs. We had the better of exchanges at midfield and got lots of the ball, but much of our shooting was inaccurate.

'The teams were level at four points each at half time. For most of the hour, which produced great hurling and lots of thrills for the spectators, the sides were neck and neck — nothing between us. Coming towards the end of the game victory was still there for either side. And then came Johnny Dunne's wonderful goal — the only goal of the day; it set Kilkenny on the road to victory. We fought with fierce determination in an effort to prevent defeat, but we failed to penetrate a great Kilkenny back line. The game ended on the score 1:7 to 0:6.'

The quality of the hurling and the spirit in which the game was played was highly praised in the papers the following day. John, who kept a scrapbook, recalled one writer commenting, 'Nothing like this final has ever been seen before at Croke Park or anywhere in Ireland.'

Were there any great individual performances that stood out in his mind? 'Yes — two in particular. The greatest outfield performance I ever saw was given by my brother Mick in the Munster final of 1936 against Tipperary at Thurles. We won the day by 8:5 to 4:6, and Mick had a personal score of 5:3. He was all over the place. He led attack after attack; he made great solo runs; he was indestructible. As captain he led by example, and it was his first time being captain in the championship.

'The second superb performance was in the 1939 Munster final against Cork. We were without our star centre-half-back, Paddy Clohessy, because of a dispute within the county. This time it was our goalkeeper, Paddy Scanlon, who was magnificent. But the word magnificent doesn't really do him justice: throughout the entire hour he made many incredible saves. We were level at half time and a point up with little time remaining, and then Cork got a goal that gave them victory on the score 4:3 to 3:4. It was a hurling classic. Words can't describe it. Cork took victory, but Scanlon took the honours. I'll never forget his display.'

Many stories have been told about John and Mick Mackey in their young hurling

Finally we came to the difficult task of selecting a team from the men of his era that John would like to have captained. His choice reads as follows:

Paddy Scanlon (Limerick)

Paddy Larkin (Kilkenny)	Con Murphy (Cork)	Larry Blake (Clare)
Johnny Ryan (Tipperary)	John Keane (Waterford)	Paddy Phelan (Kilkenny)
Timmy Ryan (Limerick)		Jack Lynch (Cork)
Jimmy Langton (Kilkenny)	Mick Mackey (Limerick)	Jackie Power (Limerick)
Mick A. Brennan (Cork)	John Mackey (Limerick)	Christy Ring (Cork)

years and the expectations their father, "Tyler" Mackey, had of them. I asked John if it was true that his late father made himself and Mick walk home behind the horse and cart because he wasn't pleased with one of their early hurling displays. 'Never happened,' said John. 'Tyler, however, always did want to see us playing a good match — by his standards — and if we didn't measure up we were likely to get a telling off.'

A photograph of John and Mick on the sideboard caught my eye. It was taken by Brother O'Connor of Artane at Limerick Gaelic grounds in 1934. I admired it, and John made me a present of a copy of it.

One of the toughest matches he ever played was against Galway in the 1936 All-Ireland semi-final at Roscrea. 'The match was unfinished. We were leading at the time by 4:9 to 2:4. Subsequently we were awarded the match.' Did he feel the game had changed? 'Hurling in my time was much different from the game we know today. There was more first-time pulling, more bodily contact. Nowadays, there's too much picking, and the ball isn't kept going like in our time. I could be wrong, but I think there was better hurling in our time.

'In the rain-ruined 1935 final, Limerick were hot favourites against Kilkenny but were beaten in a great match. It was a disappointment all right, but not a great shock. When you play Kilkenny in a final you are never too sure, and they did us by a point. I felt we were unlucky that day; things didn't go our way. But we were not downhearted: when you are young you always feel there's another day, and of course there was.

'I believe the Limerick team of 1936 to have been the best ever. The all-round standard then was tremendous for Cork, Tipperary and Waterford in Munster, Kilkenny and Dublin in Leinster, and of course Galway were always very hard to beat. There were great men too, like Tipp's Phil Purcell, John Ryan, Jimmy Cooney, and John Maher, all of whom marked me at one time or another; John Keane, the Wares and Christy Moylan of Waterford; countless Corkmen, such as Jack Barrett, Johnny Quirke, Jim Young, Seán Barrett, Mick A. Brennan, George Garrett, and Jim O'Regan. But we struck great form that year; we were very strong and always kept trying.'

Above left: Mick Mackey with the 1962 Hall of Fame Award. *Right:* with the McCarthy Cup, 1940. Portraits of John and Mick (pp.145 and 148) are from 1934.

Born: 1912

"

My greatest memory was winning the 1934 All-Ireland medal.

Some of the hurling men I admired down the years were John Maher and Jimmy Finn of Tipperary, Christy Ring and Jimmy Brohan of Cork, Ned Wheeler and Bobbie Rackard of Wexford.

"

I visited Mick in the Autumn of 1980. As I journeyed to his home my mind went back to a tribute paid to him in a Thurles programme around the mid-forties.

'There is only one Mick Mackey. Mick is probably the most colourful player that ever gripped a camán or graced the greensward of any hurling arena. Many a time he thrilled the thousands with his dashing solo runs and daring scores ... Go maire sé céad!'

There are many who saw him play and many who played against him who would say, 'Take him for all in all, I shall not look upon his like again.' I recalled too a song written in his honour (to the air of "The Star of the County Down") shortly after he retired from the inter-county scene. Three verses come to mind:

From Bantry Bay up to Derry quay
And from Galway to Dublin town,
Mick Mackey's name, his hurling fame,
Is a household word just now.

In '44 your youth was o' er
As we journeyed to Thurles field.
It was Cork again — they were younger men—
And Limerick were forced to yield.

On that July day when the Lee held sway
You burst the net three times,
But Christy Ring with a lovely swing
Won the match on the call of time.

I found Mick resting at his home, which is set in beautiful, peaceful surroundings near Ardnacrusha. He was in good spirits, and recovering from a stroke that had afflicted him some months previously.

He was still the same genial, amiable and uncomplicated Mick that I had met in Killorglin in the summer of 1953. When I asked him if he would make a written contribution to the book I was compiling he said, in true open-hearted fashion, 'Of course I will.'

Mick was a hero in his hurling days, and by the time he retired legend surrounded him and stories abounded.

It seemed to me that he had a vivid recollection of all the games he played. It was as if his mind was like a computer, with every detail stored just as it happened. And how those memories could flow from that mind! He talked freely and easily, and as I listened that lovely expression came to mind: 'God gave us memories so that we might have roses in December.'

As he recalled moments from the past, that spirit of determination and grit was evident. He loved in particular the whole-hearted stuff. He recalled matches against Cork in the early forties, particularly those of 1942 and 1944 — games that could gave gone either way. Mick felt that if fate had been kind to Limerick they might have collected a few more All-Ireland titles between 1933 and 1945.

He spoke of the defensive prowess of Mick Kennedy, the Tipperary man who threw in his lot with Limerick and gave sterling service to his adopted county. He spoke of John Maher of Tipperary and the deep study he made of the game and the many fine performances he gave at centre-back. Paddy Phelan of Kilkenny he greatly admired, and Mattie Power of Kilkenny had that "something special" in the corner-forward position. Where goalkeepers were concerned he did not know of anyone who could surpass Paddy Scanlon.

Turning to recent hurling he spoke of the great skills of Éamon Cregan, and added, 'He is always scheming.'

Among the most memorable occasions of his hurling career he rates the trip to America in 1936. Dates and details come readily to Mick, and he told me that they left Cóbh on the ninth of May on the *Manhattan* and arrived back on the *Washington* one month later, on the ninth of June. In between, 'the hospitality and welcome was incredible — celebrations everywhere we went. We won all our games, and they still say in America that we were the best hurling team that ever toured the States. A crowd of about forty thousand watched us beat New York, and the American journalists were completely captivated by the game, especially its intensity, skill, and daring.'

Mick reminded me that the Cavan footballers were also on the same tour, and that many lasting friendships were forged with the men of Breffni. 'We came home', he said, 'to a wonderful reception, and crowned 1936 by winning Munster and All-Ireland honours.'

Was there any particular game that gave him special enjoyment? Yes, there was. It was a League match against Kilkenny in the late spring of 1935 in Nowlan Park. As far as Mick is concerned this was a game of super hurling: exhibition stuff from start to finish, and yet fiercely competitive. 'If Limerick lost we would have been out of the League,' said Mick.

He went on: 'The scoring was low — never more than two points between us. It was a thriller from start to finish. I always enjoyed playing against Kilkenny. There must have been a crowd of twenty-five or thirty thousand people at the game. The park was packed, and nobody left before the final whistle.

'Towards the end of the game John and myself got a point each, to put Limerick two points up. By this time Kilkenny had moved Paddy Phelan up to left-half-forward on Mickey Cross. He sent in a high ball to Mattie Power, who was unmarked. He put up his hand to grab it and at the same time glanced back at the Limerick goal to

Mick Mackey (left) and Christy Ring, Captains of Ahane and Glen Rovers senior teams 1946. (Photo: *The Mackey Story*, Limerick GAA, 1982)

commemorative tribute to Mick from the Ahane hurling club. It read:

> We the members of the Ahane hurling club gathered together on 7.2.1962 wish to congratulate you on your unanimous election by the Sports writers of Ireland to the Hall of Fame — the highest place in the Sporting record of our land.
>
> There is no doubt that you and three generations of the Mackey family have been an inspiration to all young men of your native parish and county and indeed of all Ireland, to foster our national games.
>
> With renewed pride then, we salute you MICK MACKEY and we pray that Almighty God will bless you and give you many years of health and happiness to enjoy the signal honours which have been conferred upon you.

see where Scanlon was. Luckily for Limerick the ball glanced off his fingers and went wide, because if he had caught it he had a certain goal, and Kilkenny would have been a point ahead.

'With the puck-out the final whistle blew, and I was glad to hear it. We went on to win our second of five successive League titles.' This is a record that has never since been equalled, but as events recalled by Mick show, records hang by slender threads.

I looked through his medals and trophies as we drank tea. His Railway Cup medals had been made into a bracelet for his wife. On the wall I noticed a framed

Eventually he got around to autographing my book, recording a special memory and naming a few players he admired down the years. As I mentioned the words 'special memory' he gazed at the book, paused for a few seconds, and said, 'It's all memories now.'

He walked to the car with me and we stood for a few moments talking in the sunshine. In appearance he had often reminded me of the great Jack Dempsey, and as I bade farewell to him on that beautiful autumn day I couldn't help feeling that despite his illness he still had in his countenance that look of granite that characterised so many of his displays on the hurling-field.

Paddy McMahon in 1980 with the hurley he used in the 1936 All-Ireland against Kilkenny.

"

The 1936 All-Ireland — it was my greatest joy to win my first medal and also in 1940 my second one. It's great to be in a winning team like Mick Mackey, Timmy Ryan, Mick Hickey, Paddy Clohessy, Ned Cregan, and Mickey Cross.

Some of the great men of my day were Mick Mackey, Mickey Cross, Paddy Scanlon, Paddy Larkin, Johnny Quirke, Garrett Howard, Timmy Ryan, Mick Kennedy, and Martin Kennedy.

"

W hen I left Castleconnell having visited John Mackey, I turned in the direction of Annacotty in search of Paddy McMahon. I was lucky to find him returning with the day's shopping.

Paddy told me he was first recommended to the Limerick selectors by Willie Hough of Monagay, who was a member of

Born: 1911

the victorious Limerick team in 1918. Paddy used to play junior hurling for Kildimo, and from this level it would have been very difficult to make the county senior team or come to the notice of a panel of selectors. The selectors responded to Willie Hough's recommendation, and Paddy was given an opportunity to prove himself when he was picked to play for Limerick in a League game against Dublin. He made an immediate impact, scoring five goals on his debut.

He told me that he never left the field without scoring at least one goal. He rarely blocked a ball: his style was to pull first time.

His senior county career stretched from 1935 to 1940 — a span of six years. I asked him why he departed the scene after such a relatively short time, and he told me that his knees, which had always tended to give him trouble, no longer stood up to the rigours of an hour's hurling. It was a blow for hurling and for Limerick when he had to quit prematurely.

Paddy's arrival on the county scene coincided with the departure of Martin Kennedy. As a full-forward he was to prove himself a worthy successor to Martin. When people who remember that era talk about full-forwards they tend to bracket Paddy and Martin together in the same class.

His greatest regret was losing the 1935 All-Ireland to Kilkenny. He recalled that he had the ball in the net in the final moments of the game, but the referee blew for a 21-yards free. 'A point would have drawn it,' said Paddy, and he added, 'we would have been very hard to beat in a replay.' But it was not to be. In the atrocious conditions that prevailed that day, the ball failed to rise sufficiently high from Mick Mackey's stroke. It was cleared by the Kilkenny defence, and the final whistle blew.

Paddy then went on to recall the 1940 final against Kilkenny. 'In the opening moments it looked as if Kilkenny would run riot as they banged in a goal and sent over a point. But then Limerick steadied and settled. It was a wonderful game, with very few frees — only eleven in the entire hour. I remember scoring a goal that day that was disallowed by the umpire, John Maher of Tipperary. I argued the decision with him, in the belief that I hadn't offended against the "square" rule.'

When I met John Maher we talked about the goal in question. He remembered it well. He hated having to disallow the goal, because it was one of those close affairs.

But he was satisfied Paddy was inside the square.

One of the highlights of Paddy's career was the tour of the United States with the Limerick team in 1936. They played a series of matches in Boston and New York. They returned to a championship campaign that saw them take the All-Ireland title with a resounding victory over Kilkenny. 1935 had been avenged.

Paddy recalled with fond memories his team-mates of the 1935–40 era. He felt honoured to have been a member of a team that boasted so many greats, and felt that they were unfortunate not to have collected a couple more All-Ireland medals. In particular he felt proud and privileged to have been a member of the 1936 winning team. It was a wonderful combination, he said, a great team.

Paddy picked a selection from the players of the thirties and forties that he would like to have captained:

Paddy Scanlon *(Limerick)*

Willie Murphy *(Cork)*	Tom McCarthy *(Limerick)*	Paddy Larkin *(Kilkenny)*
John Maher *(Tipperary)*	Paddy Clohessy *(Limerick)*	Paddy Phelan *(Kilkenny)*
Timmy Ryan *(Limerick)*		Lory Meagher *(Kilkenny)*
Tommy Doyle *(Tipperary)*	Mick Mackey *(Limerick)*	John Mackey *(Limerick)*
Johnny Quirke *(Cork)*	Paddy McMahon *(Limerick)*	Mattie Power *(Kilkenny)*

Born: 1908

and John recounted two memories of the great full-forward that typify his genius.

The first was in a Railway Cup game against Leinster. A high lobbing ball came in towards the Leinster 21-yard line, Martin angled the bos of his outstretched hurley and deflected the lobbing ball into the path of the inrushing "Ga" Aherne (Ga loved to get a ball as he rushed inwards towards goal), who gave the Leinster goalkeeper no chance as he shot to the net.

The second was an occasion when Martin was marking Peter O'Reilly, the Kilkenny full-back. It was a custom with Martin to trap an incoming ball, leave it to drop to the ground, and then hit it on the drop, goalwards. This particular ball came in, and Peter O'Reilly felt it was more prudent to stay behind Martin than to go out. He knew Martin's style of play, and Martin knew that Peter knew his style of play. He trapped the ball and outfoxed Peter, who prepared to block the anticipated drop puck — only to find that Martin had on this occasion pulled as he trapped and sent the ball into the net.

The great tradition of Tipperary goalkeeping was upheld by Tommy O'Meara during the 1930 campaign. He was particularly brilliant in the Munster final against Clare. Tommy used to use a special short hurley for blocking the ball (he had a full-size one for the puck-out), but he never liked forwards going in on top of him. John told me of the instructions to the Tipperary defence going onto the field for the 1930 Munster final against Clare: 'Don't allow any forwards in on Tommy O'Meara.' They didn't, and Tommy gave an inspired display.

John then talked about John Joe Calla-

"

My greatest thrill was the winning of my first All-Ireland in 1930 in my first year in inter-county hurling. In 1928 Thurles lost the mid-Tipperary junior title and in 1929 won the senior county title. In 1930 I was on the county senior team that won my first All-Ireland medal.

It was a pleasure to have played in my day. The game was tougher and faster and more man-to-man marking. Other memories that come to mind are the victory over Limerick in the Munster final, 1937, and the win over Kilkenny in 1945.

Advice to any player: play the game for the game's sake.

"

There is a lovely timing attached to the All-Ireland titles won by John Maher during his hurling career.

His first success came at the beginning of his career in 1930. Mention of those days called to mind the great Martin Kennedy, nan, who all his life had a deep love of hurling and was captain of Tipperary in 1930. He had won a medal with Dublin in 1920 against Cork, and could also have been on the Dublin team in 1917 against his native Tipperary, but for the fact that he had played in a Tipperary championship match between Thurles and Boherlahan.

John Joe had the distinction of being the oldest holder of an All-Ireland medal to referee an All-Ireland (Limerick v. Kilkenny in 1940). Interestingly, the late Vin Baston of Waterford was the first man to referee a final (Tipperary v. Kilkenny, 1945) and then subsequently win an All-Ireland (1948).

John told me that John Joe had to make one of the hardest decisions of his hurling life in 1929 when the vote for general secretary of the GAA took place. The final contest was between Pádraig Ó Caoimh and Frank Burke. John Joe had won a hurling medal in 1920 with Dublin, and Frank Burke was a team-mate. But the Munster delegation, to which John Joe was attached, had proposed Pádraig Ó Caoimh. To add to the drama of the 1929 election, Ó Caoimh had sent off John Joe Callanan and Mickey Fitzgibbon of Limerick in a match he refereed. Would it influence the voting?

The Cork delegates approached John Joe for his vote. But even before that he felt obliged to vote for Pádraig Ó Caoimh. As things turned out it was a vital vote, with Frank Burke losing by eleven votes to ten.

John's third All-Ireland came his way in 1945, in his last year in county hurling. He feels he probably gave his greatest display that year, as he captained his native Tipperary at the age of thirty-seven to victory over Kilkenny. They were four goals up at half 'time. Jim Barry, the famed Cork trainer, visited the Tipperary dressing-room at the interval and wished them luck in the second half, but cautioned them to 'mind Kilkenny, who are never beaten until the final whistle.' And so it nearly turned out. Kilkenny banged in three goals in the second half, and would have got more but for a staunch Tipperary defence and the absolutely superb little Jimmy Maher in goal. The final score was 5:6 to 3:6 in Tipp's favour.

As part of the celebrations they visited Tommy Moore's pub, owned by the Kilkenny man who starred with Dublin hurling teams and who had won an All-Ireland medal in 1920 with a Dublin team that also included Johnny Callanan, now a Tipperary mentor. Johnny had a "blank cheque" from Johnny Leahy to fill the cup, and filled it was. Tommy was asked how much was due to him. 'Nothing this time — you can pay the next time you win,' said Tommy. It was more than just generosity; it was a special gesture of hurling comradeship.

As they celebrated John met the great Kilkenny half-back of the thirties, Paddy Phelan. 'Will you stay on? Paddy asked John, who admitted to feeling in very good trim and as fit as he had been five or seven years earlier. 'What do you advise?' he said to Paddy, whose reply was, 'When you're crossing O'Connell Bridge take the boots and bag and throw them in and then hang up the hurley.' John decided to call it a day.

Midway between the 1930 and 1945 triumphs came the 1937 success. He was very disappointed with his display in the final against Kilkenny, even though Tipperary triumphed easily on the score 3:11 to 0:3. It was only around that time he began to realise the real meaning of individual fitness. He felt very fit before the game, but once it got under way he found himself hitting the ball badly, and as the game progressed his feet grew heavy. His weight had dropped below twelve stone five in training, and he now knew that for him that was too light. He realised he was overtrained.

A few weeks later, however, he played a game that gave him great satisfaction. It was against Waterford in a tournament. In those weeks he hadn't handled a hurley, and weight loss had been restored. In contrast to his All-Ireland display he was in sparkling form. He felt in command of every situation, and he always seemed to be where the ball was. That day he finished up scoring 2:1 from the centre-back position.

John's most memorable game was the

1937 Munster final win against Limerick. In many ways this is easy to understand. Limerick were heading for their fifth Munster success in a row. They had beaten Tipperary in 1935 and 1936, and John admits that Tipperary looked none too impressive in their win over Cork in the 1937 Munster championship. So all the odds favoured Limerick. But Tipperary caused a major upset in a titanic contest that ended 6:3 to 4:3.

John considers the Tipperary defence of 1937 to be the best to represent the county during his career. It was: Dinny O'Gorman, Ger Cornally, Jim Lanigan; Johnny Ryan, John Maher, Willie Wall.

After Tipperary's 1937 All-Ireland success, and with their strong defensive set-up, they looked good for a few years and certainly looked good for 1938. But the Cooney Case brought about their downfall, when Clare successfully objected to Tipperary. It's a complicated case, that began with Cooney admitting attendance at a rugby international in early 1937. It was this admission, John believes, that brought about Tipp's downfall, because it left Tipperary with a very weak case and the GAA with no proof.

The year 1941 was another rewarding one for John. Tipperary defeated Waterford in the first round, but the foot and mouth outbreak and the restrictions that followed barred Tipperary from further participation in the championship. Cork won the All-Ireland title.

The delayed Munster final was played in Limerick in November. The beet season was in full swing, and Tipperary were forced to make some changes, as a few of their players could not get off from work.

When the Tipperary team arrived at Limerick Gaelic grounds, Cork were already on the field and being photographed. Indeed, as 1941 All-Ireland champions they were surrounded by photographers and were being snapped from all angles.

Mentally Tipperary were in relaxed mood, and as they took the field it was almost time for the throw-in, and stewards were ushering the photographers from the field. By half time Tipperary had gone seven points up against the breeze.

A surprise was on the cards: there was no photograph of the Tipperary team. "Green Flag", a Kerryman and sports writer for the *Irish Press*, attempted to get the Tipperary team together at half time for a photograph, but without success. When the final whistle blew it was Tipperary 5:4, Cork 2:5; and even though Cork were All-Ireland title holders for 1941, Tipperary were the Munster champions for that year; and John believes that no photograph of that team exists.

According to John Tipperary won the game at midfield, where Willie O'Donnell and Neil Condon held sway, with Condon having a really fine game on Jack Lynch. Strangely enough, Condon didn't have many games in the Tipperary jersey.

John then talked about the hurling philosophy of Johnny Leahy and Tom Semple. It was a very basic one. Both advocated getting rid of the ball when you got it: no dallying; no delaying; no messing. On the rule changes — well, John as an oldtimer is not too sure about their merits. The shoulder: 'not what it used to be'. The hand going up: 'if you put your hand in the fire you know you will get burned'. The man in possession who decides he will run the

---

When it came to getting John to name the team from the men of his era that he would like to have captained, the best I could get him to do was to act as non-playing captain.
His team reads:

Tommy Daly *(Clare)*

Willie Murphy *(Cork)*   Tom McCarthy *(Limerick)*   Mick Kennedy *(Limerick)*

Dinny Barry Murphy *(Cork)*   Jim O'Regan *(Cork)*   Garrett Howard *(Limerick)*

Jim Hurley *(Cork)*   Timmy Ryan *(Limerick)*

Phil Cahill *(Tipperary)*   Mick Mackey*(Limerick)*   Tommy Doyle *(Tipperary)*

Christy Ring *(Cork)*   Martin Kennedy *(Tipperary)*   Mattie Power *(Kilkenny)*

length of the field: well, in Mackey's day you stood solid and blocked him — if you were lucky — and if you weren't lucky he just went right through you. John thinks the pendulum has perhaps swung a little too far.

Turning to the present day John felt that there was far too much pressure on youth about coaching and training. He would prefer to see youngsters doing more pucking about and developing their own flair, as hurlers were wont to do in olden days.

John is still as lean and sprightly as in his hurling days, and the mind is wonderfully alert, retaining countless memories of great games, and not only from his own hurling days but right up to the present time.

Three of Wexford's, and Ireland's, greatest hurling sons, the Rackard brothers. *Left to right:* Bobbie, Nicky and Billy. See below pages 198 ff.

'In pensive mood'.

❝

Hurling was the standard topic of conversation amongst the people with whom I spent my boyhood. It was discussed at school, at church, at work, and at play. It did not require, therefore, divine inspiration to become involved in playing hurling. The environment was correct, the encouragement was forthcoming, many willing people provided the leadership, and the counter-attractions were not that plentiful.

Many played hurling in my native parish of Holycross, and I was one fortunate enough to meet with much success. I took

Born: 1930

part in winning three senior hurling county finals, seven National Leagues, four Railway Cups, and five senior All-Irelands. My first All-Ireland win against Galway in 1958 was probably the sweetest, but the final against Wexford in 1962 was the most memorable. Ned Wheeler played full-forward for Wexford on that day. It was a great hour's hurling. Interestingly, I have not met Ned since, and that is nearly twenty-five years ago. Winning an All-Ireland outshines any other achievements in the playing-field, and that includes trips to America, etc.

I also participated very much in the administration of the GAA, from club chairman to county chairman, member of county board, Central Council rep, and at present vice-chairman of the Munster Council. My contribution in this area I would hope would be a return for what the organisation has given me.

My involvement with the GAA has made for me many friendships and has given me a host of memories of worthwhile endeavours and some significant achievements. I would like to feel it was as fulfilling for many others. To be part of this compilation is indeed a great honour.

❞

Michael Maher is refreshingly candid and forthright as he talks about the GAA and his own involvement with it. The GAA has been a way of life with him from a very early age, first as a player and later in an official and administrative capacity. He feels he was fortunate to get the opportunity to play with Tipperary and to establish himself.

Being from Holycross, a club that were prominent at the time, helped. It was 1952, and Tipperary were playing Wexford in a challenge. He got his place at full-back. He was opposed by Nicky Rackard, and acquitted himself quite well. It took some time to get a permanent place on the team, but he had made the initial breakthrough.

He feels there is room for improvement on a number of fronts in the GAA. 'The organisation needs to broaden its horizons and be less inward-looking. There is room for increased sophistication and professionalism. Refereeing needs to be strict and consistent; inconsistency frustrates players.

'The referee should be supreme and unchallenged while in command of a game. Let judgement be handed out by the authorities when the game is over — but it should be a helpful judgement. Referees are hard to come by. It is often a thankless job.' Michael wonders if the terrific refereeing work and considerable sacrifice of men like John Moloney is really appreciated at all.

'When disciplinary action has to be taken with players, the punishment should fit the crime, and the punishment should hurt. No point in suspending a player for one month when in fact no game takes place within the month. Such a code of punishment is really hypocritical. We have much to learn from the soccer authorities in this regard.'

He feels that any game should be reasonably safe to play, but admits that he never personally saw any danger in hurling until he got an accidental tip on the head against Kilkenny in 1964 and was mildly concussed. He wasn't one of those players who wore the peaked cap for protection, but is now an advocate of the helmet.

He admits that up to 1960 Wexford were not accepted in Tipperary as a force in the hurling world — this despite Wexford's great triumph over Cork in the 1956 All-Ireland final, and their superb victory over Tipperary in the 1956 League final. When tickets were being given out for the post-match banquet one of the players remarked jokingly, 'Wouldn't it be very flat if we lost?' — to which John Doyle replied, 'What are you talking about? There is no doubt at all about it.' 'We were absolutely sure of beating them,' said Michael to me.

'We were waiting for the ball to be thrown in and get on with the game, but as things turned out it was worse we were getting as the game progressed. Theo English and myself finished the game in the tunnel under the Hogan Stand: we mistook a whistle with about a minute to go for the final whistle, and ran off the field. We were anxious to make a quick exit. The result was so unexpected. We stood there looking at each other like two idiots until the final whistle.'

It was after that game that Jim Ryan said, 'We must now recognise that Wexford are in the same class and pose the same threat as Cork or any of the established hurling counties.' 'It was therefore with a very different frame of mind that we approached Wexford in the 1962 final,' said Michael. 'To meet them was an honour, and to beat them was sweet.

'I can remember an awful lot of the play and action of that most memorable final. I was on Wheeler, a very good overhead hurler, and strong. I expected that the Wexford strategy would be to feed the ball to

---

This is Michael's team from the men of his era that he would like to have captained:

Tony Reddin *(Tipperary)*

Jimmy Brohan *(Cork)*	Michael Maher *(Tipperary)*	Mark Marnell *(Kilkenny)*
Jimmy Finn *(Tipperary)*	Tony Wall *(Tipperary)*	Mattie Fouhy *(Cork)*

Michael Roche *(Tipperary)*   Joe Salmon *(Galway)*

Jimmy Doyle *(Tipperary)*	Christy Ring *(Cork)*	Eddie Keher *(Kilkenny)*
Jimmy Smyth *(Clare)*	Nicky Rackard *(Wexford)*	Josie Gallagher *(Galway)*

Michael Maher, Rest of Ireland full-back, against Wexford at New Ross (1960) 'policed' by Wexford full-forward John Kennedy.

him good and high and for him to sweep it into the net. I can remember well the first ball Padge Kehoe got. He looked in at both of us and poised himself to float the ball high. Psychologically I had been preparing myself for this, and I knew that the first clash would be crucial. My plan was to pull on the ball before it reached its highest point, where Ned would have the advantage. You can imagine the great morale boost it was to me after I had pulled very hard to see the ball travel fifty yards out the field to Tony Wall.

'I remember vividly too Mackey McKenna's pass to Tom Ryan, who flashed the ball to the Wexford net. Indeed, about three minutes later he had another opportunity to score a goal, but the chance was missed. It would be impossible of course to forget our lightning opening — two goals up after ninety seconds — but we needed them, because when the final whistle blew we were only two points to the good.'

The 1958 triumph was special because it was his first All-Ireland win, but the game

against Galway was not really a very memorable one. In 1961 Tipperary beat Dublin in a cliff-hanger. They were rather fortunate to be a point ahead at the end. Dublin played some very fine hurling and got enough opportunities to carry the day; but, as Michael said, 'we were expected to win. We were given no real credit. It was the public perception of things; Dublin weren't seen as serious contenders.'

The 1964 win was special because it was Tipp's twenty-first title. In 1964 and 1965 Tipperary had blossomed into a great team, and they won both All-Irelands rather easily at the expense of Kilkenny and Wexford. 'It was the arrival of Babs Keating and Mick Roche that really turned this Tipperary team into a first-class one,' he said.

He recalled having marked Ring on a few occasions, and was particularly taken by his artistry, his strength, and his mad anxiety to win. 'His desire for victory was incredible. Once when the Rest of Ireland were playing Wexford, Ring for some reason wasn't playing but he was on the sideline, and he was full of joy when the Rest won. That was typical of him. Every match had to be won. When playing on him you had to hold your concentration for every minute of the game.

'I can remember him in the 1960 Munster final. I have great memories of that game; it's a win I cherish. There was a great finish to what had been a fierce contest. We were hanging on. Ring was running wild; he was challenging all of us in the Tipperary full-back line. It was a tactic — an attempt to unnerve and unsettle us. But we held the fort and won the day — just — 4:13 to 4:11.

'I remember too the 1957 meeting between Cork and Tipperary in Limerick. I hit Ring with a well-timed solid shoulder. He fell awkwardly, and had to retire with a broken wrist. I sent him a get-well card; he appreciated it.

'He was particularly adept with the 21-yards free. In his day, you must remember, as many backs as possible lined the goal. But Ring could place the ball where he liked, and he usually went for a spot a foot beneath the crossbar, where bodies were scarce and getting the hurley up in time would call for superb reflexes.'

Michael always believed that as far as Ring was concerned Glen Rovers came first, Cork second, and the GAA third. He considers that Jimmy Doyle possessed as much artistry as Ring. However, he wasn't physically as strong. Neither had he the same fanatical approach to the game, nor the same killer instinct.

I asked Michael if he considered Tipperary's greatest era to have been from 1958 to 1968. He felt it was, although his uncle Michael Maher, who led Tipperary to All-Ireland victories in 1895, '96, and '98, might have had other ideas. Indeed, of the thirteen finals played between 1887 and 1900, Tipperary won six of them. 'You might find it hard to believe he was my uncle,' said Michael. 'You see, he was the eldest of the family, and my father would have been at least twenty years younger. He was more like a father figure to my father than a brother. I seldom met the man, and can't really recall him as a person. He sold his farm in Tipperary and went to farm in Galbally in Co. Limerick. It was a distance of about thirty miles, but in those days it was a distance one rarely travelled.'

But to return to Tipperary in the 1958–68 years, Michael makes the point that they won all the major honours, which included five All-Irelands, eight Munster titles, five National Leagues, and five Oireachtas titles.

They had great forwards, which he feels would put them ahead of the 1949–51 team, and of course competition was much keener than it was before the turn of the century. 'No matter how good your backs are,' said Michael, 'you can't be a great team without having good scorers — and we had them in those years. Keating, Nealon, McKenna, Doyle, McLoughlin, Devaney — all scorers; all match winners.

'Another sign of our greatness was the fact that we won so much despite having several different goalkeepers. That takes some getting used to, and can put a lot of strain on a team, but we were good enough to absorb it.'

Michael agreed that the winning of medals was, by 1965, losing its lustre. The fans were no longer delirious with excitement. People were saying they have won enough; a new face would be welcome. Yes, indeed — a new face. Such is always welcome — necessary really. It is part of the life blood of the association. It has a revitalising effect; it kindles new fires. It breeds hope in those who have yet to taste success.

Tony Reddin, Sam Melbourne, the McCarthy Cup, Damien Martin, and a friend.

Born: 1946

66

When asked to write on the rise of Offaly hurling over the last twenty years, I found to give the full picture, I must go back to the early sixties.

It is important to know that hurling has always been part of life in Offaly, and in particular in the south of the county. Great hurlers were produced through the years, but never enough at the same time. Two teams in particular dominated the hurling scene, Drumcullen and Coolderry; occasionally Birr or Tullamore would emerge. Because of their dominance the rivalry was intense, and had to be seen to be believed. The result was, unwittingly, the clubs were more interested in themselves than in the county, and were suspicious of each other. Yet they were the backbone of the county teams.

When I came to the Offaly panel for the 1964 championship (to be beaten by Westmeath in Tullamore in the first round), the players did not really know each other, and a number did not even talk to each other. Neither was there even one training session or get-together. Then Brother Denis, a

Presentation Brother from Bantry, joined the Birr community. He got involved in the Offaly hurling team, and we were on our way.

The first thing he did was organise collective training, with a cup of tea and a sandwich afterwards. Over the years he built up a sense of comradeship in the panel, and made the lads proud to play for Offaly.

Development of the bogs by Bord na Móna (with the jobs created, and also the jobs in the ESB) became evident throughout the county in all spheres of life, and especially in the GAA world. One of the obvious examples was my own club in Banagher, St Rynagh's, a club that regularly produced great minors but never had a good senior team, because of emigration. Rynagh's won the junior championship in 1963; were promoted senior; got to the senior final in 1964, to be beaten by Tullamore. They won their first county senior title in 1965, and ten of the following twelve county championships. They brought with them a new approach, coached by Tony Reddin, of fast, open, skilful hurling, and still were able for the old approach of blood and thunder.

The advent of Rynagh's also made the traditional teams realise there was now a new force to be reckoned with, and they set their sights on Rynagh's instead of each other and had to raise their standards to meet the new challenge.

1967 saw the return of Kinnitty, a club in the doldrums for decades. In the twenties and thirties Kinnitty produced fantastic hurlers renowned for their skill. Most of them emigrated to New York, where they helped Offaly to dominate New York hurling for years. This new team also had fantastic skill — Johnny Flaherty a prime example. While they won only the '67 title they were knocking on the door until the late seventies, when their period of dominance commenced.

Coolderry were always there, winning the odd championship, which was very important: that the traditional teams were not just being replaced by the new but that they should complement each other. The late great Pat Carroll was from Coolderry.

Sadly, Drumcullen went into decline where the great Paddy Molloy carried the torch for years, and then only Paddy Fleury made the team of the eighties. They are now showing signs of a recovery.

Tullamore disappeared after 1964; won the 1990 intermediate championship; are now senior, and hopefully they will make a contribution again.

Birr, the main centre of population in south Offaly, won the 1970 title and have produced little since, in spite of all the great minors they produced. They had nobody on the 1981 or 1985 teams. This is a pity.

So the mixture of the old and the new with Brother Denis was taking shape in the 1968 championship Leinster semi-final v. Kilkenny at Port Laoise. We lost a man in the first five minutes, and with fourteen men were narrowly defeated.

Wexford won the 1968 All-Ireland, and in 1969 at Croke Park we beat them in the Leinster semi-final, to make Offaly's first appearance in a Leinster final since 1928. Kilkenny beat us narrowly, and went on to win the All-Ireland. The team had a lot of older players who could not keep up the momentum for further years, but we had come a long way. It is my opinion that this team was far superior to the teams of the eighties. Unfortunately Brother Denis got most of the lads too late, and by the time he had the problems previously referred to solved, they were past their best. He did bring the team a long way and made Offaly a team to be respected, and the foundations were laid for the future teams.

Throughout the seventies Rynagh's won Leinster club championships, beating the best in Wexford and Kilkenny, explod-

ing the "God-given rights" myth. This attitude passed through to the county panel — that we were as good as any — but there was still no breakthrough. In 1979 Wexford beat us narrowly in Athy in the Leinster semi-final. Brother Denis had left us at this stage to concentrate on the younger players in the county, and in particular on the lads in the Presentation College and later Birr Community School. The vast majority of the team of the eighties were his past pupils.

After this defeat we decided to make an all-out effort to gain promotion to division 1 of the National Hurling League. We did, and had a good run in the League, beating Wexford in the quarter-final.

I went to my club, St Rynagh's, and proposed an outside coach for Offaly for the 1980 championship. The proposal was carried. On behalf of my club I put the proposal to the county board. I remember making the example of Offaly being on a see-saw; I did not know what was needed to tip it in our favour, and, with respect, nobody present did either. An outside coach would be like holy water: he might do no good but he certainly could do no harm.

The proposal was carried narrowly and Dermot Healy was appointed. He concentrated on the skills of the game, and made us really believe in ourselves. Dermot's contribution is well documented. The winning of two minor championships in the eighties was a marvellous achievement, and means the future is secure.

To Brother Denis, who built the foundations, and Dermot Healy, who finished the job, Offaly's hurling world and especially the likes of myself who played under one or both men can only say 'thank you', for without them I certainly would have no All-Ireland medal.

I would like to thank Brendan Fullam for the honour of contributing to this great book and for the opportunity to thank in print the two men most responsible for Offaly's hurling success.

"

As Damien walked from the pitch at Ashford after his first senior game with Offaly in the National League against Wicklow in 1964, a young Wicklow enthusiast ran up to him and asked for his autograph. Damien, still a teenager, 'was stunned with surprise, and wondered if the youngster was serious.'

He knew of course what it was to have heroes. Tony Reddin was his goalkeeping idol, and for sportsmanship and overhead striking he was completely captivated by the hurling artistry of Galway midfielder Joe Salmon.

There was no sound reason in 1964 — based on tradition, that is — for Damien to have great expectations. A look at the Offaly record showed that the cupboard was very bare. The twenties appeared to have been relatively good times; four Leinster senior finals were contested — in 1924, '26, '27, and '28 — but without success. In 1923 and 1929 Offaly won junior All-Ireland titles, and Jim O'Regan, the great Cork centre-half-back, hurled junior with Offaly in 1924 and won a Leinster title. But decade after decade passed, and no hurling glory came Offaly's way. It fell to Damien Martin and his colleagues to change all that: to show that eventually perseverance does pay off.

Patience and perseverance mark his career. It spanned twenty-two years — by any standards a remarkable innings. It had many and varied highlights: an outstanding display in 1969 against Kilkenny in the Leinster final, when Offaly lost by two points with a team that had many top-class hurlers; the special honour of an All-Star award in 1971; the famous Fennelly flick that brought a crucial goal from out of bounds; the superb reflex save from Noel Lane in the 1981 All-Ireland final — a save that was as vital to Offaly that day as was Art Foley's save for Wexford from Ring in 1956, but somehow has never received the same prominence. And finally I can still see him heading from his goal-line against Cork in Thurles in the 1984 All-Ireland Centenary final as he took the right option to smother Seánie O'Leary, but to no avail,

for Seánie, who found himself loose inside the Offaly full-back line, took a poor pass on the blind side, resisted the temptation to handle, thus saving precious time, and with a deft trap, touch and turn finished with one of the great goals of hurling.

Damien used to travel to New York to play with the Offaly team there, and had as a team-mate Pat Dunny of Kildare. 'He was great, a fantastic hurler.' In the summer of 1967 he travelled to the United States and, without approval from GAA head office, played with Offaly. He got a two-year suspension, but was reinstated the following Easter by the Mercy Committee.

He travelled as an All-Star in 1971 and received the Man of the Tour award in the United States. He gave credit for his success to 'a superb full-back line of Tony Maher, Cork, Pat Hartigan, Limerick, and Jim Treacy, Kilkenny, that provided me with magnificent cover.'

Many of Damien's successes have made him feel very humble. He thinks of great artists of the game who never became household names or won any honours, because of the counties they came from. Among them he includes "Jobber" McGrath, Pat Jackson and Tommy Ring of Westmeath, Christy O'Brien of Laois, Gerry O'Malley of Roscommon — 'a wonderful hurler' — Paddy Quirke of Carlow, Mick Mahon of Laois, and Declan Lovett of Kerry, 'who would be handed a jersey in any county.'

The best man — and he emphasises "man" — that he played hurling with or against was Pádraig Horan of Offaly; while the best hurlers of his era were Jimmy Doyle of Tipperary and Barney Moylan of Offaly.

Special words of the highest praise he bestows on Laois goalkeeper Johnny Carroll. 'One of the best goalkeepers I have seen, but who has no honours or awards; I felt very humbled every time I played against him.'

But I must return to the rise and rise of Offaly. Some special characteristics began to manifest themselves. Tradition and reputation didn't cost them a thought: they went down to Cork and played that county in a

League game and won. Few teams ever succeed against Cork in Páirc Uí Chaoimh.

Kilkenny, Wexford and Galway were to discover on many occasions that Offaly were men of steel and sterling qualities backed up with grit, determination, and a never-say-die spirit. They had a style of their own that reflected a healthy mental attitude. They had a great capacity to hang in and stay in touch with opponents, even when they were being outplayed, each man sticking to his task, doing it manfully, playing with economy, doing the basics very well, never giving up.

Damien was with Offaly as they climbed slowly towards the top level, and the trip was not without its growing pains and disappointments. But when they did break through they made their presence felt and continued to rise and rise, growing in stature and competence and finesse. A Leinster title in 1980; an All-Ireland title in 1981; every Leinster final contested throughout the eighties — concrete proof that they had arrived in the big time; and as time passes and we look back on the eighties and Offaly we will pick out quite a few hurlers who will be remembered as giants of the ash.

It had been a long road from Ashford in 1964 to Croke Park in 1981. 'We drove in triumph in a bus through Tullamore after the '81 All-Ireland victory. The crowd was incredible. I didn't believe there could be so many people in Offaly. Pádraig Horan turned to me and said, "Wasn't it all worth while?" and I replied, "It would have been all worth while even if we didn't win." '

Surely a sentiment that epitomises what sport and games are all about.

Damien Martin, Offaly.
(Photo: Jim Connolly)

164

Born: 1899

point, 2:5 to 2:4, in an enthralling final.

And they'll oft retell the story
Of the glory that was Lory's.
For that was the day that he took away for
the first and only time the McCarthy Cup to
Kilkenny and famed Tullaroan.

When Lory died, a local friend named Paddy Fitzpatrick wrote a poem in his honour. Here is a verse that appealed to me:

Goodbye and farewell to a friend and a
*   neighbour;*
The last final whistle has parted our ways;
The game is all over and the crowds are
*   dispersing,*
And I can't help remembering those
*   happier days.*

I went in search of some first-hand information on Lory to Tullaroan, where I met his nephew Dan Hogan. Here is how he remembers Lory, lifelong bachelor, fearless critic and ardent supporter of the GAA ideals.

'My greatest memory of Lory was his intense interest in the formative or early days of the association. On visits to him at Curragh [Co. Kilkenny], when school ended on Friday evenings to Monday morning, I often tried to get him talking about his hurling career when going fishing or hunting rabbits. The question or petition to tell us something about his great days would be sidestepped with an ease that to a young mind seemed deceptively easy. He would think aloud about the early meetings in Thurles, always maintaining there was a lot of that story untold.

'His father, Henry Joseph Meagher, attended the founding meetings of the GAA in 1884, accompanied by Jack Hoyne

As long as hurling lives, the name Lory Meagher will be synonymous with all that is majestic in hurling. (No personal recollections are possible, as he went to his eternal reward in 1973, seven years before this work began.)

Lory has been described as a prince of hurlers. He preceded Mackey and Ring, and the decade 1926–35 belonged to him. He covered himself in glory in the two drawn games with Cork in the 1931 final, and his absence from the third game through injury is believed by many to have tipped the scales in Cork's favour. There is the story of the girl in the crowd from Co. Kilkenny whose emotions overflowed into tears as she and others begged of Lory with the chant 'Lory, Lory, Lory' to respond to Kilkenny's need — but he couldn't.

Some say his greatest hour came towards the end of his career, in the 1935 final against Limerick.

He was captain. The weather was atrocious. A powerful Limerick team were hot favourites; but Lory's skill and leadership at midfield saw Kilkenny through by one and Ned Teehan, both of Tullaroan. Jack was a member of the Kilkenny team that won the first senior All-Ireland in 1904.

'My visits to Lory took place about sixty years after the founding of the GAA. Lory had a fascination with those days in Thurles, to my mind to the total exclusion of his own deeds. The purpose of the visits of my late brother Henry and myself to Curragh was to stay with his mother while he cycled eight miles to Kilkenny to attend a meeting of Kilkenny County Board at the Central Hotel.

'At a later stage in his life he was often asked to give an interview to members of the national press, who often in the winter months ran a series of articles on famous players. This he was always slow to do. I think he did not like opening his mind to newspaper men. On one occasion John D. Hickey *(Irish Independent)* called, accompanied by Dick Grace (Lory's first cousin) and Sim Walton. Lory could not be found.

However, the situation was saved by his eldest brother, Willie. When Lory could be persuaded to talk he was most interesting, as John D. Hickey testifies in his article.

'Throughout his entire life Lory held the GAA in the highest esteem. He was a nationalist at heart. Memories of his childhood made him an ardent supporter of the ban, and when they voted at club level in Tullaroan as to whether or not the ban should remain, the vote was 39 to 1 to abolish it. Lory stood alone.

'He never lost the hurling artistry. I can remember when my brother and myself used to visit him in our early teens, Lory would take down the hurley and ball, hit the ball straight up into the clouds — or so it seemed to us — and the ball would come back down and land at his feet. He would repeat this several times. The skill, the artistry and the hurling were still there at sixty. Only the youth was gone.'

Lory Meagher with horse-drawn reaper and binder.

Born: 1916

Christopher Moylan

"

It was a great moment for me to win the 1948 title, having lost in 1938 and having lost several games in the forties by narrow margins. I thought we would never win a title. For me the winning of the 1948 title was particularly rewarding. It came at the end of a long hurling career, which began in 1935.

The standard of hurling was very high in the thirties and forties. All the hurling counties had very strong teams; so it was very hard to win matches or to come out of Munster. I always enjoyed club hurling with Dungarvan, and when we won the county final in 1942, by beating Mount Sion, one of my ambitions was achieved.

Some of the players I particularly admired were Jack Lynch, Christy Ring, Mick Mackey, Paddy Phelan, Bobbie Rackard, and Vincent Baston.

"

With Christy, sportsmanship is paramount. 'No medal is worth injuring a man,' he says.

As Christy Moylan reflects back on his hurling career, foul deeds come to mind that greatly tarnish the image of good sportsmanship. At club and county level he can recall incidents where he was the victim of reckless and indiscriminate pulling that left him badly injured. In these cases he is satisfied that his opponent was making no attempt to play the ball. In those days there was a certain ambivalence about what was often downright dangerous play; nowadays such behaviour would not be tolerated.

And yet, strangely enough, Christy is not greatly impressed by the elimination of the third-man tackle. He would prefer the old style of game where you could shoulder an opponent as you raced for possession. He liked it physical, but he abhorred the unsporting and the dangerous. He places great emphasis on speed, getting to the ball first — gaining possession, and taking your score.

In club hurling in his native Co. Waterford he felt he was always a marked man in both hurling and football. In one county championship match he can recall grabbing a ball in the very early stages of the game only to be hit from behind by an opponent, the injury requiring six stitches. Then he added, 'I was never a dirty player. I got a lot of injuries. I could enjoy a good physical contest. Sometimes I was forced to retaliate to protect myself. Sometimes the nasty incidents took place behind the referee's back.' Christy remembers occasions when certain players would not switch from an opponent even when requested to do so;

they took the view that if they switched, the opponent would think they were afraid or cowardly. It was an attitude of mind that was not untypical of the times.

Now he is talking about some of the gentlemen he encountered. 'Ah, they might give you a rattle but they would never pull on you. You would know going out the kind of game to expect. They would always play the ball with you. They were ball-players.' And those who came readily to mind were Bobbie Rackard of Wexford, Timmy Ryan of Limerick, Jimmy Kelly and Paddy Phelan of Kilkenny, and Alan Lotty and Jack Lynch of Cork.

Mention of Jack Lynch reminded him that Jack used to say that Christy was one of the most difficult opponents he had to cope with, and that Paddy Scanlon of Limerick was the best goalkeeper.

He feels that Waterford lost a lot of games on the sideline, and as a result perhaps Munster and All-Ireland titles. As an example he cites the 1943 Munster final against Cork, lost by 2:13 to 3:8. To this day Waterford folk believe it was a game they had the winning of. Christy Moylan was at full-forward. In a challenge game in Waterford he had performed exceptionally well on Batt Thornhill, the Cork full-back, and so he was retained at full-forward.

In the opening minutes Christy gained possession. He passed to Willie Barron, who in turn shook the net. Inside seven minutes Waterford were five points up. But as the game progressed it became obvious that switches were needed on the Waterford team. Jack Lynch was being fouled, and was punishing Waterford from frees. Christy pleaded for a switch to midfield, but without success, and in the course of the hour Jack Lynch had eight points from frees, according to Christy.

Mick A. Brennan was in the Cork full-forward line of 1943, and Christy recalled an amusing trait that he had on the hurling-field. 'He was always walking and moving — going back and forth in front of goal. Every now and again he would turn to the goalkeeper and say, "I'll pay you a visit soon." Those were the days when you could charge the goalkeeper. The visit

wouldn't be to discuss the weather.'

But 1948 was to see dreams come true. He felt all keyed up for the Munster final with Cork. He had been in England for three years and had come home to see his mother, who was unwell. He was asked if he would stay home if he got a job, and he said he would.

Then he was out on the field waiting for the parade. Jack Lynch came over and welcomed him back and wished him well. His immediate opponent was Josie Hartnett, who was reputed to be very fast. Then the game was on. In a run for possession Christy won the race, gathered the ball, and parted to team-mate Curran, who sent the goal umpire bending for the green flag. Christy's speed was proving decisive, and Matt Fouhy was brought back in an attempt to curb him. The contest was an absorbing one. Waterford were playing fine hurling; Thurles was agog with excitement.

Time was running out. Christy thought Waterford were three points up. Christy Ring was only forty yards from the Waterford goal. He knew Cork were only one point behind. He shot high, and skimmed the upright on the wrong side. It was all over. Waterford were champions.

Christy considers the 1948 Waterford team to be the best he played on; he would see it as superior to the 1938 line-out. He considers that too much experimenting was done with the 1938 team, and that the forwards got enough of the ball to win but wasted their chances.

He feels that he played much of his best hurling in the Co. Waterford championships. He had one of his proudest hours in the 1941 county semi-final against Portlaw. He was at midfield and pitted against Mick Hickey. Frees to Christy yielded a goal and two points. Mick moved to full-forward, but Christy followed. From start to finish the exchanges were furious, and at the final whistle it was Christy Moylan and Dungarvan who were through to the final.

Christy regards Charlie Ware as the best full-back he has seen. 'I admired him,' he said, 'from the first time I saw him as a chap when he was opposed by Martin Kennedy of Tipperary.' Then he added, 'I'd love to have seen Eudi Coughlan in action.'

He had great admiration for Johnny Quirke. 'He could hold Mick Mackey. He could hurl anywhere.'

But in Christy's opinion Mick Mackey was the king. 'He would go into a tussle and come out with the ball. He always got it. Once he got the ball in front of him he couldn't be stopped. He could read a game. He was physical; he could give it and take it in the same spirit.'

Christy recalled one of their meetings in a Limerick-Waterford clash. He was centre-forward on Paddy Clohessy. In quick succession he rounded Paddy and scored two points. Mick Mackey came running up the field. He sent Paddy elsewhere and, addressing Christy, said, 'I'll quieten you, Moylan.' The exchanges were tough.

Off the ball and behind the referee's back there was a wrestling encounter. The heat remained in the exchanges. There was a hold-up in play; someone ran on with an orange to Mick. 'He halved it and tossed one half to me, saying, "Here you are, Con" (he used to call me Con). That's the kind of man he was.'

Not all of Christy's feats were confined to the hurling-field. He played football too. He was a sub on the Munster football team on about five occasions, and once he was actually selected at left-half-back and was out on the field when hurling mentor Seán McCarthy rushed onto the field and took him off, explaining that he was needed for the hurling game! He regrets having missed the honour of playing football for Munster.

From the men of his time he would like to have captained the following team:

Seán Duggan *(Galway)*

Johnny Quirke *(Cork)*   Charlie Ware *(Waterford)*   Alan Lotty *(Cork)*

Bobbie Rackard *(Wexford)*   John Keane *(Waterford)*   Paddy Phelan *(Kilkenny)*

Jack Lynch *(Cork)*   Christy Moylan *(Waterford)*

Jimmy Doyle *(Tipperary)*   Mick Mackey *(Limerick)*   Christy Ring *(Cork)*

Mick A. Brennan *(Cork)*   Nicky Rackard *(Wexford)*   Jackie Power *(Limerick)*

Born: 1922

Donchar O'Murchin

"

I have been fortunate to have lived in a period when one could say I experienced the Gaelic Athletic Association growing and developing to the point at which it is today. One could say in a broad sense I met and knew very many of the tremendous people at national and local level linked with the founding and early years of the Association who in a very difficult political, social and economic climate struggled to put the Association on the right road and indeed succeeded admirably in doing so. I had the tremendous honour and uplifting experience of working with the great people in the twenty-five years from 1940, when I believe we were blessed with a very enlilghtened and forward-looking generation of leaders at all levels. This is not to say that we have not had great men in every generation. I would love to mention several names that are now part of history, but I am certain that I would leave out some. Pádraig Ó Caoimh, the then General Secretary, stood out as someone special.

This period from 1940 to which I have referred was the era when the policy of each club owning its own ground was initiated and encouraged, and we now have the fruits of this forward thinking. This was the era too of a tremendous upsurge of interest in our national games, particularly at inter-county level, which saw the courageous development of stadiums, albeit with modest accommodation.

I will never forget the years of the Second World War, when our games were really the social safety valve of our people. I remember with no little emotion — being an inter-county player at the time — the many sacrifices made by supporters to get to games; the primtive travel by today's standards; people of all ages, some indeed not so young, cycling from west Cork to Thurles and Croke Park, which took days to go and days to return. I can still see the joy on people's faces despite the hardships of travel.

In my view these twenty-five years or so consolidated the great work of the first fifty years of the Association and sowed the seed for the next twenty-five years of improved administration and organisation linked with a massive development of facilities which, for a voluntary organisation with nothing other than its own resources, has been phenomenal. One can say with justification that the GAA was ahead even of local authorities in developing the concept of local community playing and social facilities.

For the record the recent statistics for development are 1,740 club grounds, 3,500 pitches, 91 county grounds, 12 major stadiums, 300 social centres, and 720 handball courts, which have cost an estimated £220 million, and the work is ongoing. This gives some indication of the contribution the Association has made to community and national life and gives the lie to the often heard general accusation that the Association's leaders are and have been conservative and lacking in any form of progressive thinking and planning.

Central to everything in every generation has been the games, and for somebody like myself who played at all levels there is no question that playing the games was something very special. I will be forever grateful to my club, Valley Rovers, and North Monastery school, for enabling me to experience so many great occasions on the playing-field and having such abiding and cherished memories.

If I may humbly say so, I played with and against, in my opinion, some of the greatest of all time, and was fortunate to have played in many hectic inter-county hurling games such as the All-Ireland hurling final of 1947, reckoned to this day to be one of the greatest ever.

Yes, my life has been enriched by the people I met at all levels, the great memories of great games at all levels and a host of sporting players. I repeat, sporting players. I agree that some of the over-physical aspects had to be eliminated, but I will never yield ground to modern day on the great courage, sportsmanship and skill of the players of my day.

I agree that the games of football and hurling have changed since my playing days. Football, in my opinion, has changed somewhat for the better. It still has problems mainly in the application of the rules in a consistent manner, particularly with regard to the personal foul, the tackle, and off-the-ball incidents. I feel, however, that there is considerable overuse of short play, sometimes ridiculously ineffective, and all too little of the high fielding and the catch-and-kick skills of the game.

Hurling is much changed. As I have stated, I agree that the over-physical aspects had to be eliminated, but accompanying this has been a serious drop in the overall use of the range of skills so unique in hurling. Ground hurling is gone. Skilful overhead striking is gone. Direct, long, accurate striking is going too, and the ball

is no longer made do the work. We have every now and then, too infrequently in my opinion, where one's faith in hurling and its great tradition and range of skills are concerned, had our hopes partly restored by the odd exhilarating game, but the general pattern is a cause for concern.

The game, in my opinion, due to players, even top players, not having the full range of skills and sometimes as a result of team coaches' tactics, is developing into a short passing and short striking game with an overuse of handling the ball and a mixture of handball and football. I hope that this trend will not continue. If it does, hurling will lose its appeal as a spectacle. There is also more movement of players, less positional play, and a slowing down of the game in the matter of speed of the ball. In other words the ball is no longer made to do the work, which is a distinctive feature of hurling. What a pity to see this trend! Hurling has such a range of skills; and if they are fully used, it will remain the game with no equal in the world.

We must ensure that our games are developed with expertise in these changing times, but no way should this mean that their essential characteristics be diluted or changed.

As far as the Association itself is concerned, it faces great challenges as the years roll on. Society is experiencing many changes, some of course for the better. However, the values that were once cherished are either forgotten or given a changed meaning. Some changes are affecting the Association. This is understandable. Some changes threaten the overall ethos of the organisation and would be of concern to me.

The Gaelic Athletic Association was built on voluntary effort, and in my view if this voluntary effort even in this materialistic age, goes, or even if it is significantly diluted, it will have a serious effect on the future of the Association. I agree fully that if we are to be competitive in the times we live in we must have a certain amount of professional support for the voluntary worker. Regrettably, the tendency is to go beyond this. There is at times an over-emphasis on finance, and to who gets what and how much for doing this and that. We hear of some of our élite players, who were put on the road to fame by committed voluntary workers, cashing in on their fame at the expense of clubs, etc.

I fully agree that all players who devote so much time particularly to inter-county games should be treated very fairly in the matter of out-of-pocket expenses and in how they are treated generally. No way should players be paid or no way should any player or official other than whole-time be compensated by a fee for helping our Association directly or indirectly in any way.

I dread the long-term effect of supporters' clubs as they are constituted. I know that the Association is endeavouring to tackle the problem. Such clubs should be under the direct control of county boards. I fully agree that we should harness the good will and support of the general public, should we say for inter-county teams, but no way should a group with this responsibility be outside the control of the county board.

I have fears too about the long-term effect of extending sponsorship to logos etc. on jerseys. I hope that my fears will never be justified. I am not so concerned about logos on jerseys but with what may happen otherwise.

I fear that the way we are going we may have what we might call a two-tiered organisation, one for the élite players and a certain group of officials, and the other for those who promote the games and play at club level, where it matters most. One can envisage the effect this would have. I hope that we will never see the day.

Despite these pessimistic comments, we can gear ourselves to meet these and other serious challenges of the future. We have great games. We have a fund of good will and enthusiastic support for the Association and, above all, we have a great hard core of dedicated, committed workers.

If I were asked what are the simple priorities for the Association as of now and for the foreseeable future, I would say:

1. Developing a deep commitment and concentration on the promotion of the games, including coaching at youth level in the proper sense, not devising new gimmicks that are destroying our games but teaching the proper use of all the skills and, very importantly, the natural use of the body in the playing of the games.

2. Developing leadership and recruiting manpower, without which the Association cannot function.

3. Developing uniform discipline both on and off the field, to earn further respect for the Association and our games.

4. Developing good public relations.

5. Reorganising administration, particularly at county and provincial levels. Very little change has taken place in the form of administration at these levels in over a hundred years.

6. Planning every aspect of work, be it games programming or administration in order to see that our Gaelic games and the full value of the work of the Association will remain the centrepiece of Irish life and retain the attraction of Irish people everywhere, at home and abroad. We no longer have a monopoly, and things are not going to happen by chance.

If we are determined and committed I have no doubt that we can cope.

Ar aghaidh linn! Ní neart go cur le chéile!

,,

Con Murphy's lifelong association with the GAA began in his college days. He played full-back for Munster Colleges for three years in a row, from 1939 to 1941. In one of those years they were beaten by Leinster Colleges in Nowlan Park, Kilkenny, 'after extra time in a replay that produced wonderful hurling.'

His immediate opponent that day was Wexford man Nicky Rackard, and later on in the forties they faced each other again in a Railway Cup final. Also on the victorious Leinster Colleges team was Éamon Young, who was boarding at Good Counsel College, New Ross, and who later starred on Cork football teams and won a senior football All-Ireland in 1945.

Con made his senior hurling debut at corner-back for Cork in a tournament game against Tipperary in the autumn of 1941. A few weeks earlier Tipperary had defeated Cork in a delayed Munster final, and fielded the same team. Cork made a number of changes. Con was opposed by Willie O'Donnell, 'a big, strong man; he could have murdered me that day if he wanted to, but he didn't. He was a real gentleman, and I never forgot him for it.'

Con played many times on Mick and John Mackey of Limerick. 'John had many touches that Mick didn't have, and was an outstanding hurler. Yet he never scored off me; but Mick did, and he would use psychology to the full to upset you. I think it was the 1944 Munster final, and after he had scored two goals he turned to me and said, "You'll be taken off any minute now." John also indulged in the psychology antics, and particularly with little Jimmy Maher, the Tipp goalkeeper. He used have the heart crossways on Jimmy because he was always charging in on top of him, and on one occasion after three goals had been scored, John, having knocked the cap off Jimmy and replaced it again, looked at Jimmy and said, "This won't do at all, Jimmy — this isn't good enough at all."

Con's favourite position was full-back, and he 'never met any easy full-forwards.' He had special words of praise for Cork defender Alan Lotty, 'who was one of hurling's gentlemen.' He was always highly impressed by the way Jim Young encouraged young players on the team. 'He'd never criticise them — convinced them they were doing well even if they weren't — shouted words of support; and that was my own experience with Jim too.'

The outstanding goalkeepers that Con admired were Paddy Scanlon of Limerick, Tony Reddin of Tipperary, and Jimmy O'Connell of Kilkenny. 'But I had a very special grá for Tom Mulcahy, the Cork goalkeeper, who I played in front of many times, both at county and inter-provincial level.'

Con refereed many matches in his time. 'It wasn't always easy refereeing when you were dealing with hurling colleagues. But I used to enjoy observing what went on. There were occasional exchanges of banter, and at times comment that could hardly be titled banter.' He recalls that Christy Ring would on occasions, after scoring a particularly fine point, say to him, 'What did you think of that, Murphy?'

Then there was the day that Glen Rovers were playing a championship game. Ring was at centre-forward. A high ball came in between him and the centre-back. Both pulled and missed, and the ball continued inwards. Con blew for a free out. 'What's wrong?' said Ring. 'What's wrong? I pulled on the ball!' Con's reply was masterly. 'If you had pulled on the *ball*, Christy, you would have hit it.'

Con's major refereeing assignments included the National League final of 1947, the Munster final of 1949, and the All-Ireland finals of 1948 and 1950. 'I was a strict referee. I was strict on discipline. Sometimes I could be strict to the point of ruthlessness.'

His playing career coincided with a great Cork era, and he won Munster, All-Ireland and Railway Cup honours. Yet strangely enough his most memorable game was a divisional junior final replay against Carrigaline, which was lost. His biggest regrets were the losing of the 1947 All-Ireland final by a point to Kilkenny, 'because we had done enough and were good enough to win,' and the defeat by Waterford in the 1948 Munster final, 'prior to which we had been playing better than even in 1946, when we convincingly defeated Kilkenny.'

He was honoured with the prestigious office of president of the GAA from 1976 to 1978 — the association's twenty-sixth president, and the third Corkman to hold the office. He was county secretary from

1956 until he became president, and he has been a member of the Munster Council since 1956.

I wondered if he would favour a losers' group in the championship. 'No — only one bite of the cherry.' An open draw? 'No.' A sharing of the GAA grounds? 'No' — firm and polite.

He fears that hurling standards have dropped, and skills have declined. He would allow only one hand-pass, after which the ball would have to be struck with the hurley before a further hand-pass could take place. He blames some coaching methods for the drop in standards. 'Indirectly television is contributing to the decline. Youngsters are watching all the hand-passing and solo running, and tend to emulate what they see.' Con would like to see a reversion to all the old skills of the game — no gimmicks — allied to proper use of the body in positioning and covering and protecting.

He attributes Cork's catalogue of successes over the decades to 'good, sound, solid, intelligent hurling: making the ball do the work; adjusting to the demands of the occasion, and doing the right thing at the right time. Remember, we won a title in 1990 with limited resources.'

Looking to the future he fears complacency. 'We no longer have a monopoly. We must consolidate in the strong hurling areas, and encourage the spread of the game in the weaker counties; but consolidation and preservation must come first.' Con sees the game as a national heritage, and questions VAT on hurleys. He would like more Government support for our games. 'The economic spin-off from Gaelic games is very substantial.'

Con, who was a most gracious host, is an ardent adherent of the aims, ideals and aspirations of the GAA. A great number of players confine themselves to action on the field and after retirement tend to drift away from the scene; but with Con it has been a lifetime of involvement: player, referee, administrator, delegate, president.

When Tony Reddin and John Mackey selected for me their favoured fifteen, both chose Con Murphy as their full-back, but from very different viewpoints: Tony was viewing him through the eyes of a goalkeeper; John, as a famed forward, was passing judgement on a man with whom he had engaged in hectic combat and exchanges of rare abandon on many occasions.

"

The men of my time that I remember as being outstanding were Tyler Mackey of Limerick, and Matt Gargan, Sim Walton and Jack Rochford of Kilkenny.

"

Born: 1887

It was wonderful to have had an opportunity of talking with this fine oldtimer at his home near Castlebridge — the only surviving member of the victorious 1910 Wexford team. I was graciously received by a woman who showed me into the sitting-room and then called, 'Governor, you're wanted here.'

He was born around the time of the first All-Ireland championships. He had seen the game of hurling progress through many stages and evolve into its present form. He remembered in his young days hearing

older men talk about the 21-a-side game of hurling. 'There were few open spaces in those days on the pitch, and very little room for manoeuvre,' said Mick. In his early hurling years teams lined out seventeen-a-side, and this was the way in the 1910 final. Mick also played in the 1918 final, but by that time the teams had been reduced to fifteen. This was a change that Mick welcomed, because it left more room for skill and open play.

He told me that in the early years of the GAA there were many disputes about championship matches, and also disputes within the organisation itself. At one stage he recalled that Castlebridge had a row with

Mick Neville: 'Oh for one of those hours of gladness; gone, alas, like our youth, too soon.'

the GAA and left the association and affiliated to a rival group known as the National Association of Gaelic Athletic Clubs. Mick felt that the standard of hurling declined somewhat in Castlebridge and the surrounding areas following the break with the GAA. Nonetheless, they were good enough to reach the finals of the All-Ireland championship of the NAGAC in 1916 and 1917.

The 1916 final was played at Wexford Park when Limerick, with a Fedamore selection, beat Wexford, with a Castlebridge selection, by the score 1:1 to 0:1. In 1917 Limerick and Wexford again reached the NAGAC final. This time it was played at the Market Field in Limerick. Again Limerick were victorious, on the score 5:2 to 1:1.

We then talked about his two All-Ireland finals, 1910 and 1918. Coincidently, both were against Limerick. Wexford emerged out of Leinster in 1910 at a time when Kilkenny hurling was going through a golden era. Between 1904 and 1913 Kilkenny won seven All-Ireland titles, so it is easy to measure the quality of the Wexford team that emerged as Leinster champions in 1910.

The 1910 final was a milestone in the GAA, as it saw the arrival of further change and the introduction of new rules. Mick said that the changes seemed to affect Limerick, who had three goals disallowed, more than Wexford, who had only one goal disallowed. I asked him if it was true that Wexford got through for an easy goal in the closing stages because someone in the crowd had blown a whistle. He smiled and said, 'That's what they say.' Whatever about the incident, he said the game was a very sporting contest, and he paid tribute to his immediate opponent, John Madden.

Limerick were represented by Castleconnell, while Wexford standard-bearers were Castlebridge, who called on three outsiders — Jim Mythen, Seán O'Kennedy, and Paddy Mackey — to complete their line-out. The game took place on 11 November, and Mick told me it was the first time that sideline seating was provided in Croke Park. It consisted of about one thousand chairs.

What were his recollections of that final? 'I remember early on in the game finding the roar of the crowd terrifying. It was seventeen-a-side. The teams lined out seven down the centre, including the goalkeeper, and five on either wing. I played third on the right wing. I was one of the lightest of a big, strong team.

'At half time the score was Wexford 6:0, Limerick 3:1. In the second half Limerick tightened up their defence a lot and improved their performance throughout the entire field. With so many goals being disallowed I wasn't quite sure what way the game was going. Seán Kennedy, our fullback, played a great game. He was a big man.

'The game was very sporting and very hard-fought. When the final whistle blew I didn't know who had won, so I was delighted to learn that we had got through on the score 7:0 to 6:2. I felt the game could have gone either way. I thought Limerick were better-trained.' It was the only occasion so far that the winners of the hurling title failed to score a point.

Mick told me how in 1918, the year of the great flu, Wexford lined out in the All-Ireland final with a very weakened side. Many of their players were sick. Mick travelled to the game not intending to play; his whole body was covered with boils and sores; but Wexford badly needed him, and he lined out in the half-forward line. The entire game was an agony for him. The weakened Wexford side were unfortunate to come up against a very talented Limerick team that won easily.

The men who brought honour to Wexford in 1910 by capturing their first senior hurling title were: R. Doyle (captain), R. Fortune, M. Cummins, Paddy Mackey, M. Parker, Jim Mythen, A. Kehoe, J. Shortall, Seán O'Kennedy, S. Donohoe, P. Roche, D. Kavanagh, J. Fortune, W. McHugh, P. Corcoran, Mick Neville, W. Devereux.

Born: 1921

Matt Nugent

"

Hurling was and still is the greatest game in the world as far as I am concerned. For speed, skill and the expertise of all county players there is nothing in any game to equal it. While here in Clare our successes on the inter-county scene are few and far between, we still have a very healthy and virile association, which sticks to its unenviable task year after year; and maybe in the near future success will crown their efforts and all the defeats of the past will be forgotten.

During my inter-county hurling career men like Jim Young, Tommy Doyle, Mick Mackey (RIP), who had his best years behind him, Christy Ring, Joe Salmon, Josie Gallagher, Willie Walsh and Pat Stakelum were players whom I admired for their skill and sportsmanship.

"

The county's only All-Ireland success was in 1914. In 1932 a fine Clare team captured the Munster title, but failed against Kilkenny by one goal in the All-Ireland final. Since then, despite producing many fine combinations and several outstanding hurlers, no championship honours have come Clare's way.

Matt's career stretches from 1945 to 1958. He made a return in 1962 for the championship, but defeat was Clare's lot. He considers the Clare team of 1946 to be the best county team he played on. They won the Thomond Feis tournament in Limerick, defeating Tipperary in the final. They captured the Áras na nGael trophy with a win over Dublin. The 1946 team added to its stature by winning the National Hurling League — Clare's first success in the tournament.

It was won the hard way. They drew with Dublin in Limerick. The replay was in Croke Park, where Clare had a great win over a Dublin team that included such fine players as Harry Gray, Ned Wade, Tony Herbert, Seán Óg O'Callaghan, and Mick Banks, who, Matt recalls, was a very good goalkeeper.

The Clare lineout was: John Daly: Dan McInerney, P. Callaghan, Philly Byrnes: Des Carroll, D. Solon, Brian McMahon: A. Hannon, Fr Jackie Solon: Matt Nugent, Bob Frost, Michael Daly: Joe Whelan, P.J. Quane, Michael O'Halloran.

Matt believes that Clare had the ability to challenge strongly for the Munster and All-Ireland title of 1946. They met Cork in the Munster Championship on an 'awful wet day.' It was so bad that the lines were washed off the field. In a way Matt blames himself for the defeat by Cork. He was

M att Nugent would dearly love to see Clare make the breakthrough in the big time of the hurling world.

taking the ball along in front of himself up along the sideline, only to find the linesman flagging: Matt had crossed a line he could not see. From the resultant sideline cut Cork goaled, and the game swung in their favour. However, as Matt pointed out, Clare were the only team to give Cork a close run in the 1946 campaign.

It was inevitable that he should talk about 1955. Clare had a tough passage to the Munster final. They beat Cork in Thurles; they overcame Tipperary in Limerick; they looked a formidable outfit as they lined out against Limerick in the Munster final in Limerick on a sweltering hot July Sunday afternoon.

Clare had been playing great hurling in the Oireachtas games of 1953 and 1954, and in 1955 they felt that, provided they struck form, they could handle any opposition. It was in that frame of mind that they entered the Cork game.

After they defeated Cork, Matt met Mick Mackey, who enquired, 'Will you beat Tipp?' 'We will,' said Matt. 'Good,' said Mick, 'because we will beat you in the final.' Matt was confident before the game with Tipperary and their victory established them as favourites for the Munster title.

As Matt now looks back on a Munster final that they lost by 2:16 to 2:6 against Limerick, he feels that defeat was due to a number of factors. Clare failed to cope with the fierce heat of that July Sunday; in retrospect, they were probably overtrained; the mantle of favourites brought a psychological pressure. Matt was emphatic that they were not overconfident, and added that, as Clare captain, it was the most disappoint-

ing moment of his career.

His most memorable game was the 1954 Oireachtas final replay against Wexford. Played in a November downpour, the game these two teams served up was delightful hurling. Clare's tactic was to keep the ball moving on the ground and concentrate on ground hurling, swinging the ball from wing to wing. It paid off, and they won by 3:6 to 0:12. Matt recalls that a feature of the game was the wonderful display by Mick Hayes in the Clare goal.

Turning to more general matters, Matt felt that the time had come to introduce the open draw, even if only on a trial basis of, say, five years. He would also favour a closed season from November to February, inclusive. He sees little merit in playing hurling games during those months.

He praised the contribution made by Justin McCarthy of Cork to Clare hurling. He felt that Justin was especially good at giving a speech to a team before taking the field, and also at analysing opponents.

He then talked about some of the great hurlers of his era. He was a great admirer of Vin Baston of Waterford. He had special words of praise for Tim Flood of Wexford as a corner-forward.

He recalled one of Tony Reddin's many great saves. It was against Cork in Limerick. Christy Ring doubled on a flying ball from about twenty yards out from goal, 'and when he hit it it travelled,' said Matt. Reddin blocked it, and displayed one of his great goalkeeping skills by holding the ball dead on his hurley, and then clearing. Lesser goalkeepers would have let it rebound.

From the men of his era he picked the following combination as one that would appeal to him, but excluding fellow-Claremen:

Tony Reddin *(Tipperary)*

Bobbie Rackard *(Wexford)*   Nick O'Donnell *(Wexford)*   Tony Shaughnessy *(Cork)*
Tommy Doyle *(Tipperary)*   Vin Baston *(Waterford)*   Jim Young *(Cork)*
Joe Salmon *(Galway)*   Fr P. Gantley *(Galway)*
Josie Gallagher *(Galway)*   Mick Ryan *(Tipperary*   Jimmy Langton *(Kilkenny)*
Paddy Kenny *(Tipperary)*   Christy Ring *(Cork)*   Tim Flood *(Wexford*

Born: 1925

66

I remember too well that moment in the 1956 All-Ireland. We were playing Cork. Included in that team was the great Christy Ring. We were leading by two points with about seven minutes to go. Christy Ring gave Bobbie Rackard the slip; he raced towards goal. From about fourteen yards he let loose a fierce shot at goal. Art Foley saved it brilliantly. After clearing the ball, Ring went in to Foley. I remember him saying to Foley, 'Who will you leave them to?' — meaning his hands. I said to Ring, 'If we win today and you retire soon from hurling, I don't care who Art gives them to.'

In 1946 Nick O'Donnell won a junior All-Ireland medal with Kilkenny. He was a sub on the 1947 Kilkenny senior team that won All-Ireland honours by a one-point margin over Cork in a game that ended in a welter of excitement. At that time Paddy "Diamond" Hayden had arrived on the scene at full-back for Kilkenny and was filling the position with distinction. Perhaps that's why Kilkenny failed to "discover" Nicko. When neighbouring Wexford became his adopted county he threw in his lot with them and went on to win honour and great renown in the full-back berth.

Nowadays whenever great full-backs are recalled the name Nick O'Donnell invariably crops up. Many with whom I talked agreed that, while individuals may differ on their choice of favourite for that position, it would be very difficult to find anyone to surpass Nicko.

In the course of a long and illustrious career he stood out as a prince among full-backs. He had, according to Ned Wheeler, that great attribute of rarely giving away close-in frees; and in an era when many full-backs played the role of "stopper", Nicko concentrated to a very large extent on playing the ball and, as a consequence, a great deal of fine hurling.

And yet Nick can recall moments when 'Homer nodded.' In the 1952 Leinster final against Dublin he saw his immediate opponent, Alfie O'Brien, score four goals. In the opening ninety seconds of the 1962 All-Ireland final Nick had the nightmare of seeing the ball in the back of the Wexford net twice in that short time. It is not generally known that he was a sick man that day, and yet he turned in a fine performance in a final that will be remembered as one of the most exciting and memorable that the game has known.

Understandably, the 1956 win over Cork remains a special memory. But 1955 had its own uniqueness. Nick, as captain, led the county to its first All-Ireland success in forty-five years, and rejoiced as a great sense of pride spread throughout the county: through Forth and Bargy and 'o'er the bright May meadows of Shelmalier.' Indeed, back in 1910 men from Shelmalier were prominent in Wexford's first All-Ireland hurling win.

In 1960 Nick joined a select band of hurlers when for the second time he captained the Model County in its fourth All-Ireland success.

I reminded him of his role in the 1958 National League final against Limerick. It was a game that produced majestic hurling. The late John D. Hickey, reporting in the

Irish Independent, described it as the greatest game he had seen, and Joe Sherwood in the *Evening Press* said, 'It was a gripping, pulsating combat, but what a sporting game!'

It was a game of wonderful sportsmanship and full of fast, open and spectacular hurling. Fortunes alternated, and entering the closing stages Wexford were grimly holding on to a two-point lead. Limerick pressure was sustained and intense. A goal would win the game. The dying moments approached. The Limerick onslaught was fierce.

A Limerick forward sent in a piledriver. It caught Nicko on the face. He went down injured; the ball was cleared; and afterwards it was all over. Wexford had triumphed, and owed much to the skill and the strength and above all the courage of Nick O'Donnell.

The 1955 team that brought All-Ireland honours to Wexford after a lapse of forty-five years, and which Nick captained, lined out as follows:

Art Foley

Bobbie Rackard	Nick O'Donnell	Michael O'Hanlon
Jim English	Billy Rackard	Mick Morrissey

Jim Morrissey

Séamus Hearne

Paddy Kehoe	Ned Wheeler	Padge Kehoe
Tom Ryan	Nicky Rackard	Tim Flood

Jim O'Regan. Photo on page 181 is from the 1920s when he was on the Garda hurling team.

Born: 1901

Fan Larkin, Martin Kennedy, Mick Kenny, Mick Cross, Timmy Ryan, John Maher, Tom Doyle, Jimmy Doyle, Lory Meagher, Paddy Phelan, Mick King.

Hurling at its best: I was fortunate to be selected for Cork and to play with them for roughly ten years — the best years of my life. In 1926 Cork and Tipperary met at Cork Athletic Ground. The crowd invaded the pitch, and the match was abandoned; replayed in Thurles and resulted in a draw; replayed a fortnight afterwards — Cork won. Cork then played Kilkenny in the All-Ireland, and after a very hard game Cork won. Some hurling, I tell you.

Cork and Kilkenny in 1931, and it took three matches to decide. The second match of that series was to my mind the best hurling I can recall. Pity both teams could not win! I heard an old Kilkenny man say some years after that the ball never hit the ground that day.

"

I played with Offaly in the Leinster championship in 1924 and won the Leinster junior championship. I played with Dublin in 1925 against Kilkenny, but were beaten by objection. I played with Cork from 1926 to 1936. My position that I liked best was centre-back — I actually loved the position.

These games — hurling and football — are wonderful. Pity one can't stay at them longer! I think I won with others all the important events run by the GAA. Glad to have been a member and meeting such wonderful men.

Now a little story. We — Cork — played Kilkenny in the 1926 All-Ireland. We went to Mass, and the priest, Fr Fitzgerald, said at the end of the Mass, 'Boys, I have said this Mass that we might win.' The lads were wondering about having a Mass said to win a match; one of them in the finish said, 'Look, I would rather bate them fair.'

The men I admired were (excluding Cork) Mick Gill, Garrett Howard, Fowler McInerney, Mick Mackey, John Keane, Phil Cahill, Jackie Power, Paddy Larkin,

On my way back from Eugene Coughlan's I called to Johnny Quirke, who gave me directions as I set off in search of Jim O'Regan. Jim was in the back garden watering his cabbages, but he abandoned his chore and came into the house to talk with me about hurling.

Jim had no doubt about his favourite position. He was almost in ecstasy as he talked about the centre-back position and how much he loved to play there.

He had some harsh things to say about some of the recent changes in the rules. He regretted the departure of the old-style "shoulder" as you go for the ball with an opponent. He also queried the worthwhileness of penalising a player, especially a defender, for "charging in possession." He took the view that a back had little hope in the present-day game of dealing with an incoming forward. He felt that the frontal shoulder should be permitted, and said he could never recall anyone being injured as a result of a fair shoulder.

Memories of my meeting with Eugene Coughlan earlier in the day came back to me when Jim said that if a man puts his hand up for a ball, he runs the risk of having it pulled on and that he must accept the consequences. He disagreed completely with giving a free in such circumstances. The present-day rules, according to Jim, gave a player in possession, especially a forward, special privileges, and he was opposed to this.

He then recalled a day in his hurling career when he found himself in the full-back position, hemmed in on all sides and unable to swing his hurley to effect a clearance. He decided to kick the ball out instead. As he did so an incoming forward pulled, and the ball entered the net; but the opponent not only hit the ball but connected with Jim's toes afterwards. 'But,' he added, 'the forward was right to do what he did. I took the risk. I couldn't expect all opponents to stand aside as I kicked the ball clear.'

Jim, who hailed from Kinsale, joined the Garda Síochána in the 1920s and played for the famous Garda team in the Dublin championship, and won county honours. He left the force to become a national teacher, and regretted that he never had the distinction of winning a Cork county hurling medal.

I asked him about Cork's defeat by Dublin in 1927. It was a comprehensive win, on the score 4:8 to 1:3, and it happened during a golden era in Cork hurling. 'We had a good win over Kilkenny in the 1926 All-Ireland,' said Jim, 'and of course we won Munster and All-Ireland titles in '28,

'29, and '31.

'We were confident as we faced Dublin in 1927. We had a very good team, which included such greats as Seán Óg Murphy, Eudi Coughlan, the two Ahernes, and Jim Hurley. Dublin were backboned by the famous Garda team. On the day they played magnificent hurling, and at no stage did Cork really get a grip on the game. However, the outfield exchanges were much closer than the final score suggests. It was a great Dublin team — star-laden really: Tommy Daly, Fowler McInerney, Dinny O'Neill, Garrett Howard, Mattie Power, Ned Tobin, Mick Gill, to name but some of them.'

The following year saw Cork and Dublin meet in the All-Ireland semi-final. Despite the 1927 result Cork were confident of victory, and before the game Jim O'Regan decided he would have a ten-pound bet on Cork. A Dublin mentor told Jim that the Dublin team was even superior to the 1927 line-out. It put Jim thinking: ten pounds was a lot of money in 1928. He decided to keep his ten-pound note. He regretted his decision when the game was over, because Jim's recollection was that Cork won by about sixteen points, and then went on to heavily defeat Galway in the final.

Among his most treasured possessions were the miniature gold hurley presented after the 1931 triumph, and the Tailteann Games medals he won in 1928 and 1932. This dual Tailteann success was achieved by only one other player, Garrett Howard of Limerick, in 1924 and 1928.

He retired from inter-county hurling in 1936, and had the honour later that year of refereeing the All-Ireland hurling final between Limerick and Kilkenny.

Jim absolutely revelled in playing the game of hurling. In it he found a tremendous medium of self-expression. He played in a hurling era of tough physical contact, full-blooded exchanges, and first-time pulling. He loved it. As we parted he said, 'I wish I never had to give it up!'

Born: 1916

Jackie Power

❝

I was born in Annacotty, Co. Limerick, on 30 May 1916. I started hurling at national school under my teacher at the time, John Kelly, who was a hurling fanatic and had been chairman of the Limerick County Board, GAA.

The first medal I won was with Ahane in the 1933 senior county championship and went on to win fifteen hurling and five football titles with that club.

I had the honour of playing with such famous names as the Mackey brothers — Mick and John — Timmy Ryan, and Paddy Scanlon. We all played on the Limerick team, and also at inter-provincial level. When playing with Munster I had the privilege of playing with such famous men as Jack Lynch and Christy Ring of Cork, Bill O'Donnell and Tommy Purcell of Tipperary, John Keane and Christy Moylan of Waterford, and P. J. Quane and Hauly Daly of Clare.

The game of hurling meant a lot to me, as I met some lovely people through my association with it and made some lifelong friends. 1936 and 1940 will always live in my memory, and also of course 1973, when I was involved with Limerick again in winning that All-Ireland.

❞

Jackie Power belongs to a small band of hurlers who possessed an exceptional level of hurling skills that enabled them to play with great distinction in a variety of positions. His senior county career spanned fifteen years. During that time he manned with distinction at inter-provincial level for

Munster the centre-forward position in 1943, 1947, and 1948; he was at centre-back in 1944 and 1945; he was selected at centre field in 1946, and in other years at wing-forward and corner-forward. He was equally versatile and brilliant with his native Limerick. In the autumn of his career, after the Munster final of 1946 against Cork, one sports writer wrote, 'If Jackie Power is not the best ash artist in the game today, then who is?'

As we talked at Jackie's home in Tralee I glanced around the sitting-room at the wonderful display of trophies and medals that belonged to father and son — Jackie of hurling fame (although he played football too, at county level with Limerick), and Ger of Kerry football renown.

Jackie belonged to an era when hurling was a way of life and the major recreation of many in the hurling strongholds. 'There was hardly a Sunday we weren't in action. There were occasions when I played two games. There was never a question of not playing on a particular Sunday because of an important match the following Sunday. The approach to the game was not selective; players and supporters in those days would laugh at such an idea. We looked upon every game as important. There were club matches, All-Ireland championship matches, National League games, Monaghan Cup in London, Áras na nGael tournaments, church tournaments, Thomond Feis competitions, and indeed many others.'

The Thomond Feis tournament took place in Limerick every spring between Cork, Clare, Tipperary, and Limerick. 'It provided many fine games and was always a good indicator of how things might go in the championship.'

Pride of place in Jackie's memories goes to the All-Ireland successes of 1936 and 1940. '1936 was particularly special. Limerick were all-conquering; they looked the perfect team.' All counties have their hard-luck stories and might-have-beens, and Limerick is no exception. Jackie's career brought him two All-Ireland medals; with a little luck it might have been five. He reflected on how unrevealing full-time scores can be: 'cold statistics that go into the record books, hiding the splendour and magnificence of many a game; the quirks of fate; the superb contribution of the losers; the heartbreak of defeat.'

Yes, the heartbreak of defeat. Jackie still remembers the incredible depths of disappointment suffered by Timmy Ryan, captain of the Limerick team, after their one-point defeat by Kilkenny in the 1935 All-Ireland final. Nothing went right that day for Timmy. It was a day completely unsuited to hurling: weather and underfoot conditions were atrocious and no doubt contributed to Mick Mackey's failure to properly lift and strike a 21-yards free in the dying moments. The ball fell short and was cleared.

Jackie remembers too the 1931 final games between Cork and Kilkenny — tough, bone-crushing stuff that left several players injured, some seriously. 'We played many benefit games for the injured. I can remember clashes in my day when the impact of ash on ash was so fierce that the vibrations would run right up the back of your neck, and hurt.'

He feels that hurling standards have levelled out, and that the general standard is not as high as it used to be. He is critical of the amount of catching and carrying of the ball. 'First-touch performance on the ball

The 1936 Limerick team that he speaks of with such pride and fondness reads as follows:

	Paddy Scanlon	
Paddy O'Carroll	Tom McCarthy	Mick Kennedy
Mickey Cross	Paddy Clohessy	Garrett Howard
Timmy Ryan		Mick Ryan
John Mackey	Mick Mackey	Jim Roche
Dave Clohessy	Jackie Power	Paddy McMahon

has diminished. Forwards get a lot of scores in the modern game. In my day a back would be taken off if his man was scoring too much.'

Among his sadder recollections is his suspension in 1950 by the Limerick County Board. Limerick were drawn against Tipperary in the first round of the championship at Limerick, and Jackie was selected at full-forward. At that time he was based in Co. Mayo with CIE. There was some confusion about the question of transport; there was also the matter of a message sent by Jackie to the county board regarding his likely absence from the line-out. It is not clear whether the message was delivered late or not delivered at all; however, the upshot of the whole affair was that Jackie was suspended. The county was saddened that his playing career with Limerick should have ended on such a note.

But that is now in the distant past. More recent memories centre around the great joy of being associated as coach with the victorious Limerick team of 1973. 'I had a far deeper realisation in 1973 of what it meant to win an All-Ireland medal than I did at the young age of twenty in 1936.'

Jackie Power will always rank among the greats. Versatility, adaptability and consistently high performances were the hallmarks of his long and action-filled career.

Below: Jackie Power: 'The prize we sought is won' — photographed just after the final whistle had blown in 1973 with Limerick, trained by Jackie, victorious over Kilkenny.
Page 183; After the victory over Kilkenny in the National League of 1947.

66

The All-Ireland of 1923 has always been a special memory. I always wished to live to see the day they would win another All-Ireland. When Father Iggy Clarke handed me the cup on the platform in Loughrea after winning the 1980 title I felt proud and honoured — all Galway were delighted. My mind went back to over a half century when we won Galway's first All-Ireland title in 1923.

There is no game like hurling. It has been great in every decade. Long may it live.

Some of the greats I played on were Martin Kennedy, John Roberts, Mick Neville, "Major" Kennedy, and Tom Barry.

99

Jim Power remembered hurling at a time when it was dangerous to play the game — dangerous by proclamation, that is. Notices were displayed warning that anyone playing Gaelic games was liable to be shot on sight. In defiance of the proclamation Jim travelled with Galway to play a game in Croke Park. The game passed off without incident, but shortly afterwards the nation was to witness Bloody Sunday.

Those were troubled times; and because many of the Limerick players were imprisoned, Limerick refused to play Galway in the All-Ireland final of 1923. Galway were awarded the title but refused a bloodless victory, and the final was postponed until 1924.

Jim outlined for me the special intensive programme undertaken by Galway for that final. About twenty-two players assembled at Rockfield House, about three miles from Athenry, and weeks of training followed. Each day they would have a shower, a massage, physical exercise, hurling practice, and running on the sleepers of a nearby railway line. Every second evening they had a training stint that included running and jogging on the road that encircled the demesne at Rockfield. As a result it was an extremely fit team that faced Limerick in the decider. The final score was 7:3 to 4:5 — but the game was much closer than the score suggests.

Jim recalled that the teams were level at half time and that Galway had the advantage of the breeze in the second half. He felt it was anybody's game until the closing stages, when Galway found the net again. There was rejoicing in Galway and in the west; the county had won its first senior hurling title.

His 1923 colleagues — none of them any longer on this side of the great divide — he remembered with fond affection.

'For with them and the past, though the thought wakes woe,

My memory ever abides.'

Sadly he pondered on the fact that all his colleagues were now gone and that he was the only surviving member of that great team.

Mention of 1928 to Jim brought unhappy memories flooding back to him. Cork were their opponents in the final. Very early in the game Galway star performer Mick King received severe injuries to his knee that necessitated his removal from

the field. All his life Jim remained convinced that Mick King was a marked man that day. He was so upset by what happened to Mick King that when the final whistle sounded he threw down his hurley on the ground in disgust and never played county hurling again.

As we talked about Mick King's hurling ability Jim described him as magnificent and magical, and recalled his display against the United States in the Tailteann

Games, when he scored points from every angle.

After the 1923 victory Galway hurling was on the crest of a wave. They qualified for the final in 1924, and Dublin were their opponents. They had lost the services, however, of Mick Gill, who was now living in Dublin; and since under the rules of that time he was not eligible to play for his native Galway, he declared for Dublin and found himself on opposite sides to his 1923 colleagues. Dublin won, but there is no doubt in Jim Power's mind that Galway would have triumphed if Mick Gill had been on their team. But he did agree that it was a great Dublin team that triumphed on the score 5:3 to 2:6.

In the semi-final stages of that championship Galway faced Tipperary, and this is a game that Jim had very happy memories of. He held Martin Kennedy scoreless — full-backs of the day rarely did it. According to Jim, Martin never did the same thing twice in a row. He varied his game and kept his opponents guessing.

Six points divided the teams at half time, and after twelve minutes of the second half the score was Galway 3:1, Tipperary 2:3. That was how it stayed until the final whistle. But there were many near escapes. Let Jim tell part of the story: 'Following a sideline cut to Tipp, which was floated into the goal-mouth, I blocked the ball down in front of me. I had no room to swing. Forwards came thundering at me. I sidestepped. They finished up in the back of the net; I kept the ball covered in front of me. Other forwards tearing in collided with their own men who were scrambling out of the net. Eventually I succeeded in clearing the ball.

'On another occasion, and again from a sidelined cut, the ball came lobbing in. I blocked it down inches from the goal-line. A forward was holding my hurley. As Martin Kennedy prepared to strike I booted the ball clear. There were many such close escapes, but we held the fort. I was very relieved when the final whistle sounded.'

In 1982 when Jim was ill he was visited by Martin Kennedy. He deeply appreciated Martin's visit. The epic moments of the

1924 semi-final and indeed many other encounters were also recalled and replayed as they took a trip down memory lane.

Because of a disagreement within the county, Jim and some colleagues did not line out for Galway in 1925, and even though the team reached the final they were well beaten by a margin of thirteen points by Tipperary.

Jim felt that fate and misfortune may have cost him his place on the Tailteann Games team of 1924. Leinster played Connacht in a trial game, and Jim had five of his teeth knocked out from a stroke of a hurley. He was taken to hospital, where two more teeth were extracted without an anaesthetic. He rinsed his mouth and left, but for three months afterwards he suffered agony.

He loved playing at full-back, and believed that the three key ingredients for a successful full-back are close marking, possession, and first-time striking.

Jim named the following selection from the players of his day that he would liked to have captained:

J. Mahoney *(Galway)*

"Fowler" McInerney *(Clare)*   Jim Power *(Galway)*   M. Derivan *(Galway)*

Jack Darcy *(Tipperary)*   Jim O'Regan *(Cork)*   Garrett Howard *(Limerick)*

Tommy Treacy *(Tipperary)*   Mick Gill *(Galway)*

Tom McGrath *(Limerick)*   Mick King *(Galway)*   Mick Darcy *(Tipperary)*

Ga Aherne *(Cork)*   Martin Kennedy *(Tipperary)*   Mattie Power *(Kilkenny)*

Born: 1883

"

I remember 1907, Kilkenny v. Offaly at Tullamore. Jack Rochford, full-back, said to me, 'I must have two drinks or I will be no good hurling.' 'Have the two drinks,' said I, 'and wait till the match is over and you can have as many as you like.' We won the match. I considered him a great full-back.

The outstanding man of my time was Jim Kelliher.

"

John T. Power was in his ninety-ninth year when I visited him. For his years he was amazingly alert and active. When I called, at about six o'clock in the evening, he was having his tea, and enjoying it too — a wonderful sight to behold for a person of his years.

In his young days he hurled with Piltown, who, according to him, were the third-best team in Kilkenny. Tullaroan and Moincoin were the best, and Piltown, he

said, no matter how they tried, could not beat Tullaroan or Mooncoin. I asked him why he was not on the winning Kilkenny team in 1909, and he explained that because of some disagreement within the county his parish was against him playing, and it cost him an All-Ireland medal. The passage of time, however, seemed to have made him philosophical about this loss.

I had often wondered what had necessitated the replay between Cork and Kilkenny in 1905 after Cork had won the first game on the score 5:10 to 3:13. John T. had the answer. After the first game it appears that Kilkenny objected to the Cork goalie, Jim McCarthy. This brought a counter-objection from Cork, who claimed that Kilkenny's Matt Gargan had played a Munster championship with Waterford. A replay was ordered, and Kilkenny won well at 7:7 to 2:9.

John remembered as a boy going to Fiddown station with his father, where Parnell, who was travelling to a meeting in Waterford, put his head out the window of the train and spoke briefly to those present. He also recalled being in Dublin when a rally was held in support of those fighting in the Boer War in South Africa.

He told me that he played against Tyler Mackey, 'a hard, tough player,' and when I asked him if Tyler was good he replied, 'He wasn't good enough for me: he couldn't score any goals against me.' Years later he met Mick Mackey, who well remembered his father saying that in the particular game in question it was the two Piltown men who beat them. He was referring of course to John T. Power and John Anthony.

John recalled some of the great names

of the 1907 team, the year he won his first All-Ireland medal: the Doyles of Mooncoin, Matt Gargan, Jack Rochford, Sim Walton, John Anthony, and Dick Grace. Others of that time he admired were Seán Óg Hanly, who won an All-Ireland medal with Limerick in 1897 and was on the London team that lost to Cork in the final of 1903, Tom Semple, Dan Kennedy, and Tyler Mackey.

He was adamant, however, that the outstanding man of his time was Jim Kelliher of Dungourney, Co. Cork, who was not only a great hurler but an outstanding horseman also. According to John, Jim was not a big man, but he was a very commanding figure on the field and used to hurl at both full-back and centre-back.

I got the impression that he preferred to think in terms of great hurlers in each line-out position rather than of the "greatest ever". 'You know, a man can be great in one position and quite inadequate or mediocre in several other positions.'

As a young man he joined the civil service in Dublin, but after a relatively short time he gave up the post and returned to Piltown, where he farmed. As he reminisced he talked of Barrett's field in New Ross, Fraher's field in Dungarvan, and Jones's Road in Dublin. 'I played in them all and in many other pitches throughout the country as well.'

'Money was scarce when I was young,' he mused, and he went on to add that many young boys in his day made their own hurleys from ash, sally, and blackthorn. 'I well remember playing hurling on the street of Piltown with a blackthorn stick — no traffic worries then. I can remember too when the sideposts were dispensed with.'

John's All-Ireland medals were won in 1907, 1911 (a walkover from Limerick after a dispute over the venue), 1912, and 1913. He retired from hurling in 1919 but was recalled for the All-Ireland semi-final against Galway in 1925. It wasn't a happy return: Kilkenny lost heavily.

He recited poetry about stirring games, great hurling victories, and heroes of his day. There was a pause as he seemed to ponder on something, and then he said with conviction, 'I'll make the hundred.' He rose from his chair and walked over to the table where I was sitting. He stood over the book. 'I'm glad to do this for you.' He wrote with ease. The signature was strong and definite. He was carrying his tenth decade lightly.

He had enjoyed recounting his memories, and as I made ready to leave he cast his head slightly downwards, reflected, and quoted two lines remembered from his schooldays:

'Oh, God be with those happy days,
Oh, God be with my childhood.'

John T. Power with Paddy Buggy.

Born: 1929

to winning All-Ireland, National League, Oireachtas and Railway Cup medals, won 9 consecutive senior hurling county medals and three county senior football medals.

Players outside of Waterford in that period who I admired most were of course Christy Ring — the greatest of them all — and Paddy Barry, Cork; Pat Stakelum and Jimmy Doyle, Tipperary; the Rackards and Ned Wheeler, Wexford; and Seán Clohessy and Ollie Walsh, Kilkenny.

" "

66

The greatest moment in my hurling memories was the winning of the All-Ireland in 1959 after a replay with Kilkenny. Winning the All-Ireland was great, but beating Kilkenny comprehensively in a replay was special. It was the final goal of a great Waterford team who, I believe, played their own special brand of hurling, of fast ground striking, and mobility and artistry in the attack.

I was proud to be a member of such a wonderful bunch of lads, and if I mention specially my own Mount Sion clubmates Phil Grimes, Frank Walsh and Larry Guinan I believe the others will understand. In a span of ten years these men, in addition

If Waterford had beaten Limerick in the first round of the championship in 1949 they might have won two in a row. They failed, and fell on lean times. Seumas Power recalls that in the mid-1950s they drew with and beat the great Wexford team of that era in League games. They began to realise in Waterford that they had the makings of a team of considerable potential if only they could make the breakthrough.

With the arrival of 1957 they began to make long-term plans and to adopt an analytical approach to the game. They looked on Limerick as the danger team, and felt that if they overcame the Shannonsiders in the first round they would cope with the other teams.

The first-round match was a real test. Limerick had a young team, with players like Liam Moloney, Mick Tynan, Tom McGarry, Dermot Kelly, and Vivian Cobbe. Waterford had a narrow win and had to overcome adversity as well as Limerick, because Grimes suffered a shoulder injury, Austin Flynn had to go off, and

Frank Walsh wasn't on for the full hour. Seumas remembers that Johnny O'Connor was 'man of the match' and that John Barron was outstanding at full-back when he moved from the corner to take over from Austin Flynn. Yes, Waterford were on the march; their three-week training session had paid off; the glory days of the next seven years lay ahead.

Seumas's childhood heroes were Vin Baston, John Keane, Mick Mackey, and Christy Moylan — 'a player who could hit left and right with equal effectiveness.' The two games of his career that he enjoyed most were Rest of Ireland v. Tipperary in 1962 at Thurles, when he played on Tony Wall and contributed 1:4 of the 3:12-to-2:9 defeat of Tipp, and Rest of Ireland v. Waterford in 1960 at Walsh Park, when Waterford held the Rest to a draw, 2:8 all.

'In these games you could hurl with freedom and abandon,' said Seumas. 'You wanted to win, but if you lost you didn't suffer the disappointment and sense of loss that you felt after a Munster final or All-Ireland defeat.'

Seumas never enjoyed playing for Waterford in a Munster or All-Ireland final. There was so much at stake, so much to lose, so much that could go wrong. You were always afraid that some players, including yourself, might have an off day. Against top opposition a team can't afford to have anyone have an off day.

That brought us to the 1957 final against Kilkenny, when Waterford were eight points up with about as many minutes to go and they looked as if they were home and dry. Seumas recalls gaining possession and being allowed go completely unchallenged as he hit the ball. A colleague is convinced he saw one Kilkenny back give a shake of his head to another defender, as if to say, 'It's all over for us.' What happened is history. Seumas will tell you there are no words to describe the feelings after a defeat like that of 1957: 'numbed', 'shattered', 'bewildered' — all totally inadequate.

How does he see things now as he reflects back to a quarter of a century ago? He is able to look at '57 philosophically and with cool analysis and put the defeat into proper perspective. While the loss was bitter at the time, and for a long while afterwards, he now looks back and says, 'No regrets.' He found fulfilment playing a wonderful game with great colleagues and opponents.

Turning to the present he accepts that the game is changing — perhaps the word is 'evolving' — and agrees that this has to happen if the game is to survive and flourish.

He would love to have played Wexford in an All-Ireland final in the 1957–63 era. Indeed many of his colleagues share the same wish. Seumas believes such a game would have been a great hurling spectacle between two teams of very different styles. Talking of Wexford, he holds the view that it was the late Nicky Rackard who really masterminded the rise of the county team. He explains that Nicky in the UCD and Leinster jerseys had played with and against players from other counties. It began to dawn on him that with certain improvements Wexford had what it took to match the best. How right he was.

Switching to Tipperary, Seumas mentioned the late Johnny Leahy and the hospitality he had enjoyed from Johnny on several occasions, and added, 'Johnny was a Tipp man through and through: always anxious for a Tipp win, no matter what was at stake.'

Seumas feels he was fortunate to have tasted the success of League, Oireachtas, All-Ireland and Munster titles, as well as several county successes, and to have had the honour of refereeing in Gaelic Park in New York in 1965.

My own special memory of Seumas is as the saviour of 1959, when he snatched Waterford from the jaws of defeat in the dying seconds with a superb goal. It epitomised the class and spirit of the man.

Born: 1944

“

Ever from the time I was a small chap the GAA was very important to me. It has everything that a good game should have: there is competition, team effort, skill, and the excitement of a close contest. I suppose that every player will admit that there is a special thrill in playing for his county team and the possibility of winning the greatest honour in the game: an All-Ireland.

There were two men that played a major part in my hurling life: Syl Barron (RIP), Rathnure, and Ned Power (RIP), St Peter's College. Both men were a big loss to the GAA, as both gave freely of their time and both had so much more to offer.

It was in St Peter's that I first came into contact with Ned Power. He used to train the teams for the college championship. He always said that we should enjoy the game, but we found it hard to enjoy some of the stunts imposed by him! 'Fitness through final perseverance' was his motto, except that it was not Ned Power who was suffering! I suppose fitness makes the competition keener, and that gives the game excitement. During those years in college

it was practice every evening and doing the skills we were least good at until we got them perfect. We won the Colleges All-Ireland under his guidance, the first ever won by the college.

When summer came it was back to the club, and Syl Barron was the man in charge there. Syl brought me to all the matches, juvenile, minor, and senior. He always brought the Rathnure chaps to county minor matches and senior matches.

I first got on the county senior panel after the All-Ireland in 1962. I played part of the League that year, but missed out on the championship because of a broken finger. Wexford got beaten in the Leinster final. I did not play but was back for the League and played up to 1971 — but played away with Rathnure up to 1983. During those years with the county I won 1965, '68 and '70 Leinster finals, 1967 League and 1968 All-Ireland. I had the honour of being captain of the 1968 team.

During your playing days those things may not look important, but when you look back it gives you great pleasure. I suppose winning the All-Ireland was my biggest thrill, but a great thrill also was the first time in my days with the county team beating Kilkenny in the 1965 Leinster final with a very young side when we were given no hope of winning. Also during the 1970s we had a great run with Rathnure winning seven county championships, three Leinster Club finals; and my biggest regret was that we won none of the Club All-Irelands.

With regard to the present time in the GAA I think it is at a crossroad. Yes, we have appointed a coach in Wexford but that is not the only answer. Youth and times have changed. When we were young we were brought to club and county matches and the interest was intense. After the matches when we went home it was in to get the hurl and a ball and out to try to imitate those we saw at the match. We looked up to so many of the county team and used to spend hours trying to do what they could do. We never went anywhere without a hurl and ball. That all seems to be gone, and I see now that youth never go to the field to hurl for the fun. They will not go unless there is someone there to train them, and if he is not there they will lie down until he comes.

Some way has got to be found to make them play for the love of the game and not just for the competitive side of the game. I think if there were less competitions for the very young and get them to play for the love of the game it would be far better. That is where I see coaches can help to improve the game, as there would be no pressure on them to win games. I think you cannot compete in competitions and hope to improve the skills of the game at the same time, because one has to fall by the wayside: you either help the game and lose the competition or win the competition and the skills will suffer.

"

Down the decades many illustrious and famous family names have adorned the GAA hurling calendar. The name Quigley of Rathnure holds a proud and prominent place among them.

They had a unique honour in 1970 when four brothers lined out in the All-Ireland final against Cork. The Wexford half-forward line read: Martin Quigley; Pat Quigley; John Quigley. Dan was at centre-back.

But victory went to Cork, on the score 6:21 to 5:10. 'We had to line out without Phil Wilson, Ned Buggy, Willie Murphy, and Christy Kehoe — but that didn't excuse our defeat. We were caught for pace in a few positions, and we didn't adjust well to the eighty-minutes game — it was

the first such final.'

Dan made a little bit of hurling history in 1964. He played for his province before tasting championship hurling with his county, and won a Railway Cup medal at full-back with Leinster on St Patrick's Day.

Though his heart is in hurling he likes all sports, and welcomes the spirit of "glasnost" that is dawning. Gestures like sending good wishes to the Irish soccer team at World Cup time are applauded by Dan; but he wants to see more of this. He wants to see an opening of windows and doors, and he wants to see a lot of fresh air blowing through the GAA. He would like to see the playing of selected soccer internationals at Croke Park, Limerick and other venues as a source of income, and would encourage such a pragmatic policy. The fact that soccer authorities have failed to build a worthwhile stadium is a matter for them and not something we should berate them about.

He wants encouragement for the youth, and more consideration and recognition for players past and present. In particular he would like to see some definite policy on the question of All-Ireland tickets for players, and a vast improvement in the area of insurance for injured players.

His greatest moment was when he received the McCarthy Cup as captain of Wexford in 1968 — 'although the significance of the honour didn't sink in for a long time afterwards.' His boyhood heroes were the Rackards — 'inevitable, wasn't it?'

His biggest regret will always be the failure to capture the Club All-Ireland title for Rathnure after they had succeeded three times in Leinster in the seventies. 'How we lost it on at least one of those occasions I'll never know.' His special wish is that the game should never die. 'If we could only get more players involved when they retire.'

His favourite position was right-full-back, 'but I was happy too at centre-back when I was physically fit for the demands of the position.' His most fulfilling mission would be to have a coaching brief separate and apart from the responsibility of producing a winning combination.

Dan arrived at senior level at an early

age and departed prematurely. Here is the story of the unfortunate sequence of events leading to his irrevocable decision to quit the county scene. 'In the autumn of 1971 myself and three colleagues went on an approved trip to New York to play one game with the local Wexford team in the New York championship against Clare. We won the game — plenty of hurlers out there from Clare too. We were asked to stay for the next round, against Kilkenny, and agreed — after all, it was costing us nothing: they were paying for us. At home Wexford were due to play Cork in the National League at New Ross. They phoned looking for us but couldn't contact us. How could they? We were still in New York. Anyway, it rained so heavily that the game against Kilkenny was postponed, and we returned home the following day.

'Wexford were due to play Limerick in the Oireachtas final the following Sunday. They picked none of the four of us — myself, Dave Berney, Teddy O'Connor, or Mick Jacob — because we weren't available for the game against Cork. They even tried to suspend us, but they couldn't, because we had only played in the game in New York that we had permission for — so there was nothing to suspend us for.

'I felt we were being treated like schoolboys. I quit. I think I played one game after that, but that was it. I was approached a few times to come back, and some of the players came to me, but I had made my mind up: nothing would entice me back. I had hardly ever missed a match and never missed training. What really got to me though was the fact that the Cork hurlers who travelled to New York had no issue made of the matter. They just were not available for the League game and were not picked, and that was it. Us — treated like children.'

There were quite a few more hurling years in Dan. No county could afford to lose a man of his talents and calibre. It will therefore forever remain a matter for conjecture what bearing Dan's presence would have had on the All-Ireland results of 1976 and 1977 against Cork had he been in the line-out. "Significant" would be an understatement.

Born: 1911

John Quirke

The GAA is a wonderful occasion: you meet so many people and you make many friends; and it's proved that your greatest opponents on the field can become your best friends afterwards.

Some of the men I played against come to mind, such as John Keane, Jack Lynch, Christy Ring, Jackie Power, Mick Mackey, John Maher, Declan Good, Billy Murphy, and Charlie Ware.

"

"

I lived in Blackrock and grew up playing hurling on the road and any field you could take a chance in. Played a few minor and junior games; I then got my place on the famous Blackrock senior team in 1929, and we won three county championships. That famous club with their own selection had no less than ten of their own team that played for Cork from 1926 to 1931.

I got my place in the Cork team in 1932, with a very lean period until 1941. I won two Leagues and eight Railway Cup medals out of ten in a row; also four AllIreland medals: 1941, 1942, 1943 and 1944 in a row.

It would be difficult to come across a more helpful person than Johnny Quirke. His is a warm personality that radiates willingness to help, and when the task involves GAA matters his enthusiasm knows no bounds. He arranged my appointment with Eudi Coughlan; guided me to Jim O'Regan; and promised to put me in touch with Willie John Daly of Carrigtohill.

I mentioned to Johnny that I was about to visit John Joe Doyle of Clare. 'Be sure and give John Joe my regards,' he said, 'and tell him that he cost me my place on the Cork team for a considerable period in 1932.'

Johnny was born in Milltown, Co. Kerry, but when he was ten months old his family moved to Cork, and so instead of perhaps being a Kerry footballer he became a Blackrock and Cork hurler. He likes to jokingly say that he is probably the best hurler to have come out of Kerry.

He recalls that his early years in Cork hurling were very lean ones. Cork had won five Munster titles and four All-Irelands between 1926 and 1931. When Johnny arrived in 1932 Cork were beaten by Clare, and seven years would elapse before Cork would again reign supreme in Munster.

Johnny talks about his contemporaries, both colleagues and opponents, with warmth and affection. The defeats of the thirties taught him to understand deeply the feelings of players who never tasted success. He felt too for teams who had victory snatched from them when all seemed won, or who lost against the odds.

Success came for Johnny towards the autumn of his career, and when it did it came with an abundance of riches, the crowning jewel for him being the great four-in-a-row of 1941–44. For him, 1944 was a year packed with drama and happy memories. It was a year of records and close calls.

The scene of the main drama was Semple Stadium, Thurles, where the drawn Munster final and replay were staged. It became known as the "bicycle final" (cars were off the road because of the war). Johnny recalled that "Carbery" described the hundreds upon hundreds of cyclists converging on Thurles as being 'like ants on the move'.

He readily concedes that fortune favoured Cork in both games. They were behind in lost time in each game. They survived the first through a brilliant goal from Johnny. He balanced the scales in the replay with a typical point, and Ring gave Cork victory with a "wonder goal".

He wouldn't go into detail about his own superb contribution but was very happy to talk about what he saw as the turning point in the replay. Here's how he recalled it: 'It was well into the second half and heading for the closing stages. Limerick were leading by five points and hurling well and very confidently. Mick Mackey bore down on the Cork goal, and the sliotar shook the net. But the whistle had gone for a foul on Mick as he soloed through. Controversy raged for a long time afterwards, for some held that the ball was in the net before the whistle blew and that the advantage rule was abused, while others held that the whistle had gone before the ball had entered the net.

'The free, from a fairly difficult angle, was missed. That left Limerick still five points ahead. It might have been eight — it could have been six. But the failure to get the goal or the point at that stage in the game proved in the end to be the turning point for us. We were heartened by the let-off.

'It was a kind of psychological boost. We breathed a sigh of relief and felt that the gap, late in the day as it was, could still be bridged. If they had got the goal or the point I feel certain we would have lost.'

And that victory kept the road open to four in a row. The record was achieved; a great Cork era and team took its place in hurling history and the record books.

High among Johnny's special memories are the defeat of Limerick by Cork in 1938 and 1939 and the part he played in curbing Mick Mackey when he moved from his customary attacking role to the pivot of the defence. For in those days Limerick were still a renowned outfit, and Mackey was magic.

The great Cork team of '44 was as follows:

Tom Mulcahy

Willie Murphy	Batt Thornhill	Din Joe Buckley
Paddy O'Donovan	Con Murphy	Alan Lotty

Jack Lynch		Con Cottrell

Christy Ring	Seán Condon (captain)	Jim Young
Johnny Quirke	Jim Morrison	Joe Kelly

Born: 1931

Billy Rackard

66

My first game for Wexford was in 1949, my last in 1963. In between those years at club and county level I was very active, and rather fortunate to be the age I was when the Wexford team of that era came good — a team that collected every honour in the game. My sympathy always goes out to outstanding players — you will find them in most counties: players who were unlucky to be born at the wrong time and consequently miss out on the good era and especially an All-Ireland win.

Fourteen years is a long time in any game, and you could endlessly recall memories — a standard occupation for any long-serving player; and yet personally it is all just a parcel of moments. So I hope you will enjoy the memory of a certain day in 1953. It was the Railway Cup final, a trophy that hadn't been to Leinster for over a decade. There were some aging players on our side, men such as Jim Langton, my brother Nicky, Diamond Hayden, etc. — players who badly needed this win.

We were almost there after all those years — Leinster two points up; the dying minutes of the game — when a certain Christy Ring came thundering towards the Leinster goal, having rounded my brother Bobbie, who was now literally glued to Ring's right elbow. The marking was close, and Christy without question was running into a cul-de-sac. From my right-full-back position hugging Séamus Bannon I observed the following sequence of events. Ring knew he had nowhere to go — that is if we all sat tight in the full-back line — but lo and behold the fabulous Old Diamond, obsessed with the prospect of finally upending his arch-rival of many years, could not resist the temptation of such a golden opportunity and just took off like a wounded rhino to clobber you-know-who.

Ring, the maestro that he was, saw the chance, actually tempted him, then palmed the ball past the unfortunate Diamond and faded away. Meanwhile Derry McCarthy, a Limerick man and a master of the drop shot, made no mistake with a ball that was unstoppable, lifting the mist clear of the rigging.

The green flag was waved, and the resultant puck-out brought the long whistle, with Leinster yet again denied a title they had not won since the year 1941. A mistake had been made, and to his eternal credit the Diamond knew who made it. It was only afterwards in the silence of the dressing-room that the emotion became too much for him. I shall never forget a boot crashing against the wall and Diamond announcing to everyone that he really hated nobody — but nonetheless right now if he could get his hands on Ring he'd bloody kill him.

My brother Nick, laughing, defused the situation when he put his arm around Diamond and asked him for the loan of his comb, which I recall boasted about three to four teeth. Nicky combing his hair with an affectionate and consoling arm around his great rival and colleague in his moment of self-reproach and deep regret is a memory that shall never leave my mind.

99

I spent several pleasant hours with Billy Rackard at his home in Saint Helen's on the south coast of Co. Wexford, as he recorded in my book some of his memories.

Billy is a great student of the game and capable of deep analysis of all aspects of its tactics and skills. Before a game he would always analyse fully the opposing team and in particular his immediate opponent. This was confirmed by Tim Flood when I talked with him. Said Tim, 'For that reason, I never looked forward to playing on Billy Rackard. He would have it all carefully planned and thought out beforehand.'

Billy feels that every need and requirement of a team, ranging from medical guidance to properly fitting boots, should have detailed attention and should be the responsibility of specific people. He felt that neglect or inadequacy in such matters could mean the losing of a game.

He has always been a strong advocate of the closed season. He can see no merit in playing hurling from November to February, and he himself never enjoyed playing the game during the winter months.

While an All-Ireland medal is the pride of any hurler, Billy feels that visually the Oireachtas medal is more attractive.

On the question of the switch of his brother Bobbie from centre-back to full-back in the 1954 All-Ireland final, he totally rejects the viewpoint put forward by some that it cost Wexford the game. In this respect 'he is in full agreement with the views of Bobbie. Billy very readily admits that when a team wins an All-Ireland title there are usually about two other teams in the championship campaign as good as the winners. 'It is a question of who gets the breaks,' he said. He believes that there are occasions when very little can turn a

mediocre team into a good team, and equally well a good team into a great team. 'It could, for example, be the finding of an outstanding goalkeeper or centre-back, or perhaps an inspiring captain.'

Looking into the future, Billy saw the game of hurling having some obstacles to surmount. Counter-attractions will be one; the greatest problem, however, may be the cost of ash and its finished product, the hurley. He felt individuals and clubs may need some form of support to help defray the ever-soaring price of hurleys.

On the 1956 final, Billy expressed the view that one of Wexford's master strokes was the placing of Martin Codd at centre-forward on Willie John Daly. Martin's height and overhead play neutralised Willie John's potential effectiveness.

I always associate Billy Rackard with 1960. This was surely his greatest year. In the Leinster final against Kilkenny on a wet and miserable day he was majestic at centre-back, driving back attack after attack by Kilkenny. He was superb in the air, and his covering and positional sense matched his aerial performance. The late Joe Sherwood, writing in the *Evening Press* on the following day, said that: 'He strode the scene like a Greek Colossus.'

I saw him again that year in the All-Ireland final against Tipperary, who were red-hot favourites. This time the weather was pleasant. Tactically, Billy played a different game from the Kilkenny one. Throughout the hour he neutralised danger-man Liam Devaney and made a major contribution to one of Wexford's greatest victories.

Others too made an impact that day. Padge Kehoe was in great form and had an early goal from a 21-yards free taken from the Hogan Stand side of the Railway Goal. John Nolan kept Jimmy Doyle in check. Hopper McGrath went through for a goal in the second half that really clinched it. A resounding 2:15 to 0:11 success, it stirred Mick Dunne to open his report the following day in the *Irish Press:* 'The Assyrian came down like the wolf on the fold,/And his cohorts were gleaming in purple and gold.'

It was in every sense a Model victory.

Born: 1927

Bobbie Rackard

was a Doran of Moneyhore, a sister of John Doran who played on the famous Wexford football team 1914–18.

It is difficult to know where we got our interest in GAA. Neither of our parents encouraged it, but I must add neither did they discourage us. As a matter of interest my first introduction to sport was cricket, and I am sure my brothers can say the same. My father used to play it in Hilton, near Bree. Our interest in hurling came mostly through the local Rathnure club, which wasn't that long formed and was then only junior. I grew up during the war years, when everything was very scarce and rationed. I remember the first radio and Mícheál O'Hehir's early broadcasts, which probably as much as anything else helped to fire the imagination of a lot of young people, including myself.

I can remember Sundays when Leinster and Munster finals and All-Irelands were broadcast. Our kitchen, which is large, would be cleared out and extra seating put in to cater for the locals who would collect to listen to the match. Ours was the only radio in the locality at the time. Needless to say the hurleys would be parked outside, and immediately the broadcast was over we would rush out, grab the hurleys, onto the field to try and emulate the Mick Mackeys, Lory Meaghers, etc., depending on the team playing on that day.

My father traded in horses during those years, buying and selling. There were always young horses to be broken. This, I would say, was our first challenge, as anyone who has ever had anything to do with breaking horses will tell you. They are individuals just like humans, and will test your skill and courage. We became skilful

"

For a long time I found it difficult to know what to say here. I at last decided to give a short history of my family.

I was born on 6 January 1927, one of nine children — five boys, four girls — the eldest being Sally and Essie. Next came Nicky, Jimmy, myself, John, Billy, Mary, and Rita. Nicky, Billy and myself are the best-known because of our involvement in hurling and football. I mention all this to give whoever reads this some understanding of the background we grew up in.

My father wasn't interested in GAA. He came from a large family. His father was a small farmer from Ballinlug, about half a mile from Killann. Originally the Rackards came from a place called Rackardstown, near Kilmore Quay. My father went to Dublin to serve his time to the bar trade at a very young age, and came home in 1904 and bought Killann Bar and Grocery and seventy acres of land; price, I believe, £800. The house, which is very old, is reputed to be the home of John Kelly, one of the 1798 insurrection leaders (the song 'Kelly the Boy from Killann'). My mother riders, rode to the local hunt, and on other days organised races between ourselves and some locals. There sprung up between us a friendly but serious rivalry as to who was the best, who could jump the biggest fence and do the most daring deed. There was many a mishap, but none too serious that would stop us from accepting an even greater challenge the next day.

The reason I mention all this is because I believe this was to reflect itself on the playing-field later on, more especially with Nicky, Billy, and myself. Jimmy opted out quite early, and it was a pity, because he was probably more polished and skilful than any of us. John never really made the grade in sport.

When you are young and playing a particular sport you sometimes dream that one day you will get to the top. It was so in our case. On the one hand you dreamed, not really believing it would happen. It was this early rivalry, unspoken of between ourselves, which set the scene for what was to follow. It also taught us that second-best wasn't good enough.

Nick of course had natural ability to inspire others, and as most people know in later years was plagued with alcoholism. This was his greatest challenge. After a hard struggle he finally overcame it, and inspired many others to do likewise.

There is a sizable yard in front of our house. There are also some ten windows — I shudder when I think of the number of times as youngsters we broke them, having been warned beforehand not to play hurling in the front yard. However, most of our hurling was done down the road in a field not far from the house, and it is those long summer evenings I remember most: the organising, backs versus forwards; someone to keep the ball pucked in — and I can tell you the competition and marking was as keen as any championship match. There were arguments, and the odd punch-up. One thing it taught me early on: there was nothing to be gained by losing your temper, and I found to beat your opponent in the hurling skills brought far greater satisfaction, and strangely enough a respect from your opponent that couldn't be gained by

getting into a brawl with him.

The Wexford team of the fifties earned a respect and popularity on a national basis which far exceeded that of other teams which perhaps had won a lot more. This of course was largely due to their sportsmanship and the way they played the game. I am proud to have been a member of that team.

It is now thirty-one years since I played for Wexford,* so you must appreciate that one's memory may not be all that good. However, there are moments you can never forget, like the disappointment of losing the 1951 and 1954 All-Irelands — especially the '54 final, as I believe luck didn't favour us on that day. This of course was all forgotten when we won in 1955 and 1956. The nicest thing about winning is coming home to your supporters knowing that at last you have made them really happy.

Inexperienced as we were in 1951, could we have exchanged goalies I think we would have won. I can still see Nicky getting inside the Tipperary backs and letting fly from very close range, and Tony Reddin killing the ball on his hurley and clearing it outfield. Our goalie on the other hand had a most unhappy day. He hadn't been playing much for Wexford up to that. Looking back on it, I suppose it was unfair to bring him on in an All-Ireland final.

Tipperary had a great team in those years and were always hard to beat. We got our revenge in the League final in 1956 when we came from sixteen points behind at half time to beat them. Then of course Wexford beat them again in the sixties. I wasn't on that team, as I had to retire in 1957 owing to an accident.

The 1954 final was against Cork, and it is the one I am most often asked about, principally because Nick O'Donnell was knocked out and I was changed from centre-back to the full-back position. I was having one of my best games ever, and a lot of people hold the view that I should have been left centre-back and we would have won. It is a question that can never be answered.

* This was written in 1988.

You can of course speculate, as a lot of people do, and most people feel we would have won had I not been changed. My own view is that I honestly don't know. Had Nick O'Donnell not been knocked out I have no doubt but we would have won. Billy put the question to Christy Ring; he claimed had I not been moved back Cork would have won by a lot more. I would certainly have a lot of respect for Christy's opinion. Needless to say I had great respect for him on the field, and consider him one of the finest players I ever met.

99

There is a tide in the affairs of men
Which, taken at the flood, leads on to fortune;

That moment came for Bobbie Rackard in the 1954 All-Ireland final against Cork. With about twenty minutes remaining, Nick O'Donnell, the great Wexford full-back, broke his collar-bone and had to leave the field. Wexford reshuffled their team and took Bobbie Rackard to full-back.

He proceeded to give a power-packed and impeccable display of defensive hurling that will forever have a special place in hurling history and will be talked about whenever great feats of individual brilliance are recalled.

As we talked at his home in Killann he traced the rise of Wexford in the hurling world as the forties ended and the fifties dawned. A sample of the kind of hurling that Wexford would serve up for over a decade was seen to advantage in the 1951 final against Tipperary. Wexford were bringing to perfection their own particular style, which was basically lift-and-strike and catch-and-strike.

There were moments early on in the 1951 final when it seemed that Wexford would win, but it was not to be. All during the 1951 campaign Wexford failed to come up with an established goalkeeper. Four times that year they changed goalkeepers. That is not the kind of recipe that estab-

lishes the relationship and understanding between goalkeeper and backs that is essential for victory in top-class hurling. This proved to be a contributory factor to their defeat at the hands of Tipperary in 1951.

But in defeat Wexford were glorious, and Gaeldom rejoiced at the arrival of a new face — a face that would illuminate hurling and add honour and glamour to the game.

Bobbie recalled that 1952 was a sad year for Wexford. They faced Dublin in the Leinster final, and after their performance in 1951 it was generally felt in the GAA world that Wexford could go one step further in 1952. Followers in Wexford wouldn't hear of defeat. For two weeks before the game they were talking about victory. Some even talked of an easy victory. Bobbie was convinced that this attitude among the supporters filtered through to the team. He believed that mentally the team approached the game in a gear lower than they normally would.

Very early in the game it began to dawn on the Wexford players that there was far more hurling in the Dublin team than Wexford followers had given them credit for. On the field Wexford were now really up against it. Dublin found gaps in the Wexford defence. Goals began to come. Wexford failed to seal the gaps; Dublin ruthlessly exploited the position.

The final score told a sorry tale for Wexford. It was nine scores each. Wexford had scored 3:6 — but Dublin had found the net seven times. The two points were incidental to the outcome.

'I have no doubt,' said Bobbie, 'that overconfidence and an ill-prepared mental approach cost us the Leinster final. Many lessons were learnt that day.'

Supporters had travelled in their thousands. Every means of transport was used. The atmosphere on the journey to Nowlan Park was carnival-like. They returned crestfallen, the journey home like a funeral procession. Dublin had triumphed against all expectations. Wexford, with the potential to win the All-Ireland crown, were caught in a kind of trap of immaturity.

As we talked about those early disap-

Nick O'Donnell had retired injured. He would disagree with the view that it cost Wexford the match. He puts it this way: 'Consider the score: Cork 1:9, Wexford 1:6 — a very low-scoring game, which suggests defensive supremacy or forward inaccuracy, or perhaps a combination of both.'

As it was, the Wexford defence was outstanding. The Cork defence was tight, but outfield Wexford dominated the play and won an abundance of possession. They failed, however, to capitalise on this superiority, and missed numerous golden scoring opportunities. Late in the game when Cork did get their only goal — which proved to be a winner — Wexford ought to have been well in front. 'It was a game,' said Bobbie, 'that should never have been lost.'

He then went on to pay special tribute to the often "forgotten men" behind the scenes who work with such dedication and commitment to promote and foster hurling. These men are to be found at all levels of the association: club, county, and province. Without them the GAA as we know it could not function; yet as Bobbie pointed out, we tend to take these people for granted.

Inevitably, the name Christy Ring entered the discussion. There was only one of him, said Bobbie, as he reflected on the length of time that Christy had played in top-class hurling at club, county and provincial levels; the consistency with which he produced outstanding performances even after he had turned forty; his phenomenal scoring records; his dedication and commitment; his sacrifice for the game; and the intensity of his competitiveness. This quality of competitiveness at times seemed fanatical, and we wondered as we talked if it was this that in the end may have cost him his life.

Bobbie from his boyhood had always placed tremendous emphasis on good sportsmanship, and all through his hurling career it had been his objective to set a high standard in this regard. He feels a special sense of pride in the acclaim Wexford won in the fifties for their great spirit of sportsmanship.

The All-Ireland triumphs of 1955 and

pointments Bobbie felt that it wasn't only on the field of play that weakness and inexperience manifested themselves. Wexford mentors too were inexperienced in the big time, and this tended to leave Wexford at a disadvantage when they came up against the seasoned campaigners of Kilkenny, Cork, and Tipperary.

As he reflected on those early days Bobbie recalled the casual and easy-going Wexford approach as compared with the detailed, intensive and at times almost fanatical preparation of the established hurling counties. 'We must really have been a great team to have won what we did in those days,' he said.

Turning to 1954, he believed that the right decision was taken by the selectors when they switched him to full-back after

1956 compensated in some degree for the many disappointments of the early fifties. Bobbie remembers meeting the late Tom O'Rourke in Enniscorthy one day after those victories and being congratulated on the great successes of '55 and '56. That took Bobbie back to his boyhood days, when Tom O'Rourke was a Garda sergeant in Bobbie's native Killanne. Tom was a Clareman who had played with the Garda hurling team in Dublin and had been a member of the star-studded team who defeated Cork in the 1927 final. In those days in Killanne Tom used to be very critical of the Wexford style of lift-and-hit and catch-and-hit. He used to tell them that they would never win anything with that style and that they wouldn't have a hope in Munster. As he saw them perform with a style that was alien to what he was accustomed to, he used to shout at them, 'Whip on the ball — whip on the ball!' But the Wexfordmen did not change what for them was a natural style of play; and Tom had to eat his words after the successes of '55 and '56.

Bobbie had reservations about collective training. Where he himself was concerned he would prefer to do his own training and reach peak fitness in a manner best suited to himself as an individual. He felt too that the ordinary supporter has really little idea of the incredible mental pressure that some players are likely to feel on All-Ireland day or even for that matter on a Leinster or Munster final day. This mental strain can weigh heavily on some. Because of this, Bobbie felt that players should be trained and coached and tuned to anticipate the pressure and therefore cope more effectively with it. He would see mental and psychological preparation as being just as important as physical fitness and training.

Before I left Bobbie I asked him how long more he felt he would have continued at county level but for his unfortunate accident in 1957. He felt he could have played up to 1962.

If that had been so, there are many of us who feel that Wexford might well have brought the McCarthy Cup on a few more visits to Slaneyside.

See also photograph of the Rackards on page 156.

Born: 1919

Tony Reddin

"

* I started my career in 1940 with Galway against Cork in junior; played Galway senior in 1943/44. I went to Tipperary in 1947; played for ten years with Tipperary — won three All-Irelands, five Railway Cups, six National Leagues, three Munster medals.

I enjoyed my hurling career, and have many memories of great games.

"

As Tony Reddin entered his thirtieth year it is unlikely that he had All-Ireland medals on his mind. After all, it was an age when many would be contemplating retiring. But great things lay ahead.

The year was 1949, and before that he had never really won the limelight at county level. A native of Mullagh, Co. Galway, he first played senior in the early forties for his native county, and was also on the Connacht Railway Cup panel. There was a gap in his inter-county career until 1946, when he played for Galway against Tipperary in the Monaghan Cup in London.

He played full-forward on Flor Coffey. 'I hit the crossbar; I hit the upright — any shot I hit goalwards was saved by Jimmy Maher. I'm not going to score, I thought to myself, so I changed my tactics. I began to play the ball outwards to the wings so as to feed the incoming forwards. It brought results — but not enough to win the game.'

In 1947 he went to Lorrha in Co. Tipperary in search of work. It was a momentous move; it set the foundations for the emergence of a goalkeeping wizard. A series of superb performances for Lorrha in the North Tipperary championship of 1948 and for Tipperary in League games made him a must in goal when the selectors sat down to pick the 1949 championship team to play Cork in the first round in Limerick. And for Tony what a baptism of fire it was to the fury that can be the stuff of Munster championship encounters!

It took 150 minutes to dispose of Cork — a draw; a second draw, and then extra time. In those two-and-a-half hours there were a hundred battles in front of the goal.

'I was four yards out from goal, covering and watching as backs and forwards tussled. A bulletlike shot flew by me and rebounded from the crossbar and out under my arm before bouncing off the ground and being cleared. It was at a crucial stage in the game. Ring was furious. He maintained the ball had hit the cross-section at the back of the net. But I know from where I was standing and the angle at which the ball passed out under my arm that it had to be the crossbar.

'As Ring exchanged words with the umpire he threw his hurley into the net. It

205

flew in over my shoulder and nearly hit me. I wouldn't let him in for the hurley. "Don't fight," said Tony Brennan, my full-back. "I'm not going to fight; I don't want to fight — but I won't let him in. Let him stay out." The game continued, and Ring got a different hurley. Then a Cork County Board man came round to the umpire. "Ask Tony for the hurley." "Is the time up?" I asked. "Ah, 'tis all over — you have it." I handed out the hurley. "Thanks, Tony, for the hurley," said the Corkman. "Thank you very much."'

On another occasion there was frenzied activity in front of goal, backs and forwards pulling and pushing and falling and covering and shouldering. And suddenly, just nine yards out, Ring loomed up with the ball and prepared to let fly. Tony's mind and reflexes went into simultaneous action. 'Oh, no hope at all — no hope — no hope — no hope. The ball flashed shoulder-high to my left; up went my hurley; it was driven back with the fierce force. I didn't know where the ball was; I felt panicky; then I saw a Cork forward looking up. I looked up and grabbed the ball as it came down in front of goal; I got a belt in the neck as I attempted to clear. Mickey Byrne evened things up for the belt I got in the neck, and the ball was cleared.'

I interrupted his train of thought to ask if it bothered him when players went in on top of him and if he ever felt he had to take care of any of them before they got him. 'No; I always kept my eye on the ball. I never blocked the ball down in the goal: I either caught it or deadened it, and I was good at the side-step. The forward coming in never really bothered me. I felt I could anticipate every situation and instinctively do the right thing.' He stood up to re-enact for me some of the goal-mouth incidents and saves. He gave a commentary on the activity between the backs and forwards and his own positioning as his goal was threatened. The drama of the past came alive again; he re-created the excitement and relived it again. I was able to detect exceptional powers of concentration and anticipation. Add to this his cross-country training, his fearlessness, his deft side-step

and his ability to clear left and right and you have a goalkeeper of tremendous mental alertness and physical agility.

Probably his most horrifying ordeal was at Killarney for the Munster final of 1950. A tense encounter on the pitch was further fuelled when a hostile element of the crowd gathered around Tony's goal. He was pelted and threatened and even obstructed by the blackcoats (a name used in Galway for supporters) in the course of the game. At one stage when he looked back the net was gone — pulled off by the crowd. It was that kind of day. But it ended with a Tipperary victory, and it took three hours before Tony was able to make his way out of the pitch.

There was no hurling tradition in Tony's family; his father's interest was in football. So Tony had no hurling heroes as he grew up. He can't remember his first inter-county game, but he does remember his last, which was played in New York in 1957, when Tipperary won the League. And he remembered too the League final against Wexford in 1956, when Tipperary won the toss and played with a gale in the first half and led by about fifteen points at half time. Despite such a commanding lead, he didn't want to go out for the second half — he was feeling quite sick that day

— but he was prevailed upon and he went out, and Tipperary lost and Tony was dropped.

He is proud to have coached Damien Martin, the great Offaly goalkeeper, and he is delighted that Damien is now passing on Tony's goalkeeping philosophy to the present Tipperary net-minder, Ken Hogan.

In retirement it sometimes happens that an opportunity arises to relive the excitement and the ecstasy of the playing days. This happened for Tony when the Centenary hurling team selected by popular choice was announced in 1984. It was the day after his daughter's wedding, and he was drinking a cup of tea before going to Mass. People started calling and congratulating him. He thought it was about the wedding. Then someone said, 'Did you hear about it? You got it: you're top goalkeeper.'

'I couldn't believe it. I didn't think I could get it — not with Tommy Daly of Clare and Paddy Scanlon of Limerick and Ollie Walsh and Noel Skehan of Kilkenny in the running. I walked up and down the kitchen. I was filled with excitement. I wasn't able to finish the breakfast.

'I set off for Mass. Everyone in Banagher was congratulating me; pulling my coat and slapping me on the back and shaking hands with me. I said no prayers at all at Mass that Sunday — the distraction was too great.' It was the ultimate honour for Tony.

He closed his eyes and his mind went back to the past: to Limerick; to Killarney; to Croke Park. He stood between the posts again; beneath the crossbar; he heard the strains of "Amhrán na bhFiann"; the hurley was firmly gripped; he was standing on the goal line, 'the very spot where many a time he triumphed.'

His ideal fifteen reads as follows:

Tony Reddin *(Tipperary)*

Willie Murphy *(Cork)*	Con Murphy *(Cork)*	John Doyle *(Tipperary)*
Jimmy Finn *(Tipperary)*	Pat Stakelum *(Tipperary)*	Jim Young *(Cork)*
Seán Kenny *(Tipperary)*		John Killeen *(Galway)*
Christy Ring *(Cork)*	Mick Ryan *(Tipperary)*	Jimmy Kennedy *(Tipperary)*
Jimmy Doyle *(Tipperary)*	Nick Rackard *(Wexford)*	Willie John Daly *(Cork)*

Great action from the 1956 All-Ireland Final between Cork and Wexford, showing Christy Ring, Bobbie Rackard and Mick Morrissey with Ring's team-mate Paddy Barry on the ground.

Sports photographer Jim Connolly's classic portrait of Ring in action. A goal about to be scored.

Born: 1920

I failed to get Christy Ring's personal contribution for this book. Not that he refused, but rather that the Great Scorer himself intervened, and Christy was "imithe ar shlí na fírinne" when I began this work in the autumn of 1980. If he had lived he would have been a must for this collection.

Instead I had hoped to settle for the very next best: a written contribution from his brother, Willie John — Christy as seen through a brother's eyes. Unfortunately, when I visited Willie John he felt precluded from making a written contribution. We did, however, have a very pleasant few hours chatting and looking through enormous scrapbooks. Christy is referred to in other parts of this book; but here are some of Willie John's comments about a beloved brother.

'The artist would surface regularly as he practised in the field at Cloyne. For example, the ball would be sent across the goal, and Christy would stretch out the hurley; angle the bos; and the ball would deflect into the corner of the net. He was always emphasising the art of hooking, and the block-down (as distinct from the chop). He could hit the ball going backwards, and make room for himself — and of course he could hit left and right.

'His first game in the Cork senior jersey was against Kilkenny in the League in 1939, as I recollect. His senior championship campaign began in 1940.

'The games that I regard as his greatest were: 1944 against Limerick in the Munster final replay; 1946 versus Kilkenny in the All-Ireland final; 1951 versus Tipperary in the Munster final on Bannon at midfield; 1954 versus Wexford in the All-Ireland final (of Cork's 1:9 that day he scored five points and "made" the goal); 1950 versus Tipperary at Killarney in the Munster final; 1954 versus Galway in the All-Ireland semi-final, and a Railway cup game against Galway when he ran riot.'

His greatest era? 'He didn't really have one as such. He played over a span of twenty years and was always as fit as he could humanly make himself. He was liable to hit a peak and rise to great heights at any time in his career. He never underrated a man — "He is there for a purpose",' he would say.

'Hurling was his whole life.'

These are just a few recollections from a multitude of memories about the "Wizard from Cloyne," who sometimes would spring suddenly on the scene like a hawk or a din of thunder and leave the opposing defence bewitched and bewildered, dumb and dazed, as he did to Limerick in 1956 in the Munster final in Thurles. His cue to swoop was a weak puck-out, and within ten minutes he had hammered home three goals. For good measure and to add drama to drama he grabbed the green flag and waved it in glory to signify one of those goals.

When I was leaving, Willie John told me to stop at the Cloyne hurling pitch and survey the scene where Christy had practised and perfected his hurling sorcery. He had said to me, 'We were very close, very close altogether,' and his eyes had filled with tears.

See also page 95 above.

Born: 1895

"

I loved the game of hurling. I cherish the 1922 All-Ireland win.

Two full-backs that I admired were Johnny Leahy and Fowler McInerney.

"

John's memory was incredible. He painted clear, vivid pictures of games played over half a century ago. He recalled minute details. He still remembered the flight of the ball; the men who combined to make memorable movements; the verbal banter between players; the margins of victory and defeat.

As he talked to me he recalled some of the great names of his day: Johnny Leahy and Martin Kennedy of Tipperary — he said Martin was a great ball-player; "Fowler" McInerney — 'a big, strong hurler — probably the best full-back I played on'; Sim Walton and Mattie Power of Kilkenny

— 'Mattie was one of the great corner-forwards the game has known'; Dr Tommy Daly of Clare — 'a wonderfully consistent goalkeeper'; Jim O'Regan of Cork and Willie Hough of Limerick — 'both rock-like defenders'; Seán Kennedy of Wexford and John T. Power of Piltown — 'both fine athletic figures, who always played the ball and were gentlemen on the hurling-field'; Jack Walsh of Laois — 'a most skilful exponent of the game'.

John would on occasion stand up during our chat to demonstrate how goals were scored and how movements were executed on the field of play. His great enthusiasm for the game surfaced as we recalled the past. Hurling and the GAA were central to his life. He spent ten years on the Leinster Council. He refereed many matches, and had charge of the 1928 All-Ireland hurling final.

His county hurling career began in 1915 when Laois, who were preparing for the All-Ireland against Cork, requested a challenge game so as to get them in trim for the final. It was played at Port Laoise. Kilkenny lined out with nine Dicksboro players and six from other clubs; John recalled that it was a good Kilkenny combination, and they surprised Laois in winning by eight points. Laois, however, went on to beat Cork and record their first All-Ireland win. 'It was a fine Laois side,' said John. He added that Laois had some wonderful hurlers, and he often wondered why they did not win more All-Irelands; he regarded their one All-Ireland triumph so far as poor reward for their efforts down the years.

It took until 1918 for John to establish himself firmly on the Kilkenny team. In a tournament final against Limerick at a

Waterford venue Kilkenny fielded quite a few of the 1908 team. John got his place on the team, replacing Mick Doyle of Mooncoin. He remembered the 1919 Leinster final against Dublin. Sim Walton, veteran of many campaigns since 1904, was recalled. It was hoped that his presence would bring victory, but time had taken its toll, and he was unable to save Kilkenny from a 1:5-to-1:2 defeat.

The unfolding memories brought us to the name of J. J. Hayes of Littleton, who hurled with Tipperary in the 1922 and 1925 finals. John told me that the Hayes family farmed a large holding and employed so many men that at dinner time it was customary for them to spend some time playing a hurling match or practising.

The year 1922 was very special to John: it was the year of his only All-Ireland triumph. If we look at the records we find that Kilkenny won in 1913 and in 1932; in between Dublin and Cork had golden eras, and 1922 stands out in Kilkenny's hurling triumphs. Yet seven minutes from the end of that final against Tipperary they trailed by seven points and to many must have seemed like losing.

John told the story as follows: 'I was playing at full-forward for Kilkenny and was opposed by the renowned Johnny Leahy. Being lighter and less experienced, I wondered how I would best cope with him. The first ball that came in was cleared first time down the field by Johnny as I tried to match him man to man. I changed tactics; when the next ball came in I backed in on Johnny. He was deemed to have fouled me, and from the free a goal was scored. "If you do that again, Roberts, I'll cut the head off you," said Johnny Leahy with a ring of devilment but no malice in his voice. And so the game progressed. It was a very sporting encounter — great ground hurling. There wasn't a scratch on any player; it was fast and free-flowing and most enjoyable.

'With about seven minutes to go we were seven points behind. In a short space of time we got two goals, and with very little time left and Kilkenny only one point in arrears we forced a seventy. Johnny

Leahy and myself decided then that it was going to be a draw, and at that stage both of us were happy to settle for a draw. Dick Grace took the seventy but instead of going over the bar it lobbed into the square.

'I had the ball in front of me and tried to move goalwards, but Johnny Leahy blocked my way; the forwards were like a swarm of bees in the square. I tipped the ball to Dick Tobin on the right. He sent it back to me; I moved it to the left, where Mattie Power was on hand to send the ball to the net.

'From the puck-out the ball went downfield, and a shot from Martin Kennedy went over the bar, but it might just as easily have gone into the net. Before the final whistle Kilkenny added a point to give us a two-point victory over a stunned Tipperary team.'

I asked him if he liked playing full-forward, and he said, 'Not particularly. They played me there because I was able to get scores. I liked the left-half-forward position best; it suited me. I weighed ten stone five and had the speed for the wing.'

John was proud to captain Leinster against Munster in the 1927 Railway Cup final. It is remembered as one of the great games in the series.

I knew he had refereed the 1928 final between Galway and Cork, and I enquired about the controversy surrounding Mick King's injury in that final. John told me he was quite close to the incident when it happened. He remembered that Mick King was moving goalwards for Galway when the ball came across the wing. It was pulled on first time by Jim Hurley and cleared, but in the process of following through he hit Mick King on the knees and he had to be removed from the field. John saw the incident as a genuine accident.

John always admired sportsmanship. He believed that hurling was a game to be enjoyed: a game where you learnt to win, lose or draw with dignity — to cope with life; a game that fostered friendships and good fellowship. His motto always was 'Play fair at all times, and if you lose under that maxim you go down with honour.'

companied by a few friends we cycled the sixty-mile return journey to see it. The names of Lory Meagher, Mattie Power, Paddy Phelan and Padge Byrne of Kilkenny, Mick Mackey, John Mackey, Jackie Power, Timmy Ryan and Mickey Cross of Limerick will live for ever.

Hurling during that period was of a high standard when you consider that the five subs on the Munster Railway Cup team of 1938 were as follows: Timmy Ryan (Limerick), Johnny Ryan (Tipp), Jack Lynch (Cork), John Maher (Tipp), and Jim Ware (Waterford).

It was a great honour for me to play with and against all those great players of that period, and indeed as the years pass by what an occasion it is to meet again with some of those greats! Hurling was and is a way of life for me, and without it life would be much drearier.

Tommy Treacy was my boyhood hero:

The work done at midfield by Treacy was
  grand,
And the cheers for that hero which came
  back from the stand
Will live in our memories until we are dead,
And the crimson-stained bandage he wore
  round his head.

99

❝

I was born into the great hurling parish of Moycarkey-Borris in 1914. Many were the tales I heard as a youth about our great hurlers who represented our parish and county with distinction. I heard of Paddy Maher (Best), Jim Bourke, Ned Hayes, and Matt Ryan. Matt Ryan was an uncle of mine and won his All-Ireland in 1900.

There were seven brothers in my family, and hurling was a second religion to us. The game was played in a small field behind the house whenever the opportunity became available — be it morning, noon, or night.

The best hurling game I have seen was the 1935 League final between Limerick and Kilkenny played at Nowlan Park. Ac-

Hanging on the wall in the sitting-room was a frame containing Johnny's medals. As we browsed through them he told me the stories and the memories that lay behind his favourite one.

'I get a great kick out of having that

medal: it's very historical,' he said as he pointed out one that he referred to as the Black-and-Tan medal. The set of medals was first played for in 1918, with Limerick and Tipperary in opposition. The game ended in a draw. Boherlahan had the Tipperary selection. The replay didn't take place until 1922, and again the game ended in a draw. Shortly afterwards the Tans stole some of the medals, but they were later recovered.

In 1941 Boherlahan regained the Tipperary title and had the selection of the county team in 1942. One of the first things they did was to revive two Gold Medal tournaments of 1920 and 1922. The Black-and-Tan medals were played for and won by Tipperary, and with Johnny it was a treasured possession.

The second medal of special value to Johnny was the Jubilee medal of 1934, won with Moycarkey in the Tipperary senior championship. It is shaped like an All-Ireland medal and bears the heads of Croke, Davin, and Cusack.

Next we came to the 1941 Munster medal. Apart from the fact that Tipperary were delighted to have defeated Cork, the reigning All-Ireland champions, in the "delayed" Munster final of that year, Johnny had the personal privilege of being captain of the team.

Then came the All-Ireland medals of 1937 and 1945, and for these we will let Johnny tell the story. 'I remember well making preparation for the All-Ireland title with Kilkenny in 1937. The game was played in Killarney, as the Cusack Stand was under construction in Croke Park. We felt confident of victory, particularly after our great win over Limerick in the Munster final.

'I had seen Kilkenny two years earlier in 1935 against Limerick in the All-Ireland final. They were two super teams; anyone will tell you that. The game could have gone either way. There was only a puck of a ball between them. The game was over, or so it seemed, while you would be smoking a cigarette. It was great.

'Kilkenny won by a point in torrents of rain. Earlier in the year Limerick had won a League game by two points in beautiful sunshine. As I said, just a puck of a ball between them. I reckoned in '37 that Kilkenny were still a great team. It was the thrill of a lifetime to beat them in Killarney. But '45 was different. At least it was different for me.

'We met Waterford at Fermoy in the first round. Jim Barry was the referee. Ring and Johnny Quirke were two of the umpires (Lord have mercy on all three of them now). It was a hard, tough game. We were getting it heavy. After fifteen minutes the score was Waterford 0:2, Tipperary 0:0. Some of our players were down injured. At a break in play Ring ran in to me and said, "Don't be killing yourself in this game. Admit it now: wouldn't Cork beat the pick of the two of ye by a cricket score?"

'Well, we won the game, and on the way out I met John Mackey. "We had heard great things about ye, but ye're not good enough. It will be left to Limerick again to try and stop Cork," he said.

'Three weeks later we played Cork in Thurles. It was a roasting Sunday. Cork were heading for their fifth All-Ireland in a row. I was playing on the flying Joe Kelly — Irish sprint champion. We confounded all the critics and beat Cork by seven or eight points.

'Then came the Munster final against Limerick. We knew we were up against it. In the first five minutes we got a goal. The game finished with that goal between us on the score 4:3 to 2:6. Peter Cregan was great for Limerick, who had most of the play out the field, but our backs were superb.

'After the game Jack Rochford, the great Kilkenny defender, paid tribute to the Tipp defence when he said, "I often saw backs hold out for ten or fifteen minutes, but that back line of Tipp's today and their defensive play for half an hour was as good as I have ever seen. You were bombarded by Limerick but still held out."

'Our next game was against Antrim and we won by about twenty points, and I was looking forward to the first Sunday in September.

'For seven years in inter-county hurling I hardly got a scratch, but in '45 I got a number of injuries, and also suffered from pneumonia early in the year. Shortly before the All-Ireland I had fluid taken from the knee. I then went for a trial. Thurles Sarsfields, who had the selection, left the decision to me as to whether I would play or not. I was very fit; I wanted to play; but I was afraid I might lose the game for Tipp in the first ten minutes. I would be playing on Jack Mulcahy. I decided against playing, and took my place in the subs.

'And then came the moment of heartbreak: time for the photograph before the match, and I was told to stand back — only the fifteen players. It nearly broke my heart, after all I had gone through in the '45 campaign: Waterford, Cork, Limerick, Antrim, and now stand back.

'If I could go back again I would definitely have lined out.'

For the next five or six years Johnny was always nursing injuries. He was on the fringe of the team on many occasions; he was on the 1949 panel, but a poisoned finger kept him out of the game. As the fifties dawned he was still on the fringe. In the Tipperary county championship he was able to hold his own and often outhurled the regulars of the county team; but at county level Tipperary were now a real force, and getting on the team was a difficult task. He felt he was good enough to have made the Tipperary team that won the League and trip to America in 1950.

He recalled the outstanding display of Tommy Doyle, in the autumn of his career, at left-half-back for Tipp in the 1951 All-Ireland final against Wexford. 'He gave an exhibition,' said Johnny, and a stranger beside me asked who was the young fellow playing for Tipp, 'and there was I the same age and feeling as fit as a fiddle, but by then I knew the end of the road had come for me at county level.'

He recalled a tournament game against Cork in 1950, the O'Donovan Rossa Tournament, played in Cork. Tipp had Jimmy Maher in goal. Jack Lynch, who some time earlier had been elected a TD, went in on Jimmy, as was allowed in those days. Jimmy ran out after him and, putting the hurley up against him, said, 'If you do that

again.there will be a by-election in Cork very soon.'

After the game Johnny met Jim Hurley and Mr O'Neill, who was chairman of the O'Donovan Rossa Tournament committee and who in earlier times had been in charge of the number 7 section of the ambush at Cross Barry. They got to talking about *Guerilla Days in Ireland*, the book newly published by General Tom Barry. 'I'd love to meet Tom Barry,' said Johnny. 'If you ever get a chance to introduce me to him I'd appreciate it,' he said to Jim Hurley.

'Well, I hadn't long to wait,' said Johnny. I was an umpire at the mid-Tipperary final between Holycross and Thurles Sarsfields. An announcement was made over the loudspeaker stating that there were two outstanding personalities at the game: Tom Barry of [old] IRA fame, and Jim Hurley of [old] IRA and GAA fame. After the game Jim Hurley called me and introduced me to Tom Barry. "I wouldn't know you in your clothes," said Tom, "but I'd know you in your togs. Many's the time I cursed you." There I was,' said Johnny, 'in the company of Tom Barry — a man quite small in stature, yet an inspiration in the struggle for independence.'

Johnny then talked about the players he admired. In his boyhood days he had three in particular: Paddy Scanlon, the Limerick goalkeeper, and Tommy Treacy and Phil Purcell of Tipperary. 'Phil was an outstanding hurler. He rarely hit the ball from his hand, nearly always off the ground — same as Mickey Cross, a great man too. Phil could hit the ball left and right. There was power in his clearances. He was the kind of half-back that inspired a team.'

Then there were Paddy Phelan, Mattie Power, and Lory Meagher; Mark Marnell, 'who was able to make things so difficult for Paddy Kenny'; Tim Flood, 'a lovely ball-player with great footwork and who could weave around opponents'; Johnny's brothers "Sweeper", 'who had a great pair of hands,' and Mutt, who beat Limerick in the '45 Munster final; the three Rackards and Padge Kehoe; Willie Campbell of Cork, 'a hurling genius'; Jimmy Doyle, 'a hurling stylist'; Mackey, Ring, and Keher,

Jackie Power and Jack Lynch, John Keane and Garrett Howard — 'the list could go on for ever, but it goes to show how many great hurlers there were,' said Johnny.

He recalled the comrades, the friendships, and the rivalries. 'John Maher, Jim Lanigan, Tommy Doyle, myself, Willie O'Donnell and Dinny Gorman were great buddies. Dinny Gorman and myself were both eight years on the right flank of the defence for Tipp. Not many goals came from that wing; we had great understanding, and knew each other's play inside out.'

Corkmen whose company he often enjoyed were Willie Murphy, Mick A. Brennan, and Johnny Quirke. He recalled visiting Johnny Quirke's pub shortly after he had opened his business, and a sign on display read, *A Quiet one, a Quick one, a Quirke one.*

'Ring and myself used to get on well,' said Johnny. 'He gave me one of his jerseys as a souvenir. It is one of my prized possessions. He was a very different personality to Mackey, who tended to be cavalier and very sociable.' Other Limerickmen with whom he forged great friendships were Jackie Power, Garrett Howard, John Mackey, and Timmy Ryan. 'Yes, that's how it was. Friendship and comradeship off the field; but on the field rivalry could be intense.' Johnny remembered a Gold Medal tournament match in Fermoy between Limerick and Tipp. Parading around the field Timmy Ryan and John Maher had their arms around each other. Then the throw-in — and murder. Any time they clashed it was fire and fury; but coming off the field it was arms around each other again.

In a Gold Medal tournament in North Tipperary, again between Limerick and Tipp, Timmy Ryan was admiring Johnny's hurley at half time. 'I like that pattern,' said Timmy. 'Will you swap with me?' 'I won't give it to you now, but after the match you can have it,' replied Johnny. 'Well, with about seven minutes to go Timmy came out to clear a ball and I went in to meet him. We both clashed, and finished up with the handle of a broken hurley in our hands. We looked at the hurleys; we looked at each other. We went off laughing.' This is the kind of sporting rivalry that Johnny remembered and liked to recall.

For his most memorable games he chose ones at which he was a spectator. He remembered the torrid clash between Cork and Tipperary in the Munster final of 1960, when Tipp came out on top with two points to spare on the score 4:13 to 4:11. It was an extremely tough game, reminiscent of clashes of twenty years earlier. It was a game in which Jimmy Doyle was outstanding.

Johnny felt that the energy Tipperary had to expend in that Munster final, coupled with the hard training they subsequently did, was one of the factors that caused them to fail to Wexford in the final of that year. For the other games he went away back to 1940 and 1944, to the Munster final games between Cork and Limerick. Each went to a replay; all four games were epic encounters that oldtimers talk about whenever those years are mentioned. In 1940 it was Limerick by two points after the replay. In 1944 Cork had a goal to spare — a goal that came from the stick of Ring on the call of time.

But Johnny gave pride of place to the Limerick v. Kilkenny League game of 1935, played at Nowlan Park. This was a game of non-stop delightful hurling. There was never more than a puck of a ball between the teams. It was a game of great sportsmanship. Both line-outs were adorned with some of the greatest hurling artists the game has known. It was a meeting that left a lasting impression on all who saw it.

Johnny used to visit Thurles on the eve of a Munster final. The crowd would be gathering. The atmosphere would begin to build. There would be an expectancy in the air. Fiddlers would play music on the streets; there would be singers too, giving renderings of Irish songs and stirring ballads. It all added up to a fitting overture to the great occasions that would take place on the following afternoon.

Johnny had great praise and admiration for the press. 'Without them there would be no records; I regard them as very important people,' he said. He always loved reading the previews and reviews, and remembered some of the comments and phrases, such as 'Frayed tempers marred the game towards the closing stages.' Seán Coughlan, writing under the pen-name "Green Flag," after the 1937 Munster final in which Tipperary surprised Limerick, didn't write Limerick off but instead said, 'Limerick big guns failed to fire.' Before the 1937 All-Ireland final the heading was as follows:

'Rival captains' opinions; Lanigan pins faith on current form; Experience will tell, says Jack Duggan.'

Paddy Mehigan, who wrote under the pseudonym "Carbery," was perhaps his favourite columnist. In 1945 the Munster hurling selectors were regarded in some quarters as not having chosen the best team in the province, and a second selection was made to challenge the official fifteen. The result vindicated the selectors. In his column Carbery wrote that it was every hurler's ambition to win an All-Ireland medal; but in his opinion the best honour for any hurler was to get on Munster's chosen twenty: to be chosen for your province — the greatest honour of all. It should be 'the proudest feather in any hurler's cap,' in Carbery's opinion.

'Moycarkey for a hurler' was a well-known saying in Tipperary in bygone decades. In Johnny Ryan Tipperary had a hurler who personified this belief.

And then we got to selecting the fifteen that Johnny would like to have captained, and after he had picked it he glanced through it and said, "Oh, dear lord, where did I leave Paddy Phelan, and John Keane, and Jackie Power, and lots of others too.'
His team was as follows:

Tony Reddin *(Tipperary)*

Dinny O'Gorman *(Tipperary)* Tom McCarthy *(Limerick)* Jim Young *(Cork)*

Johnny Ryan *(Tipperary)* John Maher *(Tipperary)* Tommy Doyle *(Tipperary)*

Timmy Ryan *(Limerick)* Jack Lynch *(Cork)*

Christy Ring *(Cork)* Mick Mackey *(Limerick)* Jimmy Doyle *(Tipperary)*

Jimmy Langton *(Kilkenny)* Martin Kennedy *(Tipperary)* Mattie Power *(Kilkenny)*

216

Born: 1910

66

My special memory of matches was to captain the Limerick team in the jubilee year of the GAA, 1934. My regret was that we should have won 1935.

My best players that were in my time were Mickey Cross, Mick Kennedy, Mick Mackey, Jackie O'Connell, Jim O'Regan, Paddy Phelan, Paddy Clohessy, and Jim Hurley.

99

Timmy Ryan's most abiding memories of his hurling days were the sheer enjoyment he got from playing the game, the people he met, the friends he made, and the

friendships that endured. It was a pleasure to reminisce with Timmy about his hurling days. Hurling was a way of life with him; he went to the field to practise every evening and played a match every Sunday.

This great midfielder and model of sportsmanship played for sixteen seasons in the midfield position for his native Limerick. 'It must constitute a record for a midfielder,' said Timmy to me.

We talked about the ban, and Timmy felt that it probably lasted too long. He added, 'Strangely enough, some of our greatest supporters and admirers were rugby players and rugby followers.'

He felt that we had seen many great games of hurling in the last decade, and bemoaned the fact that potentially very good teams go out of the championship in the first round. To overcome this he would have liked to see a losers' group introduced. He visualised this group operating on an open-draw knockout system, with perhaps two teams joining the provincial champions at the final stages of the championship.

While Timmy welcomed changes that help to "clean up" the game, he felt that hurling had become 'a little too refined — too much like tennis. Forwards have too much scope; the backs should be allowed the frontal shoulder.'

He then turned to memories of his playing days. One of the greatest individual displays he saw was given by Mick King of Galway at centre-forward against Clare in the 1932 All-Ireland semi-final.

He felt Limerick were raw in 1933 when they faced Kilkenny in the final. True, they had come to Croke Park with good results in Munster — Limerick 6:8, Clare 1:1;

Limerick 2:9, Cork 1:6; Limerick 3:7, Waterford 1:2; but Kilkenny were battle-hardened and experienced: three finals against Cork in 1931; victory over Clare in 1932; National League champions in 1933. Yes, by comparison Limerick were "raw".

In the second half they put on fierce pressure, but a great Kilkenny defence and goalkeeper held firm. Indeed, so persistent was the Limerick pressure that the backs had moved out towards midfield. It was this set-up that enabled Johnny Dunne to break through for the only goal of the game. Spectators on the sideline shouted, 'Lovely, lovely, Johnny Dunne.' From then on in hurling circles he was to be known as "Lovely" Johnny Dunne.

Timmy remembered Jack Rochford, a Kilkenny stalwart of earlier years, being very impressed by Limerick. Jack felt it was the best team he had ever seen come out of Munster, and wondered how they were beaten.

After the 1933 defeat 1934 had to be a crucial year for Limerick. Timmy was captain, and he dearly wanted to lead Limerick to victory and collect those specially struck All-Ireland medals to commemorate the jubilee year of the GAA. His ambition was fulfilled, but only after a very difficult and testing campaign, involving six games.

In Munster, Clare, Cork and Waterford were overcome. Galway presented stern opposition in a tough and hard-fought semi-final.

It took two games to overcome Dublin in the final. In a great drawn game Timmy recalled that Limerick were fortunate enough to survive a fierce Dublin rally that saw them come from five points down to force a second meeting. 'Dinny O'Neill, a Laois man based in Dublin, played superbly for Dublin,' said Timmy.

The replay, according to Timmy, was even more exciting than the drawn game. But this time it was Limerick who staged the final rally. They drew level with a goal with ten minutes to go. Two minutes from the end it began to look like another draw; but then Limerick struck. Points by Mick Mackey and Jackie O'Connell and a goal by Dave Clohessy carried the day. For Timmy it was a day never to be forgotten. The coveted Jubilee medals had been won. Commenting on the game, one reporter wrote, 'Great men won and great men lost.'

Timmy attributed the 1937 Munster final defeat at the hands of Tipperary to the fact that Mickey Cross was desperately upset following a fire that burned the family property and horses on the morning of the match. Also the goalkeeper, Paddy Scanlon, was unwell that day. In retrospect it was probably unwise to have lined out with both men.

Timmy was always proud of his club, Ahane, and its players, and liked to remind people that a Munster Railway Cup selection in the mid-thirties numbered seven Ahane men in its ranks.

I asked Timmy if he would like to select an ideal team, including himself as captain, from the men of his era. This is his selection:

Paddy Scanlon *(Limerick)*

Johnny Ryan *(Tipperary)*   Seán Óg Murphy *(Cork)*   Mick Kennedy *(Limerick)*
Garrett Howard *(Limerick)*   Paddy Clohessy *(Limerick)*   Paddy Phelan *(Kilkenny)*

Timmy Ryan *(Limerick)*   Harry Gray *(Laois)*

Mick King *(Galway)*   Mick Mackey *(Limerick)*   Jackie Power *(Limerick)*
Johnny Quirke *(Cork)*   Martin Kennedy *(Tipperary)*   Mattie Power *(Kilkenny)*

Joe SALMON

1949-1964   Galway, Eyrescourt and Liam
Mellows (Galway) and Glen Rovers (Cork)

Born: 1931

"

We are blessed with the most wonderful field game in the world. No sport is more skilful, more graceful, more revealing of those who play it, and nobody who has seen hurling played by its greatest exponents can be in any doubt about what beauty is, or graciousness or courtesy either.

There is something else that is innate to hurling: the spirit in which the game is played. You can hurt, maim or even kill a man with a blow from a camán. You can certainly intimidate an opponent more persistently and to more effect in hurling than in any other game. The camán can be a skilful instrument or a bloody weapon; that traditionally it has been the former rather than the latter is something to be proud of — something to be properly cherished and nurtured.

Without a certain decency of spirit hurling would be rendered ugly. Decency in this sense is, like the game itself, distinctly Irish.

"

What age are you? said Vin Baston of Waterford to Joe Salmon in the closing stages of a Railway Cup semi-final. 'I'm twenty,' said Joe. 'You'll be great,' replied Vin. It was prophecy that came true.

Joe's father was a great hurling enthusiast and followed his son's hurling career with deep interest. After a particularly good performance Joe would test his father for reaction, and he often remembers being told, 'You're not as good as Timmy Ryan yet.' In Joe's father's eyes, Timmy Ryan of Limerick was the complete midfielder.

In 1984 the Galway County Board set about finding the Galway Hurler of the Century. A very professional assessment approach was adopted to meet a very difficult task; the chosen player would have to be a man of many skills and in many ways a man apart. The honour fell to Joe Salmon, and he was presented with a magnificent Galway crystal trophy by Seán Ó Síocháin. It was a fitting honour to a great sportsman and hurling artist.

Joe always played for the love and enjoyment of the game. Above all, he played sportingly. He took the view that everyone has to go to work on Monday and meet as sporting friends in future years. He learnt early in his career always to have a healthy respect for his opponent and never to underestimate him.

He recalled the All-Ireland semi-final of 1950, when he was opposed by Tommy Doyle of Tipperary. Joe had won a few Connacht sprint titles. He had the speed and energy of youth. Tommy was in the autumn of his career. After all, Joe was only six years old when Tommy won his first All-Ireland in 1937; he should leave Tommy standing. But no, he was in for a shock and a lesson. The ageless Tommy was as fit as ever, and was beating Joe in the short sprints.

Joe's boyhood heroes were John Killeen and "Inky" Flaherty of his native Galway, and Christy Ring. He played his first game in Croke Park in 1947 when Galway minors were heavily defeated by Tipperary. He watched Ring in the senior final; little did he think then that he would one day be a colleague and team-mate of Ring in the Glen Rovers jersey.

Joe always enjoyed playing against Kilkenny and Cork. These counties played the fast-flowing type of game that suited his style of open hurling, where you kept the ball moving and let it do the work.

He found games against Clare and Tipp 'difficult'. There was a local derby flavour attached to games between Clare and Galway. Tipperary tended to close a game down and make it tight. It was usually close man-to-man combat. Almost every ball was hard-fought and hard-won. He found Theo English a difficult opponent to handle. Ned Wheeler of Wexford was difficult too, but in a different way. Ned had strength and enthusiasm; Theo played it tight and first-time.

But the midfielder he admired most was Phil Shanahan of Tipperary. 'He was great under a dropping ball. Standing over six feet, he was strong and would double first time. He was the best I played on at midfield,' said Joe.

He was on the losing side in three All-Ireland finals. The victories of Wexford in 1955 and Tipperary in 1958 were fairly decisive; but in 1953 when they lost to Cork it was a different matter. Tactically Galway erred that day. A late goal made it 3:3 to 0:8 for Cork. Man for man and as a unit, Galway had superior resources, but did not make use of them wisely.

The previous year, in 1952, the same teams met at the semi-final stages at the Limerick Gaelic grounds. It was a close, low-scoring game with Cork getting the decisive and only goal early in the second half. Joe felt that Galway in 1952 were a better team than the 1953 line-out. In later years he often discussed the 1952 semi-final with his Glen Rovers colleagues; they always agreed that it was a game they would have bitterly regretted losing if they had been wearing the maroon jersey of Galway.

Strangely enough, none of the All-Ireland losses that he himself experienced on the playing-field left him with the same deep sense of disappointment that the defeats of 1981 and 1985 at the hands of Offaly did. 'But,' said Joe, 'all credit to Offaly for their tenacity and never-say-die spirit.'

To a lesser degree he was disappointed with the failure against Kilkenny in 1979. Galway on that day were somewhat better than their opponents in the outfield exchanges, whereas in the games against Offaly they dominated the outfield for long periods but failed to an incredible degree to register that superiority on the scoreboard.

Joe is satisfied that Galway were good enough to have won three in a row from 1979 to 1981, and added that 'ironically, they beat the best team of the three in their historic victory over Limerick in 1980.'

I was particularly interested in Joe's years with Glen Rovers and Christy Ring. When Joe took up duty in Cork he was asked to play for the "Glen." He gave it a lot of consideration, and then accepted. He felt it would help to heal the "sundered friendship" that existed between Cork and Galway after the hostilities, both on and off the field, that surrounded the All-Ireland meeting of those counties in 1953. Ring was anxious to heal the rift. He used to call to Moore's Hotel for Joe and say, 'Come on, we'll go to the pictures.' They struck up a close friendship and a unique relationship. Their personalities blended. There was a bond of trust.

On one of those early calls to Moore's Hotel Ring spent over an hour on the stairs explaining to Joe in great detail his version of the 1953 affair. Joe listened. Christy talked. There was unconscious psychology — a reciprocal empathy — at work. It led to a great clearing of the air; it cemented a friendship and gave Joe a deep insight into Christy's personality.

'Where hurling was concerned Christy was dedication and fanaticism personified. He would be very keyed up beforehand about a game. He would always be quite prepared to listen to a viewpoint or suggestion, but it had to make sound sense. When the reasoning was sound and constructive Ring was a very good listener. Otherwise he could be very dismissive. He had a high code of honour and loyalty, and valued real friendship.'

Christy on occasions used to analyse Joe's hurling talents. He would refer to the speed with which Joe could execute a variety of strokes — strokes that Christy felt he himself might not do as quickly — and then he would add with emphasis, 'But you would not be as strong as I am.'

There is one aspect of the evolving game that bothers Joe. A player puts his hand up for the sliotar; the opponent pulls on the ball and hits the hand as well, and has a free given against him. 'Not cricket,' says Joe. 'Hurling is about pulling on the flying ball. I learnt that in my early years. I was nineteen playing for Erin's Hope against Castlegar. I soloed in from midfield and sent a pass to the winger. I continued into an open space and called for a return pass; it came — a high looping one instead of a fast shoulder-high one. As I grabbed the ball Stephen Connor, the Castlegar full-back — a big, hefty fellow — connected first time and cleared the ball upfield. I shook my bleeding hand — the cut was nasty. The full-back took a look at it. "It will be all right," he said. "Don't put it up again, a mhic."

'I never forgot it. It was a classic example of ciall cheannaithe.'

This is the fifteen Joe would like to have captained:

Seán Duggan *(Galway)*

Bobbie Rackard *(Wexford)*	Pat Hartigan *(Limerick)*	Jim Brophy *(Galway)*
Jimmy Finn *(Tipperary)*	Pat Stakelum *(Tipperary)*	Tom McGarry *(Limerick)*
Joe Salmon *(Galway)*	Phil Shanahan *(Tipperary)*	
Seán Clohessy *(Kilkenny)*	Christy Ring *(Cork)*	Tim Flood *(Wexford)*
Paddy Kenny *(Tipperary)*	Nicky Rackard *(Wexford)*	Josie Gallagher *(Galway)*

Born: 1931

ton, Nicky Rackard, Tony Wall, Jimmy Doyle, Tim Flood, Jimmy Finn, Joe Salmon, and John Doyle.

99

66

No matter how good a player is, he has really lost if he doesn't "play the game". It is vital that he can approach his opponent after a game to shake his hand; it gets more important as the years roll onward.

Tull Considine (Ennis and St Flannan's) was my inspiration. He was doing forty years ago as a coach and trainer what we are now encouraging clubs to do in 1981. He was Ireland's greatest mentor. I never had the pleasure of seeing him play.

Clare must be the most loyal of hurling counties. After years of disappointment and frustration they are still strong in hurling.

Hurling in 1981 is as skilful as ever. Why do we do such grousing?

I had the pleasure of playing with Christy Ring for ten years. It would be interesting to see if many Corkmen, and how many, have played beside him for as long.

My most important memories are of winning five championships with my own parish, Ruan. Players I admired were Christy Ring, Pat Stakelum, Jimmy Lang-

Jimmy Smyth was a true hurling artist. His prowess with a camán demonstrated itself very early on. He went to college to that great hurling nursery, St Flannan's of Ennis, and had the rare distinction of winning three successive All-Ireland college titles in 1945, 1946 and 1947.

His brilliance was spotted by the Clare minor selectors, and at the incredibly young age of fourteen he was selected for the county team. He played county minor hurling for five seasons, thus creating a record in this grade that may never be equalled. I wasn't surprised therefore when he told me he made his senior debut in 1948 at the age of seventeen. He continued to adorn the hurling scene for a further nineteen years until 1967.

During that time if he had been a Tipperary man he would have won eight All-Ireland medals and joined the élite ranks of John Doyle and Christy Ring. In the Cork jersey he would have shared in four All-Ireland successes. If he had been born by the Noreside and donned the black-and-amber, three All-Ireland victories would have come his way. As a Wexfordman he would also have won three All-Ireland medals, and who knows but he might have hung on for a fourth in 1968, and this would have set a record for a Wexfordman in hurling. But with his native Clare, All-Ireland senior hurling success was not to be, even though there were occasions in the fifties when Clare gave displays that suggested they had All-Ireland material.

Jimmy knows only too well what it is like to hope and wish, and fail to reach the promised land in hurling. But for him there are more important things. He has his own philosophy about hurling. Good sportsmanship he regards as most important.

Tull Considine was his inspiration, and Jimmy regrets that he never saw him hurl. He regards Tull as having been far ahead of his time in his coaching and training methods.

Like Brendan Considine, Jimmy is loud in his praise of Clare's loyal supporters, and he feels the game is still very strong in Clare. In Jimmy's opinion hurling at the present time is as good as ever and he welcomes the changes that have tended to open up the game and shift the emphasis from the physical to the skilful.

Looking back on his hurling days some special recollections come to mind. The first was the wonderful feeling of pride he felt on each of the five occasions that he won the Clare senior hurling title with his native Ruan. Then there was that great victory over Wexford in the Oireachtas final of 1954 that went to a replay. It was special because a wonderful Wexford team were on the threshold of a great era.

In 1949 he captained the Clare junior team. They were beaten by London in the All-Ireland final in Ennis. Jimmy's recollection is that they were six or seven points up with about five minutes remaining but a number of 21-yard frees to London saw victory snatched from Clare. A great hurler and captain knew disappointment.

Jimmy Smyth (Cl), on left, and Johnny McGovern (K), centre, and J. Maher in the 1958 Railway Cup at Croke Park, Leinster v Munster.

Finally there was the great honour of having played beside Christy Ring for ten years on the Munster team. His last Railway Cup victory with Ring was in 1963. Here was the Munster line-out:

	Mick Cashman *(Cork)*	
Jimmy Brohan *(Cork)*	Michael Maher *(Tipperary)*	John Doyle *(Tipperary)*
Tom McGarry *(Limerick)*	Tony Wall *(Tipperary)*	J. Byrne *(Waterford)*
	P. J. Keane *(Limerick)*	Jackie Condon *(Waterford)*
Jimmy Doyle *(Tipperary)*	Tom Cheasty *(Waterford)*	Dónie Nealon *(Tipperary)*
Jimmy Smyth *(Clare)*	Christy Ring *(Cork)*	Liam Devaney *(Tipperary)*

Born: 1927

Pat Stakelum:

66

The aims and ideals and construction of the GAA were lost on me until I had finished my playing career. For me hurling was everything in sport from a very early age. As one of a family of ten with modest means, growing up in the depression of the thirties, I do not know what I would have done without the great happiness which I experienced from playing hurling. We were encouraged by my father to play hurling, and to play it well. You were a bit of a joke until you could strike both left and right. I vividly remember that part of the development.

Hurling was the most topical conversation in our house. People who made the parish team were our heroes. The one, Dinny Gorman, who made the county team — he was God in our youthful eyes.

We thrilled to hear people who were at big games talking about the happenings there. Radio and Mícheál O'Hehir had a big influence on us. I would say that I learnt to read from studying the Monday reports from "Carbery" (P.D. Mehigan), "Green Flag," etc. I was never in Dublin until I

played a minor All-Ireland in 1945. The game helped me to make great friends. Hurlers are a special breed of people. The parish team victories are happy memories for me. The three-in-a-row team-mates are also very special friends. Opponents from all counties are also good friends and happy memories. I did not make one enemy that I am aware of.

When I finished playing I spent a few years in administration, and then I drifted into a kind of limbo. I became involved in juveniles, and now I am "cured" again.

There are times I fear for the games, and hurling in particular. There are many other attractions, and we must be prepared to ensure that our young players are cared for. Many players quit after playing, and the central authorities must find a way to get ex-players involved in training young players. CBS schools and colleges must be encouraged and respected for what they are doing. We have an obligation to future generations to pass on the great game as healthy as we got it from those who went before us.

The Limerick and Cork games of the late thirties and early forties were the greatest games of hurling I ever saw. Mackey, Scanlon, Timmy Ryan, Clohessy, Power, Donovan, Lynch, Ring, Quirke, Lotty — they were all great.

When the final whistle for me has blown
And I stand at last before God's judgement
  throne,
May the Great Referee when he calls my
  name
Say, You hurled like a man — you played
  the game.

Good luck, Brendan. You have brought

back many memories. God be with those who are gone, and God speed the camán in the future.

,,

'I was only a garsún,' said Pat to me, 'as I watched the drawn and replayed Munster final of 1940 between Limerick and Cork in Thurles. I was there again in 1944 watching another draw and replay between the same counties. Those were the greatest games I have seen. They were super teams — they were mighty men. They had a major influence on my game. Hurling reached a pinnacle then that has not since been equalled; if we had videos of those games at present they would be on television every week.

'After those games we used to go home and go out hurling, all ten of us — even the girls in our house played hurling — and we were all Mick Mackeys and Paddy Clohessys and Johnny Quirkes.

'My father, who was the finest man I ever met, encouraged us all to play hurling, and some say he was a better hurler than I was. There was always a feeling that we were safe and involved in a healthy activity when we were hurling. We were very happy playing the game. We made our own hurleys, and hurleys were handed down from the oldest to the youngest. I can remember one Christmas when my uncle sent three hurleys for the "chislers." I was fourth in line and had to settle for a hand-me-down.

'In our family there was great comradeship and team spirit and great respect for one another. It enabled me in later life to fit easily into a team; it also made me tolerant and considerate. It helped me too to encourage others and to praise honest endeavour.'

There are moments now when Pat fears for the future of the game. 'The Government is blind to a national culture and heritage as it imposes VAT on hurleys. It is an example of lack of foresight and vision — they should be encouraging the game and encouraging the youth to play it.'

To really succeed, Pat is convinced that we must begin with the youth. He believes that the decline in Tipperary's hurling started with the decline of the game in Thurles and the surrounding parishes, coupled with the absence of a youth policy. 'It is as natural for a kid from Thurles to hurl as it is to walk,' says Pat, and he believes that our approach to youth and their playing of the game must be one of "Mol an óige."

For about seven years now he has been involved with Durlas Óg, a club that caters for young hurlers up to sixteen years old. Pat has found that it brings its own special rewards and joys, both in victory and defeat — like the occasion when a little fellow of twelve jumped high into Pat's arms after winning and cried with happiness, or 'to watch a smile and a face light up following a word of appreciation and to see them go home with a buzz in their little hearts. To be out in Boherlahan or Knockmore with juvenile teams might be lacking in glamour and far removed from media coverage and publicity, but I have found it more rewarding than my work as senior county selector.'

He has a special word of praise for the Christian Brothers, especially in Thurles, where he says they never lost their love and commitment for the game. He mentioned in particular Brother Keane from Clare and Brother Higgins from Cork, and wondered if the time and sacrifice and energy given by them to our national game was appreciated by the powers that be. They used their own small incomes to subsidise hurleys for their young teams; Pat contrasts this with the vast sums spent by the GAA on concrete and development and other activities, and wonders if the priorities are a little unbalanced.

His hurling days with his native Holycross always conjure up the happiest of memories. Being on the parish team was something special. Hurling was the topic no matter where you went in the parish: at the crossroads; at the forge; after Mass; at funerals; at the threshing; and at the hay-saving, of course. Club victory united the entire parish. It bred a sense of pride; it elevated people. Pat recalls the supporters in victory expressing themselves in the noblest and most simple of ways, with a depth of sincerity and an open innocence. It was reflected glory at its best.

The most dramatic scene Pat ever witnessed in a dressing-room during his hurling career was in Limerick in 1949, after the replay between Cork and Tipperary had ended in another draw. Here is how Pat recalls the occasion.

'When Holycross beat Lorrha in the final of the Tipperary senior championship in 1948, they had a large say in the county selection. They cast the net wide in an effort to find a blend that would put Tipperary back on a winning trail. There was a good blend of experience and youth in the team that played Cork. The game had been played under a scorching sun. Extra time would be a test of character and endurance.

'As we headed for the dressing-room I was beside Paddy Leahy. Reddin was limping. "Don't limp," said Leahy — the psychological battle was now on. Passing by Jack Lynch, Leahy said, "Isn't it great stuff, Jack? How will we decide on it at all?" "I don't know," said Jack, "but I have enough of it." On hearing this comment Leahy put a spring in his step and made haste for the dressing-room.

'Tipperary were the younger team. Someone had overheard Con Murphy, the Cork full-back, declare that he was having some difficulty handling Sonny Maher. It was more sweet music to the Tipperary ears.

'The question now was would extra time be played or not. The dressing-room was crowded. It included two priests — Fr Barry, a Passionist, and Fr Dwyer. In the normal way these priests would be vying with each other before a game as to who should bless the ball. Now they were united: there would be no extra time; it would be immoral to demand any more of the boys. It was then that Paddy Leahy spoke. "This is a moment of crisis," he said. "All out except the players." "Aye, aye," said the two priests. "Sorry, but that includes you, father, and you, father, too," said Leahy.

'Now only the players and Leahy remained. Leahy assumed supreme command. High drama was about to unfold. Some of the players were mumbling that they had enough and there should be no extra time. Leahy called for silence, and commanded that all those prepared to do battle in the Tipp jersey to move to his right, and those who couldn't cope to stand to the left. The left remained empty.

'It was now time to move out again under the evening sun. Seán Kenny's voice was heard to say, "I can't go out." "What's wrong?" said Leahy. "The bandage is falling off my head," came the reply. "Tear it off," said Leahy. 'Twas done. "Out now," he said. There was a charge — we got stuck in the door going out. Within the hour we returned through the door bearing victory. It was the greatest moment of my career.

'Back in Thurles I collected my bicycle and headed for Holycross with my boots and socks on the handlebars, and would you believe it, the Munster Senior Hurling cup too was taken on the bike after the victory over Limerick in the final. I have the bike still — I got it done up. I'm mad about that ould bike.'

The 1949 Tipperary team that was fashioned out of Holycross's county win in 1948 gradually matured. They had their share of good fortune — which must be with you in the championship — as they triumphed in Munster over Cork, Clare, and Limerick. By 1951 they were a formidable outfit. Sound and solid, they had developed a confidence in each other and had knitted together in a manner that brought them three All-Irelands in a row.

Pat had come a long way in the hurling world since that day in 1947 when Holycross awaited with trepidation the throw-in in their championship game against Thurles Sarsfields. Paddy Leahy said to Fr Fogarty, 'Come here and wish luck to your native boys.' 'I hope ye win, we need a change,' was his terse good wish, and win they did.

And he remembers too the day in 1947 that they went down to play Tullaroan in a friendly and Lory Meagher refereed the game, and they all felt honoured to be in his

Top: The changing sliotar, 1886 to 1990s.
Below: Protection for the captain as Pat Stakelum leads out his team.

presence. It was a milestone in Pat's hurling life. And memory lane had lots more too. Tony Reddin was discovered during the 1948 Tipp championship, and his many great performances between the Tipperary posts makes him Pat's number one goalkeeper.

He sees Kilkenny as the county of great stylists and purists where they live the game and where it is a religion. His work took him to Kilkenny for over twenty-one years, where he met and talked with the greats — Jack Rochford, Dick Grace, Sim Walton, Paddy Phelan, the Byrnes, Jack Mulcahy, Jimmy Kelly, Jimmy Walsh, Jimmy O'Connell, and Jimmy Langton — and loved it all. The Mackeys, Timmy Ryan and Paddy Clohessy were childhood heroes who left a lasting impression.

He has always felt that the arrival of Wexford gave the game a fabulous lift. 'They brought something new to it. They were mighty men with a sense of fair play that was quite remarkable. The Rackards adorned the game, and so did Padge Kehoe, Ned Wheeler, Tim Flood, and Nick O'-Donnell,' he said.

And then he talked of other hurlers. 'Jackie Power of Limerick was a tremendous player who could play any place and with great authority. Paddy Barry of Cork was a most under-rated player. Josie Hartnett of Cork, who was often my immediate opponent, was a tough opponent: a useful team man, hard to stop, hard to excel on; he would knock his rights out of you. Ring was a major influence on the game — a man of incredible determination, blind fury, and commitment to victory. Tommy Doyle was a fitness fanatic, a good ambassador for the game, and a fine example to youth.'

He had memories too of the centre-backs of the game: John Maher of Tipperary, 'a most dedicated player, who copperfastened the great Tipp defence of 1937'; Paddy Clohessy of Limerick, 'a striking figure on the field who dominated many games in a great career'; Bobbie

Rackard of Wexford, 'a marvellous sportsman who always demonstrated authority in his style'; and Tony Wall of Tipp, who opened up his hurling career as a moderate player. 'He was tried in many positions and was persevered with until he eventually found his true position at centre-back. He was a deep thinker of the game. He made a detailed study of the centre-back position and emerged as a highly accomplished player and one of the great centre-backs the game has known.'

For an assessment of Pat Stakelum as a centre-back we can look at what some of the sports writers of the early fifties had to say. 'Pat Stakelum is perhaps the greatest centre-back since Jim O'Regan of Cork or Paddy Clohessy of Limerick,' said "Pato" in the *Irish Times* of Tipperary's return to form, which, he added, 'was as rapid as it was remarkable.' After Tipperary's victory over Limerick in the 1951 championship, one commentator wrote: 'The laurels of the day must go to Pat Stakelum who was invincible in the half-back line.' And another writer said, 'In defeating Limerick 3-8 to 1-6 on Sunday Tipperary put up their best performance for a long time. Man of the Match was Pat Stakelum of Holycross whose individual brilliance both in defence and long range scores inspired his fellow defenders at a time when Limerick were going great guns to crash their way through the champions' lines.'

Pat retired from the game in 1957 at the relatively young age of thirty. (He did return in 1959 for the game against Waterford, but Tipp lost.) He found himself slowing down, and he was fearful of perhaps getting 'ugly'. Good sportsmanship was always important to him. It is his proud boast that he was never sent off the field, nor was his name ever taken by the referee.

He feels privileged to have played the game at the highest level. It brought him great enjoyment. It made many friendships. It enriched his life. Pat says he is always at home with people who are interested in hurling.

Born: 1920

When Dick Stokes was thirteen years of age he witnessed the arrival of a great Limerick hurling combination in 1933. They were to be his boyhood heroes, and in particular Timmy Ryan and Mick Mackey. He was destined to join them in 1940 and share in the glory of Munster and All-Ireland victories.

He still had the programme of the Munster final of 1940 between Cork and Limerick; he made me a present of it. It cost him three old pence — just a little over a present-day penny. Admission to the field was a shilling (five new pence); stand, one shilling extra; sideline, two shillings extra.

Limerick gave a completely different positional line-out from the team they actually fielded, so as to mislead and confuse the Cork officials — it was a ruse that would meet with severe censure from the media nowadays.

The programme reproduced Dr Croke's letter of December 1884 to Michael Cusack (reprinted at the end of this book). Its content reflected the mood of the times. How different in tone and spirit was the address in 1940 at the Munster convention by the chairman, Seán Mac Cárthaigh, which the programme also carried. Here is his address:

'What a pride and glory it is to witness the stirring scenes associated with a well played, cleanly and keenly contested Gaelic match, especially in hurling; to feel the thrills coursing through one's veins as the springy ash camáns crash in the air above and on the sod below; and to realise that here is being enacted before our excited and admiring gaze a vivid symbol of long ago, a sure reminder that Knocknagow is not dead; and a striking and soul stirring

"

I would consider the following to be the highlights of my playing career:

The privilege of playing with so many of the great Limerick team of the thirties who continued to play on to 1945; and my association with the Limerick All-Ireland team of 1973.

The winning of an All-Ireland medal (1940) might be regarded as the high point in any player's career; however, the ups and downs of playing the game is equally important as a most valuable asset towards personal development and objectivity, in coping with real life situations.

The large number of very sincere friends amongst players and officials which are made and have lasted over the years in all parts of the country.

There were so many great hurlers down through the years that I would hesitate to mention just but a few.

"

guarantee that by Shannon, Suir and Lee and by hillside and glenside throughout the province, the virile manhood and traditions of our race are keeping a firm hold on their hard won inheritance.'

It also contained an address from Rev. Father Meagher, chairman of Tipperary County Board. It reflects a mood of the times that the present generation may find difficult to understand and identify with. He was exhorting a yet infant and emerging nation to have pride in its heritage. Here is an excerpt:

'There is an old saying with a little change: 'Let me sing a nation's ballads and I don't care who makes its laws.' Let us sing the nation's ballads at our big matches. It would help us very much if suitable songs were printed in the official programmes as is done in Croke Park. How grand and inspiring it would be if all joined in and sang these songs of yore that kept the flame of nationality alive and incidentally helped to make Ireland what the Warrior Bold once called it — Land of Song.'

It was Dick's first year in inter-county hurling, and he was rewarded with a Munster medal and an All-Ireland medal. There followed in the early forties some close riproaring encounters with Cork — games that might have gone either way; games that were won with a score on the call of time; games that took Cork on to easy All-Ireland victories and left Limerick talking about what might have been.

There were so many occasions down the years since 1940 when Limerick appeared to be plagued with ill luck against Cork. They lost games that they seemed to have won and on occasions should have won. All that would change, however, in the Munster Final of 1980. It was the first time that Dick saw Limerick getting the breaks against Cork. It is interesting to recall them.

Limerick's first goal came early in the first half. A ball was floated into the Cork goal-mouth; the goalkeeper failed to hold it. Backs were lying across the Cork goal-line. Éamon Cregan with all the experience of a veteran spooned the ball up into the roof of the Cork net: a magic score, a dream start. Midway through the second half

came the second Limerick goal. A long free by Dónie Murray went down the right wing towards the Cork goal. Two Cork defenders went for it and collided. In a flash Ollie O'Connor gathered, soloed goalwards, shot hard, and the green flag waved. This was the crucial score. It came at a time when Cork were pressing hard and reducing Limerick's lead.

Fierce Cork pressure followed. They had narrow misses. They missed a seventy; they even hit the upright with a rasper. At the final whistle it was Limerick 2:14, Cork 2:10. Limerick had won, and for once the gods had smiled on them.

Dick felt that Cork and Kilkenny hurlers possess what he described as 'a sense of movement in their style' that has tended to give them something extra that stands to them, particularly in close encounters. The Galway side of the present time has, he felt, that same quality.

Dick was most reluctant to single out any one player above another for the title of the "best ever" in a given position. He said that in any decade several players can adorn each position on the field with rare distinction. He was, however, prepared to admit that it would be very difficult to find anyone to surpass Nick O'Donnell at fullback, and talking of full-forwards he took the view that Paddy McMahon of Limerick 'was as good as any of them.'

Dick himself has a unique record that may never be equalled. He was the only player to have the distinction of winning Dublin county senior hurling and county senior football titles with UCD. The football title was won in 1943, and the hurling success was achieved in 1947.

Dick had all the attributes of a first-class hurler, among them versatility and outstanding sportsmanship. His dedication was exceptional. A Munster GAA correspondent wrote as follows: 'In seeking the outstanding player of 1951 I am not looking for the individual that thrilled Croke Park crowds or proved the main factor in bringing great success to his Club or County. Rather I am seeking the man who by his example and self sacrifice did most for the games of the Gael during the season just concluded. Dr Stokes has never failed to answer the call of Club or County sometimes at great personal inconvenience, and already knowing that many of the "regulars" would be absent ... playing his part with earnestness and a do or die spirit that nothing could quench.'

He has a fund of hurling stories, and two of them are worth recording. Some decades ago a hurling match took place in Maynooth among the clerical students. While thoughts and acts within the college centred mainly on heavenly things, it seems that on occasions all hell would break loose on the hurling pitch. Early on in the game a student who was injured made his way to the matron's surgery. 'What happened you?' she asked. 'Kinnane hit me,' came the reply. A little later another wounded player arrived at the surgery. The matron asked the same question. The reply was the same: 'Kinnane hit me.'

Before long another injured player arrived at the surgery. By now the matron felt she had grasped the trend of things. 'I suppose Kinnane hit you too,' she said as she looked at a pretty dazed youth. 'No,' came the reply. 'I'm Kinnane.' Years later this student was to become Archbishop of Cashel.

The second story relates to a day when Limerick went to play Cork in a National League game. On arrival in Cork they discovered that they had only fourteen men, and they called "Leftie" O'Brien, who used to carry the hurleys and jerseys, to go into goal. "Leftie" protested, but in the end agreed to stand between the posts. Those were the days when forwards used to sweep ball, goalkeeper and anything else that came in their way into the back of the net. "Leftie" had visions of nightmares. He kept turning around in his mind the enormity of the task facing him. He was wondering how he was going to cope with the job of keeping his eye on the ball and blocking and clearing it, and at the same time cope with the inrushing forwards.

After some deliberation he obviously decided it was better to specialise and do one aspect of the job well, because when the backs came back into position he went out to Mick Hickey, the Limerick full-back, tapped him on the shoulder, and said, 'Mick, you can let the forwards in — keep the ball out.'

Dick won his second Railway Cup medal with Munster in 1943 in a team that comprised some of the giants of hurling. This was the line-out:

Jimmy Maher *(Tipperary)*

Willie Murphy *(Cork)*   Batt Thornhill *(Cork)*   Peter Cregan *(Limerick)*

Andy Fleming (Waterford)   John Keane (Waterford)   Jim Young (Cork)

Jack Lynch (captain) *(Cork)*   Dick Stokes *(Limerick)*

Christy Ring *(Cork)*   Jackie Power (Limerick)   Tommy Doyle *(Tipperary)*

Johnny Quirke *(Cork)*   Willie O'Donnell *(Tipperary)* Mick Mackey *(Limerick)*

(During the game, John Mackey of Limerick replaced Willie O'Donnell of Tipperary.)

Born: 1943

When he was young he used to watch a car call at Johnny McGovern's home. He would see Johnny climb in with his hurley and togs and be driven off to hurl for his native Kilkenny. Jim used to dream that some day he too would be collected and taken to play for his county. That dream came true.

Being captain in 1967 was a wonderful honour. The victory had special significance: the Tipperary bogey was laid. It was forty-five years since Kilkenny had beaten Tipp in an All-Ireland.

The statistical fact sounds worse than the reality. Since 1922 they had only met four times in finals, but each time victory went to Tipp. The green-and-gold jersey was becoming a nightmare in Kilkenny. Some were even saying that the black-and-amber would never cope with the Tipperary jersey. In 1922 Kilkenny were seven points down with about as many minutes to go, but they put in a storming finish to win by two points. Little did they think that forty-five years would elapse before they would again triumph in an All-Ireland over Tipp.

It was interesting to recall with Jim those four defeats. In 1937, when the final was played in Killarney, a Kilkenny fifteen that had many a household name in its ranks went down heavily to Tipperary on the score 3:11 to 0:3. Eight years later Tipperary halted Cork as they headed for five in a row, and accounted for Kilkenny in the final by 5:6 to 3:6. But the game was closer than the two-goal margin might suggest.

Came 1950, when Jimmy Langton's shooting was off target and one point separated the sides on the score 1:9 to 1:8. It

> **"**
>
> My greatest memory was the 1967 All-Ireland hurling final against Tipperary. I had the honour of being captain on that occasion. It was a great honour for me to receive the McCarthy Cup from a Tipp win. It was the first time Kilkenny beat Tipperary in a final for over forty years.
>
> All the success I had in hurling I owe to my club, Bennettsbridge. We had some great hurlers in our club that I looked up to: to name a few — Dan Kennedy, John McGovern, Mick Kelly, and Séamus Cleere.
>
> **"**

At about five o'clock on the first Sunday in September 1967, Jim Treacy, captain of the Kilkenny hurling team, held the McCarthy Cup high as he stood in the Hogan Stand and listened joyfully to thousands of Kilkenny fans chant cheers of victory. It was a great moment for this left-full-back from Bennettsbridge.

was no consolation to Kilkenny folk that they had plenty of chances to win the game. The next meeting was 1964. Tipp had a powerful fifteen; Kilkenny were reigning champions. For the black-and-amber the result was humiliating: 5:13 to 2:8.

But it's a long road that has no turning; and the turning came with the final whistle in 1967. It was sweet music to Kilkenny ears, and a moment of elation for Jim Treacy. Kilkenny had played some very fine hurling in an hour of tense excitement. Ollie Walsh was outstanding; the cover from his backs was excellent. The scoreboard read Kilkenny 3:8, Tipperary 2:7. A county's pride was restored. For Jim Treacy no other successes would be quite the same.

The Kilkenny teams that bridged the 45-year gap were as follows:

1922

Walter Dunphy (captain)	Edward Dunphy	M. McDonald (goal)
John Holohan	James Tobin	Thomas Carroll
Richard Grace	William Kenny	Patrick Glendon
Pat Aylward	Martin Lawlor	John Roberts
Pat Donohue	Mattie Power	Richard Tobin

1967

Ollie Walsh

Ted Carroll	Pa Dillon	Jim Treacy (captain)
Séamus Cleere	Pat Henderson	Martin Coogan
Paddy Moran		J. Teehan
Eddie Keher	Tommy Walsh	Claus Dunne
J. Bennett	J. Lynch	M. Brennan

Dublin Senior Hurling Championships 1947 — the UCD team of which Dick Stokes (p.229 above) was a member.

Born: 1904

**
There were four players I had a particular admiration for: Mick Mackey, Christy Ring, John Maher, and Mick Gill.
**

Tommy Treacy was resting in bed and recovering from the effects of a stroke when I visited him at his home in Phibsborough, Dublin. Energies that in his younger days were channelled into hurling were now being directed towards regaining his health.

He told me that hurling colleagues would call to see him from time to time and that he particularly enjoyed recalling the past with them. I told him that I had visited Mick Mackey, who was also recovering from a stroke. He enquired with deep interest about Mick's well-being and rate of recovery. He seemed very pleased to hear that Mick was progressing well and was out and about again.

In between conversation Tommy used to whisper a prayer: 'Thank God for today, please God for tomorrow.' He said this many times. Speaking in a quiet, almost sad voice he recalled moments from the past, especially 1930, when he won his first All-Ireland title with a Tipperary team that included greats like John Maher, Martin Kennedy, Phil Purcell, and Phil Cahill.

'Martin Kennedy was a household word in my day. He gave so many great displays for Toomyvara, Tipperary, and Munster. 1930 was a great year for Tipp hurling, for they won the three All-Ireland titles. We toured America in September of that year and won all our games. We were called "world champions." I have very happy memories of that great tour.'

Tommy played with Dublin in the 1934 championship, and was critical of a decision by the Dublin mentors in the final of that year. 'They brought on a one-armed man,' said Tommy to me, referring to Charlie McMahon, who had an injured hand and whom the Dublin selectors introduced as a sub during the game. Tommy felt it cost Dublin the match.

A game he recalled with particular satisfaction was a League encounter with Limerick in 1936, 'and we were proud to beat such a great Limerick team. I recall Paddy Clohessy, the Limerick centre-back, as one of the best and toughest opponents I used to encounter.' The way times have changed is illustrated by the fact that one Sunday in 1937 Tommy played a Dublin championship match with Young Ireland and then took off with Jimmy Cooney to play a Munster championship game against Cork. The game had started when they arrived, but they were happy to see their native Tipperary win by one point. Later that year Tommy played a major part in Tipp's unexpected defeat of Limerick in the Munster final.

In hurling circles Tommy was seen as a player who epitomised typical Tipperary steel in his wholehearted and full-blooded approach to the game. He regretted that he had departed the scene when Tipperary won the 1945 title: he would have liked to share that third medal victory with John Maher.

Mick Gill, the great Galway hurler, who died some days after Galway's All-Ireland victory over Limerick in 1980, was a life-long friend of Tommy's. There was a feeling of pride in his voice as he told me that Mick Gill used to tell him that he 'was the best he ever played on.'

We looked through photographs and some cuttings, and then we came across a Christmas card that he cherished with affection. He had received it at Christmas 1980 from his great friend Brother Joseph Perkins, a Christian Brother. Written on the card was: *To Tommy Treacy, the Greatest ... 50 years ago – 1930*: and then he quoted a verse from a song that was composed to commemorate the 1930 victory:

'The work done at midfield by Treacy was grand
And the cheers for that hero come back from the stand
"T will live in our memory until we are dead
And the crimson stained bandage he wore round his head.'

These stirring lines recalled characteristics of courage and vigour. Now I was observing qualities of resignation and deep faith.

Talking with Tommy had been a special experience, most enjoyable and deeply rewarding. As I prepared to go he talked again about Mick Mackey's rate of recovery. I felt he was searching for hope for himself, and as I left thea room I heard that whispered prayer again: 'Thank God for today, please God for tomorrow.'

Here is the line-out that gave Tipp and Tommy Treacy one of their greatest hurling victories by defeating Limerick 6:3 to 4:3 in the 1937 Munster final:

		Tommy Butler		
Dinny Gorman		Ger Cornally		Jim Lanigan
Johnny Ryan		John Maher		Willie Wall
	Jimmy Cooney		Jack Gleeson	
Jimmy Coffey		Tommy Treacy		Tommy Doyle
Willie O'Donnell		"Bunny" Murphy		"Sweeper" Ryan

The same team beat Kilkenny in the All-Ireland final at Killarney — 3:11 to 0:3.

Ollie Walsh rises to clear the ball. (Photo: Jim Connolly)

Born: 1937

to be the goalkeeper on the team.

The next step in my career was when I was selected to play for the Kilkenny under-fourteen team in 1949. This was the first inter-county schools championship match to be played, and we beat Dublin at Harold's Cross.

In 1953 I was selected to play for the Kilkenny minor team — again against Dublin, but this time we got to play in Croke Park, which is the dream of every hurler. I can still visibly remember standing at the dressing-room door under the Cusack Stand and looking out onto the hallowed ground. Little did I think as a boy in Thomastown listening to Mícheál O'Hehir describe the Canal End and the Railway End and the exploits of the famous men of that era that I would get to represent my county and play in what is the mecca of Gaelic games.

Three years later — 1956 — I was selected on the Kilkenny senior team and got a baptism of fire when I had to face the wonderful Wexford team of that time — Nicky Rackard and all. Unfortunately we were beaten that day, but one year later I achieved what every schoolboy in Ireland dreams of — an All-Ireland senior medal — when we defeated Waterford.

I went on to play for eighteen years in

66

Hurling has been a way of life for me as long as I can remember. Even as a little boy going for the messages for my mother I had to have the hurley and the ball with me. I was fortunate that my mother and father loved hurling, and I was encouraged and helped in every way. I was also very lucky in that the local schoolteacher — Peadar Laffan — was a fanatic for the game, and any of the local boys who showed any promise were encouraged all the way.

The first great moment in my hurling life came when I was nine years old. After the school had trained from the previous September we were all called into the classroom after school on a March day in 1947, and the team for the forthcoming championship was announced. My joy knew no bounds when it was announced that I was

---

The team that I would pick to play in (only players I played with and against) would be:

Ollie Walsh *(Kilkenny)*

Jimmy Brohan *(Cork)*	Pa Dillon *(Kilkenny)*	Billy Rackard (Wexford)
Séamus Cleere *(Kilkenny)*	Mick Roche *(Tipperary)*	Martin Coogan *(Kilkenny)*

John Connolly *(Galway)*   Frank Cummins *(Kilkenny)*

Jimmy Doyle *(Tipperary)*	Tom Cheasty *(Waterford)*	Eddie Keher *(Kilkenny)*
Tom Walsh *(Kilkenny)*	Nicky Rackard *(Wexford)*	Christy Ring *(Cork)*

goal for Kilkenny, and during those years won every major honour in the game. While winning was and is the name of the game, the enjoyment and the friends I made during the years are even more important, and wherever I go in Ireland now I meet with friends and acquaintances and we reminisce on those years. It has been wonderful to be involved all those years in the game that I love so much, and I still keep in touch with affairs by training and coaching teams in the county.

,,

It was Ascension Thursday in 1956, and Ollie Walsh was enjoying the swing-boats at a carnival in his native Thomastown when a Kilkenny mentor shouted up at him: 'Come down — you're on the panel to play against Wexford.'

He was only out of minor ranks, but his superb goalkeeping qualities had been in evidence as early as 1951, when he had the remarkable distinction of playing for Thomastown in the under-fourteen, under-sixteen, minor and junior championships.

Ollie lined out at Walsh Park, Waterford, against Wexford, and Kilkenny won the Dr Kinnane Tournament. It was the beginning of an illustrious and distinguished career that saw him wear the number one jersey for Kilkenny until 1971. The trophy he won that day was a Waterford glass goblet with *An Tóstal* inscribed on it. It is still a cherished possession.

His career is dotted with achievements: All-Irelands, Leinster titles, Railway Cups, National Leagues, Oireachtas titles, twice Puc Fada champion. But a county senior title eluded him, even though his club, Thomastown, contested two county finals.

His memories of the people he met are more vivid than the games he played. However, two games stand out for the sheer effort and endeavour of team contribution. The first was the 1957 All-Ireland final, when Kilkenny defeated a dashing Waterford fifteen; the second was the 1967 All-Ireland — a sweet win that broke a 45-year

Tipperary hoodoo. Ollie played that day with an injured hand, which was kept secret until after the game.

He regards the 1966–69 combination as the best of his career. 'This was a great bunch — we could have won four in a row. We had the ability to do it. We lost to Cork very much against the odds in 1966 — a little too confident perhaps. In 1968 we went down to a strong Wexford team by one point in the Leinster final. That Leinster final was a difficult one for me. I watched it from the sideline; about two weeks before the game I was dished out a six-month suspension for an incident in a League game against Tipperary in which I was a completely innocent victim.'

Ollie was sidelined too for the 1960 Leinster final against Wexford; he had broken a finger in training. He has, however, happy memories of a sporting gesture that day. As the teams lined up for the parade Nick O'Donnell came over to shake his hand in sympathy, and was followed by all the Wexford players.

While an All-Ireland medal is the dream of every hurler, Ollie received two awards in 1957 that have always been very special to him. One was the Cú Chulainn award, a unique trophy in bronze carrying an image of the legendary warrior and inscribed *Curadh Mhír na hIománaíochta*. This was a journalists' award. The second was the People's Choice award; this came from a radio programme presented by Mícheál O'Hehir on which the people of Ireland were requested to pick the sports person of the year from all sports. Ollie was top choice, with Galway footballer Seán Purcell second. Mícheál O'Hehir presented a silver cup to Ollie. He has the cup — still very proud of it — and a photograph of the presentation.

His idea of a good full-back in his day was a "stopper": the full-back who kept the forwards at bay and allowed the goalkeeper to concentrate on the ball. In this regard Ollie was always very happy playing behind Pa Dillon and "Link" Walsh.

Growing up he had two model goalkeepers: Tony Reddin of Tipperary, and Seánie Duggan of Galway.

In 1959 Ollie participated in a little piece of hurling history when the All-Ireland final went to a replay. It was only the fourth time in the history of the game that this happened: the other occasions were 1908, when Tipp played Dublin; 1931, when Cork played Kilkenny; and 1934, when Limerick played Dublin. Strangely enough, the Leinster team lost in all the replays.

As I talked with Ollie at his home he was savouring his first success as trainer of the Kilkenny senior squad following the previous Sunday's win over Dublin in the League. He was, however, philosophical about it. 'I know only too well that the difference between success and failure is a very thin line.' He has had remarkable success with the county junior team, guiding them to All-Ireland victories in 1984, 1986, 1988 and 1990. Several of his pupils — including Pat Dwyer, Bill Hennessy, and Mick Cleere — moved successfully to senior ranks.

While it is the lot of many a hurler to fade from memory as the years roll on, there are always some who live on in legend. Such a figure is Ollie Walsh. His flamboyant and swashbuckling style attracted scores of youngsters to the back of his goal in games at Nowlan Park. His brilliance between the posts, the lynx-like eye, the cat-like agility, lifted his defenders above themselves, enabling them to perform gaiscí. It bred confidence in colleagues. It deflated opponents. His brilliance won many a game for Kilkenny.

If he had an Achilles heel it was probably the ground ball, but then, as the adage says, 'Ní bhíonn saoi gan locht.'

Born: 1903

"

I recall my first Munster final, when Tipp gave us, Waterford, a fair good beating — the year 1925.

Martin Kennedy of Tipperary was the best full-forward I played against.

"

As I sat in Charlie Ware's sitting-room, a picture of a hurling team on the sideboard caught my eye. On examination it turned out to be the victorious Munster Railway Cup team of 1931. What a galaxy of stars it contained, all household names — John Joe Doyle and Tull Considine of Clare, Micky Cross and Garrett Howard of Limerick, Tommy Treacy, Phil Purcell, Phil Cahill, Martin Kennedy and Tommy O'Meara of Tipperary, Dinny Barry Murphy, Jim Hurley, Eudi Coughlan, Fox Collins and Ga Aherne of Cork.

The full-back on that team was Charlie Ware, and that of itself speaks of his prowess as a full-back. Phil Grimes had

described him to me as one of the great full-backs the game has known, and added, 'for a small man he was amazingly effective.' His brother Jim was sub goalkeeper on the 1931 team.

For one of his favourite recollections Charlie went back to the' Munster final of 1925, when Waterford played Tipp and lost 6:6 to 2:2. He was opposed by Martin Kennedy, who he rates as the best full-forward the game has known.

Charlie had no regrets. 'I enjoyed every moment playing the game,' he said. Defeats and the fact that no All-Ireland came his way never interfered with his enjoyment of each game.

His favourite hurling personalities were Micky Cross of Limerick, Martin Kennedy of Tipperary, Tull Considine of Clare, Jim Hurley of Cork, Mick King of Galway, and Tommy Carroll of Kilkenny. He considered Phil O'Neill of Cork the best GAA writer of his time.

In bygone decades "suit length tournaments" used to be a great attraction. One such tournament was always recalled by Charlie whenever he reminisced about the past. The venue was Cashel, and his club, Erin's Own, were playing Clonoulty of Tipperary. It might seem to have been an encounter of endurance — the kind you might read about in Irish mythology. The game began at four in the afternoon and finished with the Angelus bell. Maybe it was just as well; maybe it was time to say a prayer. After all, they had run out of first aid.

We then turned to some of the great moments in his hurling career, and he named three. There was something special about the first county title he won with

Erin's Own in 1927. At the age of forty-four he felt proud when he won his last county title with his club in 1947. Then there was 1948 — a great year for all Waterford folk.

Ten years earlier Charlie had known the disappointment of failure when they went under to Dublin in the 1938 decider, a game he felt was lost on the sideline. But 1948 brought compensation. Charlie was on the selection committee that steered Waterford to its first All-Ireland senior title, and it was a great feeling to see his brother Jim captain Waterford and return triumphant with the McCarthy Cup.

Born: 1908

66

My first proud memory was in 1931 when I was picked as a sub on the Munster team, which included many of the best men I have seen hurling.

I feel it was an honour to have played between 1926 and 1949, when I played against the great Limerick, Cork, Tipperary and Clare teams of that era. A lifelong ambition was achieved in 1948 when we beat Cork in a Munster final thriller, and then went on to win Waterford's first senior All-Ireland against Dublin.

Players of my time that I particularly admired were Mick Mackey and Timmy Ryan of Limerick, Martin Kennedy of Tipperary, Dinny Barry Murphy, Christy Ring and Jim Young of Cork, Christy Moylan, Phil Grimes, John Keane, Vin Baston and Mick Hickey of Waterford.

99

Jim Ware had a long and illustrious career with Waterford stretching over more than twenty years. It wasn't an uninterrupted career. He was injured in 1937 and replaced by M. Curley, but he returned again in 1940.

He is remembered for two particularly outstanding qualities: his long delivery from goal, and his confidence and dependability in dealing with the high lobbing ball. He felt that not sufficient credit has been given to the Waterford team of 1931, who drew with the famous Cork team of that era in the Munster final. That Waterford team was made up of fourteen Erin's Own men.

Jim still felt angry about that drawn game. The referee, Willie Gleeson, allowed play to continue well into extra time, and in the eighth minute of extra time Cork got the equalising point, following which full time was blown. The combination and understanding of the Erin's Own men caught Cork by surprise in the first half, when they conceded four goals, and Waterford folk still question the disallowing of another goal scored by "Locky" Byrne. Jim told me that Willie O'Donnell, who was later to win hurling renown with his native Tipperary, played with Waterford in 1931.

Like his county team-mate Andy Fleming, he felt they had a very good team in 1943 and with a little luck might have beaten Cork in a Munster final that was lost on the score 2:13 to 3:8. A deflection about ten minutes from time when Waterford were ahead turned the ball into the net. Such happenings are a goalkeeper's nightmare.

Was there any particular save that came to mind that he thought was special? Yes, there was. Jim recalled that at one stage in the 1948 Munster final against Cork they had fallen five points in arrears in the first half. Cork mounted another attack, and from about twelve or fifteen yards, Jack Lynch sent in a rasper. It hit Jim low in the chest; he gathered and cleared downfield, and Waterford broke through for a goal and proceeded to take a grip on the game. It had been a crucial save.

Every goalkeeper has memories of goals that should never have gone in, and Jim recalled one of these — adding, with a smile, that there were many. This one happened in the 1948/49 National League campaign against Kilkenny at Dungarvan. Jim Langton took a free for Kilkenny, and from the flight of the ball Jim Ware felt sure it was heading over the bar and stood casually where he was. To his consternation the ball seemed to dip at the last moment and finished up in the net.

For Waterford 1948 was a memorable year, when they took the Munster title and went on to win their first All-Ireland victory. Jim had the great honour of being captain. To add to Waterford's cup of joy, the minors also won the All-Ireland title; and since this victory was achieved at the expense of Kilkenny, it made it all the sweeter, said Jim.

There was a wonderful feeling of achievement in Co. Waterford after the 1948 triumph. Jim would like to have taken the cup to many parts of the county and displayed it to the loyal supporters and well-wishers, but in 1948 things were not as well organised as nowadays, and transport was not always readily available.

Jim's wife, Alice, a great GAA enthusiast, told me that after the 1948 triumph they received a great deal of letters from Waterford emigrants from all over the world. It is impossible to describe the sense of joy and elation the 1948 victory brought to these emigrants overseas. They wanted to hear and read about the men who brought the honour to Waterford, and they felt a sense of loss that they were not at home to share in a great occasion.

So great was Alice's enthusiasm for hurling that it found expression in a play, called *Blaze of Glory*. It was staged in 1958 at the Theatre Royal in Waterford, and an abridged version was produced on radio. The central theme was hurling and hurlers, with the main character a dedicated and committed player. The point of conflict in the play was the ban, which was in operation at the time.

I asked Jim to pick a team he would like to have captained from the players of his era. This is his selection:

Jim Ware
(Waterford)

Mickey Cross	Charlie Ware	Willie Murphy
(Limerick)	*(Waterford)*	*(Cork)*
"Builder" Walsh	John Keane	Vin Baston
(Kilkenny and Dublin)	*(Waterford)*	*(Waterford)*

Christy Moylan   Jim Hurley
(Waterford)   *(Cork)*

Christy Ring	Mick Mackey	Dinny Barry Murphy
(Cork)	*(Limerick)*	*(Cork)*
Josie Gallagher	Martin Kennedy	Jackie Power
(Galway)	*(Tipperary)*	*(Limerick)*

Born: 1932

"

Wexford v. Tipperary, 1956 — Tipperary leading at half time by fifteen points, and Nick Rackard was in very bad form, as we all were. In the dressing-room he paced the floor and banged the hurley on the table, calling us a crowd of camogie-players. His speech that day fired us to great heights, and we beat Tipperary by four points in what was to me a great game.

The game of hurling to me is the greatest field game in the world. No other game has the speed and thrills when it is played with verve and dash. It brought me in contact with some wonderful people from all over Ireland, and especially with the great Wexford team of the fifties and sixties, who were all gentlemen. I have special admiration for Pat Stakelum, Jim Langton, Jack Mulcahy, Bill Rackard, Christy Ring, Bob Rackard, and Tim Flood.

"

In a galaxy of Wexford hurling stars, Ned Wheeler was a giant among giants — gentle giants; gentlemen. Just look at some of the names: Nick O'Donnell, Bobbie Rackard, Billy Rackard, Jim Morrissey, Paddy Kehoe, Padge Kehoe, Nicky Rackard, Martin Codd, Jim English.

I can vividly recall Ned's giant frame on the field. He was a versatile performer, having played half-back, centrefield, half-forward, and full-forward. Despite his titanic clashes at full-forward with "Link" Walsh of Kilkenny, and his many fine scores from that position, I always thought he was best suited to the half-back line. I can remember too the quality of his sideline pucks: long, high, floating balls that switched play from defence to attack. It was a hurling skill he brought to a high degree of excellence.

Hurling was in his blood. His Uncle Paddy had played with Laois back in the thirties — an era when Laois produced many fine hurlers. At the age of five Ned left his native Laois and took up residence in Slieverue, Co. Kilkenny. Ten years later, at the age of fifteen, he would leave Kilkenny and settle in Co. Wexford. His adopted county had gained a new son who in the purple and gold would adorn the hurling scene and leave a lasting imprint.

It was delightful talking to him, and as we chatted he unfolded some of the memories that have remained uppermost in his mind. He will never forget the 1956 League final against Tipperary. Playing against the wind in the first half, Wexford fell further and further behind, until at half time they were fifteen points in arrears. In the first half Ned felt that almost the entire Wexford team were unsettled and completely at sixes and sevens.

Very early in the second half Ned recalls doubling on a pass from Jim Morrissey. As he followed the flight of the wind-aided sliotar, he saw it travel between the posts and rebound off the wall at the back of the goal — a distance of well over a hundred yards. That point heralded a change into top gear by Wexford. They were on their way back from the grave. The forwards began making full use of plentiful supply of the ball. Slowly, surely, relentlessly they chipped away at Tipp's intimidating lead, and as they did the atmosphere became supercharged. When the final whistle blew the score was Wexford 5:9, Tipperary 2:14. The Model County had won an unforgettable victory.

Ned's sweetest victory was the 1956 All-Ireland triumph over Cork. Wexford stamped their class on the hurling scene in that game.

Ned's most memorable game was the 1954 Railway Cup final against Munster, when he played at centre-half-back. He recalled that Leinster had not won this trophy since 1941; but this 1954 Leinster team, drawn from Dublin, Wexford, and Kilkenny, blended beautifully, and in a hectic encounter in which the ball travelled first time up and down the field they triumphed over a star-studded Munster team on the score 0:9 to 0:5. According to Ned it was full-blooded hurling, which thrilled the attendance of fifty thousand for the entire hour.

His most bitter disappointment was the 1954 All-Ireland defeat at the hands of Cork in a game that Wexford dominated everywhere except on the scoreboard.

Over his long career the team he liked to play against most was Tipperary, and he particularly enjoyed playing on Theo English at midfield. Ned regrets the downgrading of the Oireachtas tournament, and recalls the great games of hurling this tournament has served up, in particular those between Wexford and Galway and between Wexford and Clare in the early fifties.

Ned agreed that if All-Ireland titles were the ultimate measure of a team's contribution to hurling then Wexford would fare rather poorly. But, like Limerick in the thirties and early forties, the Wexford team of the fifties and early sixties put infinitely more into the game than they got out in the form of All-Ireland medals. Their sportsmanship was of the highest quality. They had a glamour that was the envy of all other teams. They had a flair for the big occasion, and Wexford at their height turned every occasion into a big occasion. They were as gracious in defeat as they were glorious in victory. And Ned was part of all that.

Proudly displayed in a barber's shop in Wexford that I used to visit was a photograph of the 1956 team. The caption was taken from Peadar Kearney's ballad "Down by the Glenside":

We may have great men
But we'll never have better.

Ned could have picked many teams from the stars of his era, but after much thought he opted to captain the following selection:

Tony Reddin *(Tipperary)*

Bobbie Rackard *(Wexford)*   Nick O'Donnell *(Wexford)*   Mark Marnell *(Kilkenny)*

Jim English *(Wexford)*   Pat Stakelum *(Tipperary)*   Tommy Doyle *(Tipperary)*

Jim Morrissey *(Wexford)*   Phil Grimes *(Waterford)*

Jimmy Doyle *(Tipperary)*   Ned Wheeler *(Wexford)*   Christy Ring *(Cork)*

"Hopper" McGrath *(Wexford)*   Nick Rackard *(Wexford)*   Jimmy Langton *(Kilkenny)*

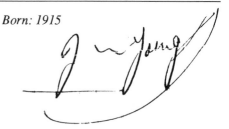

Born: 1915

During his hurling career he won all the honours in the game, and was part of the great Cork team that created a record-breaking four-in-a-row hurling triumph from 1941 to 1944. In 1945 his brother Éamonn was a member of the victorious Cork senior football team, repeating a success his father, Jack, had achieved in 1911 — and Jim followed with a senior hurling medal in '46. So, collectively, the Young household equalled Jack Lynch's six All-Ireland senior medals in a row.

Among his most cherished victories are the Fitzgibbon Cup successes in hurling in 1939 and 1942 and the Sigerson Cup football wins in 1943 and 1946.

In the earlier part of the century many Gaelic players took part in the struggle for independence. Jim's Uncle Ned was one of those, having taken part in the famous Kilmichael ambush.

While Jim makes no secret of the fact that he is a GAA man first, he had other sporting loves too. In Muskerry Golf Club he played off a handicap of four. He mastered squash sufficiently to be Munster champion in the fifties and his brother Éamonn succeeded him. He loved tennis. Two mixed-double players he held in very high regard were Ann Delaney and Nan Connor. But, according to Jim, the best mixed-doubles partner he ever had was his mother, then hale and hearty. Partnered by his father he won the men's doubles in 1932, and in 1967 he had the distinction of being non-playing captain of the Irish Davis Cup team in Monaco.

In the many encounters between Limerick and Cork in the forties Jim invariably found himself marking John Mackey. We joked about the clashes between them, for

"

There are too many wonderful hurlers that come to mind; to leave out any would be an injustice. I shall never forget the Fitzgibbon Cup matches when I played with UCC, and of course I shall never forget my four-in-a-row comrades, many of whom are gone to the happy hurling ground, sad to say.

The greats: Mackey, Ring, Lynch, King, Kennedy; and more than likely the others were just as good. A special word for John Mackey and Andy Fleming!

Le gach dea-ghuí.

PS: The game is slower today. No man can carry a ball as fast as a ball hit by a hurley!

"

Jim Young was one of hurling's and indeed sport's greatest enthusiasts. He took the positive rather than the negative view. He praised where others might criticise.

it is well known that in all their meetings the exchanges were of a supercharged nature, where no quarter was asked or given on either side; and yet John and Jim were always the best of friends.

'Do you know,' said Jim to me, 'John was a fine-looking fellow,' and he added, 'so as to keep the contest even, as it were, I wasn't a bad-looking fellow myself either.' Even the Cork women admired him, admitted Jim, and it was not only John's hurling ability he was talking about. It therefore seems that when Limerick and John Mackey used to lose to Cork — coupled with the intensity of the exchanges between John and Jim — there were certain women in Cork, known to Jim, who used to feel a sense of sympathy for John Mackey and used to show it by not talking to Jim for several days after the Limerick-Cork encounters.

He considered hurling at the present time to be as good as ever — though perhaps not as fast, mainly because of too much carrying of the ball. Looking back on the seventies he said, 'Look at all the great games we witnessed, both in the League and championship.'

He felt that the game had benefited from the resurgence of Limerick and Galway, the revival in Clare — 'a most unlucky team' — and the arrival of a new force, Offaly.

Talking of great games reminded him that his father used to say that the greatest game he ever saw was the second game between Cork and Kilkenny in the 1931 All-Ireland final.

I asked Jim what game or games he would want to play all over again if he could go back in time. Without hesitation he mentioned two. The first was a "suit lengths" tournament in 1939 at Milford, Co. Cork, between Glen Rovers and Ahane. This was non-stop, uncompromising stuff, where club pride was very much at stake. Jim recalled that for a period of twenty minutes in this game the ball never crossed the line.

The second game was in the first-round Munster championship clash between Limerick and Cork in 1942 at Limerick Gaelic grounds. It was an epic, ranking with the great games between these two counties. It produced twenty scores, nine of them goals — Cork 4:8, Limerick 5:3. Cork had the first and last say. In the first minute they goaled via Derry Beckett. Entering the final minutes it began to look like a draw, when Charlie Tobin gave Jim Young an unforgettable memory with a one-handed swing from about fifty yards that gave Cork a point lead. A further Cork point followed.

In between these Cork scores there were thrills and spills, heroics and casualties, clashes of the ash and flashes of genius. In the second half in particular the pace was hectic, and in one spell of less than ten minutes the crowd was dazzled by a four-goal barrage, two each to either side, that brought excitement to fever pitch. On the call of time it was Cork by two points. During the hour of superb hurling Jim recalled that the teams were level twice; Limerick were ahead twice; Cork were ahead three times and, most important of all, were there at the finish.

His greatest regret is the losing of the 1939 final against Kilkenny, a game he feels Cork might have won. Without elaborating he mentioned a free given against Cork for an alleged jersey-pulling offence at a crucial moment. By inference it appears to have had a bearing on the result.

His team read as follows:

Skinny O'Meara *(Tipperary)*

Bobbie Rackard *(Wexford)*   Seán Óg Murphy *(Cork)*   "Fox" Collins *(Cork)*

Jackie Power *(Limerick)*   James Kelliher *(Cork)*   Paddy Phelan *(Kilkenny)*

Jim Hurley *(Cork)*   Mick King *(Galway)*

Christy Ring *(Cork)*   Mick Mackey *(Limerick)*   Dinny Barry Murphy *(Cork)*

Josie Gallagher *(Galway)*   Bob McConkey *(Limerick)*   Mattie Power *(Kilkenny)*

He then told me of an amusing story linked with the "star choice" team that he picked for the *Sunday Independent* during 1981. At that time he said, 'I am giving what I consider to be my best fifteen men to have wielded a camán, but then I could probably pick another side to beat them.'

When "Fox" Collins met Jim he said to him, 'You never saw Bob McConkey play — how do you know he was the best full-forward?' Jim's reply was a classic. 'You don't have to see a man to know he was the best. Did you ever see Jesus Christ?'

When I read *The Spirit of the Glen* I was particularly taken by the last paragraph of Jim's address as president of the club, and feel it is well worth reproducing here, as it reflects the depth of feeling he holds towards his club and the GAA: 'May our future match our past. May we always be loyal to the Gaelic Athletic Association, and may we always be proud of the Spirit of the Glen.'

The Hurler's Prayer

Grant me, O Lord, a hurler's skill,
With strength of arm and speed of limb,
Unerring eye for the flying ball,
And courage to match whate'er befall.
May my stroke be steady and my aim be true,
My actions manly and my misses few;
No matter what way the game may go,
May I rest in friendship with every foe.
When the final whistle for me has blown,
And I stand at last before God's judgement throne,
May the great referee when He calls my name
Say, You hurled like a man; you played the game.

Séamus Redmond

Some great teams

Above: LIMERICK 1936
Back row left to right : Paddy Clohessy. Tom McCarthy. Jim Roche. Dave Clohessy. Paddy O'Carroll. Paddy Mc Mahon. Mick Mackey. Garrett Howard. Sgt Major Brown (Trainer)
Middle Row- Timmy Ryan. Mickey Cross. John Mackey. Mick Kennedy. Paddy Scanlon.
Front Jimmy Close. Mick Ryan. *Inset* Jackie Power.

Below: WEXFORD 1956
Back row left to right: Billy Rackard. Nick O'Donnell. Ned Wheeler. Jim Morrissey. Martin Codd. Nicky Rackard. Padge Kehoe. Bobby Rackard.
Front row: Tom Ryan. Mick Morrissey. Jim English. Art Foley. Tim Flood. Tom Dickson. Seamus Hearne.

Some great teams

Above: WATERFORD 1959
Back row left to right: Larry Guinan. Jackie
Condon. Ned Power. Johnny Kiely. John Barron.
M. Leacy. Seumas Power. Phil Grimes.
Front row: Tom Cheasty. Donal Whelan. Charlie
Ware. Frankie Walsh. Austin Flynn. Martin Óg
Morrissey. Joe Harney.

Below: KILKENNY 1972
Back row left to right: Ned Byrne. Mick Crotty. Pa
Dillon. Pat Henderson. Eddie Keher. Frank
Cummins. Kieran Purcell.
Front row: Pat Lawlor. Jim Treacy. Liam O'Brien.
Noel Skehan. Pat Delaney. John Kinsella. Eamon
Morrissey. *Inset:* Phil Larkin.

Some famous hurling families.

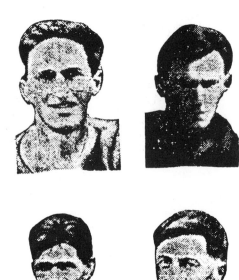

Among the Giants of the Ash interviewed for this book are these 'hurling families' — the famous Mackey brothers from Limerick, the Ware brothers from Waterford and, more recently still, the three Rackards from Wexford. Here are pictured — sourced from a 1934 feature in the *Independent* which I gratefully acknowledge — some earlier hurling brothers:

above left : The Graces of Tullaroan, Co. Kilkenny (l-r: Pierce, Dick and Jack);
above right, the Leahys of Boherlahan, Co. Tipperary (l-r: Paddy, Tommy, Mick and Johnny);
and below the Doyles of Mooncoin, Co. Kilkenny (l-r: Mick, Eddie and Dick.)

Some household names from the early days of hurling

TWO GALWAY SUPREMES

Michael Gill *(above centre)* and Michael King *(below left)* of Galway represented 'the best of Galway hurling.' Both played together as young hurlers, Gill staying the field to become one of the greatest and most consistent of mid-field players the game has known. Unfortunately King fell victim of a 'shattering accidental knee-crash' that led to a year in hospital, a brilliant career nipped too soon. He continued to play afterward however, featuring in the Tailteann and Railway Cup.

A WEXFORD HERO

Hurler and footballer, Sean O'Kennedy *(above right)* of New Ross was an all-rounder with few equals, and held All-Ireland medals for both hurling and football. He led Wexford through a record series of football victories from 1915-1918. He was noted as a master tactician, unerring in piercing the opposition's weaknesses.

He had a loose easy hurling style, and specialised in very effective drop-pucks, establishing a vogue for drop-pucks at that time.

A CORK FULL BACK

'Kelleher *(above left)* was certainly the brainest back that ever came out of the South. His judgement was uncanny. He could sense a forward's movements and proceed to outplay him by brains rather than brawn. He could turn on his

tracks like a hare,' wrote the *Independent* about this hurling and hunting farmer from Dungourney in East Cork. Versatile and nimble, he could play in most positions but settled for centre or full back.

TOM SEMPLE OF TIPPERARY

Prince of hurlers, handsome, tall (6'3"), brown curly hair, striker of 90 yard 'grounders', fierce and fearless, 'his private life honest and good as his hurling was bold and clean' — so sang the reviewers of this renowned sportsman from Thurles. Commemorated forever in the naming of Thurles pitch, Semple Stadium, Tom Semple *(below centre)* was a winger with the great Tubberadora men, with the Mahers, Gleeson and the Hayes'. He played every championship from 1900 to 1912, winning three All-Irelands among his sixty gold medals.

'A LIMERICK GIANT'

Against Tullaroan in the All-Ireland final of 1897, Sean Óg Hanley *(below right)* was the best man of the thirty-four, and his fame and prowess that day in Tipperary spread nationwide. 6'1", and fourteen stone, he depended on skill and art to win — a talent handed down from another very famous hurler, Sean Hanley, his grandfather. In Dublin in 1899 he played for Commercials, and later helped build the London Irish team of 1902–04 — a team which sensationally beat both Cork and Tipperary. He died in his early fifties.

Extracts from Dr. Croke's letter, 1884

The following extracts have been taken from the letter — now known as the "Charter of the GAA" — received by Michael Cusack from Dr T.W. Croke, Archbishop of Cashel and Emly.

Its relevance today is perhaps primarily as a historical document, but Dr Croke, in 1884, was speaking on behalf of a people who were mainly under-educated, down-trodden, dispirited, searching for leadership. He saw in the GAA a vehicle for that leadership.

December 18th, 1884.
MY DEAR SIR — I beg to acknowledge the receipt of your communication inviting me to become a patron of the Gaelic Athletic Association, of which you are, it appears, the Hon. Secretary. I accede to your request with the utmost pleasure.
. . .
Ball-playing, hurling, football-kicking, according to Irish rules, "casting", leaping in various ways, wrestling, hand-grips, top-pegging, leap-frog, rounders, tip-in-the-hat, and all such favourite exercises and amusements, amongst men and boys may now be said to be not only dead and buried, but in several localities to be entirely forgotten and unknown. And what have we got in their stead. We have got such foreign and fantastic field sports as lawn tennis, polo, crocquet, cricket and the like — very excellent, I believe, and health-giving exercises in their way, still not racy of the soil, but rather alien, on the contrary, to it, as are, indeed, for the most part, the men and women who first imported, and still continue to patronise them.

And, unfortunately, it is not our national sports alone that are held in dishonour and are dying out, but even our most suggestive national celebrations are being gradually effaced and extinguished, one after another as well. Who hears now of snap-apple night, pan-cake night, or bon-fire night? They are all things of the past, too vulgar to be spoken of, except in ridicule by the degenerate dandies of the day. No doubt, there is something rather pleasing to the eye in the get-up of a modern young man, who arrayed in light attire, with parti-coloured cap on and racquet in hand, is making his way, with or without a companion to the tennis ground. But, for my part, I should vastly prefer to behold, or think of, the youthful athletes, whom I used to see in my early days at fair and pattern, bereft of shoes and coat, and thus prepared to play at handball, to fly over any number of horses, to throw the "sledge" or "winding-stone", and to test each other's mettle and activity by the trying ordeal of "three leaps" or a "hop, step and jump".
. . .
In conclusion, I earnestly hope that our national journals will not disdain in future to give suitable notices of these Irish sports and pastimes which your society means to patronise and promote, and that the masters and pupils of our Irish Colleges will not henceforth exclude from the athletic programmes such manly exercises as I have just referred to and commemorated.

I remain, my dear Sir,
Your very faithful servant,
✠ T. W. CROKE,
Archbishop of Cashel.

All-Ireland and National League champions, 1887–1990

Decade		Clare	Cork	Dublin	Galway	Kerry	Kilkenny	Laois	Limerick	London	Offaly	Tipperary	Waterford	Wexford
1887 – 1900	All-Ireland		4	1		1			1			6		
1901 – 1910	All-Ireland		2				4			1		2		1
1911 – 1920	All-Ireland	1	1	2			3	1	1			1		
1921 – 1930	All-Ireland		3	2	1		1		1			2		
	National League		2	1								1		
1931 – 1940	All-Ireland		1	1			4		3			1		
	National League		1	1	1		1		5					
1941 – 1950	All-Ireland		5				1					3	1	
	National League	1	2						1			2		
1951 – 1960	All-Ireland		3				1					2	1	3
	National League		1		1							6		2
1961 – 1970	All-Ireland		2				3					4		1
	National League		2				2					4	1	1
1971 – 1980	All-Ireland		3		1		4		1			1		
	National League	2	3		1		1		1			1		1
1981 – 1990	All-Ireland		3		2		2				2	1		
	National League		1		2		4		2			1		
All-Ireland Total		1	27	6	4	1	23	1	7	1	2	23	2	5
National League Total		3	12	2	5	-	8	-	9	-	-	15	1	4

And, departing, leave behind us
Footprints on the sands of time.

Longfellow ("A Psalm of Life")